FlightLog

FlightLog

The Novel Adventures of a Stewardess Wannabe Who Becomes a Flight Attendant

· · · · · · · · ·

by

Suz

FlightLog: The Novel Adventures of a Stewardess Wannabe
Who Becomes a Flight Attendant

Printed in the United States of America.

FIRST EDITION

ISBN 979-8-9859691-7-7

I would like to thank the many artists, readers, editors, and friends, who with love and kindness, shared their skills, insights and valuable time with me on this project. I hope someday that I can repay all of you in a worthwhile way.

THIS BOOK IS DEDICATED TO ALL YOU BIG-OL-JET-AIRLINER PEOPLE WHO…

Were there with me when I took off with United Airlines in 1978, including gate agents, ticket agents, supervisors, mechanics, trainers, reservationists, pilots—and of course, those who worked beside me in the aisles and in the galleys: my flight attendant brothers and sisters, who like me, wanted to have fun for a living. It was mostly because of you, my peers, that I did indeed have so much fun.

It is also dedicated to the many airline people I've met since—not just at UAL but at (in alphabetical order) Aero Mexico, American, Braniff, British Airways, Continental, Delta, Eastern, JAL, KAL, LATAM, Lufthansa, Midway, Pan Am, PSA, Southwest, TWA, etc. May your journeys always be joyous and turbulence-free.

Contents

Dreams of a
Wild Blue Yonder

All through my little girlhood, I wanted to be a stewardess. One of those high-heeled, tight navy-blue-skirted smiling sweeties with shiny pins displayed above perky breasts. Those were my memories of the girls I'd seen on the flights I'd taken with my family in the 60s and early 70s. Those were the looks of the pencil-drawn stewardesses from the cover of my favorite book, *Coffee, Tea or Me*, which I'd read three times.

Pro 'Log'

It was 1978. People didn't have home computers, video players, or answering machines. We rented our telephones from local phone companies and hand-wrote letters. The terms 'politically correct' and 'African-American' had not been coined. 'Eating disorders' and 'alternate life styles' were not yet common household phrases. Only strippers wore thongs, which made perfect sense to me, as they only caused one to gyrate their hynie in a desperate attempt to dislodge the bothersome wedgie. Famous department stores hadn't crossed borders. If you wanted to shop at Bloomindales, you had to go to New York. Harrods—London. Nordstroms—Seattle or Portland. To gamble legally in the US, one had to be in the state of Nevada and if you wanted to buy Fannie May Trinidads, you had to go to Chicago.

Wines came in red, white or rose, and the Gallo Brothers reigned supreme. Screw tops and plastic champagne corks were perfectly suitable. Starbucks and other specialty coffeehouses hadn't gone global; if you wanted a decent cup of Java, you had to go to Europe or South America. The most popular female stars in our country were white, chopstick-thin blondes. Girls like: (It was still ok to say girls) Cheryl Tiegs, Suzanne Somers, Farrah Fawcett, Christy Brinkley, and the braided-bombshell beauty of them all—Bo Derek, the world's Perfect 10. Though considered beautiful, brunette and redheaded stars of any skin color were just a notch below these light-eyed blondes (with rare exceptions) until ideas about beauty changed. Let's put it this way: in the 60s and 70s, blonde movie stars never, ever, dyed their hair dark, unless it was for an 'ethnic' role.

Only weirdoes didn't eat meat. They were 'health nuts' and perceived, as Woody Allen put it, to eat mashed alfalfa sprouts. Only fanatics or competitive athletes 'exercised.' They didn't run, they 'jogged.' Nobody twerked. Normal people had never heard, 'Namaste.' White people didn't dine on Thai, Japanese, Moroccan, or Vietnamese food yet, though we did eat French toast and French fries. Mexican food meant tacos. Italian food meant pizza, spaghetti or lasagna and all had to be smothered with meat sauce. Chinese food only came in white cardboard-boxed containers. For the most part, Anglo-America's taste in food and drink was familiar-vanill-iar. Life was white-bread bleak; we just didn't know it.

*

I was nineteen years old. The government had deregulated the airlines—the big birds were hiring and muscling out the small regional carriers, taking over long-established routes. Minority quotas were overdue. Companies looked for a sense of parity in their employee groups with (in alphabetical order) Asians, Blacks and Latinos. Most of us had never seen a female cop or a female doctor, just as we hadn't seen male secretaries or male nurses. Gender-specific fields were opening their doors to the opposite sex. Yes—men were becoming 'stewardesses,' and that was my first eye-opener about the job. Since ninety percent of the applicants were single white girls, (I was there for interview after interview—thousands upon thousands showed up for hundreds of jobs) I was elated to make the many callbacks (they called them interviews, I called them tryouts—like cheerleading) and get hired.

Part I:

· · · · · · · · ·

Taxi

Chapter 1:

. . . .

Leavin' on a Jet Plane!

"*A*LL MY BAGS ARE PACKED, *I'm ready to go,*" I sang to my soon-to-be ex-boyfriend Toby as we stepped outside, letting the screen door slam behind us. He didn't think it was funny. I *kissed him goodbye and smiled for him* while my family watched from the idling station wagon; they were all taking me to the airport.

* * *

My Gateway Airlines flight to Cleveland was just minutes from boarding. "You know Sherri," my father stated importantly as we took seats near the gate, "all the stewardesses I've ever known seemed to be running away from something."

"Well Pops," I said, "guess I'm all set then, my track shoes are already packed." He frowned. I had taken to calling him by his first name which he hated. However, since my new job was a sore subject, I didn't use it here—especially after the track shoes remark. He was not going to give me his blessing. Only men should have exciting jobs—especially ones that involved travel to wonderful destinations. Women should get married, have babies, stay home, raise their children and read books like *The Total Woman* by Marabel Morgan. That's what my perfect sister Shannon did.

Waving 'so long' to my tearing mother, my head-shaking sister and my smiling kid brother, I boarded. I was finally leaving Wichita's Mid-Continent Airport for inflight training in Cleveland, Ohio, with a major airline. There was joy in my heart and a skip to my step; the airplane couldn't get me out of Kansas fast enough. Unlike Dorothy, I would not be wandering around any city—Emerald or otherwise—lamenting that, 'there's no place like home.'

They put me in first class. *Yes!* I loved my new job already. It was a Boeing 727 aircraft and a gal approached me right after takeoff with a knowing look. I was in the first row. "You're a new hire, aren't you?" I grinned from ear to ear. "Would you like a cocktail? I'm working up front; I'll get you a drink right away, serve everyone else then come back and chat; K?"

"Up front?" I asked, not understanding.

"In first class—where you're sitting." She smiled again.

Oh, man! This was great! She didn't even ask me if I was twenty-one. After the first few sips of my Screwdriver, I got nervous and slowed down; didn't want to be tipsy on arrival. There's nothing like the smell of underage drinking in the morning! Her name was Madge and she'd been flying for five years. *Wow, a long time.* She told me that she had a note on her 'manifest' (I asked again—it was her list of passengers, along with any special instructions) to instruct me to go to Gateway Airlines lower-level exit door number four and that a bus would take me to the training center. She also told me that Denver was her domicile—the city she was based in.

"Hopefully you'll get based there right out of training," she said, "it's so close to Wichita, you could commute no problem."

"Oh I don't want to commute," I said. *Don't know when I'll be back again.* I really think I'd like to be stationed in London or Paris." I was kidding but she missed that.

"We don't fly there silly girl," she chuckled. "This isn't Pan Am. Our bases are all stateside." She counted them off on her fingers. "New York, Cleveland, Miami, Denver, Houston, Los Angeles, and San Francisco; there, that's seven."

I enjoyed every minute of her; she was pretty, nice, attentive, fun, and knew how to count to seven—exactly how I hoped to be. She kept looking up to see if any of the other first-class passengers needed anything. If they flinched, she hustled over, leaping with glee in her mauvy-plum-eggplant and beige uniform. It was awful I noted; and dated. It wasn't sharp; the colors didn't seem flattering to anyone. *Whatever.* We were on time; the flight seemed so quick. Madge gave me a hug and wished me lots of luck. I turned a little red, no doubt in part because of the vodka, and left the plane in search of exit door number four. When I veered a little left, I stopped and took a piece of gum along with my white go-with-anything sunglasses from my purse; best to hide the evidence.

I found several other incoming new hire attendants assembled at the lower level waiting for our bus. It was the first Saturday in May and I knew the 104th running of the Kentucky Derby had taken place at Churchill Downs earlier. Looking around the arrival area, I listened to the other trainees. I asked if anyone knew who had won the race but they were all too excited about training to talk sports. Many knew details about what lay ahead. We had an orientation in a few hours. Classes would begin at 8 A.M. on Monday. There were going to be forty new hires in our group. Forty new trainees started each week. A tall lady stood on the bus and collected money to tip the driver. She was much older, maybe even thirty-five, with wide hips and teased brown hair about the color of mine. I thought she must be an instructor but after we arrived and she handed the driver his stash, she introduced herself to all of us as Jane in a boisterous, jovial tone. She was one of our classmates and volunteered with a smile that she was probably the oldest. Actually, several of the trainees were old—as in twenty-seven and up.

"That's a great read," said the gal next me as she tapped the Linda Goodman *Sun Signs* book on my lap. It had been on the *New York Times* bestseller list for months. "What sign are you?"

"Gemini."

"Me too!" She pressed her shoulder into mine. "My name's Mara. We don't look much like twins," she giggled. *No kidding.* Mara looked like a Filipino American to me. Her teeth were the most perfect I'd ever seen and she had waist-length black hair. I made a mental note to pop out my retainer before orientation; I looked like a high-schooler compared to her. She had worked for Gateway Airlines for three years as a reservationist before being hired for inflight. She told me she had to undergo all the same hiring interviews that we had, and was so happy to finally start flying. "Reservations was awful," she confessed. "I couldn't wait to get out of there."

"Glad you're here; as someone who's already an employee, you can probably teach us a lot."

"Sure, sure. You know they put four of us in each dorm room," she said. "If they haven't assigned people already, you want to be roommates?"

"You bet," I said. "I'll room anytime with a fellow Gemini."

At the training center, we gawked at the other trainees who'd been there for one, two, three or four weeks already. They were the seasoned vets and ready to tell us what they'd learned. *Seniority was everything; the trips you got to fly, your pay, benefits, and even getting on a flight as a standby on your days off all depended on your 'senior-ity.'* Since their start dates were prior to ours—they would all be senior to us. We had to have a well performing watch upon grad-uation so that we could announce arrival times to our passengers.

That night, we assembled in the cafeteria to meet our instruc-tors and get our class schedules. Each of us was to stand up, give our name, age, and tell 'a little bit' about ourselves. There were married people. Some were parents. There were former soldiers, nurses, stewardesses from small lesser-known airlines, beauty queens, political science majors, statisticians for professional ball teams, cops, Playboy Bunnies, scuba-diving instructors, zoo workers, and school teachers. Very few like me, had little to say about themselves. We were twenty-five gals and fifteen guys strong. Five Asians, five Latinos, ten Blacks, and twenty of us were White. *Bravo Gateway Airlines. You get it.*

I decided not to say anything about dad—and didn't want to mention that I still lived at home. I would have to make my job at the bank sound interesting.

I noticed a real cute guy across the long table from me. When I looked at him, he smiled. His turn came quickly; when he stood to speak, I was all ears. "Hi everyone, I'm Danny Orr. I live in Seattle and I'm twenty-four. I was born in Canada and yes, I did play hockey all through my childhood and in school." Everyone laughed. "And I worked at a Radio Shack before joining you." It was easy to hear his Canadian accent.

The lead instructor, a fine-looking blonde named Pauline, interrupted him. "Well Danny, there's another Orr from Canada you may have heard of..."

"Bobby?" Danny grinned. "He's my oldest brother."

Pauline practically flipped. I was focused on Danny. *I like you!* Cute, an athlete, brother of a famous Hockey great, *neat.* Pauline couldn't contain herself; she blurted out that she was from Boston and she was a huge hockey fan. There was a lot of murmuring through the next several speeches as some learned from others in whispers who Bobby Orr was.

When directed, I stood and pretended to be eager to tell 'a little bit about myself,' a simple task, as there was little to tell about me, Miss Sherri Van Ness, nineteen, born and raised in Wichita.

"I love to read and I write some too—mostly for myself and I've worked at a bank for one and a half years." *And I just started drinking liquor!* "Six months ago, I was promoted from teller to the 'Rejects and Returned Items' desk…"

Danny from Seattle laughed out loud; others followed. Immediately I hated him. I rubbed my collarbones with my right thumb and middle finger.

Pauline smiled at me. "Sherri, then you'll be having your birthday while you're here with us?" She knew this, because all trainees had to reach their twentieth birthday by graduation. I nodded, smiling, but was still red from Danny's laughter. She asked if anyone else would be having birthdays while in training. Mara and two others raised their hands.

Each of our four instructors took a turn speaking when the trainees finished. They delighted in talking about themselves, bragging about their years of flying, all the fabulous places they'd traveled to and all the exciting people, including famous celebrities, they'd met. We oohed and awed appropriately, especially when Alan told us he'd had Elvis Presley on a flight only months before he'd passed away. Lydia, the most senior, had flown for eight years! I wondered why I hadn't seen a black stewardess like her before. Then I realized I hadn't seen a male steward before either. Now I had two as instructors. Alan was short, balding, and funny—the kind of guy everyone likes immediately. Mike was more of an efficient type in his dress shirt and tie—hands on his hips with a confidant stance and a business-friendly grin.

Pauline changed the mood with her next announcement. "For four weeks you'll be in and out of classrooms, dressed in business attire with your hair styled appropriately for flying—which means *Up* if it touches your collar. You'll learn everything from how to make a martini to how to recognize each aircraft type. You will not be late—ever. Airplanes don't wait. You will have one weekend day off. On the other you will go out to the airport and ride along on observation flights. You are to observe quietly and do what you're told. However, most of the crews will let you work and we encourage you to do that. Your fifth and final week will be in the airplane mockups learning FAA and Gateway Airlines safety requirements. You will be evacuating airplanes; well, the mockups of course but they are very real; you'll feel like you're in an actual plane. There's a lot of physically demanding stuff during Emergency week training, so you can wear casual clothes. Jeans are fine. You will be tested on everything and you must score an eighty percent or better on each test. If you do not pass, you must re-take the test. Numerous re-takes will get you sent home so this is serious folks; you're in for some hard work. Don't neglect your studies."

"Not working as a group will also send you flying and I don't mean on one of our planes," Alan added. He made funny faces to make us laugh, placed his first finger over his top lip to represent a mustache then fell into a Gestapo rant as he continued. "We will ask you to leave training if you do not cooperate and help each other out." He goose-stepped around the room. "We don't want tattle-tales and we don't want to hear irritating complaints about each other." Falling back into normal speech he said, "Look guys, you'll be working every flight for the rest of your career as a team so learn to resolve your differences amongst yourselves and learn that lesson now. Even our largest airplanes are cramped—you're not going to escape each other—don't fight, argue, or get into power struggles. That's one of the best tips I can give you. The *Other* best tip I can give you is run to the galley as soon as a passenger gets sick because *Nothing* kills the stench of throw up faster than gobs of used coffee grounds!"

"What?" One the trainees asked with real surprise.

"It's true," Alan said. "Get those big coffee cans of used coffee and dump a couple of pounds of them on top. Then the cleanup is bearable because it knocks out the odor." The other instructors were smiling and nodding yes. *They obviously weren't big on stench.*

The Contracts test was the one everyone dreaded and the test that required the most re-takes, Mike said. He would be instructing us for that module. "Our Contracts module is tough and thorough but it's info you must know. You will learn how to figure out your flight pay, calculate your hours, meal expenses and most important, when you are 'legal' to fly again after returning home. Like pilots, you will be expected to record all pertinent data in a logbook and carry it with you at all times."

Alan interrupted Mike to warn us about the evil 'Crew Desk' which he referred to as the 'Screw Desk' and how they, the employees giving us or changing our flying assignments, would pull fast ones—especially on green new hires who didn't know their legalities. We would also be learning about special add-ons such as: understaffing pay, First Flight Attendant pay, and galley pay, when applicable.

Lydia took over. She was nearly as tall as Jane. "Speaking of contracts, I need you all to pick up the first sheet in your blue folder and hold it up for me like this," she demonstrated. "Do you all have one?" We shuffled our papers and nodded. "I want you all to hold it up—now. Ok I see every single person holding it, right? This is a binding agreement between you and Gateway that covers the specific rules and regulations while you're here at the training center. You need to read and sign it. Give it to Pauline tonight."

She put her paper down. "I want to draw your attention to item number five. It states very clearly that men are not allowed on the women's floors, and that women are not allowed on the men's floor. We still have more females coming to the training center than men, so the female dorms are on the second, third and fourth floors. Obviously the first floor is for classrooms, the cafeteria and conference rooms. The top floor, number five, is for men only. Does everyone understand this?" Giggles broke out. "I want to see your hands in the air now if you understand this—I will not put up with anyone telling me later that they did not read this or that they weren't aware. Let's see everyone's paw and I'm going to repeat this because sometimes people don't hear me. *Men are not allowed on the women's floors and women are not allowed on the men's floor!* Sign those papers. Don't let me catch anyone breaking that rule! It better not happen. If it does, I will not be a happy camper, and Lordy, you all do not want to be around me when I am not a happy camper." She laughed and stepped back, leading all of us into a moment of comic relief.

"As soon as you hand me your signed form, collect your handouts and schedules. Go to the store by the check-in desk to purchase your first logbook." Pauline pointed. "All of your observation flights need to be recorded and your pay figured as if you're really out there on the line working. That will be part of your contracts class."

"We have to do math?" asked Georgia, a former Miss Alabama and second runner-up for Miss America. I rolled my eyes at the southern beauty and we both laughed. *Fast friends.* "Math is a four-letter word for me," she drawled. "Didn't someone tell them I left a lousy four-letter word job for this glamorous one?" She turned toward me. "I'm Georgia," she said, giving me a genuine pageant-quality smile.

I smiled back. "I didn't picture pouring over pay certs. I just want to have fun for a living, that's why I left the bank. But I'm pretty good at math," I said perking up for her. "Shouldn't be more than a little addition or multiplication. If you need help let me know."

"Thank you," she nodded with real gratitude. "Being a good team player already."

"Listen up everyone," Pauline called out as too much banter had broken out. "I know you're getting restless but I need a few more minutes. I want to impress upon you something of utmost importance and that is—just how far our job has come in forty years." She seemed taller, suddenly beaming with pride. "Gone are the days of being called 'stewardesses,'" she exclaimed. "Gone are the days of being grabbed by male passengers, *and*, being pinched by supervisors to insure we were wearing girdles! Thanks to years of hard work, enduring prejudice and sexism and thanks to our unions who fought tirelessly for fair working conditions, good pay and respect, we have shed the image of the fun-loving bimbo stewardess of yesteryear and turned this job into a respected career. Ladies and gentlemen," she said, as if moments away from presenting the president of the United States, "we are *'Flight Attendants!'* Neat, attractive, professionals."

Some clapped, some cheered. Others beamed, sitting up high in their seats. *Yeah baby*, we've arrived, their smug looks said. I pursed my lips and looked at Georgia. "I don't want to be a Flight Attendant," I whispered. I never wanted any such thing. "I want to be a Stewardess!" Georgia laughed hard, throwing her head back. I had checked off the days, months, and years as my boring life had dragged by until I was finally old enough to apply. I didn't want to be a neat attractive professional… I wanted to be a sex symbol.

I'm too late; I sank into my chair. I'd missed the era—it was over. Why couldn't I have turned twenty in the 60s? No more glamour, no more sexiness, only… professionalism. What kind of crap was that? I wouldn't be swishing down the aisle with a smile serving snacks and cocktails in a sharp military ensemble answering calls for 'Oh Stewardess' from scores of gorgeous men who all wanted me. Instead, I'd be a no-nonsense-faced prude in that miserable, mauve-eggplant beige barfy thing Madge had worn answering calls for 'Oh professional.' Some ugly chick with hairy legs must've put them up to it. I slunk out of the meeting after finding out more bad news. Class seniority was ranked by date of birth. I was the youngest: the most junior in our class.

"Why you're the baby," Georgia said in her accent. She made why sound like a baby's cry: whah.

Then like a good 'flight attendant,' I got in line to purchase my logbook.

Danny raced up and gave me a friendly push. He really was cute; he had tanned skin and wild sun-bleached feathered hair. "Hey Rejects," he said—a nickname others picked up on quickly—"seniority first," he stated loudly. Everyone thought this was a great idea so right off the bat, we could all honor the pecking order. We lined up by age; Jane was first and I kept stepping further behind. By the time I got to the front, they were out of logbooks.

"It's ok," the clerk said sympathetically. "You're only required to record your flight info in one place; it doesn't matter what you use."

Everyone else had walked away proudly holding a cool slim three by four-inch faux leather-bound book with 'Logbook' embossed in gold lettering on the front. Some were red, some were black. I got an eight by five steno pad with sixty-pound stock paper covers like secretaries use for dictation. It was yellow and had a metal binder at the top. Using a pencil the clerk wrote, 'Logbook' on the front. *Wow, gee, real neat.*

Upstairs, while listening to Mara exchange the details of her life with our other two roommates, Amy and Cheyenne, I organized my materials. Next week when the new shipment came in, I'd buy a real logbook. The clerk had told me they were expecting more by Friday, before the next class arrived. I may be young, but I'm not stupid. I'd get one before that group lined up in seniority order. I opened the steno pad. It was perfect for shorthand and I smiled thinking I could write secrets about everyone in it that no one could read—like Danny. *That's it!* I erased the penciling, grabbed a permanent marker and wrote, *'FlightLog'* across the front instead. I liked the way it looked with two capital letters but no space between the words. Then I turned to the first page and scribbled with a regular pen:

• *Danny is a dork.*

I ended up writing in longhand. It had been way too long since my sophomore high school shorthand class—I couldn't remember enough of it. My secret log would be perfect to record the details, observations and life-altering events of my flying career, which I guessed would last two years until some rich, dashing, handsome man swept me off my feet and made me his bride. *I'd wear his wedding ring.* Our ceremony and reception would put Shannon's to shame. I went over to my closet and tucked *FlightLog* into my suitcase where none of my roommates would see it. Then I went into the lounge across the hall from our dorm room. After much channel surfing, I learned that Stevie Cauthen, the 18-year-old six-million-dollar jockey riding 'Affirmed' had won the Kentucky Derby, beating the favored horse, 'Alydar.' Only one other person in the room seemed to care. Many hadn't known who Bobby Orr was. Next observation for my disguised journal:

• *Few of my fellow flight attendants seem to be sports fans.*

Chapter 2:

. . . . ♫

My Sweet Lord

As 'junior' roomie, I got last dibs in the bathroom. I took the news cheerfully, refusing to let anyone see how the junior stuff was bothering me. It wouldn't have been so bad, but the others always ran past their allotted times. Usually, I had less than ten minutes to shower and dress.

Girls were scheduled for 'Female Appearance One' while guys attended 'Male Appearance One' thus missing our makeup lectures where all my mistakes were pointed out. I wore my rouge too low—it needed to be higher on my cheekbones, which I couldn't find on my round face. My lipstick was too light. The blue mascara I used wasn't flattering to my brown-hazel eyes. I should take advantage of foundations—that gross pancakey stuff because it would help my makeup set and last longer. I tried to act as if I cared about all of this, but I didn't. I spent five minutes doing makeup whether I was going to the grocery store or to the prom. *A lie;* I didn't wear makeup to the store; for work or proms, it was five minutes. I wasn't going to spend hours before each trip sculpting cheek bones on my face with thick rouges trying to copy Vogue models. We received samples from manufacturers and were urged to 'experiment.' I made sure my roommates saw me trying.

"You'll never be a makeup artist," Amy said with disdain. As a Barbie wannabe, Amy collected anything that 'Mattel' color. Her robe matched the pink sponge curlers she often wore.

We were warned about the drying qualities of the aircraft cabins and the training center itself. "Keep your skin hydrated," Lydia said, "Don't skimp on moisturizers. Buy good products."

In the first few days, we were fitted for our uniforms. The seamstress, Rosie, pinned and fussed. *Rosie the riveter; making it all fit and snug.* I was impressed and in spite of finding our uniforms ugly, I looked forward to wearing mine.

"They won't be ready until the week you graduate," she said as she placed my chalked and tacked items into a bag bearing my name. "Gateway doesn't want anyone trying on their final fitted ensemble until they've passed everything, including Emergency training."

"That is a great T-shirt Rosie; where did you get it?" Printed across her front was: *'Marry Me, Fly Free'* in flowing letters.

"An instructor was wearing one a few years ago; I loved it so she got me one at the airline store at the airport. I work for the airlines too," she gushed. "I get passes, just like everyone else."

Lessons I did much better in included the twenty-four-hour clock and airport codes. The clock was simple—dad used it all the time. 'Dinner will be ready at seventeen hundred hours,' he'd say. Subtract twelve numbers—it's 5 P.M. But it gave some in my class headaches. Poor Georgia. The three letter airport codes were also easy—most were obvious. San Francisco: SFO, Atlanta: ATL, Denver: DEN. Some were odd and required a little memorization. Kansas City: MCI, Chicago: ORD, Cincinnati: CVG. Our test would be to fill in a dotted map of the US using the correct three letter codes for all the cities Gateway serviced. We were not expected to learn international cities; we didn't fly abroad except for occasional charters. Though large, Gateway was a domestic carrier.

This brought us to 'bidding.' The process could be tedious—no way around it. Each month the schedules were different. Some would be turnarounds, (one-day trips) some would be two-day trips, some would be three-day trips, and many choices (called 'lines') would be mixed. Some would be the same cities and same days of the week for the whole month. Others would have to be mapped out on a calendar because every trip differed. Therefore, the only way to really inform yourself about the options was to read each bid 'line' carefully because each one was unique.

"As new hires," Mike pointed out, "you will be on reserve every other month. It's easier bidding those lines because you're only bidding for days off. You don't have to look at specific trips or positions. Lots of this is not going to make sense until you're out there. Just take my word for it, it's only one part of your test so don't spend too much time on this."

Cheyenne raised her hand. "I'm confused," she said. "You talk about reserve, then you talk about ready reserve, what's the difference? If I'm on reserve and they're allowed to call me in the middle of night, does that mean I have to sleep with my uniform on?"

Danny and Tom howled. Tom rubbed his hands through his uneven long Afro. "Only you have to Cheyenne," he said. Danny smacked him on the back. "You probably shouldn't sleep at all," he continued. "Sit up all night in your uniform so you're ready to go," he finished.

Mike gave Tom a cool glance. "Of course not Cheyenne," he said. "If you're called, you have four hours to get to the airport. There are 'short call-outs.' That's anything less than four hours' notice—you aren't required to make those trips. But you have to show up. If the plane can't leave because you will be filling the FAA minimum crew required, they will hold the plane for you. Just go to bed and when they call, get dressed and go. This is what a good contract and a good union gets you. Four hours is a lot. Used to have to show up in thirty minutes no matter what or you were fired. Learn this stuff guys! To answer your other question, yes, it is confusing. Reserves are usually told the night before what they're going to fly or what the next day's 'trip' is going to be. If the crew desk thinks they may have last-minute assignments, they can covert you to 'Ready Reserve' where you either wait by the phone, or you go sit at the airport in case you have to cover a trip fast. For those of you who are always on ready reserve, get a beeper! They're fifty bucks a month but they're worth it. This will all come to you. Read this contract!" He handed out bid sheets displaying our weekend flight options. There were forty lines. "These are your observation flights," he said. "You're going to bid them just as if you're bidding next month's schedule. Try to fly at least one narrow-body trip (planes with one aisle: Boeing 727, Boeing 737, or the McDonald Douglas DC-8 aircraft) and one jumbo jet, or wide-body trip (planes with two aisles: the MacDonald Douglas DC-10, or the Boeing 747 aircraft). That will maximize your exposure." There was a charge in the room as my classmates examined the bids.

"Look at this one," said Jane. "Work one leg out to LA then deadhead back! Think I'll take that one!" We already knew that 'Deadhead' meant simply flying as a passenger, taking a seat and enjoying the ride. These were done when they only needed you to work one way, either work out and deadhead back or deadhead out and work back.

"I think you'll probably hold it," Mike laughed, "seeing as you're the most senior."

I glanced at the 'lines of flying' then pushed them aside.

"Sherri, aren't you curious about the bids?" Mike asked.

"Sure," I said. "I'm looking forward to my training flights but I don't have to bid. I'll get the last line no matter what."

"You shouldn't look at it that way. You should bid just for the practice."

"Think I'll get plenty of practice on the line."

We were interrupted when Pauline came into the room. Behind her was a scowling, beautiful redhead. "Everyone I'd like you to meet Jeanna," Pauline said, motioning toward the gal taking a seat near me. "Jeanna was in a previous class and had to return home for personal reasons; she will be joining us. Please make her feel welcome."

"Welcome back Jeanna," Mike retraced his footsteps and gathered materials for her. "Ok. Any other questions about the lines of flying? About bidding in general? All the answers are in your contract! I want you to know it like you know the back of your hand."

* * *

I knew my roommate Amy would be looking for information about our new classmate, and I was right; she was talking about Jeanna when I stepped into our dorm room.

"She's from LA," Amy said to the others. "She's a manicurist and *Cher* used to be one of her customers! After we talked for a while, I asked her nicely why she had left training and you know what she said?"

"What?" Cheyenne asked obediently. She was Amy's shadow.

"Things," Amy complained. "Just… 'things!' That was all she said."

"She doesn't want to talk about it," I flopped across my bed as I spoke.

"That's not really in the team spirit, is it?" she countered. "How can we help her if…"

"Let it go Amy," I'd grown tired of her. She had harsh opinions and was often unpleasant. In class she acted sweet but Amy was a phony. She backstabbed and whined. I had not heard her say one nice thing about any female in our group, including our instructors.

"You're just happy because there's probably someone junior to you now."

"You got me all figured out." With that, I leapt off the bed and left the room. And, I ran right into Danny in the elevator.

"Rejects!" As much as I hated the nickname, Danny always seemed happy to see me. I tried to stay mad but I took one look at his outstretched arms as if inviting me to hug him, and I laughed. "What's up?" he asked.

"Had to escape Malibu Barbie before I threatened to blow up her Dreamhouse."

"Close quarters can do that. Remember what Alan told us…"

I gave him a warning look; he stopped. "Are you hungry?" I asked. "Let's get something to eat." The cafeteria was open from 5:30 A.M. to midnight. To avoid the stuffiness of our tiny room, cramped with four girls, I'd taken to spending lots of time there. The food was free and it was good. Danny had his bids. Each line had several letters; I remembered that they corresponded with where each flight attendant would sit and where they would work. "These letters don't matter to us. We are just observing, we aren't going to be assigned to actual positions. You're making it hard. We'll be sitting in passenger seats. We're not safety qualified yet; we can't sit in jumpseats. Ignore all this." I grabbed the blue Inflight Handbook he was studying and slammed it shut. Handbooks had to be carried on every flight. The binders had large fasteners because revisions were common; we would update our manuals constantly we were told, removing old pages and putting in new ones. We scoured the bids; I helped him pick and choose what he liked. At twenty-four, he really wasn't that senior to me; he had to bid thirty-two times to cover himself.

"Heard you helped Cheyenne and Georgia," he smiled sweetly at me.

"You almost sound nice Danny; that possible?"

"Guess I just expected you to be all needy—being so young and inexperienced. You surprised me. You give the instructors a run sometimes."

"Look who's talking? You and your friends are always cracking jokes."

"That's different than *Challenging* them. Like today with Mike. Why didn't you just say, 'Ok Mike, I'll bid!'"

"Because there are always other things to do. We haven't started anything really hard yet; I'm not going to waste my time. Besides, I just got practice helping you. Now stop talking and let me eat!"

In week two we covered aircraft memorization, onboard services, and basic safety procedures. We were shortening the names of planes too, learning 'the lingo.' A Boeing 727 was called a '727' or a '27;' a McDonald Douglas stretch DC-8 was an '8' or a 'stretch-8.' Finally, we were setting up galleys and serving dummies propped up in passenger seats. Our instructors tried not to laugh as we answered questions written out on the dummies' trays.

"Danny," Alan called. "You're in the middle of a combined cocktail and meal service when the captain comes over the PA and announces that they've picked up lots of time and they will be landing the plane in ten minutes. Half the cabin has meal trays; what do you do?"

"Fix myself a cocktail and sit down in the first available seat."

Services pushed us, but it was fun. It was also a relief to be up doing something instead of sitting at desks. There was much laughter as we worked together in cramped galleys, running into the aisles, smashing into each other, dropping food and drinks;

having fun using the Public Address (PA) systems—it was terrific. The 737 had many configurations; it was difficult remembering the service flow. Three of us found ourselves on a particularly strange 737 mockup.

"Jeanna," Alan called out. "How are you going to work this flight? You've only got one galley that first class and coach share. Some coach customers are in front of the galley like first-class customers and some are in back of it. There's one liquor cart. What do you do? It's not going to be feasible to have three people working out of the galley at the same time, especially if one is working with first-class glasses and large wine bottles."

Jeanna turned red and looked at me.

I prompted her, "toward the galley…"

"Well," she said slowly, "you always serve… toward the galley…" I could see her working it out. "The A serves first class in rows one thru three, then serves the coach people at the front of the plane, rows four through ten, working directly out of the galley. The other two take the cart to the *Back of the plane*, and serve aft to forward, rows twenty-two to eleven."

"Excellent!" Alan cheered. "Did everyone hear that?"

We had a lot of re-takes for our inflight services module. My classmates moaned but the instructors held their ground. Anyone with a seventy-nine or less had to re-take the test. Jeanna passed; she was ecstatic.

Next, we learned how to make drinks. There were interesting tidbits such as, when Japanese businessmen asked for 'Whiskey,' they meant Scotch. I struggled with Cocktails. I didn't know Jack Daniels from Crème de Menthe. Coach drinks were easy; fill a plastic cup with ice, hand over the unopened miniature liquor bottle and the mix—like Coke or Tonic Water—and charge a buck fifty. But in first class we made the drinks by hand. They were complimentary *of course.*

"I'll help you," Jeanna said, "used to wait tables." She taught me how to swirl Vermouth with ice in the first-class glasses then toss everything out and straight-pour the gin or vodka with fresh ice.

"This isn't how they tell us to do it," I pointed out.

"Trust me," she grinned. "The snooty people up front will love you if you do it this way."

Jeanna started showing up at our room, knocking and asking me if I wanted to go get a cup of coffee or take a walk. I felt squeezed—Mara and I were good pals but Mara caught on quickly. She had lots of other friends. On the other hand, I was Jeanna's only friend, so I'd go off with her. Some in our class called her 'Jeanna Meana' behind her back.

Basic safety put us back in the classroom. "What is it we must stop and check whenever the seatbelt sign comes on?" Lydia asked. "Georgia?"

"Seatbelts," she said.

"What else?"

"Lavatories," someone else added.

"And?"

"Infants in the first row if passengers are using bassinets," Amy said. Gateway had portable bassinets that screwed into the bulkheads (front walls) in first and coach on many of its airplanes. That way customers could put their babies in and take a break from holding them.

"I'm never going to remember that," Jeanna whined. "It's Thursday! We test on this plus all the other stuff tomorrow! Everything's thrown at us so fast."

"Remember the three B's," I said. "Babies, belts and blue rooms (shop lingo for bathrooms)."

"You need to tell everyone that Sherri; it's so much easier."

"What's that Jeanna?" Lydia asked, hearing us talk in the back.

"Sherri has a good way of remembering that; it's really helpful."

"Share your methods Sherri. Let's hear it."

I flushed as everyone looked at me. "Um, I would call it the three B's?" I sort of asked. "If the seatbelt sign blinks, I visualize it as blinking to remind me of the letter B, check your three B's: babies, belts and blue rooms. It helps to put them in alphabetical order."

"That's wonderful Sherri; you should share more often. Remember we're a team here. How did you come up with that so fast?" Lydia asked.

"My mother's a part-time teacher; one of her classes is study skills." *I was going to reference the mnemonic device 'King Phillip Came Over From Geneva Switzerland' (Kingdom Phylum Class Order Family Genus Species) but that would be showing off.* Amy was glaring at me. *Great.* By now I wasn't confused; she hated my guts. I'd helped some of the others and was well liked. And I hadn't had a re-take. After every test she'd jump at me, 'What did you get?'

That weekend we set out for our first observation flights. Everyone had been issued a Gateway picture ID and even though we weren't in uniforms, we waltzed past security flashing our badges, just as inflight and cockpit crews did. *It felt so good!* Several of the bid lines had two or more positions so my fellow 'training' partner was… Danny. He looked great and I looked pretty cute myself. I'd saved my best 'business-attire' for the OB flights but as we moved through the concourse, I noticed things felt a bit snug.

"You always wear your skirts tight?" Danny asked, as if reading my mind.

"Danny…"

"I'm not complaining; my Lord, you look nice."

"Hello." A gal in a long, flowing, hippie-style skirt was suddenly all over Danny. She put a flower to his chest and pinned it on him. "A lovely flower for a lovely human being," she said. "We believe in peace and love," she smiled in an 'I'm so pious' way. She showed him a thick book about the Hare Krishnas. "And we don't ask for handouts but if you would like to contribute a little something, I would like to give you this gift in return…"

As she conned, I noticed other Hare Krishna followers in the terminal approaching other travelers—especially those in military uniforms.

"You want me to buy this book? How much?" Danny asked.

"It would be wonderful if you could donate ten dollars. You would be…"

"Ok," Danny pulled out his wallet. "Tell you what, since *I really want to be with you,* I'll buy your book for ten dollars if you buy mine for twenty." He held up his inflight manual. "I don't ask for handouts but I do accept cash gift contributions." Then he sang, *"Hare Krishna,"* and I laughed. He could hold a tune. She unpinned his flower and walked away.

Soon we were at our gate, but we had to move aside quickly as a sprinting gentleman fled past us. Obviously, he was late for his flight further down the concourse. "Go OJ go!" Danny yelled; others in the concourse laughed as Danny made reference to the many famous Hertz Rental Car commercials OJ Simpson had made. The passenger threw him a thumbs up without breaking his stride. He looked like the kind of guy who raced for flights often. I was sure he'd heard that encouraging line before. "He's probably just trying to get away from that Hare Krishna chick," Danny said.

We met our crew in the boarding area. "I'm Suzanne, the A," said the oldest. Completely relaxed, she sat in the boarding area with her crew enjoying a cigarette. She had long legs and stretched them out unabashedly for all to see. Being the 'A' meant the same as being the First Flight Attendant. "Narrow-bodies are easy," she said. "The A always works in first class, takes care of the cockpit and helps out in coach as needed. Are either of you interested in doing the announcements?"

"We haven't really practiced that," said Danny as I shook my head no. "We'll do the safety demos though if that's ok."

"Anything you like," she looked Danny up and down. "Aren't you two cute," she added. "If you feel bold enough to try any announcements on the return, let me know. First time's the hardest." She gave me a wicked smile. She looked like she had lots of fun and I wished we were going to fly a real trip and have a layover with this crew.

"Where are you guys based?" I asked.

"New York," she said. "I wouldn't live anywhere else."

Danny would work with Suzanne up front on our flight from Cleveland to Denver while I worked in the back. We would switch cabins for the return flight. As soon as we got onboard, the coach crew started moving. They checked everything on the 727: megaphones, safety kits, air pressure in the slides, doors, handles, buttons, phones, fire extinguishers. Then they set up their galley. Popping off big, heavy doors, they began counting trays, opening the warming drawers, counting entrees, loosening bags of ice, checking liquor, making coffee... busy. I wasn't a lot of help, but I did what I was supposed to: observe. When customers started on, I stepped into the aisle and offered magazines and pillows. It was easy to smile; it felt great to be on a real airplane and away from the training center.

Seconds after takeoff the pilots turned off the 'No Smoking' sign and the coach attendants immediately lit up. We'd been airborne about twelve seconds. I was in the last row. One of them offered me her pack but I shook my head. Under their jumpseat, they had set down a paper coffee cup with water in it. It was their ashtray. After their last drags, they jumped up. We served a full cocktail service then a meal service with a choice of beef or chicken, and another beverage service. I loaded the hot entrees onto the trays, stacked the foil tops back into the ovens, helped run them out and worked from the back galley serving drinks while the two of them worked the drink cart.

After all the passengers deplaned, we only had thirty minutes before we headed back to Cleveland. Gateway Airlines changed out Suzanne's front galley six minutes before we closed the door. There was much more to do in first than in coach before takeoff. We offered drinks on the ground, hung coats, marked the hangars with seat numbers, stashed luggage, took inflight drink and meal orders, and made sure the cockpit had beverages too. I mixed the pre-departure drinks while she ran them out. The agent headed down with our final manifest and shut the door.

In the galley, I was feeling like hot stuff in Suzanne's name-monogrammed inflight apron. "Sooo," I asked her. "Any celebrities aboard? The Pope? Joan Rivers? Al Pacino?"

"They were all up here on the last flight having drinks together," she said. "Sorry you missed it. You know, the name Suzanne suits you. Have you done any emergency training yet—Suzanne?"

"No," I laughed.

"When we close the door we hook the door slides to the fuselage—the body of the plane," she explained. "Let me show you." She bent down in front of her door and pulled up a flat metal strip. It had been attached to the bottom of the door. "See the hooks in the floor? You place this bar inside them. Then the slide inflates if the door is opened. We do this just as the plane pulls away. That's when you hear 'prepare for departure.'"

"Ohhh," I'd heard it many times but never realized that was their queue to hook the slides so they would inflate if the door was opened in an emergency... made sense.

"Want to connect them? While I make the announcement," she asked.

"Sure," I said, still feeling fun loving. "Let *Me* hook 'em this time."

Suzanne laughed, "Ready?" she picked up the PA but instead of saying, 'prepare for departure' she said, "Hook 'em girls."

I could hear Danny laughing from his coach seat. "Hallelujah!" he cried.

Suzanne pulled a folded cart out of a thin cabinet behind the first-class seats after takeoff. I recognized it. "This is what we call a queen cart and we use it upfront a lot instead of a heavy drink cart. They use them in back too on the all coach 737s…"

"I've set them up before," I said, recalling our services module and how weird the 37s were.

Suzanne used the cart first for her linen, silverware, glassware, salad and rolls. We prepared the salad in the aisle for each passenger, laying down a linen tablecloth, giving them glassware, napkins, flatware, salt & pepper shakers, butter dishes, and rolls she had carefully warmed in foil.

First class wanted drinks! We served cocktails first, then wine with dinner; coffee after dinner followed by after dinner liqueurs—all in three hours. Suzanne stripped the cart after the salad presentation and reset it for a roast she carved in the aisle. She worked fast. After we collected all the main course dishes, she stripped the cart again and set it up for ice cream sundaes. There was so little room—it was an education so much more valuable than any of our service classes at the center. When everyone seemed satiated, she fixed four bowls of ice cream and put them on a tray. I was exhausted and my feet hurt.

"Here," she said, handing me the tray. "Take these to the cockpit and sit with them awhile. They love company, especially someone as young, cute, and friendly as you are."

"What's the code?" I asked. We knew there was always a 'secret' code between the inflight crew and the cockpit. Usually, it was two knocks. Sometimes it was three.

"Two knocks," she said, eyeing the tray I held. "Use your foot; you'll get good at it."

The three pilots were thrilled to see me. They peppered me with questions about myself, training, and being a new hire, while we all enjoyed the sundaes. I didn't say a word about my dad.

"Sherri," the second officer asked. He was behind the first officer and I was sitting in the seat to his left. "Would you like to join the Mile High Club? I could get you in," he grinned.

"What's that?"

When they laughed without answering I knew I'd been had somehow, so I dropped it. Suzanne came in to have a cigarette. As I gathered up the dishes, the second officer turned his attention away from me and began singing, "Oh Susie Q baby I love you—Susie Q. I like the way you walk; I like the way you talk…" I rolled my eyes and left.

After we landed, Danny and I got our start and end times for both flights from the cockpit and recorded them in our logbooks before saying goodbye. I called my private one, *FlightLog* and the real one, my logbook. I loved its shiny red covers. Danny's was black, of course.

"We have an hour and a half before the next bus," Danny said. "Want to get a drink?"

"Yes." I was beat; a real drink would hit the spot. There wasn't any liquor at the training center, just bottles filled with water for practicing. "You know what else I want? I want to find SOPs. The store for airline employees. I think it's in this concourse."

We found the store and I bought myself and Mara *'Marry Me, Fly Free'* T shirts. Danny bought a folding alarm clock. Then we had drinks at the concourse restaurant and reminisced about our day, the crew, and Suzanne, the gal I now affectionately referred to as, 'The Happy Hooker.'

"What the heck did you guys learn in Male Appearance?" I asked.

"Gateway won't let stewards wear earrings. Couple of guys have to let their holes grow in."

"We have male classmates with piercings?" I'd never seen a man in person who wore earrings.

"Yeah Sherri; we've got a few… you know." He looked at my puzzled face. "Oh my God," he laughed. "Sherri, don't you know that most of the guys in our class are gay?"

I stared at him. Then I put my drink down. "Really? How do you know that? You mean…" I thought about Tom. "Is Tom gay? He can't be."

"He may not be openly yet," Danny said. "But once we get on the line, he's going to come out of the closet so fast we're all going to get splinters."

"We need a class on identifying who's gay," I said. "We gals are allowed to have *One* piercing in each ear—that's it. Guess if you have more you look too…"

"Contemporary?" Danny grinned.

"Danny," I teased. "Big word!"

Back at the center, Danny asked me if I wanted to go downtown. "Sherri, lots of us go out on the weekends; you sit in the cafeteria and study. Don't you want a break?"

"I'm not going to study. I'm really tired. That turnaround was work, especially in these shoes." I slipped a foot from my high heel and rubbed my aching arch. "I want to put on sweats and relax. I also want to know who won the Preakness. Danny?" I asked. "What's the Mile High Club?"

Upstairs I unburied *FlightLog* and wrote about Suzanne, Danny, the Hare Krishnas and falling for some old airline joke. Danny had explained it to me with raucous laughter.

- *'Sherri,' he'd said. 'When you're ready to join let me know; I'd love to be the one who initiates you.' Then he sang again, 'My sweet lord, hm my lord, I really want to see you; I really want to be with you!' Why do men start singing whenever they like someone?*

Chapter 3:

· · · · · · · · · · ♫

Just the Way You Are

IN WEEK THREE, WE MOVED ON to 'Appearance Two.' There wasn't going to be an 'Appearance Three.' I was relieved that all the staring in the mirror stuff would soon end. A local beautician, Avnos, dragged posters of the latest dos into class. Most required blow-dryers. I wasn't very good with them. Those of us with long tresses would get a much more 'professional' look if we chose a shorter style, he said, prancing around the room. Now *This* guy was spot on gay!

Avnos approached Jeanna. "Let me show you what I could do," he reached for her head.

"I'm not cutting my hair," she stated loudly while pulling away. Jeanna, like me, was forced to wear her hair up. But she always wore it in a different style and it looked terrific. I pulled mine back in a tight ponytail, wound my rubber band around it, and pinned it to my head with dozens of bobby pins. If I sprayed the short loose pieces my head looked bald, dark and shiny. If I didn't, I looked like I'd stuck my finger in the toaster while standing in the bathtub.

Avnos moved toward me and gave a short spastic cry. "Ah! My God, what is this?" Within minutes, he had convinced the class that I should try a chin-length cut. The front would be longer and taper up at an angle until it reached the back. I nodded, even though I hated the idea.

"Really Rejects," Amy said. "You need an adult haircut."

"You know what Amy?" Jeanna's brow rose; she smiled diabolically. It was the first time we had seen her teeth. "You need a muzzle, and *You don't* get to call Sherri *'Rejects.'*" Though our beauty queens and Playboy bunnies were lovely, Jeanna was the real looker in our class.

"Now girls," Avnos clapped his hands. "No disagreements. I'm here only to offer advice."

At the end of class, Lydia highlighted the finer points of our Appearance modules. "Remember," she said. "Reapplying lipstick and blusher inflight *Is* part of your performance evaluation! Make sure you do this when you get your check rides. Always look your best girls; you're the neat, attractive, professional face of Gateway Airlines."

Later, with Mara in the lounge, I kidded about all the things it was 'recommended' I change. "They really love me *just the way* I am, don't they?"

She was putting the latest revisions in her handbook; loose, dated, removed pages filled up a trash can beside her. "It's just part of the class; you're so darn good-looking Sherri; I wouldn't change a thing. Everyone loves you. Danny can't keep his eyes off you."

My mouth fell open; I was surprised by her words. We'd been at the center a long time; I'd been busy and stressed about not getting along with Amy, and surrounded by many gorgeous gals, not only in my class but in the other classes—I hadn't felt attractive at all; just the opposite. Everyone seemed older and stylishly more sophisticated. But Mom had taught me to accept compliments graciously. "Thank you Mara; that's so nice to hear."

"I know you don't look at yourself that way," she said. "But you are really pretty—beautiful Sherri, just beautiful. Fresh, sweet and you smile all the time, even when you're walking down the hall, you do it naturally. People want someone they can talk to, and you're there. There aren't many who can compete with you."

I floated all day. That night I pulled out *FlightLog* and listed Mara's virtues. She was quieter, gentler, more poised than I, and I wrote it all down and finished with:

- *I love you Mara. And that's forever.*

And I did. Suddenly, I started to cry. It embarrassed me at first; then I let the tears come freely. I didn't need to change anything for Gateway; just mature a bit and not take things so hard. I wanted to get out of here and start my flying life; the training center was getting old—fast.

Week four was reserved for lectures and for our toughest class: 'Contracts.' We attended presentations on spending, saving, planning for our financial futures, healthcare, personal safety in hotel rooms and on layovers—which was a totally bizarre unit, and on 'Superior Service Skills' presented by Alan. He wanted to introduce us to Gateway's 'Sea to Shining Sea' first-class service— anything from a point on the Atlantic to a point on the Pacific or vice versa: New York to LA, Washington DC to San Francisco, Boston to Seattle. He was proud of the first-class linen because each had a button hole so that businessmen could prevent spills from staining their shirts. Alan wrapped linen around carts, buckets, wine bottles and trays. He placed first-class wine glasses upside down around the perimeter of a bowl filled with ice, assuring us that we would all find bowls like this in any first-class pit.

The 'pit' was a mysterious airplane galley that was hidden from view—you had to go down an elevator on the 'jumbo' or 'wide-bodied' aircrafts (the 10s and the 47s—our aircraft 'lingo' terms were getting shorter all the time). There were two pits on the 47s and one on the 10. One attendant was assigned to work down there alone; it sounded intriguing. Working the pit position required special training. Alan told us not to worry; we would be qualified for that later after we'd flown for at least three months. We could not be forced (junior-manned) into working a premium position until we had received proper training. Basically, if you were in charge of the first class or coach service on a jumbo airplane, or downstairs in one of its pits, these constituted 'Premium Positions' he tried to clarify—only confusing us more. We scratched our heads.

"Never mind," Alan said, seeing us squirm. "You'll get it when you're on the line."

"What does that mean; on what line?" Cheyenne asked. "Is this on our Contracts test?"

"No," he said. "Just the pay differential. I was trying to be helpful, sorry."

Danny threw a pile of linen at him. "Here," he said. "These are for your wine bottles at home and for your guests so they can keep their suits clean."

"I'll ignore that," said Alan. "Now let's get back to my presentation. After you let the glasses sit for a while upside down on ice, you lift each one quickly, flicking them up like this!" He grabbed two glasses by their stems then flipped them right-side-up beside his face with a silly look of glee. "They fog up nicely, don't they? Just like chilled glasses coming out of the freezer! This is called 'wafting the glasses' and those of you who become marvelous flight attendants like me, will take the time to do little steps such as this to enhance your service." He put the glasses down and took one of the many napkins he'd folded, put it on his head like a woman's scarf, and tied it under his chin while raising one foot behind him playfully like a silly girl. A great performance; we laughed hard.

* * *

"It's been an interesting day," Jeanna said after our lecture. "First we learn that we should look under the beds and behind the shower curtains of our hotel rooms for dead bodies before we get comfortable, then we learn how to 'waft' glasses."

"That could come in handy," said Danny. "Wafted glasses are probably what the dead bodies in your room would prefer because they're ice-cold. All part of the first-class service."

* * *

Mara and I tried breaking the contractual pay into smaller steps for Georgia and Jeanna. First, multiply your hourly pay by the hours the trip was worth. A turn was worth at least five hours, a two-day trip: nine hours, and a three-day trip: seventeen hours.

"That's the easy part," Jeanna whined. "It's when a three-day trip has two duties periods, and all the other exceptions kick in! You have to divide all the hours you were away from home by three and a *HALF* to get your minimum! I mean, three and a half? Who came up with that! I hate this!" It sent her screaming into the bathroom. She hollered to us anyway from out of view. "Add that we're guaranteed at least half of all the hours we're on duty—we have to figure out which is the most then we get two dollars more per hour for any time we fly 'A,' one dollar more any time we work pit or 'B,' four dollars more per hour anytime we're short staffed; you have to be a calculus major to do this and we're just getting started!" She returned from the bathroom with a cold washcloth on her forehead.

"It sounds like you're getting it Jeanna," Mara said encouragingly, rubbing her arm.

There was much moaning and groaning from the library and lounge rooms that week. Friday arrived and we took the test.

Mike called me up to his desk. "Sherri," he said quietly, "you didn't miss one question; excellent."

When we walked into our room, Amy was waiting; I could tell she had flunked. "What did you get?" she asked me. I saw a look in her eye that was cloudy and strained. This was our last written test before Emergencies, which was all hands-on testing; this part of our training was over.

Before I could answer, Jeanna said, "She aced it Amy; get over it!"

Danny made a big deal about me getting a perfect grade. He also found out I hadn't had a re-take and that there were only two others who hadn't: Mara and David.

"Rejects," he asked. "How'd you get so smart?"

"I made it a point to stay away from people like you Danny."

Later that night, Danny and his roommates, Tom and Yosef, knocked on our door. Amy huffed over to answer it. She wore bigger curlers now; they were the size of rolling pins, intended to straighten her hair. "Guys aren't supposed to be on this floor," she said. "What do you want?"

"We want to talk to Rejects. Hey," Danny said, as I walked over. "Congratulations on your perfect score. This is for you." He doused me with water then sprayed my front and face with whipped cream. Tom and Yosef whooped and hollered before they all took off down the hall. After I caught my breath, I took off after them. Amy and Cheyenne followed me. The guys passed up the elevators and disappeared into the stairwell.

"You bastard, Danny!" I yelled. Throwing open the stairwell door, I ran right into Pauline and collided with her outstretched arm.

"What's going on," she asked. I froze; my two roommates piled into the back of me. "You girls aren't supposed to have gentlemen down here. Did I just see Danny, Tom, and Yosef leaving this floor?"

"Yes!" Cheyenne shouted. "They came to our room and pounded on the door. They wanted to talk to Rejects, and…"

"Sherri did you invite those boys to your room?"

Uh oh. I turned and gave my roommates a 'be quiet' look. "Well… I did… ask… them for something… I might have given them the impression… that I needed it right away?"

"Clean yourself up and report to my office immediately." Pauline spun around and headed up the stairs.

As soon as I got into my bathroom, I heard Amy open our front door. The hallway payphone was ringing. None of the rooms had regular phones; just one per floor—in the hallway, that needed coins. I heard her shout at the caller, "you guys are in big fat trouble, you know that?"

"Give me the phone," I raced out and snatching it from her hand.

"If I were you Sherri," she said, using my real name so I'd know she was serious, "I'd nail them. And don't get whipped cream on the phone."

"Danny?"

"Reej!" He reduced my nickname to one syllable. "We're to go to Pauline's office right now!"

"Me too."

"Sorry," Danny apologized. "I didn't mean to get you in trouble."

"Don't go in until I get there… don't say anything."

"What are you going to do?"

"I don't know, but *You* should be calling your hotshot brother right now, and telling him to get his *Ass* here as soon as possible so he can charm Pauline; she loves him!"

"Did you just say ass?" Amy poked. "And *bastard* before that? Such a potty mouth."

"Shut up Amy."

My two roommates stood at the bathroom door as I washed up. "Tell her the truth Rejects," Cheyenne said. "You didn't do anything wrong."

Mara came in and Amy started flapping her lips immediately, dramatizing the whole affair. Mara studied me as I changed out of my pajamas. "What are you going to say?"

"We're supposed to be a team," I said.

"Good girl Sherri." She patted my hand.

"You better not get us into trouble," Amy said pointing to herself and Cheyenne.

On the first floor, I saw the three pranksters coming around the corner. I nodded and went in first. Pauline sat at her desk and told me to sit down. Danny and the others followed.

"Want to tell me what happened?" Pauline asked.

"Well," I cleared my throat. "I told Danny that I was having trouble with my skin, with the dry air and all. And uh, he told me he knew about a good facial that his mother uses."

"Is that right," she played with her pencil; I could see she was surprised by the stupidity of my explanation. Here I was, baby of the class, and instead of blurting out the truth, I was making up a ridiculous story. Did she really expect me to rat? I also knew my face was red as a poppy.

"Yes…" Danny said. "It's a secret recipe I can't share, so I had to mix it myself. I tried to sneak it down. I'm sorry, I know I shouldn't have, but I didn't go into her room or anything."

"So… you gave Sherri a facial in the hallway?"

"Sort of."

"Then why were you, Sherri, chasing after him with said facial still applied, calling him a *Bastard*, might I ask?"

"It ended up burning my face. I have sensitive skin and I got nervous, thinking it might have been a prank or something."

"Nervous," she repeated while squinting her eyes, "a prank."

"Must have been the Pepto-Bismol," Danny said.

"Pepto-Bismol?" Pauline frowned.

"It's an important ingredient," he stated emphatically. "Usually it cools the skin."

"I see. And why—this question is for Tom and Yosef—were you two there?"

"Danny didn't know which way to go," Tom blurted out. "We're on the other side of the training center, so I showed him the way."

"What about you Yosef?"

"Oh, I ah… I helped carry stuff," he said.

Pauline brushed off her sleeve. Remnants of my 'facial' remained near her wrist. She brought her hand to her nose and looked at him. "So, you carried the whipped cream?"

"Oh that," Danny laughed. "The homogenized, pasteurized properties are good for pores."

Pauline sat back and stared. "You clowns can go. Don't let me catch you on one of the girls' floors again," she said. "I don't care if someone is having a heart attack and needs CPR."

The guys scurried out—I was right behind them.

"Sherri," she said, I stopped and sheepishly turned to face her. "Take a deep breath. I wasn't going to dismiss anyone. We know you guys are in each other's rooms all the time, but I do appreciate your camaraderie. I put you on the spot—asking you if you'd invited them. You handled it well—a bit over the top but that's fine. If I'm ever in a bind flying," she pointed her pencil at me, "I hope you're on my crew."

Danny was waiting for me, pacing at the elevator.

"Homogenized pasteurized properties, Danny?" I held up my hands and rolled my eyes.

"You were the one who came up with the facial idea," he countered.

"You're an absolute jerk, you know that?" I pressed the elevator button.

"I know," he paused. "What'd she say? After we left?"

"You three will be dismissed and sent home tomorrow." I entered the elevator and pushed the button for the fourth floor.

Danny remained in the hallway. "Will you marry me then," he said, his old grin returning. "So I can still fly for free?"

"Thought you'd never ask." As the door closed, I peered up at him with as evil a look as I could muster, but he was still grinning.

Chapter 4:

. . . .

Will You Still
Love Me Tomorrow

SATURDAY MORNING WAS WONDERFUL. I was the only one in my room who had an observation flight that day—the others slept in. The bathroom was *all mine!* I didn't have to rush. The pretty skirt I'd worn a couple of weekends ago was impossibly tight; I was gaining weight. After donning my all-purpose black pants, I selected a bright magenta blouse and a white jacket. It was a good look on me, even though the blouse was a hot shiny number and not exactly understated. I needed the focus above my waist; not below it. I liked wearing pink tortoise shell sun-glasses with the top but it made me think of Amy, so I grabbed a black pair instead—*more professional anyway*—and put them on.

I saw Sheldon in the boarding area watching the crowd—and watching me closely as I approached. Since we had Gateway training badges on, it was easy to spot other trainees. I already knew who he was, I'd seen him around. He was scrumptious to look at but withdrawn—every girl at the training center was *Curious* about him. He was in the class above ours: a handsome, private blond with stunning blue eyes. I'd caught him looking at me too; I'd always had to turn away because I'd felt fiery red.

"Hi, there," Sheldon said. *Great smile too.* He stood up as I walked over. "I'm Sheldon; are *You* observing on the flight to SanFran?"

"Yes; how do you do, I'm Sherri. Nice to meet you." I held out my hand. Whenever I had a strong attraction fast, butterflies whirled in my stomach. I'd either speak formerly or get quiet. *Please don't be gay. Please don't be gay.* Sheldon held my grip for a long time, sitting down and pulling me into a seated position beside him. The butterflies increased their speed. "I'm surprised we're working together," I said. "Thought I'd always be with someone from my own class." He had such an intense gaze; he was gorgeous.

"Couple of things," he said. "I was sick last weekend. Have to do another OB flight tomorrow as a make-up. Then, Jeanna was in our class," he explained, "but left, now she's back and they probably didn't know whether to include her OB trips on our schedule or yours… we've lost a lot of classmates." He opened his eyes widely. "It's been bad. You guys?"

"Not one," I told him.

"That's unusual. Most classes lose at least three people in training. We've had seven go home; four during the first few weeks then three more yesterday during the Emergency practicals." He sounded sad.

"I'm sorry," I offered.

"Me too," he smiled, but in a forlorn way. Sheldon had been a paramedic; I had to pull the information out of him. He was different: quiet, calm, whereas the guys from my class were loud—more gregarious. *Please don't be gay. Please don't be gay.*

We boarded the DC-10 with eight working flight attendants. The A, Betty, explained that jumbo trips required briefings and were mandatory. "You don't just waltz onto the airplane like narrow-bodies trips," she said. "There's lots to cover. But we've already had our briefing. Here in Cleveland, we meet in a room beside gate six," she told us. "If you have any more jumbo OB flights, go there and knock so you can sit in and listen. Stand near this door," she pointed to where we'd entered at door 2Left, "and watch me set up this galley." She received carts and supplies from her pit person below. I eyed the galley elevators with excitement. I was dying to go down, and see this 'pit' once and for all. One elevator was short—about three feet high—it was for carts only. The other was tall enough for a crew member. It had a shelf at the back that folded down so if it was used for a cart, you could also pull the shelf down and pile up supplies. Both elevators were thin with glass doors. Up, down, up, down they went. Carts for trash, liquor, meal carts, which Betty plugged in to keep the entrees warm. Large silver bins filled with sodas, juice cartons, milk, and bags of ice were sent up. Next came coffee cans, pots, creams, sugars, Sanka packets, tea bags, sleeves of coach plastic glasses and paper coffee cups. The very familiar queen cart came up next. The pit person had already decorated it beautifully with linen, champagne, orange juice, flowers, first-class wine glasses and napkins. Alan would have been proud.

"You two can help with pre-departure Mimosas up front; it's our biggest first-class cabin: forty passengers so they can use lots of help up there," Betty said. She pushed the cart toward us. "Go on," she urged. "Take it and go help out."

Sheldon and I were welcomed by the two first-class aisle attendants. We offered mimosas, stashed coats, hung suit jackets, tagged hangars with seat numbers, passed out magazines, pillows, blankets, and started taking meal orders; it was feeling familiar. I loved the room on the jumbo plane. It was more spacious with the extra aisle and higher ceilings; not as suffocating as the narrow-bodied aircrafts. The atmosphere was classier and the passengers seemed to appreciate it too—I think they felt more pampered. Near door 1Left there was a dial for onboard music. I'd never heard music played on a flight before. 'Hit the boarding music,' Betty had said. One of the first-class aisle attendants turned it on and we heard Gerry Rafferty's "Baker Street" hit. *So cool.* Sheldon and I never stopped moving once we were airborne and out of our seats. This was a 'Sea to Shining Sea' service. As Gateway's headquarters, the airline treated Cleveland as if it were a true East Coast City on flights to/from the West Coast. 'Competition,' Betty had explained. 'We want to offer our hometown flyers the same service people on the Eastern Seaboard get flying coast to coast.'

The return flight had such a light load, Betty offered to let us both take seats in first class and deadhead. "Have a drink," she said, "take a load off. You won't get much opportunity for that once you start flying. Believe me, you'll be working six crappie legs a day, setting up and breaking down queen carts for full cocktail services on the 37 or the stretch-8, and if you're lucky, you'll get thirteen-hour layovers after sixteen-hour duty days; more like ten-hour layovers. Do you know where you'll be based?" she asked.

"Here, Cleveland," Sheldon said. Most of the recent trainees had ended up in Denver or Cleveland; the coast cities had not been opening up for new hires.

"I don't know," I told her. "We haven't found out our domicile openings yet, but I'm sure I'll end up here. I'm the most junior in my class." Sheldon and I both wanted to work at least some of the flight back, so Betty let us help in first class after takeoff, then she let us each work one side of the cocktail carts in coach, and each of us work a tray cart in coach during the meal service. Finally, we got to go down into the pit and take a look. It was so tiny! There were floor to ceiling doors and drawers that housed everything: the ovens, carts and supplies. When all the doors were closed, the floor space was six feet by twelve feet. It was easy to see that with only two or three carts pulled out, the place was tight and confusing to work in; one had to be organized. Across from the elevators was a two-person jumpseat, emergency oxygen masks, extinguishers, a safety kit and a tiny sink. Only two people were ever allowed in the pit at one time.

Once Sheldon and I took our seats, we got great service; the two attendants up front liked us. We ate, drank, laughed, and, of course—talked. I was suddenly really hoping I'd be based in Cleveland. First-class headsets were much bigger than the chintzy plastic ones in coach that hurt your ears. Customers in back had to rent them for three dollars. Up front they were free. The featured movie was, *The Goodbye Girl.* I wanted to see it but I couldn't ignore Sheldon.

"What happened with Jeanna?" I regretted the question immediately; thinking I sounded like Amy. "Ah… if you know and don't mind my asking?"

"Actually, I do know. She slept with an instructor," he started. "Look, I haven't told anyone else that so don't say anything."

"How did you find out?" I asked. "Why are you privy to secret information?"

"I know someone in the company who's not at the training center. Jeanna flew in for training, ran into an instructor before classes started, and they went downtown to some fancy hotel," he said. "It was before orientation so they didn't have anything on her. They had to reinstate her. Frankly I think they just didn't like her."

"That's weird," I said. "How did they know?"

"Our lead instructor found out. The guy Jeanna was with is gone—he knew better, we haven't seen him since. You're not going to tell anyone, are you? This is the most I've talked in five weeks," he said.

"No," I said, shaking my head. "Jeanna's my friend; I don't care who she did what with and I don't think it's anyone else's business. Not even sure why I asked." But I did know why; I didn't want him to watch the movie.

"Tell me about *You,* Rejects," he said with a warm smile. I was suddenly thrilled I had the stupid nickname, because it was flattering to know he knew it. *He's noticed me.* He leaned closer; we were in 4E & F and I liked feeling the side of his arm on mine. He was strong and sexy. *Please don't be gay. Please don't be gay.* "You look cold," he pulled my blanket tighter. "Let me help you." He took my hands and rubbed them in his. *Yum.* "Sherri, on your observation flight today," he teased, mimicking the instructors, "what did you notice most?"

"Jewelry," I said honestly.

"Jewelry?"

"Yes," I said. "I'm not a fashion hotshot by any means, but I love jewelry. Especially when it's unique. I've noticed that flight attendants have the coolest stuff. Did you notice Betty's necklace? It's from Hawaii and it has her name in Hawaiian scripted in black enamel over gold with designs of Hawaiian flowers." I made a mental note to wear the checkerboard-like ebony, malachite, lapis and tiger's eye ring Toby had given me. He'd found it at an art festival vacationing with his family in Santa Monica; everyone loved it.

"Hmm," Sheldon hummed, completely bored by my words but gazing at me with a penetrating stare. He sighed deeply. *There was magic in that sigh.*

"What was your greatest observation?" I asked.

His eyes lit up as he leaned closer. "You." He lifted my chin with a crooked forefinger. "Ah… look at you blush! How cute!"

Soon enough I was blabbing about Toby and admitting I felt guilty for not having called him. "Deep down he knows it's over," I justified. "I made it clear I have no intention of going back to Wichita. Though I probably could have called him a couple of times."

Sheldon was making it so easy; he felt like a great friend and someone I could confide in. "He's better off," Sheldon said. "When I get dumped it's a lot easier if I don't see or hear from the person I'm missing."

I nodded and looked out the window.

"What are you doing tonight?" Sheldon asked suddenly.

* * *

I raced to my room back at the center and tore through my clothes. What the hell should I wear? Sheldon was taking me to a nearby bar where he said everyone danced; it wasn't all the way downtown and I liked that. Mara walked in as I was rifling through my closet; I stood up straight, my mouth agape and my eyes wide. "You cut your hair!"

She laughed and twirled for me. It was so short! With her cute face, any cut would have looked good on her but I loved her waist-length locks. "Do you like it?" she asked.

"It looks so pretty," I said, which was true, "I love it!" *I lied.*

"I'm going downtown tonight. I feel like having some fun," she said. "Want to come? We're sharing cabs. Jeanna's coming too."

"No go ahead," I said too loud, excited that I wouldn't have to explain my whereabouts. "I'm going to break down and call Toby." *I lied again.* This was good news; not only was Mara on her way out, but Jeanna was too. This was working for me; the center would be as barren as it usually was on weekend nights, when many stayed out late.

Sheldon had a sports car. He held the door open and I felt all delicious; it had been four weeks since I'd been in anything besides a bus or a plane; his 280Z was immaculate. He liked to dance as much as I did, and he swung me around all night. When slow dances played, he held me close but gently; I had to make sure I kept my breathing even. "Your hair is sooo pretty down," he said. "It smells wonderful," and with that he pulled me in a little tighter. Like many discos, the club's final song was "Last Dance" by Donna Summer. I loved it; by now Sheldon wasn't even asking me to dance. He'd just take my hand and lead me onto the floor knowing I'd follow.

Later, as we made our way to the training center elevator, I said, "That was the most fun I've had since I've been here; even longer than that. Thank you so much…"

"Me too Sherri. You're great. The night is young you know," he said. "You're not going to leave me now, are you? Why should the fun stop? We don't have class tomorrow."

"You have another OB flight in the morning," I said.

"That's nothing. Please? Don't be afraid."

"I… there's nowhere…" I caught myself. Why the hell had I said that? I should be saying goodnight.

"Let's go to my room," he said, putting his arms around my waist. "My door is right by the stairs. No one will see you if you come up that way."

The elevator door opened on my floor. "Come on," he said, taking my hand. We ran; he led me toward the stairwell. Once inside, we raced up to the fifth floor. "Stay here. I'll make sure no one's in the hall and open my door. Even if someone leaves their room, you'll be in mine in two seconds." I stood there in fear; worried that someone would come into the stairwell. With a rush, he opened the door and help out his hand. "Here," he reached for me.

"I can't."

"Come on!" In one step, his arm was around my waist again and I was in the hallway. I couldn't possibly fight him there; we would get caught, so into his room I went.

"Where are your roommates?" I asked as I looked around. On the window sill was a partially stocked bar.

"Don't have any," he smiled happily. "We had ten guys in my class; two rooms with four each and there were two of us in here. My roommate was sent home yesterday. I felt bad... 'til now. What would you like to drink?" he asked me. "Another screwdriver?" Sheldon also had a tape player in his room; the band Free filled the air. It was nice to hear rock after all the disco music. He put a drink in my hand and soon, the necking started, followed by an invitation to stay. "Please Sherri, please. It's been so lonely in this place. You feel so good... please don't go. You're so wonderful... amazing, I can't get enough of you. I have felt more comfortable with you than anyone else these last long five weeks. You're so nice and sooo pretty," he joined the perfectly timed lyrics to "All Right Now," and sang, "I took her home, to my place, watching every move on her face..."

The rush inside me was out of control. *He's not gay!* I hadn't been with anyone except Toby—this wasn't how I pictured the encounter with my next sexual partner. "I can't stay, no way. Look what happened to Jeanna. I'm not supposed to be in here, I've already been in trouble with Pauline. If she finds out..."

"Pauline? Your class's crazy lead?" His eyes widened. "She and Mike do it every night. They're probably in his room right now."

"How do you know all this stuff?" I said, remembering that Pauline said she wasn't going to dismiss anybody for being in anyone else's room. I also remembered she'd been in the stairwell; now I knew why.

"I just do. They are the last two people who would care about us being here."

"This isn't right Sheldon. We barely know each other. I have to do the right thing; I have to be smart."

"Don't do the right thing," he pleaded as he put his wonderful hands all over me. "Do the wrong thing; it's not wrong for me. You won't feel like it's wrong later, trust me." He stroked the back of my neck and felt me respond. "Don't be smart; be foolish like me; make me feel better. I'll make you happy you stayed." With that, he planted the best kiss on me so far.

"Ohhh, you have to stop Sheldon. I'm scared… I don't know…"

"I can tell," he said. "Don't be nervous. *Tonight you're mine, completely,*" he sang, making me giggle again. "Just relax. It'll be wonderful, I promise. And, *I'll still love you tomorrow.*"

"Sheldon… I want to love *Myself* tomorrow."

"You will," he stroked my hair and smiled; *was that the light of love in his eyes?* "It's you who will soon forget me. Every handsome successful guy on your airplanes will be chasing you. Doubt you'll be thinking about some dumb steward you met in training."

He'd put his hand somewhere and I'd say no and move it, but I'd keep kissing him and his hand would return. His kisses were so good my mouth burned; I couldn't get enough. I kept saying no until it was stupid to say it anymore; we'd slowly pulled each other's clothes off. The nos stopped, and the lack of them glaringly said yes. I closed my eyes, stopped worrying about everything, and shook off my fear. I was hoping already this would grow into something special and not end up being my first one-night-stand. Giving myself permission felt like floating through the air on a warm breeze, over flower beds, through clouds, and back again, and being touched by butterflies. I just… let go.

The song's lyrics hypnotized me; encouraging me. "All right now, baby it's all right now."

Chapter 5:

Third Rate Romance

I MET SHELDON IN THE CAFETERIA after his OB flight on Sunday. He burst into a welcoming bright smile when we saw each other. I felt like a puppy dog wagging its tail. "Hiii!" I squealed.

"What's up you gorgeous girl?" He was at me in no time. "Missed you today," he whispered. He threw his arm around my neck in front of everybody. I didn't care who saw; we were all getting friendlier as the weeks dragged on; lots of my classmates hugged and walked with their arms around each other now. After dinner we slipped into a hallway for hungry kisses. We *both knew what we wanted*, but I told him I couldn't stay with him at night; too many people around. I had thought about it all day. He whined and begged but I stood firm. The weekend was over. We probably wouldn't get any more time alone, since my class would be at the hangars all week and he'd be graduating on Wednesday. Soon enough, I'd be seeing him—flying out of Cleveland together. Before bed, I eagerly scratched in my log like an adolescent.

- *Dear FlightLog; who would have thought? I've met someone so special; he's absolutely perfect in every way. I'm too afraid someone else will find you here at the center so I won't give details while I'm still in training, but you are going to hear a lot, lot, more about him, and a lot, lot more about us! That's for sure. I LOVE this job!!!! I'm sooo... HAPPY!!!!*

We were a boisterous crowd climbing onto Gateway buses Monday morning. A week away from the training center sounded like a holiday. We had 'casual' clothes on, which meant: Calvin Klein, Vidal Sassoon, Gloria Vanderbilt or Sergio Valente 'designer' jeans, which were the latest-greatest worldwide fashion craze phenomena.

Sunday, I surprised myself by telling Jeanna all about Sheldon. "I feel it's something special." *This isn't a third-rate thing. I've never done anything like that before.* "I just know it's right." There was no way I could keep it all in—I was bursting inside.

"He's interesting," Jeanna said. "A little distant maybe but so was I. Remember this while you're making your plans though: he's going to be a *Flight Attendant* Sherri. Don't close any doors." I frowned so she changed the subject. She told me everything about her removal and reinstatement, so I didn't have to pretend I didn't know. She had met the instructor on her flight from California to the training center; he'd gone west for the weekend. "I figured he was in management," she said. "He was an instructor." She also said she felt as if she was going to make it through training. "Thank you Sherri; you have no idea how much you helped."

"Jeanna," I told her, "I'm the one who needs help now. I've... gained some weight. We weigh in right before graduation; I'm nervous."

"How close are you to your max?"

"I was exactly ten pounds under when I got here; I weighed 115 in my clothes and shoes. My max is 125 in full uniform garb. I'm sure I've gained five pounds; probably more."

Gateway wanted their attendants to be at least ten pounds under their max. If they were closer than that, they would be considered on 'weight check' and any supervisor could weigh them at any time. If they were over their max, they were removed from flying and faced permanent dismissal. The process had three steps, but the bottom line was this: if you were over your max and didn't lose the weight in a predetermined amount of time, you'd lose your job.

"You have to drop the extra weight Sherri; they'll fire you. I don't think anyone has a scale so you're going to have to be careful. You should start smoking right now; you don't want to live up to your nickname by being *Re-jected,*" she clowned, pulling out one of her long Virginia Slims cigarettes from its pack. Apparently, she had come a long way, baby.

I smiled as I watched her leap onto the bus. A nice bonding had taken place over the last week between Danny, his roommates Tom, Yosef, and David, with me, Mara, Jeanna and Georgia. I wish it had happened earlier; the first weeks had been so lonely.

"Ooh baby!" David exclaimed as Jeanna approached the back of the bus. Her long hair swung freely; many hadn't seen her with it down. "Why don't you sit on my lap Jeanna Meana and we'll talk about the first thing that pops up. I could wipe that scowl right off of you."

"That would take too long David," she said. "Wouldn't have anything to discuss for days."

* * *

"Come on in," encouraged a great-looking guy as we headed down the halls of Gateway's classrooms near the hangars. "Half of you step across the hall and settle in with Mary," he said. "Rest of you in here. Doesn't matter; format's the same and we'll all be together in the planes and in the mockups anyway; got it? I'm Steve! So," he said as we took seats. "Gonna miss the training center?" Everyone laughed. "This week will be a blast. It's a lot of work but we are going to have a great time. When we're finished, you will have completed everything necessary to be a professional flight attendant. It's Monday morning. By Friday night it'll all be over." Everyone cheered. "Most important thing is this: Friday after classes we're going to have a talent show—that's right! Start thinking about your act. Everyone participates, no exceptions. See? Fun already!"

Oh crud.

"How many of you are there?"

"Forty-one!" Danny shouted with pride. "We're all still here!" Again, everyone cheered. Our class had made a name for itself; no one in our group had been asked to leave.

"Forty-one? Every other class loses people but your class gained one? I knew you were special the moment I heard you all coming; just look at you!" Steve raised his arms. "I'm in the presence of greatness," he said. "Let's keep that perfect record. Very few can't get through Emergencies but I will admit the rules are tougher because we have no flexibility here. You can have two re-takes on Friday—that's it. After the second, if you fail either test, no more re-takes. It has to do with FAA requirements. But I know that's not going to happen, right? Let's get started."

By lunch everyone was chattering away loudly. Gateway had a hot airplane entrée cart filled with food and a full airplane tray cart sent over for us; we ate what coach passengers might get on a 'Sea to Shining Sea' flight.

"Isn't this cute," Georgia held up her salt/pepper and cream/ sugar packets. "We each get our own little everything."

"There are different meal choices in here," Yosef said, as he searched through the entrée cart, lifting up foil tops to check the meals. "Does that mean the most senior get first pick?"

By the end of the first day, our heads were reeling. We'd covered operating all the different fire extinguisher types and everything about the safety kits. We hooked slides on all the narrow-bodied aircraft and latched doors on all the wide-bodied planes. We needed to know which slides were double and which were single, as that dictated how you commanded people in an evacuation.

We also needed to know how to command people at the window exits. The procedure for directing people as a plane crashed, whether we knew we were going to crash in advance or not, was always the same. 'Grab your ankles! Keep your heads down til the plane stops! Grab your ankles! Keep your heads down til the plane stops!' After two full commands, we shortened it to: 'Grab ankles! Heads down! Grab ankles! Heads down,' which we repeated until the airplane came to a complete stop. Then we shouted, 'Release your seat belts and get out! Release your seat belts and get out!'

The rest differed depending on which exit you were at and on which airplane. While shouting, we would be notifying the cockpit we were evacuating by ringing the button at least five times and assessing if it was safe to open our exits by checking for fire/ water first. After opening our exit or exits, we pulled the manual inflation handles as backups and held customers back until the slides deployed. Finally, screaming at the top of our lungs, we literally shoved passengers out the doors. Each step had very specific commands and come Friday, every single one of us had to evacuate a 727, 737 and a DC-8 door and the back stairwell exit on the 727 perfectly, not missing one step or one command.

On the 747 we each had to evacuate an over-the-wing exit and a regular exit just like we did on the DC-10.

"We're going to make sure you know these procedures better than your ABCs," Steve promised. We practiced and we shouted and we screamed. "Take your last break and report back in fifteen minutes," he said. We scrambled out; I was fighting hunger. We'd done a lot of work on dummies: administering oxygen and performing CPR—I had burned some calories. I accepted one of Jeanna's cigarettes; a girl had to do what a girl had to do.

"Good news," said Mary as we walked back into the classroom.

"Your base openings have been announced. Are you ready? Eight openings for Cleveland, seven openings for Denver, and… twenty-six openings for *New York!*"

The class went wild; again, we were the unusual group. New York had not opened all year for new hires. I froze. Twenty-six openings in New York; that was a lot. Many of my classmates had settled into the idea of being based in Gateway's headquarter town of Cleveland and I knew all the west coast people would pick Denver; I was going to be sent to New York. No way were twenty-six people out of forty-one going to bid the Big Apple. Life was so funny; I would have been excited only a week ago but since I'd met Sheldon, I wanted to stay here.

"Oh my God," Jeanna shouted. "We're going to New Yooork!" She hugged me. No one yet had found out what Gateway was doing with Jeanna's seniority, but everyone standing in the hallway knew New York would go junior—there were too many openings. And if she did end up being the senior person in our class, as she should be, she could have her pick.

"What do you think?" Mara asked me with a concerned look. We had planned to be roommates; Cleveland was close to her home, in Illinois. This would change everything.

"Bid what you have to bid Mara," I said with a lump in my throat. "Don't worry about me."

"We've got another surprise," Steve wheeled a queen cart into the room with a large birthday cake on it. "Four of you had birthdays while in training," he said. "Mara, Jake, Tom last week and Sherri this Wednesday. Sing another 'happy birthday' instead of using all the names. Here we go, one, two three: 'Happy birthday to you, happy birthday to you! Happy birthday, happy birthday… Happy birthday, to… you!'"

I tried to smile but I felt sick. Even though I dreaded going back to the center and facing Sheldon with this news, I was grateful we hadn't found out sooner; I could never have concentrated on our material.

* * *

I found Sheldon; we'd agreed that he'd stay downstairs somewhere so I could find him, as I couldn't possibly be on his floor just as our class was returning; too risky. He'd eaten and I was skipping dinner. We went out to his car, slipping on the very late May snow; it was the only place we felt completely safe and alone. I sobbed and blew my nose.

He was *staring at his coffee cup*, then handed it to me. "Here, take this. It'll be fine," he tried cheering me up. "Sherri, New York? That's exciting, come on. Remember girl, we work for the airlines. We're going to have at least twelve days off a month and we've got flight benefits. Gateway probably has five legs a day between Cleveland and LaGuardia. It's an hour each way." He was wonderful and sweet and said all the right encouraging things, but I wanted him to be… sadder.

"I know you're right," I said. "It was a long crazy day, we screamed so much."

"You'll dream about evacuating airplanes," he promised. "All of us did."

And he was right. By Tuesday night, after we'd practiced both 'planned' evacuations (when the crew knew there was something wrong and prepared the passengers for a crash) and 'quick and dirties,' (when no one in advance knew a crash was coming) the dreams came.

"Happy birthday Sherri!" I woke to Jeanna, Mara and Georgia at my bedside. They had a bran muffin with a lit candle in it. "Twenty years old," Mara said with a smile. "You have your whole life ahead of you. And you're going… to New York!" She acted as if I'd be thrilled. "Congratulations," she beamed. "Bids were posted by the cafeteria fifteen minutes ago."

"I'm going to New York too; most of us are!" Jeanna pushed on my shoulder. "I promise you girlfriend; we are going to have a great time."

Mara was staying in Cleveland, like Amy, while Cheyenne was going to Denver. For the first time, I felt a pang of jealousy toward Amy. At least she'd never know. I knew it was the right decision not to tell anyone—*no need to talk about it*—except Jeanna. Amy would have been delighted to know how much I was smarting about Sheldon and me going separate ways.

I couldn't find him anywhere; his class was busy preparing for their graduation. It would be at noon and only about an hour; then they would all be flying off. I didn't know when I'd see him again, but he promised to call that night after we got back from Emergencies. I'd given him the number to the payphone on our floor.

"Head for the 27 mockup," Steve shouted when he saw us coming down the hall. "We're doing real evacuations today."

Half the girls in the class already had a crush on Steve. He was wonderful and fun. I probably would have been all goo-goo over him myself, but all I could think about was Sheldon. Groups of four flight attendants were told there would be an evacuation, that's all. The rest of us sat in any seat in the aircraft mockup. We were the passengers and told to do as instructed by any crew member. The mockup rocked, shook, went completely black, and filled with fake smoke; these drills were going to feel as real as possible. Steve and Mary would be the cockpit crew so everyone was to listen to their announcements. Steve and Mary set up different scenarios for each drill. In the first, not one single exit opened. The poor crew ran up and down the plane after it crashed, not knowing what the hell to do. We, the passengers, screamed at them that we needed to get out. Suddenly, Steve opened the cockpit door.

Tom, one of working crewmembers, raced inside screaming, "There are windows in the cockpit!" He went in and opened both windows, then directed passengers up. He had the cockpit ax with him and pounded beside the windows to make the exits wider and more useful.

"Good work!" Mary said afterward. Following each drill, we would discuss what happened—what went right, what went wrong, what we'd learned. There was no grading; this was practice and I realized right away—it was very helpful. "If you can't find an exit that works than by all means make one!" Mary said. "Most crashes are survivorable," she said. "But planes burn fast; we need everyone out in ninety seconds."

"Is that a word?" Danny asked me.

"No. Survivor is a noun," I said. "You don't put 'able' after a noun. You use the verb, which is 'survive.' Survivable is a word."

In the second drill, certain classmates were told secretly to 'go crazy' during the crash and race up and down the aisles screaming before the airplane stopped. Our classmates in their jumpseats survived the test; they did not get up when the 'crazy' passengers did.

The fourth drill threw everyone. In each of the first three, we went through a 'takeoff' then a minute or two of flight, then a crash. Each crewmember sat in their jumpseat, waited for the plane to rock and pitch, realized they were 'crashing' then they began their commands. But this time the crew was simply checking the plane before takeoff. They had just finished the demos and were getting ready to strap into their jumpseats, probably wondering what would happen during the crash. But there was no crash.

Steve came over the PA and in a calm voice said, "Flight Attendants, evacuate the airplane."

As we, the passengers watched Jane walk down the aisle, it didn't even register with us at first. She and the crew were checking the cabin, heading to their assigned jumpseats. Then I heard Jane repeat Steve's words softly, *"evacuate the plane,"* she stopped and her eyes bulged. She threw her hands up and turned toward the front of the plane and screamed at the other crew members. "EVACUATE THE AIRPLANE!" She raced to the back of the 27 and started the later commands. It had to be tough because in all the other drills, the crew had strapped in, waited for the crash and begun with: 'Grab your ankles, keep your heads down til the plane stops.' She had to improvise and go out of order: what to say? She went to the exit and looked outside; no fire. Mary and Steve put red flags outside the exits if there was fire and blue flags outside the exits if there was water. That meant you didn't open it; you re-directed your passengers toward other exits, usually the windows. She pushed her button to notify the cockpit and others she was evacuating. "Come this way! Come this way!" She realized she'd gone out of order. "Release your seat belts and get out," she corrected herself. "Release your seatbelts and get out!" She opened the two door exits at 2Left and 2Right then she let the stairwell down in the center of the back. "Come on!" she screamed. Some of us were confused too. "Move your ASSES!" she hollered.

Afterward, Steve and Mary praised our senior classmate; they'd pulled a fast one on this group. "Ok," Steve said. "Jane's commands got a little confused and a bit out of order, but don't you think it's damn important to realize that you could be sitting on an airplane before it takes off, thinking about the movie, your service, how much fun you're going to have on your layover when all of a sudden you have to get everyone off? This is why we do this; you have to be ready for anything. As for her telling you all to move your asses," he laughed and we laughed too. "Wouldn't you listen to that if you were sitting there stunned and frozen in fear? This is the only time Gateway wants you to yell at your passengers people," he said with much animation. "Get their attention and get them the hell off that airplane."

We finished three more drills before lunch. Everyone was starved. As we shoved our food in, Mary came into the break area. "We don't normally do this," she said, "but we are racing through today. We're going to really treat you since you're our most favorite class ever," we awed as she laughed. "And take you back over to the center to see part of today's graduation." Everyone jumped. "They're very special and each of them is different, so finish up and meet us at the buses in five. Let's go." We took off.

Back at the center, our class raced into the auditorium. We could see the graduates standing on four tiers of stacked bleachers. Everyone was watching old airline commercials on a screen. I remembered every single jingle. TWA's, "Would you like to ride, in my beautiful balloon? Way up in the air, in my beautiful balloon!" Eastern commercials, American's, "Doing what we do best," Continental's, "We really move our tails for you," and two from United: The dance halls girls inside a prop shaped like an airplane, holding the plane over their torsos with only their kicking legs visible. They sang, "United Airlines," then the director screamed, "Higher girls, higher," but instead of kicking their legs higher, they sang the jingle in higher-pitched voices, "United… Airlines!"

Next we saw the 60s 'stewardess' graduation commercial with Peter Paul and Mary singing in the background, "I'm leaving, on a jet plane." It had been my favorite as a kid, followed by Eastern and Delta ads. The show ended with wonderful Gateway Airline ads we'd all seen through the years. The best one was rushing closeups of first-rate city skylines like New York, San Francisco, Washington D.C. and St. Louis. Gateway airplanes raced through electric 'gateway' arches over the cities; a beautifully crafted ad. It was a moving presentation and there wasn't a dry eye by the time the lights went up.

Sheldon's lead instructor, Doris, took the microphone. Each graduate had a special someone 'pin' their wings on. Sheldon was the best-looking guy up there. He was the best-looking guy in the training center. Actually, he was the best-looking human there. *In the world.* "From San Antonio," Doris said. "Carmen Maria Gonzales. Carmen's mother, Elisa, will be placing on her new wings today." We watched the pinning, the two hugged, we clapped, and then Carmen returned to the bleachers while her mother returned to the audience. Sheldon was nearly last. "Sheldon Lee Mayfield, from Cincinnati," Doris announced with a flourish. I lifted my head and shoulders high so he could see me. "Today, Sheldon's wife Jessica, who is already a Gateway Airlines flight attendant, will be doing the honors." *Suddenly, he wasn't good looking at all.*

There was a murmuring throughout the room. I went white.

Jeanna looked at me and muttered, "Jesus."

From the crowd's response, it was clear that like me, no one else had known Sheldon was married either—until now. I was close to an exit; I made a run for it.

Chapter 6:

Smoke Gets in Your Eyes

M Y CLASSMATES PILED ONTO THE bus fifteen minutes later and found me curled up in a ball near the last row, hiding behind my sunglasses. "Sherri," Jeanna said, "You must have eaten something that made you sick; which entree did you have?" *Thank you Jeanna; nice save.* I told everyone I'd kept food from the cafeteria in my room, and that must have been what it was. Like a zombie, I made my way back to the 727 mockup. Everyone was still prattling about how great the graduation ceremony had been.

"Wasn't that fantastic?" Steve asked. "Like we said, we rarely get to take off on a Wednesday and see a graduation, but you guys are tearing through this stuff. Next up," he looked at his clipboard, "Sherri…" Mara cut him off and told him I wasn't feeling good. Steve offered to let me take a pass but I shook my head. I wanted to get it over with. I had to get my mind off of Sheldon and off the image of his wife stepping forward all proud, smiling, beautiful, to pin his new wings on… it was disgusting.

Cheyenne was the third attendant and I was the fourth, so she and I sat on the back jumpseat—her by the door and me by the galley and… we crashed. "Grab your ankles," we shouted. "Keep your head down til the plane stops!" It took forever for the plane to stop. It was black and smoky and our classmates started screaming. My primary exits were through the galley and the aft stairwell. I got out of my jumpseat and banged the button alerting the cockpit. "Release your seat belts and get out! Release your seat belts and get out!" Cheyenne wasn't moving. *Great!* Obviously, Steve and Mary had told her to 'play dead on landing,' which meant I was going to have to move her body and open her exit, then take care of her assigned window exits too. I got the galley exit open, elicited a helper to guide people out, got the aft stairwell open and did the same, then had a passenger 'help' me move Cheyenne's limp body. *For a split second I wished it was Sheldon's.* It was getting harder to see; the phony smoke vent on the mockup was near my face. Thankfully Cheyenne made it easy—though she was 'dead,' she helped us by not being too stiff or unmovable. We got her door open. "You!" I grabbed Tom by his sleeve. "Hold onto this handle! Make people form a single line and tell them to jump!" Tom did what I said.

I couldn't get close to the window exits—so many people were racing toward me as I had three exits operating in the back; I had to assess from where I stood. Danny was close to the window exit on the right. "You in the red shirt!" I screamed at him. We were told to give short but specific commands when getting an aide and not to use classmates' names. He pointed at himself. "Yes you!" I yelled. "Grab that handle at the top of that exit and pull the door onto the seat! Exit feet first…" He hesitated. He wasn't moving fast enough. "Do it!" As he grabbed the handle, I noticed the red flag outside the window. *"NO!"* I screamed back but it was too late. He opened the window and then he and two others did dying acts worthy of an action film. *Shit!*

"Ahhh!" They screamed. They flailed backward and grabbed their chests and faces as if being smacked by hot flames surging into the aircraft and engulfing them. Falling into the seats and aisle way, they flopped and writhed, trying to put their fires out. There was absolutely nothing I could do to save them. I couldn't get to a fire extinguisher. *Move on!* I told myself.

The window exit on the other side had no flags. I ordered someone to open it. The plane was empty in twenty more seconds. We were to run through the plane one more time if feasible, and make sure everyone was off, including the cockpit, then exit ASAP. Finally, I exited from door 1Left. The class was clapping—they always did after a drill. But Danny and two others were splayed out face up lying on the mockup's airplane wing as if dead. I fell to my knees and threw up in front of everybody.

"Get some used coffee grounds!" Yosef screamed.

Now, laughing friends deride…

* * *

As soon as we got back to our floor, someone yelled from the payphone, "Sherri, you have a phone call!"

"Who is it?" I asked.

"It's Sheldon," a girl from the class a week behind us said smiling brightly. She cocked her head and held the phone out for me. Mara looked at me quizzically. Jeanna's brow went up. I took the phone and slammed it into the receiver so hard, everyone jumped. "Whoa…" the junior girl said.

There were flowers on my desk/vanity when we entered our room. Mara lifted the note and read aloud, "Happy twentieth birthday you gorgeous girl. With love and fond memories, Sheldon." She turned with her mouth open and gaped at me, holding the note up.

"I'm getting rid of these," said Jeanna. She already had the vase in her hand.

- *Dear FlightLog. I couldn't possibly tell you how wretched today was. Suffice it to say that it was the most disgusting day since I've arrived, one of the most miserable days of my life, and the worst birthday I've ever had. Are all who love really this blind? How'd this smoke get in my eyes? I had the shortest relationship ever – five days, and my first one-night stand, which I didn't even know I was having and, I'm an adulterous – let's just say it: I'm a whore! Oh, and I'm moving to New York. At least there everyone knows people are rude, so I won't be shocked when I'm stabbed in the back; instead people will just spit in my face – I think it'll be easier. And I'll fit right in. I am also a murderess!*

On Thursday we practiced evacuating each door one more time in prep for the final exams Friday. "When do you, the flight attendant, leave the plane?" Steve asked.

"When everyone's off, the fire gets too hot, the smoke gets too thick or the water gets too deep," we chimed in unison.

"Good," he said, looking around. "You are not heroes, people. Every single one of you is different. One level of heat or smoke may be tolerable for one person but not another: when your brain says 'get out' then 'Get Out!' As far as the water being too deep, for me that would be high humidity," he teased.

The rest of the tests were easy: administering oxygen and then CPR to dummies. Operate each piece of safety equipment and identify where they all were on each craft. In the afternoon, we watched films about real crashes, listening to flight crews and safety inspectors give us the details and share what they'd learned. Everyone was hoarse from screaming all week, so Steve and Mary passed out lozenges.

The last thing we did was board a 747 at the hangar to jump down the slide in the cockpit. The 747 had two stories. Because it was so large, and because the winding staircase was the only way to get from the first floor to the second, the plane had an evacuation slide in the cockpit. It was five stories high; if we couldn't make the jump, we were out of training.

Cheyenne froze when she looked down. "Come on," we all squealed in strained hoarsely calls. "Jump!" And she finally did.

"Feel older?" Danny asked as we watched her pick up speed on her five-story descent.

"Quite a bit," I smiled more than I wanted to for his sake. He felt horrible about my birthday and I knew it. "I also feel wiser," I said with a croak.

"Sherri, I feel terrible. I keep screwing you…"

"Please Danny really. I ate something awful; it was only a matter of time before it came up. You probably did me a favor. Everything's fine." I told him.

"Ok…" he said. "Do you know what you're going to do for the talent show tomorrow?"

* * *

Friday morning all forty-one of us ran up and down the hanger halls, laughing as we passed each other and letting each other know which doors we'd just finished testing on. "Got the 8-door done!" High five. "On my way to the 47 overwing!" High five. It didn't stop 'til lunch. A few people were missing as we tore over to the food carts.

"There are five people back in the mockups doing re-takes on the doors," Jane said to all us. "Let's wish them luck. They should be here soon." Danny came striding into the break room. "Yeah!" Jane shouted. Within minutes, two more classmates came running in with relieved grins on their faces. A minute later, one more.

"I had two re-takes," David said, wiping his brow. "You know how nerve-wracking that was?" Everyone cheered for him. We were all seated, chatting, laughing, describing our tests and how scared we were. It had been terrifying. Though the instructors told us not to be nervous, go slow and just think it through, it was awful. It was great to be done; it was all over.

"Hey," Cheyenne said. "Where's Mara?" The room went quiet. We all looked around for a few moments, then no one moved. We sat still for half a minute before anyone said a word.

"She was right behind me," David said, sounding strained. "She had two re-takes…"

I looked down the hallway searching for her but she didn't appear. I glanced at Jeanna then at Georgia, who started to cry. My heart was on fire. Soon, many of us were crying.

Back in the classroom, we found Steve at his desk looking downcast. "I'm sorry," he said. "I'm sure you all know by now that we lost Mara." Gateway didn't allow anyone who flunked out a moment with other classmates. They were escorted to their rooms immediately and told to pack. "While you were eating," he said, "Pauline and Lydia came over and got her. She's already at the airport," he volunteered, probably knowing that would be our next question.

"She didn't even have one re-take before today," Yosef protested.

"Happens to some of the best trainees," Steve said. "We see it often unfortunately. Emergencies is a different animal than regular procedures and services; that's why it's separate."

Numbly, we went back to the testing rooms and finished our tests. Everyone passed. Mary told her group to follow us into Steve's room. He made his way toward a cart in the back with a tape player on it.

"We need to perk up this place," Steve said. "Who is going to change the mood and begin the talent show?" He fiddled with the dials. "Respect" by Aretha Franklin blared. The volume was loud. I sprung up out of my seat with a cry of joy and danced in place; some of my classmates did the same as others urged us on. Steve let the song play out. "Anyone ready yet?" he asked when it was over.

"I'll go first," said Georgia. She sang "Amazing Grace." Her voice, though hoarse, sounded lovely. No doubt her talent had helped her earn that Miss USA runner up title.

Danny and his friends did a hilarious skit impersonating our instructors at our orientation. They had studied hard; they had Lydia's, Mike's, Alan's and Pauline's movements down. A trainee in the skit was invited to stand and 'tell a little about herself.' Suddenly I was watching someone impersonate me. My line about being promoted to the 'Rejects and Returned Items' desk was part of the skit and it brought the house down. It sounded so outrageously funny to me now; I laughed so hard I cried. There was *something inside that couldn't be denied.*

We watched card tricks, listened to more songs and saw dances. I led everyone into the hallway where I did a round off followed by a back handspring; years of cheerleading had given me that great skill.

Jeanna went last. She took a sultry stance and pretended she was evacuating an airplane, but instead of screaming and yelling—

she used a 'come hither' voice. "Release your pant belt and get up, release your pant belt and get up. Come… this… way, come… this… way," she said all slow and breathless. She motioned with her forefinger for Steve to approach her. He played along perfectly, putting a look of delight on his face and going toward her eagerly. She pulled a rope off the floor—it was supposed to be an inflation handle, and spun it around like a stripper several times, swinging her hips and making hilarious faces at him. Everyone in the room was dying with laughter. She whipped the rope around his neck and pulled him toward her, face to face. "Hey there, big boy," she rubbed her torso on his and pointed down as if toward the bottom of a slide. "I want you to jump down that slide, get naked and in the horizontal position and wait for me!" Then she gave him a push, put a hand on her hip and another by her head, and took a well-deserved bow.

"Jeanna! Wooo!" Danny got to his feet and lead us all in a standing ovation. He put his fingers to his mouth and whistled.

That night, I wrote serious comments in *FlightLog*.

- *Compared to Mara's loss, I know I have nothing to be sorrowful about. She has to go back to her old job and face her co-workers. They probably had a party for her before she left. She hated that reservations job, taking monotonous phone calls all day. It's heartbreaking; she even cut off all her hair. These tears I cannot hide. I love Mara, I will miss her. I would have been proud to serve with her; Gateway, you blew it!*

Then I recorded every word of Jeanna's skit.

Monday and Tuesday were light days. We filled out forms for human resources, got information about our domiciles, including names of attendants in each city to call for help finding apartments and received our final lecture. It was delivered to us from the head of Inflight Services—Debra McPherson—the first female to be a Gateway VP. She welcomed us to the company, congratulated us and said, "Perhaps one day I will be honoring one of you at our annual awards celebration for being Flight Attendant of the year." She made some points that I wanted to remember. One was that while we were off-duty, leaving our homes, racing into cabs, subways, cars or trains—or even planes if we were commuting, that the public still saw us as representatives of Gateway Airlines whenever we were in uniform. "You might be so caught up in a task that you forget that," she said. "But they're watching you." She also said that no matter how polished, professional or friendly, sometimes people were not going to like us. "They may not like you because you're black," she said, looking at us with conviction. "They may not like you because you're white, or female, or because you look like their math teacher in high school whom they hated." The point was that when you'd done all you could and there hadn't been a conflict, just hold your head high and let it go. As for conflict, "If you're having real difficulty with a particular passenger for any reason," she said, "switch aisles or cabins."

It was time for my final uniform fitting. Although mine was tight, Rosie said she wouldn't have to let the seams out. "I always leave a little space," she said, "just in case." Dressed in my Gateway skirt, jacket, vest, blouse, scarf and regulation shoes, I went over to Pauline and took a deep breath as I stepped onto the scale.

"One twenty-two," Pauline said. "Hmm, Sherri do you realize that being so close to your max puts you on weight check? You've gained seven pounds in five weeks." I nodded, stepping off and looking away. "Come here," she said. "Let's sit." She led me away from the mirrors and scale and we spoke quietly. "You're so young," she said. "I'm going to admit that when we saw your age, we had our doubts. We couldn't imagine how you'd gotten through so many tough interviews, but you did. You impressed them and there was a lot of competition. Then you got here, everyone loved you and it was obvious that you're very bright." She paused a long time. Too long.

"And?" I urged her on.

"When we didn't see you mingling at first, we were afraid you weren't going to be a team player. We thought you might be the kind of person that had to do everything yourself which won't work on a plane. You have to be the kind of person that trusts others to do their job. You rarely left the training center on the weekends with the others. You were alone often. We also heard that you had written distasteful things about Danny in a notebook."

I stared at her, my tongue was dry and my face was crimson. That *bitch!* Amy had snooped through my stuff! They said they didn't want tattle-tales; what the hell was she? Why was Amy still around? "That's laughable," I choked, rubbing my collarbones. "Danny is one of my best friends! What I wrote wasn't mean or unkind…"

"Never mind," she said. "We were wrong. It was Georgia who first mentioned how helpful you were. Others followed and of course after that silly incident with Danny, and you sticking up for him, I knew that you were unique Sherri; beyond your years in some ways. If you'd had it out for Danny, you were given a perfect opportunity to hurt him. So, I want you to have the best career ever. I meant it when I said I'd want you on my crew. We're co-workers now. You will get your wings tomorrow and I will no longer be your instructor, I'll be your peer. But in these last few moments, let me impress upon you how important weight is.

Numerous flight attendants have lost their jobs over this issue. They fight it in court but they never win. None of the carriers tolerate heavy attendants. Do whatever it takes Sherri; don't lose your job over this. You're going to be one of the best! I have to report to your supervisor that you are officially on weight check. All probationary flight attendants have to weigh in once a month anyway during their first year, but being on weight check means they can ask you to step on the scale anytime."

She must have seen how shaken I was because she added, "I do have good news! You will not be the most junior graduate tomorrow. Gateway has determined Jeanna's start date to be one day after all of yours. Technically she'll graduate with you but her adjusted start date is later; you're senior to her."

Like that was going to make my life any better. Jeanna was getting a raw deal but that wasn't my fight. My fight was the battle of the bulge.

Walking back to my room, I thought about Amy. If I said anything she would know that she'd won on some level; that the instructors had heard her and confronted me. I decided to ignore it. I could survive being her roommate for twenty-four more hours.

That night I penned:

- *They thought I wasn't a team player; can you believe that? My instructors are SO ARROGANT! I'll show all of them – Pauline, Alan, Mike and Lydia. How dare they! I know what my goal is: I WILL be flight attendant of the year someday, I WILL! Only one more night in this wretched place; I can't wait to get the hell out of here. Yeah, training center – it's been real!*

Falling asleep with *FlightLog* safety tucked under my pillow, I thought about Danny. *Life is funny.* There was a good possibility his stupid stunt had helped me keep my job. I hadn't seen my instructors' doubts.

Chapter 7

Start Spreading the News

A S A GRADUATION PRESENT, Jeanna did my nails and fixed my hair. I should have been packing, or calling Gateway Airlines to see if my family had made it in but I could not stop looking at myself in the mirror. My hairdo was sophisticated; I didn't know how she had done it, but there was a little height on top, a bit of fullness on the sides and the back view was totally picturesque in a smashing French twist. Danny entered our room boldly; he was carrying a gift. Since we were only an hour from graduating, everyone was breaking the 'floor/gender' rule.

"All you need now is a flower in your hair," Jeanna said, watching me stare into the handheld mirror as I turned my head side to side.

"Only flight attendants working to and from Hawaii are allowed to wear flowers in their hair," said Amy. "It's not considered professional looking with the domestic uniform."

"You know I think you're perfect Reej," Danny said. "But I have to admit; that style does a lot more for you than…"

"The spinster's bun I put it in?"

"Yeah," he said.

"Flattery will get you nowhere; I'm still mad you couldn't get your brother here today."

"Really Danny," Jeanna added, giving him a disappointed look. "I wanted to meet him."

"He's going through a tough time," Danny said. "Sat out last season. He's trying to make a comeback—my brother's a world hockey great. A flight attendant graduation isn't that big a deal. But he did send this; it's for you Sherri. I told him all about the crap I put you through. Said I should get you something, and then he said he'd handle it for me."

"Oh my God!" Jeanna gasped as I opened the beautifully-boxed watch. "It's a RAYMOND WEIL!" She examined it admiringly.

"Danny," I stammered, not knowing who Raymond Weil was, but understanding this was an extraordinary present, "I can't accept this!"

"Course you can; it's nothing to him," he said. "Wants to make sure he doesn't lose a potential fan. Celebrities," he laughed. "Put it on," he reached to help me, then he stepped back. "There, you're complete now; a perfect, 'Neat, Attractive, Professional' *Flight Attendant!*"

"That's right," Jeanna added. "And I need a perfect flight attendant to pin my wings on me today. You're *Top of the List* Sherri; meant to ask you sooner; will you do the honors?"

Tears welled at the inside corners of my eyes. "Jeanna, that's such a sweet thought; but they don't let classmates pin each other…"

"Seasoned flight attendants are allowed to pin new hires. You're a day senior to me! If I were going through the ceremony next week, you'd have been allowed to—they had to say yes. Believe me, they owed me one!"

I wiped a tear away. "I'm so flattered, of course I'll do it."

"If you cry, I will kill you."

Our ceremony was outdoors. Though windy, it was nearly a perfect day. Gateway had set up bleachers, fold out chairs, speakers, mikes and refreshments on a grassy area surrounded by flower beds. Heading out in single file, I looked for my family members among the crowd. They weren't there yet. Jeanna didn't have anyone coming from home. She brushed it off as if it was no big deal, but I knew it bothered her.

Being the shortest, I was on the bottom bleacher. In order to be an attendant for Gateway, you had to be at least five feet two inches and no taller than six feet. The six-foot maximum was because of the low ceilings in the pit and because of the jumpseat designs. The five feet two inch minimum—I'd just made it—was so we could reach the overhead bins. I watched my classmates line up in their new uniforms and laughed. *We all looked like cookie-cutter Barbie and Ken dolls.* And wow, what smiles. That was it! That was the single common-denominator we all had—beautiful smiles! Gateway must have impressed that upon the interviewers they flew all over the country for their hiring events. 'Make sure you hire people with great smiles so the passengers will think they're friendly.' Even Amy had a great smile the few times she used it; Danny, Tom, Yosef, Cheyenne, I did, Mara did, Jeanna did… our instructors too, who were all flight attendants on special assignments: Pauline, Lydia, Alan, Mike, Steve and Mary— infectious smiles as well as an acceptable 'height-to-weight ratio.'

I was already in place and many of the guests were seated, when I saw my family running across the lawn. The breeze sent my brother Shane's jacket, my mother Sheila's and my sister Shannon's skirts floating; they looked like a Norman Rockwell painting. I wanted to dart across the grass and hug them all, but I stayed at attention and grinned. It was so nice to see them. I had never been away from my family for so long.

Our ceremony 'surprise' was the appearance of Mike Evans and Isabel Sanford who played Lionel and Louise Jefferson on the highly-rated smash hit TV sitcom, "The Jeffersons." They weren't introduced at first, instead we heard the show's theme song, "Well we're moving on up, to the East Side," and the two of them came dancing out, to everyone's delight. They did a hilarious act pointing out why the other one couldn't be a Gateway Flight Attendant.

"You're too fat!" Mike, playing Lionel, said to Isabel.

"You're too mean and ugly," Isabel, who was playing Louise, shot back. They were in character. Alan, who had done lots of theatre, joined the act; we all laughed merrily.

When it came time for me to pin on Jeanna's wings, I felt a little shaky; this was all finally happening. She radiated; our class was moved that she had asked a fellow classmate to 'do the honors.'

I wasn't sure who was going to pin on my wings. My dad hadn't made it; he was working so it was going to be Shane, Shannon or Sheila. I had asked my mother but she hated being in front of crowds. Just being in front of a classroom was pushing it, so I assumed it would be Shannon, and it was.

"From Wichita Kansas, Sherri Ann Van Ness," said Alan. "Sherri's sister, Shannon, will be pinning on Sherri's wings today." I stepped down as Shannon rose and came forward. She had on a flowered sleeveless dress with a full skirt. There was a delicate, feminine, chiffon second layer on top. I heard some of the males in my class behind me comment about her looks; *what a surprise*. She smiled directly at them—not hiding that she knew they noticed her.

Shannon fumbled with the pin; she stabbed herself and made a small "ow" sound and put her finger to her mouth to catch a drop of blood. People started to giggle. She got the clasp working, positioned it above my heart, and then a wild gust of wind blew her dress up; the full layers danced to the sky—high. There was no way she could catch the back in time—everyone seated in the audience got an X-rated view. The crowd erupted. The tailored skirts of our uniforms kept us safe; they were unyielding. They stayed in place, keeping us new graduates covered, modest.

"Guess I'm on the wrong side of this show," said Alan loudly into the microphone; he stood in front of Shannon. The audience roared. Shannon laughed and turned, then gracefully returned to her seat unfazed. *Brat.*

Afterwards, in front of the refreshment table, Shane gave me the biggest hug I'd had from him in years; I got a lump in my throat. I'd forgotten how much I'd missed the affection a loving family brings; I had to wipe more tears away. "Look at you," he said like a grownup, holding my hands out but stepping back to give me a once over. "Toby's not going to be happy about this," he teased. "Or happy about you going to New York."

"Who's Toby?" asked Jeanna.

"Her boyfriend," said Shane.

"My *Ex*-boyfriend," I corrected.

"Is Toby rich?" Jeanna asked.

"Nooo…" Shane said with a furrowed brow. He and Shannon eyed each other.

"Don't worry about him honey," Jeanna exclaimed, turning to me. "We're going to be meeting *All* kinds of eligible bachelors now. New York, here we come! *Start spreading the news, we're leaving today!*"

Shane laughed. He liked this tough chick.

"We'll be living the life of Riley," she boasted.

"I thought you were going to be living the life of flight attendants?" Shane asked. Shannon groaned at him. He added, "Who is Riley anyway?"

"Someone who knows how to have fun," Jeanna said with a loud whoop, "And in New York, I'm going to find men just like him."

I properly introduced Jeanna to my family starting with my mom, Sheila, Shannon and Shane.

"Everyone in your family have a name that starts with the ess-aich sound?" she asked.

"Yep," said Shane. He made a lousy joke about her having to change her name to Sheena if she wanted to be adopted. I stared at him. My 15-year-old brother was drooling all over Jeanna; it was so cute!

Danny also gave me a congratulatory hug. Before he'd let go, he was telling Shannon that just like Alan, he wished he had witnessed the 'leg' show. He was jumpy; something was on his mind.

"Danny," I interrupted. "This is my mother Sheila, and my brother Shane."

"I have to tell you," Danny put a hand on my mother's shoulder. "Rejects here, the baby of our class, ended up being the only one who didn't have a re-take. It doesn't sound like a big deal, but it is. She's amazing." He didn't wait for a response; instead, he turned to me and Jeanna. "We need everyone in the class to meet over there by the last bleacher for our last 'hurrah.' Get over there as soon as you can. Nice to meet everyone," he shouted, scurrying off.

"Who is 'Rejects?'" asked my little brother.

*   *   *

"Our award for the instructor most-likely *Not* to be invited to a nudist colony is: Lydia," Danny said. He, Tom, and Yosef had dreamed up some outrageous, nonsensical awards. The prizes were packets of first-class Macadamia Nuts wrapped in Gateway napkins folded like bunny ears; something we'd learned from Alan. No one wanted to know how they'd gotten hold of the napkins or the nuts.

Jeanna looked at me, "I don't get it."

"Had to be at our orientation," I told her.

"You always call your mom by her first name?" Jeanna asked.

I laughed. "Both my parents. Started doing that after high school—they find it shocking. They're convinced I'm turning into a Gloria Steinem worshipping woman's lib fanatic. If we were Catholic, they would have scheduled an exorcism by now."

"This special award goes to the flight attendant least likely to ever *Be* a pilot," said Danny. He made drum roll noises before announcing, "Kevin! Ready for the next one? Our award for the most-likely to *Make* it with a pilot while he's flying the airplane is: Jeanna!"

She smirked and stepped forward. "Not unless he's flying his own personal Lear jet," she said. "Then… probably. I'll have your nuts now Danny," she added, snatching her prize.

"And," Danny waited for us to calm down. "The award for the flight attendant most-likely to swear at passengers and call them *Asses* is: Jane!" His grinning subsided after she received her award. Quietly he said, "This last award comes from our hearts gang, seriously. We did some secret polling. We couldn't get to everyone, because we didn't want to give anything away, but our award for the friendliest classmate is… Sherri." Yosef handed Danny a flower. He stepped forward and placed it in my hair above my right ear. More tears. Keeping my eye makeup smudge-proof was impossible. Then Danny pulled me close and gave me a big smack on the lips in front of everyone. I started to smile and tried pulling away but he held me tight; everyone was laughing, even me, though I had trouble curling my lips because he was pressing so hard. *No tongue please Danny!* The more I struggled the more everyone cheered and hoorayed. Danny didn't let go or unlock lips for a long, long, time.

- *Dear FlightLog; Today was <u>My</u> special day and yet Shannon stole the show. She even tainted my 'virgin' wings before they were pinned on me, before I'd even touched them. She often does this – get all the attention, but since everything else went well, and I feel so good about being chosen the friendliest, I'm going to forgive her. That's what the 'friendliest' should do, right? If I hadn't gotten that award, I might have to slug her. Now I'm a 'neat attractive professional' and I'm going to act like one. I'm also a big-city girl who is ready to roll. Ok, I probably should avoid the rolls for a while. I'm on weight check. But – I'm gonna make a brand-new start of it. I'm leaving today; I want to be a part of it! I've got my 'blood' wings baby and I am ready for whatever you want to give me. It's up to you New York – New York. Come on, come through for me; these small-town blues are melting away. Come through for me, you big-bad-beautiful place!*

Part II:

. . . .

Takeoff

Chapter 8:

· · · · · · · · · · 🎵

The Lights are Much Brighter There

"Looks bad," Jeanna told me, as she made her way back from gate A-thirteen's counter. It had been twenty-four hours since we'd graduated and we were trying to ride on company business passes to New York. The flight was oversold. "Gate agent said we should consider putting on our uniforms in order to ride the jumpseats—it's really that full. They must be understaffed if there are two jumpseats open. Remember what we were told Sherri."

The summer of 1978 was crazy-busy. Trainees were warned that understaffed inflight cabin-crews were coercing pass-riding new hires into working. They promised them they would be paid, but that in fact they never were. 'You are *Not* a working crew member when you are on a pass reporting to your base,' Mike had stated. 'Do not work those flights no matter what the crews tell you.' Jeanna and I hustled into a washroom to change. Like most of the female flight attendants, Jeanna had purchased a metal foldup set of wheels—a contraption with several bungee cords. 'Wheelies' we called them, to hold her suitcase. That way she could roll her bag instead of carrying it. I opted to carry mine, as did all the male attendants. We didn't even bother going into the stalls; we changed in front of the sinks.

"Wish we'd gotten on earlier," Jeanna said. The other New York bound grads in our class had gotten seats on flights last night or earlier in the day; we were the last two left.

Back at the gate, an announcement blared. "Ladies and gentlemen, for those of you awaiting the departure of Gateway flight 726 to LaGuardia, we are going to have a delay…" Passengers in the boarding area groaned loudly.

"Well," said Jeanna. "That will help our chances of getting on. Some of these people will split and take flights on other carriers or wait until tomorrow."

We sat down and lit up; I was smoking Jeanna's brand now and had purchased a few packs of my own. I wasn't really sure if it was helping me lose weight, but I was certainly starting to like it. Fifty minutes passed with a couple more announcements; then, they started boarding.

"Campion and Van Ness," the agent called. We were assigned 24B and 27E, middle seats in the back.

"Which one do you want?" Jeanna asked me playfully, as if it really mattered. "You're senior, so you get to pick."

I grabbed a boarding pass without looking. "At least we don't have to ride jumpseats."

In the jetway we lined up behind a crowd of slow-moving passengers. I could make out an American Airline's pilot crew just as they got to the aircraft door.

"See those three at the front?" I told Jeanna. "They're American Airline pilots."

"How can you tell from here?" she asked me.

"I… just know."

Greeting them was a tall, friendly, steward with a short afro. He was boisterous and he seemed to be having a lot more fun than anyone else. Most of the customers were grouchy because of the delay; we were going to get in very late. "Whoa," he said as the pilots stepped onto the plane. "Check it out! How is it going over at American Airlines, gentlemen?"

They all seemed tired but nodded. One mumbled, "Fine thanks."

"Oh! I'm so *Sorry* to hear that," the steward said, making everyone in the jetway laugh. As Jeanna and I got closer, he eyed us with approval. "My, my," he said with a broad grin. "Happy to see reinforcements."

"We're not working the flight." Jeanna held out her boarding pass and waited until he took it from her. "Not gonna happen."

"That is some gorgeous red hair you got there," he barked, unfazed by her curt manner. "You let me show you around New York City tonight and I won't make you work nothing. Ever been there before? *No finer place for sure.*"

Jeanna kept walking.

Obviously, they could smell new hires coming. I was behind Jeanna and as I passed the first-class galley, the gal setting it up turned to me. She grabbed my arm. "Listen, we are really short-staffed tonight…"

At the back of the plane, I stashed my suitcase under the last row of passenger seats after pulling out my inflight handbook and my apron. I would be the number four FA on this 727 which meant I'd be responsible for the galley exit and the aft stairwell… *hmm, very familiar. Please don't die on the jumpseat,* I thought, looking at the attendant in the galley. *Don't want to cover your door at 2Left and the overwing exits if we crash.*

Jeanna had followed me after putting her bag under her seat. "You should not be doing this Sherri. You are not insured; that's what they said. If you work a flight and get injured, Gateway is not going to cover your medical bills; are you listening to me?"

"It's only an hour; I don't care if I'm not paid, I know the risks. Frankly, being up and in the aisle beats sitting in a middle seat in the smoking section anyway." I moved into the aft galley toward the number three attendant who was counting long rectangular snack trays. Though snacks were different than meals, we still ran them out on formal trays, uncovered; the only thing easier was we didn't have to stack entrees on them first. "Hi, I'm Sherri," I said. "I'll be helping you out back here tonight."

"Scuze me," an elderly lady said, holding out her boarding pass. "There's already someone in my seat; we both have 28D."

The other attendant took the woman's boarding card and said to me, "Welcome to the real world of flying. I'm Louise and you're about to start learning all the stuff they *Don't* teach you rookies in training, like on full flights, we have *Way* too many double seat assignments. Want to handle this?"

"Sure," I said. "What do I do?"

"Find the other person who's in 28D, take their boarding pass with this one out to the gate agent and have one of them reassigned."

As I made my way up the aisle, I ran into two other double seat assignment problems. Collecting all six boarding cards, I fought my way up the jetway and over to the gate agent.

"These three aren't going to be happy," the agent said, handing me back all the cards after he had clicked away on his computer for several minutes. "Had to give them middle seats when they thought they had aisles. We've got to shut this door, let's go." He gave me a little push and down the jetway we strode. Then he picked up the PA at door 1Left and began his predeparture announcement.

I passed the first-class galley and this time, the afroed steward stopped me. "Hey," he said. "Thanks for helping out, really. I'm Darryl; you are?"

"Sherri."

"Sherri-girl it is so cool to see two of you that did not fall for all that pressure in training to cut your hair," he said. "I cannot stand those 'stew dos'—just a shame how they get so many new hires to butcher themselves. Say… what's your friend's name?"

When I handed the three people in the aisle their 'new' boarding cards and they realized they were in middle seats, they started whining. "Please!" I begged them. "I'm sorry, but for now, just take your seat so we can take off, all right? We can't leave the gate until everyone's seated. I *Promise* all of you I will get you a free drink; that's all I can do. We have to go; now."

Seconds after takeoff, the no-smoking sign went off and Louise lit up. She too had a paper cup filled with a small amount of water under our jumpseat propped up against the back of the plane ready, to serve as her ashtray. I was afraid to join her. We were told that we could not smoke on the jumpseats; only in the cockpit if the flight-deck crew permitted it or in the back galleys in smoking sections *After* the service was completed.

"This is a fast service," Louise said. "Flight's an hour; have about forty-five minutes to get snacks out and do a beverage service. You familiar with this 27 setup?"

I had written the seat numbers of the people forced to move on a cocktail napkin. "Make sure these passengers get free drinks—please," I said, handing the napkin to Louise.

Louise told me to start running snacks. I got to the front and discovered that the first row of passengers didn't have tray tables; the customers behind them had ones that folded down from the seatback in front of them, but the first row didn't have any.

Darryl came striding back and laughed as I looked around frantically with three trays in my hands. "Looking for their tables?" he produced two for me. "They're behind the last row of first class." He folded down the legs and stuck them into the armrests of the six passengers in the first row. "Now we got you all locked in," he teased. "We'll try to remember to set you free sometime after we land." I set down three trays and took off for the back to get more. Darryl and Louise pulled the heavy beverage cart out from its spot near the back galley, placed the things they needed on the top, and dragged the cart to the front of coach. "Sherri?" Darryl stopped before leaving. "After you're done running the trays, serve drinks from the galley starting at the back until we catch you."

"I know," I smiled. I did know; the flow of services had been an easy unit for me.

I kept running. I was smiling easily, the angst of our passengers after the delay had subsided; they were happy to have a snack in front of them and to think about something else. I locked eyes with a man in 12C. *Oh boy*—Sheldon-level good looks and definitely, *Definitely,* watching me. I made an attempt to slow down and not show that I was feeling a fast exhilaration inside. He kept staring at me and out of the corner of my eye, I could tell he knew that I knew he was staring at me, and from the look of his grin he knew it was getting to me, and that he found this amusing. "Will you be having a snack with us tonight?" I asked all the passengers in his row. A and B nodded and I set down their trays with another smile.

"No thank you Sherri," the handsome man said.

I set down his tray.

"I'd just like some coffee," he said.

I started to walk away, then realized he didn't want the tray so I came back and leaned over to pick it up with an, "Oh…"

He held onto the tray. "But if you really want me to have this, that's quite all right."

"I… no. I was moving too quickly, I'll take this for you," I said, lifting it up.

"I'd just like some coffee if you don't mind," he let go.

"The two behind me will have the cart here in a moment," I said, motioning with my head toward Darryl and Louise who were at row eight. "There is a coffee cup on this tray."

He reached up and took the tray again with a grin. "Ah, so there is Sherri."

"How do you know my name?" I asked.

"It's on your apron," he smirked. A few passengers laughed.

"Oh." I looked down at the lettering over my heart. I'd forgotten that Gateway had our names embroidered on our new aprons; it was the first time I'd worn mine.

"How long have you been flying?" Way too many other passengers were watching us now; it was unnerving.

"Probably shows by now," I said a little too loud—starting my return to the galley with a fake smile; I was trying to appear confident and light-hearted instead of embarrassed and self-conscious. "It's my first flight." Some of the passengers cheered. I gave them two thumbs up as I hustled to the back. *Oh God! 'There's a coffee cup on the tray; how did you know my name?' Why had I said that? What an idiot!* There were paper coffee cups on the beverage cart; he didn't need a tray to have coffee. He was having way too much fun with me; I was going to ignore him the rest of the flight.

At row twenty-three a customer stopped me. "I'm sorry," she said. "My ashtray's full and I'd like to have a cigarette. Could you empty this?"

"Sure." I leaned over to ply the metal ashtray out of her armrest. Suddenly people all over the back of the plane wanted their ashtrays emptied too. I made three trips back and forth to the trash cart, but other passengers kept handing me full ones. The cabin cleaning crew in Cleveland had either neglected this task, or they had been told to hustle. No doubt they were already off the plane before the delay was announced. Darryl came to the rescue.

"Ladies and gentleman," he said. "We have exactly twenty-two more minutes to get the rest of you fed and watered. Let us finish our service and we'll take care of these ashtrays shortly."

As soon as Louise and Darryl returned with the cart, Louise handed me a full pot of coffee and a tray lined with creamers and sugars. "Go start second coffees," she told me. "Darryl, I'll start picking up if you break down the cart." He was nodding and had already started doing so.

Jeanna stopped me as I raced toward the front. "Pardon me Miss," she said, holding out her flimsy plastic coach soda cup. "Could you *waft* this for me?"

"More coffee? Any more coffees here?" I laughed at the private joke as I refilled cups in the aisle.

The first flight attendant came through the curtain dividing coach from first class. She put her hands on my hips and gently but firmly pushed me right up against the aisle seat. "When you're doing second coffees," she said, "get right up against the seat so the rest of us can pass you." She picked up the first group of trays and slipped past me toward the back. On her return, she didn't have to ask; I was pressed up against the aisle seat and I watched her move fast, like Louise, who was now storing the odd portable tray tables in the first row that Darryl had installed.

The service was quick but I was having fun. Smiling was easy again. There was no turbulence but I rocked anyway—my jet legs would come with time. 'Always be prepared for turbulence,' our instructors had said. 'Especially in the summer. Clear air turbulence hits without warning.' The best course for me was to refill my now-empty coffee pot from the first-class galley. I was only at row ten. The back galley was across from row twenty-five, but the first-class galley was across from row one, so up front I went. I placed my empty pot into the coffee maker, started brewing a fresh pot, put more cream and sugars on my black tray, grabbed a full coffee pot off a hot plate and stepped into the aisle. But the first-class passenger in 2B asked me to refill his martini. Back into the galley I went. I got stuck refreshing other drinks in first before I could get back to coach.

The airplane started down and the first or second officer announced that we had begun our descent. Half the cabin still had trays; I hadn't even finished a third of the cabin with second coffees. I could see Louise, the A, and Darryl move into high gear.

Since we were hurrying it was easy to ignore 'him.' But soon I was there at row twelve, and I could feel his eyes on me once more.

"Coffee, Tea or Me?" he asked. The two passengers next to him chuckled.

"I think that's her line," the man in 12A said. "You should see the look on your face," he said to me. "You're blushing."

"You're cute when you blush," 12C said. "What do you say?" he asked.

I shook my head and smiled, looking down; what else could I do? "Do-you-want-some-more-coffee?" I said carefully. "No hurry; you've got two seconds."

He plopped his plastic cup onto my tray. I poured, but barely gave him enough time to grab another sugar before moving on. When I'd finished, I saw that my crew had picked up everything, counted the liquor, the cash, filled out the paperwork, locked up the liquor cart and had stowed most of the galley doors.

We each grabbed a small bag and emptied the rest of the ashtrays in the smoking section. There were eight minutes left; customers were standing, stretching, using the bluerooms and handing us empty cups. Darryl and Louise were arguing about the new language in our latest union contract.

"If they're only going to pay reserves half pay for deadheading," Louise said, "then senior line holders will have to work all reassigned trips while junior reserves deadhead," she said. "That's not fair."

"And if they're only getting half pay," Darryl said. "Then they *Shouldn't* be working."

"It's going to be a problem in the future," Louise said.

An elderly gentleman came into the galley and asked if we had restrooms. We looked at each other—the line for the blue-rooms was two feet away.

"No sorry," Darryl said loudly. He pulled the man into the galley and handed him an empty ice bucket. "Use this. We'll close these curtains here to give you some privacy…"

"Don't pay any attention to him!" Louise grabbed the bucket. The man's lips curled up; he grinned. "He's just *Awful,*" she added, swatting at Darryl. I emptied the last coffee pot and started wiping down the counters.

"Hello." It was 12C, standing just outside the galley. He handed me his half-full coffee cup. I noticed his brown Elvis-like hair; it made him look like the singer. Bet he heard that all the time; bet he liked it. I wasn't going to say anything.

"Is it cold?" I asked. "I could warm it up."

"It's fine, I'm finished, thank you. Thank you for the nice service and the beautiful smiles." Louise suppressed a grin. "You live in New York?" He asked all of us.

Darryl crossed his arms and grinned too, leaning against the exit door; watching us.

"Yes," I said. "I'm reporting now; just finished training."

"I'm a New Yorker from way back," Louise said in a thick accent. "Best place in the world to live." She elbowed me. "You're lucky you got here right outta training. Beats *Cleveland*, that's for sure."

"I hear you," Darryl said.

"I love New York," 12C said. "I get there regularly. Sherri, are you done when we get in tonight?"

Oh my God! Was going to ask me out? What was I supposed to do?

"Since it's your first evening here, why don't you let me show you around? We could have a nice dinner, maybe listen to some music. I *know some little places to go to where they never close.*"

"Got my own car," Louise said with a laugh. *She's funny.* "Live in Brooklyn. But thanks anyway." She elbowed him.

"No, thank you," I said. "I'm staying with an aunt and I need to go straight there. I haven't seen her in a while and my parents will want me to call." *Why did I Say that? Why did I have an aunt?* He must be thinking I am a total baby. I reached up and rubbed my collarbones with my right hand. My face felt flushed.

"How about another time then; could I call you?"

"I'd feel funny giving out her number… you know, without her knowing you."

"No chance you'll change your mind?"

He was prolonging this. I thought men got ticked off when you said no, but it all seemed to be amusing him. *Go Away.*

"Too forward?" he asked, stepping back a little. "There's a lot of room in my car, so if you or the whole crew would like a ride, I'd be happy to accommodate you. A ride would be safe, wouldn't it? Is there anything you're dying to do in New York?" His green eyes shone beautifully; he was an attractive, polished man. *And he smelled good.* "There's *no finer place for sure* than *downtown,*" he teased.

The seat belt sign went on. The cockpit crew made an announcement. Louise turned to our passenger and said, "Sorry sir. You'll have to take your seat now."

"Too bad," Darryl said. "This was getting good."

"Of course," 12C said. "I'm Roman Palermo," he took my hand and placed his business card in it. "How 'bout I take you to Greenwich Village? What's your last name anyway?"

"Van Ness," I said. Then while raising one brow I added, "Actually I'd like to go to Belmont," I pulled my hand away slowly and slipped his card into the pocket of my apron.

"Sherri Van Ness," he said. "That's a lovely name. You're a horse-racing fan? I was lucky enough to be at Pimlico this year; wish I could have taken you," he paused. "Look, I'm staying at the midtown Hilton the next couple of nights. Give me a call."

As soon as he was out of earshot Louise scowled. "Sherri, don't *Ever* tell anyone your last name, do you hear me? What the heck is Pimlico?"

"Racetrack in Baltimore," Darryl told her. "The second leg of the 'Triple Crown' just took place there." He grinned at me. "Dude's hitting on you hard; he looked all right to me," he said. "*Yes* give him your name. You're with the airlines now; meeting all kinds of people. That's called *Fringe* benefits! Dressed sharp, staying at the Hilton, knows race tracks; ain't no low-life." Darryl put his face close to mine. "Didn't take you long, did it? The world loves a beautiful woman. *Everything's waiting for you.* Tell that hot redheaded friend of yours that if you're gonna hang with that guy tonight, I'll take *Good* care of her."

The no smoking sign came on; the A made her announcement and we headed into the aisle to do our last cabin/passenger checks before landing. I caught Roman's eye and we exchanged smiles. I felt excited but scared—he was worldly; I didn't want to get hurt again.

The passenger in 12A clapped as I walked by. "Let's give Sherri a hand," he said, "for completing her first flight and not pouring hot coffee on anyone." I curtsied, looking left and right as I hurried back, making sure the aisles were clear and strapped into my seat seconds before the wheels touched down.

After everyone had deplaned, I relaxed. The flight had been quick; we had scrambled. It was a relief to be done and I was grateful I didn't have three or four more legs just like it to follow like a regular crew might. I started gathering my things.

"Thank you so much for helping us," Louise said as she grabbed her own belongings. "I'll make sure you get paid. Hope to fly with you again soon."

"No problem," I said. "I can see that it would have been tough with only three people."

"Sherri!" Jeanna had gotten back on the plane and was walking toward me. "I think the guy you were talking to is waiting for you to get off," she said. "He's standing by the door. Did you tell him you'd meet him after the flight?"

"No! Oh no… what do I do?" I could feel my face redden. "Jeanna, I can't face him, he's too pushy. Makes me nervous, the way he's super sophisticated and stuff."

"Yeah," she said. "Pierre Cardin suit, Rolex watch. What's the problem? He's hot."

"I'm talking about his manner… how do you know all that stuff anyway? What he's wearing? Jeanna… I'm going to my aunt's; it's late. I can't show up after my first flight with some stranger I just met. He's probably thirty! She's waiting up for me."

"Too bad," Jeanna shrugged. "He's really good looking."

"Make sure he leaves then come get me."

"I'll go," Darryl said. "They always disappear when a dude shows up."

"It's too fast," I said to Jeanna, rubbing my collarbones again. She was frowning. "I'm only twenty, give me a minute or two before I turn into a fearless New Yorker, all right?"

She and I hopped into a cab in front of the terminal, and headed into Manhattan, after Jeanna successfully fought off Darryl.

"Good grief," I said. "Is it always going to be like this?"

"I hope so." She could not stop talking about Roman. She had also caught that his shirt was monogrammed and that his shoes were very expensive.

"Darryl likes you a lot," I said, taking a drag of my cigarette and trying to change the subject.

She laughed out loud. "Not a chance in hell. Are you kidding? A black male flight attendant Sherri? Get serious. I'm a New Yorker now; it'll be a Wall Street guy for me and I'm going to start looking for him right now. Sure you don't want to go out tonight?" she asked. *"Things will be great when we're downtown,"* she sang.

I shook my head. "Family duty." Then I looked out the window for a long time. "Jeanna, what about that instructor you were with?"

"I told you; didn't know he was a steward. Figured he was management; come on."

I giggled at her snobby bitchiness. It was her trademark and she was proud of it.

She was staying at the Sheraton for five days; that was the amount of time Gateway allotted us for finding a place to live. We exclaimed over the noise, the lights, *listening to the music of the traffic in the city,* the people walking, the clubs, restaurants, hotels; it was great.

I let the driver drop off Jeanna first then we headed up town. The ride was twenty-five bucks before I got out. I gave the driver thirty and climbed out. My aunt's building was fifty stories. Doing a 360, I looked all around me at the movement, action, traffic; *where all the lights were bright. An inviting neon naughtiness.*

Whatever came to pass, it was going to be worth it. Turbulence, irates, stranded away from home for long periods of time, alone on holidays, flying on airplanes with no water or meals or electrical power to make coffee or show movies; I could take the tradeoff. I lived in the Big Apple now; like Jeanna, I was a New Yorker. And, I too secretly *hoped I'd find someone kind to help and understand me.* The city smelled wonderful. Couples passed, laughing, *forgetting their troubles, forgetting their cares,* dressed to kill. *Yes, it was true: this is where the beautiful people are; they are here. I'm gonna wake up in a city that doesn't sleep!*

Chapter 9:

Camptown Races

"Sherri!" Aunt Harriet flitted into my bedroom without knocking. "Here's your uniform," she said, holding out my plastic draped clothing. "I had it dry cleaned so you'll be all set for your first real trip." She placed the items in the closet.

"I only wore it for an hour," I said. "You didn't have to do that but thank-you."

"Will you be able to go to church with me on Sunday?" This was the second time since I'd arrived that she'd asked me that question.

"It'll depend on if I find a place in the next few days or not." I looked away, knowing what she was going to say next.

"There's no hurry dear! You're welcome to stay here as long as you like… what are you doing," she asked.

I lifted the plastic bag and examined my uniform jacket. "Did you take off my pins before you took this to the cleaners? I also had a small flashlight on the vest too. Do you have them?"

"Oh no," she said with a tsk. "I'm afraid I didn't dear; but don't worry, I'm sure Gateway can replace them for you with no problem."

I wonder if this 'anything goes' city will go easy on me if I murder my aunt.

- *Dear FlightLog. For weeks, I agonized at that miserable training center to earn my wings. Now, before my first official trip, they're gone. So is my union pin and the Gateway Airlines issued flashlight. I'll probably be reprimanded. I have to report for duty for the first time with an incomplete uniform, walk into the offices at Kennedy Airport in front of the whole world and tell my super, the first time I meet him, that I've already lost these valuable items that I worked so hard to earn. And, I'm going to turn bright red. Is there a physical remedy for that? I HATE how people think it's just 'so cute' when I blush! Please let me find an apartment I can afford in this city soon; PLEASE let me get away from this crazy old lady; sorry, I know she's family but she lives in the dark ages and I cannot survive this much longer.*

The apartment manager's office was in the basement of the old brick building. He sat down at his desk and set one arm across his bulging abdomen. "So ah—you interested?"

"How much is it again?" Surely I had not heard him correctly.

"Five eighty."

Five hundred and eighty dollars a month for a four-story walk-up in a roach infested claustrophobic studio with an ancient, rotting, squeaking, Murphy bed along the longest wall—which wasn't long. There was a bathroom but you couldn't stand in it unless you closed the door. The closet was maybe eighteen inches wide and the 'kitchenette' had an old small sink, a miniature refrigerator under the counter, and two burners above a stove that surely had not been cleaned in twenty years. The best part of the apartment was a large window. However, the view was completely obstructed by the metal fire escape stairs which was probably good, considering the only thing behind it was the window-less brick wall of the neighboring building.

He was giving me a funny look that made me feel uncomfortable. "You're a stewardess, huh?" He raised his eyebrows twice.

Oh My God, He's flirting with me.

"A flight attendant," I said, correcting him and trying to look older and serious. "We're called flight attendants now."

"Well scuze-the-hell-outta-me!" He sat back quickly, scraping the legs of his chair against the floor and making a loud obnoxious sound. "You taking the apartment?"

"I'll have to think about it," I lied. I didn't want to say no, he was already offended.

"It won't last long. It's a nice studio," he said. "I been in this business a long time. You better call before five if you want it."

All the talk about the rents in New York was true. There weren't any affordable apartments available. The only hope one had was to find a roommate who had lived in the city for years, because New York had rent control laws. Landlords could not raise rents more than established percentages which kept 'old' tenants' costs affordable but 'new' tenants' costs exorbitantly high. When people moved out of the city, they kept their leases and sublet the apartments for a profit. *I need to find a roommate or a sublet or both.*

My Aunt Harriet was driving me insane. Not only did she want me to go to church with her on Sundays, she couldn't understand why I couldn't just 'tell' Gateway Airlines that I needed to have every Sunday off so that I *Could* go to church. *Please God, make her disappear.*

Jeanna had taken a two-bedroom two-bath hardwood floor apartment on the Upper East Side with three others from our class. They were paying $2400 a month. The place was small but clean, with a one-room living/dining area and a tiny balcony. $600 each. I had told her she was nuts, but after seeing the studio, I got it. At least I'd gotten to *See* it. By the time I'd arrived at the several apartments listed in the newspapers, most had already been rented.

Despite my pressing need for a place to live, there was something even more important to take care of.

*   *   *

"Is this it?" I asked the bus driver, standing to grab the overhead bar to steady myself.

"Hold on!" he shouted, "don't worry, I'll let you off! Yes, you're here; this is the track lady: *Belmont Park!*" Many piled off. "Good luck today."

I got my first look at the outside of a racetrack grandstand— *it really was grand!* Whoever or whatever was in charge of my life definitely wanted me to be here today. It was the 110th running of the Belmont Stakes. Stevie Cauthen was vying for the 'Triple Crown.' It had been an irresistible story in the press. A young jockey only eighteen years old in a sport that suited and rewarded older, seasoned pros, was attempting to win the third race in the historic challenge—a feat that had only been accomplished ten times in a hundred years.

I'd just arrived in New York and watched the story with interest. I had five days off from flying and even though I hadn't found an apartment yet, I *Knew* that *Of Course* I had to come. Paying a few dollars to enter, I made my way up to the open grandstand level past the tiers of stadium seating and fancy boxes. Someone handed me several sheets of paper listing the race numbers, horses, jockeys, odds. I immediately got in a long betting line. At the window I told the man, "For the next race I'm betting two dollars on the seventh horse. To win." He frowned at me but took my money, knowing I had absolutely no idea what I was doing. Right after he gave me my ticket, I heard a loud horn. "What's that?" I asked.

"Means we're not taking any more bets on this race. Made it just in time. It will start soon. Better push your way to the front if you want to watch."

"When's the big race?" I asked. "You know, the Triple Crown?"

He laughed in spite of himself; I could tell he didn't want to, but my eagerness and naiveté was too funny for him to resist.

"You got a few races to get your feet wet first. Fourth race from now," he said.

"Thanks!"

In the grandstand I quickly mingled with the crowd. Soon, I was telling three older men who looked like serious gamblers about working for Gateway, being in New York City—'Manhattan,' they called it, and searching for an apartment.

The one in the checkered shirt talked the most. "I wouldn't live in that crowded roach-infested place for all the money in the world!" he declared.

"Where do you live?" I asked.

"Here, in Queens!" he said.

"I thought I was on Long Island?" I said honestly. They laughed.

"How did you get here; you said you were staying in the city?"

"I called information, got the number for New York City transportation information, and someone told me which subway cars to take and which buses to connect to."

"Where you from?" the guy in the checkered shirt asked.

"Kansas."

That was the next funniest thing they'd heard in a while. Then the next race started. Suddenly they weren't paying any attention to me. They were watching their horses. When the race was over, all three were jumping up and down and slapping each other's hands. The checker-shirted guy had picked the first, second, and third winners and he had bet eighty-five bucks. His winnings were going to cover all of his expenses for several months it seemed. *Wow; neat!*

Checkers burst into song, *"Camptown Ladies sing this song, Doo-dah, Doo-dah! Camptown racetrack's five miles long, Oh! Doo-dah day."* Then he leaned over and gave me a pinch on my upper arm. "I think you brought me good luck today Ms. Dorothy from Kansas," he said. "Your beginner's luck wore off on me."

They tried to show me what I should look for in a horse when it came out onto the track, and counseled me on the jockeys and horses they knew and had studied, but in the end, I told them I was going to stick to my 'sure' method of 'eenie-meenie-minee-moe, catch a tiger by the toe' on the next few races and save some bucks for betting on Stevie Cauthen in the big race.

It's awful hard for one horse to win the Triple they explained, because Belmont's track was a mile and half. The horses that won the Kentucky Derby and the Preakness were shorter-distance runners but to win Belmont, a horse had to be an endurance runner. Plus, the first two races usually tired a horse. It was fatiguing, therefore very hard to be their best in the third, longest race. A fresh horse that hadn't run the first two would often enter and win the Stakes.

"That's why so many horses have won two out of three; but all three—that's a long shot," Checkers said.

"It's going to happen today," I said confidently. "I just *Know* it!"

"Do you also know which horses are coming in second and third?" he asked.

"Well," I thought about it before finishing. "Alydar will come in second like he always does, and… let me see that," I looked at the racing sheet. "This one," I said. "This one here I think. Can't be positive, I wouldn't *Bet* on it," I added, "but that's my gut feeling."

"Woman's intuition?" one of them suggested. "Beginner's luck?"

"Both."

"Why do you think 'Darby Creek Road' is going to come in third?" Checkers asked.

"Because there are three words in his name… it's a sign."

The three of them looked at each other. "Sounds like the best reason for picking a horse that I've heard in a long time. Sounds absolutely outstanding," Checkers said. "I'm putting money on those three for the trifecta to win, place and show. I'm giving you a cut if I win Dorothy."

The crowd was as excited as I was approaching the big race. Everyone sang, "The Sidewalks of New York," as the horses and jockeys walked in front of the crowd, strutting their stuff before they lined up at the starting gates. I had never been anywhere with this much energy before. This was the biggest world-class event I'd ever attended.

Holding my ticket tightly in my hand, I watched as the race began. Affirmed took an early lead. Everyone in the seats below were standing. Though it only took about two and half minutes for the horses to cover the mile and a half track, it seemed much longer. The crowd was whipped into an uproarious frenzy. The race was exhilaratingly close right from the start and all the way through. Affirmed and Alydar were neck-in-neck. With a minute to go, it was already clear that one of the two favored horses would win. They sped right beside each other for the last minute—either horse could take it—and crossing the finish line, directly in front of me, Affirmed beat Alydar by a nose! *Now I know where that expression comes from.* I couldn't stop jumping up and down. The crowd was crazed. As we watched the standings post on the marquee, we saw the final results: First Place: Affirmed; Second Place: Alydar; Third Place: Darby Creek Road.

Checkers was out of his mind. "*Two* trifectas in one day! *Two!*"

When I went to the window to collect my winnings, the grouchy betting attendant burst into a smile. "You won! Good for you!" I had bet ten bucks and got sixteen back. A six-dollar profit. It could have been a million I was so thrilled. My first gambling winnings; ever.

Checkers was beside me, collecting his money at the next window. He squealed with pleasure when they gave him his cash. I had no idea how much he had bet but he was happy. Shoving several fifty-dollar bills into my hand he said, "Here babe. This is for *You.*"

"I can't take this…"

"Ahhh!" he cried, pushing my outstretched hands away. "Take it! Don't care what you do with it but it's yours!" He turned toward the stairs to leave the grandstand. Then he whirled back around. "Take that back," he said. "I want you to take a *limo* home, understand? No more subways or buses for you today. *Ride In Style!*"

"Ok," I said, smiling back, wondering how someone arranged for a limousine.

"*Gonna run all night,*" he sang. "*Gonna run all day! I bet my money on a bob-tail nag, somebody bet on the bay.*" Then he was gone.

Chapter 10:

Over My Head

"LADIES AND GENTLEMEN, THIS IS Charlie your first flight attendant. Captain Nichols is about to take us out onto the active runway so my *'Angels'* back there, Sherri, Donita and Gwen, are going to sweep past you and make sure your seatbacks and tray tables are in the upright and locked positions and that your carry-on items are stored properly. Today we're aboard one of our old but faithful 737s, and as you can see, the bins above you are not enclosed! Therefore, the only items you can put above you are light ones, such as coats or hats. Of course, we're awfully friendly here at Gateway so we *Do* make exceptions for Newlyweds. If we see you climbing up there, you won't even have to tell us you're just married—we'll figure it out all by ourselves."

I had made it to the center of the aircraft; Donita and I came face to face—we exchanged glances to let each other know that all was good and that it was safe to retreat to our jumpseats.

"You girls really think you're something," a male passenger sneered. "Charlie's Angels," he rolled his eyes. "Fat chance."

"Yep, we do," said Donita, putting her hand on her hip. "*She* thinks she's Jacqueline Smith," she said, pointing at me. "And I think I'm Farrah Fawcett." Listeners laughed because Donita was

1) quite a bit older than Farrah, 2) quite a bit heavier than Farrah, and 3) she was black.

Other than the flight Jeanna and I had taken to report for duty, I had not worked any trips in or out of LaGuardia yet—only Kennedy. I couldn't go home when we landed because I was working back to Cleveland with Charlie's crew and laying over. His crew was based there—they would be going home. There was something very disheartening about flying into your base city but not being finished; it was a sore tease. As a junior 'reserve' I was getting lots of mixed trips. I flew with several different crews and often laid over alone. I was anxious to have a 'real' line, work with the same crew all month and enjoy good times in an exciting city. Cleveland, well… after training and Sheldon, wasn't alluring.

After takeoff, Charlie made another funny announcement and lit up. We were on the first jumpseat—in front of all the smoking rows and in front of first class. I donned my apron and clipped my flashlight into one of the pockets. Every time I grabbed my flashlight I smiled. 'That'll be a dollar for each pin and five to replace the flashlight,' they'd told me when I showed up without my hardware. It was insulting. All that work to earn my wings and it was only a dollar to replace them? Surely a flogging was in order.

Charlie had taken first-class drink orders on the ground so I prepared the first few and delivered them. He joined me soon enough. "Relax Sherri; we haven't even leveled off yet. You're going to ruin those beautiful legs and get *very gross veins* before your time."

I laughed. "Just… ready to go," and I took off with the next two drinks. The customer in 3B had a deep voice; I made small talk with him just to hear him speak. One of my goals was to *Stop* and enjoy little things; a pretty lady, a handsome man, a cute kid, a loving couple, a beautiful family, an excited first flyer, a funny expression, a gorgeous day, a perfect sunset, a delicious breeze—to take notice. Made the days brighter and my passengers seemed to sense it; it was all about your attitude. I liked finishing my flight days and feeling as if yes, I had made a difference by making someone's journey a little brighter.

In coach I joined Donita on the cart. The customers around our sneering man watched with dread or with anticipation. It was an automatic dynamic. Whenever there was a grouch aboard, the people around him or her would focus intently to see how any further exchanges went down, quieting their own conversations to listen. I was waiting on the gentleman across the aisle from him. "Can I get you something to drink today?" I asked, spreading a big smile across my face.

"Coffee please," he said.

"How would you like it?"

"I'd like it white and sweet," he said. "The same way I like my women."

Donita groaned; a couple of passengers joined her while a few others snickered. She turned to our grouchy guy and asked, "What do you want?"

"I want *Coffee.*"

She put her hands on the cart for a second, then glared at him. "You want it the *Same* way? White and sweet?"

"No," he said. He looked out the window for a moment then back at her. "I like it black and strong; the same way I like my women."

"Good comeback," she told him with an amused smile. "Welcome to the human race."

After the service I went back to first class. I wasn't needed up there, but it was a natural thing to do when you were sitting on the front jumpseat. The aft galley on the 737 was tiny anyway, and the two in back didn't need me either.

"Sorry you got based in that hell hole," Charlie said, after I told him I was based in New York. "After a year you can transfer out; gotta tell ya, I'd a quit if they'd sent me to that dangerous filthy place."

"I love it so far," I confessed with a laugh.

He laughed too. "Wanna take care of the cocks in the pit for me?" He smiled when my eyebrows rose. "Obviously, you have a high tolerance level."

"Sure…" I'd learned that many of the male attendants didn't care to mix with the cockpit. Most of the pilots were former military; too many macho men. They weren't crazy about male cabin-crew members either. I learned the secret 'knock' and rapped on the door three times.

"Hellooo there," cooed the second officer as I entered.

"Hi guys," I said, giving them my standard greeting. "I'm Sherri and I'd be happy to get you something to drink if you like."

When I returned to the cockpit with one coffee and a juice, I took a seat behind the captain. The flight-deck crews didn't like it if I left too soon. They *Loved* company and I could certainly understand why; they worked in the cockpit alone most of the time, men with men. I didn't even bother to ask if it was ok for me to smoke; no one ever said no, so I lit up.

"How long you been flying Sherri?"

It was pretty much the first question I always got.

After small talk, the captain turned around and took a good look at me. "How old are you?"

"Old enough."

"No offense," he said. "But you look like a baby. You being careful? Bet men are all over you. What about your flying partners, like Charlie; he hitting on you?"

I was so surprised by his remark, that I didn't answer at first. "No," I finally stammered. "No, he's… just a nice guy."

"He one of those swishy types?" Captain Nichols asked.

"Uh, I don't think so, no, he's… not. Not at all."

"Well then there's something wrong with him," he continued. "If I was working back there and you stepped onto my airplane, I'd sure be taking a shot at you."

It had been an awkward start. I tried veering the conversation in other directions but to no avail. The second officer gave me looks that told me he was in pain, listening to the captain talk creepy, so I gave him an appreciative smile to let him know I didn't care.

"You remind me of how it used to be in the old days," the captain said.

"The old days?"

"Yes-sir-ree! All the stewardesses were young and cute; they couldn't even *Be* married back then. Now there're all getting up there in age and some are downright chunky."

I blushed when he said that.

"And we've got all these guys! What is wrong with this world when the airlines let a bunch of grown men become… *Stewardesses?* Take's all the fun out of everything. Let me tell you something, when I first became a captain, I actually let one of the girls land the plane for me. I got on the PA and told the passengers, 'Ladies and gentleman, your head stewardess has just landed the airplane!' Couldn't get away with that now—they'd fire all of us. It was so much better back in the old days."

"What was her name?" I asked him.

He turned around and held onto the back of his seat, studying me. "I don't remember. You know, no one's ever asked me that before! You're pretty bright for being… how old did you say you were? Don't believe me, do you? Supposed to be impressed, but instead you ask me her name." He started laughing. "I like you Shelly."

"Sherri."

Back in the first-class galley, Charlie was taking off his service apron. "Have a good time up there?" he teased. "Heard this one yet? How was the Grand Canyon formed?" He didn't pause long. "A pilot dropped a quarter," he finished with a proud grin.

Flight attendants constantly cracked jokes about pilots; especially ones about how cheap they were.

"Are all pilots really cheap?" I asked.

"Nichols is," he said. "He's also…"

"Old school?" I offered. "Seems to be living in the past."

"No, that's still the culture Sherri—it's not the past—yet. We need to make it that way. Hey," he said, picking up his manifest and pointing to the name by 3B. "Does this guy, John Hutchcroft, seem familiar? Think maybe he's someone we should recognize."

"No," I started, "but let me take another look…" I went through the first-class cabin collecting empty glasses. Hutchcroft thanked me as I studied him; such an amazing voice, I could have curled up by his feet and listened to him all day.

"Think he just has a great voice," I told Charlie a minute later. "I don't recognize him."

"Something about him," he said. "What are you going to do tonight?"

"Watch baseball."

"Me too. You know 'Stretch?' He's going for his 500th homerun," he said.

While he spoke, I nodded.

"You really are a sports fan," Charlie gave me a swat on my back. "We're flying over your new home now," he said, looking out the galley door window. "Have you seen Manhattan yet from this position? You'll get a better view from the other side."

I raced to door 1Left and looked out the exit window. *God!* I saw the island of Manhattan below. Slowly, we made our way north to south, passing all the landmarks: Central Park, The Empire State Building, The World Trade Center, the Statue of Liberty… what a spectacular view, and it wasn't one we got to see this well flying in or out of JFK Airport.

When Charlie made his last announcement, I took off my apron and stashed it in the overhead bin above 1A & 1B. Glancing down at the passengers, I saw that they were staring up at me. I stifled a laugh—there *Was* something provocative about someone standing so near with their thighs pressed against the seat side and their arms raised high, shoving something into the overhead bins over their heads—especially if they only had on a light blouse. No one ever stared at my chest; there wasn't much there, but from that angle, with the neck and face lifted—it was probably impossible not to look.

* * *

"Charlie!" Donita said as the four of us walked up the jetway once all the passengers had deplaned. "Need to cut that "Charlie's Angels" crap out. Some of our passengers don't find it amusing."

I looked around the unfamiliar terminal trying to find any sort of sign for our small ops area at LaGuardia.

"We're going over to the Host café to get something to eat," Charlie said. "Got more than an hour before we have to be back. Wanna come?"

"No, thanks," I said. "I want to find our op center; I have a few things to take care of."

"See you in an hour."

I walked toward the end of the concourse. I had been told our offices were between the eighth and ninth gate but nothing stood out.

"Looking for operations?"

When I turned, an attractive black man stood in front of me, maybe around twenty-five. He looked dashing in a lavender shirt and a fetching tie. I realized right away he was a Gateway flight attendant—he carried the same suitcase I did.

"Yes. Hello."

"Follow me." He strode over to a small stairwell in the floor surrounded by a gate and opened it. I watched him from the back. *Very nice.* He seemed… different than the other stewards but then, I'd thought that about Sheldon too. Nevertheless, I was suddenly aware of my appearance and my posture. "I'll lead." He motioned for me to follow. Behind him I quickly popped out my retainer and put it in my jacket pocket. At the bottom of the stairs, he waited for me. "It's at the end of the hall, just one room really; nothing like Kennedy," he said. We passed several rooms with mechanics and ramp personnel talking loudly and taking breaks between servicing aircrafts or loading and unloading luggage. "What do you need here?" he asked.

"I was hoping to run into a supervisor," I explained.

"Skip's probably around; usually is. New to Kennedy?"

"Yes, I'm Sherri," I said. "Finishing my second month."

"Anderson Jeffries; nice to meet you."

At the end of the hall, Anderson pushed a door open and let me in first. I passed quite close to him and that feeling of a little *something* loomed. The room was small, with one desk, a phone, a big glass window on one wall where one could see the bottom of the plane at gate sixteen, a mirrored counter with lights and 'appearance' items: makeup, brushes, curlers; then a rack of books, papers, and a table with four chairs. Beside the mirror was a scale. I eyed it carefully. Anderson took my suitcase out of my hand and placed it along with his in an opening in the wall, clearly designed for luggage.

"Don't you use wheelies?" he asked.

"No, I don't like them."

He laughed. "Don't see many female flight attendants without them."

I stood in the middle of the room and didn't know what to do. "No one's here," I said.

Anderson moved toward a cabinet and pulled new revisions off a shelf. He studied the pile of papers. "Want me to call Kennedy? See where Skip is?" Before I could answer, he had picked up the phone on the desk and dialed. "George, hi. Anderson Jeffries over at LaGuardia. Is Skip in today? Got a new hire here who needs to talk to him." There was a pause. He looked at his watch then up at the wall clock. "Ah, huh. Good, got it." He walked around and leaned against the front of the desk. "He's here all right; probably taking a break."

"Ok," I took a seat in front of the mirrors and examined the lipsticks, pretending to be interested. I glanced at the scale then at Anderson. He had opened his suitcase and taken out his inflight manual. Apparently, he hadn't flown in a while because he had a lot of revisions to catch up on. It didn't look as if he was going to leave the office anytime soon. "Have you been on vacation or something?"

"Yeah, went out to Hawaii to see my dad," he said.

"Are you Hawaiian?" I asked. I was not able to hide my surprise.

He laughed. "Part," he said. "But I'm from Chicago really; that's where I grew up." He set his manual down and slid up onto the desk, facing me. Then he rolled up his shirt sleeves. "Where you from?"

"Kansas."

He looked at me without laughter; he didn't make a foolish remark about my home state like most people. "You're a long way from home. Miss your family?"

All of sudden there was a lump in my throat; I turned away. I could feel tears coming so I stepped over to the intimidating doctor scale and played with the top weight, sliding it back and forth. "Yes," I said. "I miss them." After several moments, realizing that Anderson wasn't going to say any more, I asked him, "Did you need to talk to a supervisor too? You seem like you're waiting."

He shook his head. "What do you need Sherri? Aren't all the new-hire supervisors over at Kennedy?"

"I need… to weigh in," I confessed. "It's been a month since my last check and today's the last day."

"Oh." I could tell from the sound of it that he understood. "How you doing with that?"

"I… I'm on weight check." I turned away from him and looked down, ashamed.

"Me too," he said. "Usually anyway. I'm up and down."

"You?"

"Sure." He slid off the desk and walked over to the scale. "Lots of stewards are if they work out. Standards are harsh." He stepped onto the scale and adjusted the slide. "See," he pointed to the marker. "One eighty-five. I'm not supposed to be over 178, so right now I'd be on weight check, but I don't weigh in until next March. It's ridiculous; I'm not tall but I'm…"

"Muscular," I said, eyeing his biceps through his shirt fabric. His hair was shaved very short. Must have made working out easier. For someone who was on weight check, he looked damn-near perfect. I looked up and he was looking at me too, we locked eyes and smiled, then we laughed out loud. *God he's cute!*

"Want to check your weight? Before Skip gets here?" He made it sound like he was guessing, but I knew he knew that was what I wanted. I nodded, so he stepped down. But he didn't move away.

"Do you mind?" I asked, making a swirling motion with my forefinger.

"Want me to turn around?" He suppressed a grin and retreated.

I stepped on and moved the first weight on the bottom to one hundred. Slowly I slid the top weight over but the bar wasn't dropping. One hundred twenty-one, 122, 123, *Damn;* 124, 125. I let out a gasp. It finally fell at 126 pounds. "Oh…" I said, "Oh no!" I had gained *Another* four pounds since training. All the fancy food in New York and on the planes was staying with me.

"What?" Anderson asked.

"I'm a pound over my max," I could hear my voice crack as I stepped off the scale and slammed the top weight back to zero. "I'm still on probation. I don't know…"

Anderson flew over to the door. He opened it and looked out, then closed it quickly and turned off the lights. My eyes went wide; it was very dark even though there was a huge window on one wall. "What are you doing?" I backed away as he came toward me in a rush.

"Get on," he said. He pulled a Swiss Army knife out of his pocket and pried a flathead screwdriver head out. "Get back on the scale."

I stepped back up, breathing hard.

"Balance it," he ordered. "Hurry."

I set the scale at 126 and stood there. Anderson placed the flat head screwdriver bit into the left side of the scale by the weights. Slowly the bar dropped.

"Move it back 'til it's balanced," he said.

I moved the top weight; 125, then 124, then 123 where the bar leveled off evenly.

"Is that good? Keep it close so it won't be obvious the scale's off," he said.

"Yes, as long as I'm under 125…"

He raced back to the door and switched the lights back on. "Put it back a bit but not on the zero; then move away."

As soon as I settled in front of the mirrors again, the door opened. Anderson was at the desk hovering over his manual and working on his revisions.

"Hi!" said the person I was sure was Skip.

Anderson stayed busy while I introduced myself, exchanging pleasantries, then Skip weighed me for my second monthly weight check as a probationary flight attendant—123 pounds! Three months since training began and I was flirting with losing my job.

I gathered up my suitcase; Anderson was right beside me. I was drenched, elated, and giddy. I skipped through the hall and up the stairs. Anderson laughed the whole time. *He's great!* He had *taken me to minute-long paradise*, and it sure felt nice. "Thank you so much Anderson!" I gushed when I felt safe enough to talk about it. "I don't know what I would have done without you. I was *over my head.*"

"No, you're over your weight," he stopped me and put a hand on my shoulder. "Be careful. I think you look great. No, I think you look sensational… you're young and on your way." I felt tingly all over listening to him and following his eyes as they made their way around my hips. "But Gateway—they don't go by looks; they go by numbers. I've been there. Get the weight off, get through probation, make sure you're ten under your max, then you only have to weigh in once a year. What we all do. But you've got to get through probation. Be a shame to lose this job over a couple of pounds."

I kept nodding as he spoke; I knew this already. The lump in my throat returned. I put my suitcase down and put my face in my hands, fighting back tears. Anderson put his suitcase down too. When he reached for my arm, I leapt at him and gave him a hug. *Hold me tight.*

"Whoa," he laughed. "I'm gonna hang here at LaGuardia when all the new hires come through and help all the young sweet things with the scale."

I laughed out loud. "I'm sorry. I couldn't help it, I'm so relieved."

"Don't apologize."

"Thank you again. I don't know what else to say, really."

"You need a ride?" His smile was dynamite. "I've got a car," he said.

"I'm not done," I told him with disappointment. "I'm working the six o'clock flight back to Cleveland and laying over; I don't get back 'til tomorrow."

I had walked all the way past security with him, distracted by my close call and happy to be by his side. The gates were behind us and we stood near the ticket counter; no wonder he thought I was leaving the airport.

Then out of nowhere I heard a familiar voice. "Sherri?"

An American Airlines cockpit crew near the ticket counter was walking fast toward the next terminal. "Sean!" I hollered. I left my suitcase on the ground and ran over to him. Throwing myself into his arms too, I gave him a huge kiss. "What are you *Doing* here?" I asked.

"We deadheaded in hours ago; got a hotel. I called but obviously you weren't home. Now we're racing over to cover a flight that's delayed; crew went illegal. They're waiting for us," he said in a short breath. "Sherri, sweetheart, you look good. Wish I could talk… gotta run honey, love you!" He scurried off to catch his coworkers.

I turned back with a huge smile on my face. Anderson's head was cocked, his arms were folded. "Sherri," he sounded cold. "Don't leave your suitcase like that."

"Sorry." I scurryed back to him, still smiling. "That was…"

"Pilots move in fast, don't they? Always hitting on new hires."

My jaw dropped.

"Hasn't anyone warned you about them yet?"

"You know I'm getting *Real* tired of all the ugly things I hear about pilots," I admitted.

"That's why they nail the young ones quickly—before you figure it all out."

"Actually, it's been stewards who have been total jerks to me."

"How old is that guy anyway? He married?"

"He is." My face was beet red.

"How'd you meet him so soon? He doesn't even fly for us; he with American?"

"How'd I meet him? Well, he's my dad!" I could feel my cheeks swelling and the blood rushing to my face. *I'm wasting all of my time here.*

"Shit. I'm sorry."

Turning to go, I didn't look back. He *can be cold as ice.*

Chapter 11:

• • • • • • • • • •

Pretty Woman

IN MY CLEVELAND AIRPORT HOTEL ROOM, I kicked off my shoes before checking under the bed and behind the shower curtain. *No dead bodies. Must be a good hotel.* Grabbing the ice bucket, I left the room in my unbuttoned skirt with my shirttail hanging out, my nylons, and shoeless.

Reclining in bed with my head propped up against my pillows, I enjoyed a room service meal of a burger and a salad while catching the second half of the Braves/Giants doubleheader. Even though the Giants had lost the first game, Willie McCovey, affectionately known as 'Stretch' had hit his 500th homerun. I had missed it. I had not eaten the bun; they had also given me a roll with my salad but I hadn't eaten that either. *Good girl Sherri. One hundred and fifteen pounds, here I come!*

On the next commercial break, I heard a familiar voice. "IBM presents, 'You Make the Call.'" I sat up and focused hard on the television. *That's him!* It was the voice of our first-class customer in 3B.

"Charlie," I cried out loud, "this is your guardian 'Angel,' Sherri calling. Hope you're watching the game or at least listening to the commercials." The commercial featured a questionable play from a previous game. John Hutchcroft's voice explained the scenario then challenged viewers to: make the call. Was the runner safe, or out? Then IBM did a short ad, and the playback returned. Hutchcroft explained that the runner was out. I was surer with each word he spoke. *Yup, that's absolutely Him.* Tickled with myself, I picked up the roll, slathered it with butter and ate it with great satisfaction. *One hundred and thirty-five pounds, here I come!*

- *Dear FlightLog. When I learned that I was going to be a flight attendant, I was a little leery about getting too close to attractive male customers or pilots right away. That's what Sean warned me about. I know I'm young, I know I can get hurt. But I didn't expect to get slam-dunked by of all the types out there: two stewards in a row – three if you count Danny! The second one was married, and he did steal my heart or at least make it go pitter-patter, and the third one was just as wonderful at first until I found out he was also a jerk – just in a different way. Oh well, I do think my parents would have been uncomfortable with me dating a black man, though he's really Hawaiian. My lesson is clear – no more stewards – male flight attendants – whatever we call them. On a much higher note, I ran into Sean – you know – dad, at LaGuardia today. AND, I've finally had my first celebrity onboard! He was a sneaky one. I wouldn't have known if I hadn't watched the last half of the Braves/Giants double header. John Hutchcroft.*

I have finally had a 'brush with greatness' and now have something to brag about!

*　*　*

It was still dark when I plopped down to sit on my sturdy uniform issue mauve Samsonite suitcase. Outside Aunt Harriet's apartment building, I waited for a taxi. Carefully I shifted my crossed legs. They were still clammy in the thigh area from forcing on my support hose immediately after showering. It's refreshing to sit outside in the cool air. Flying sucks the moisture out of you. Dry aircraft cabins with re-circulated oxygen suffocate you after several hours, especially when half the airplane smokes.

I had phoned the recorded reserve tape last night at 8 P.M. as soon as it was available. After six busy signals, I got through on the seventh try. 'Sherri Van Ness' the pre-recorded announcement finally got to my name. 'Eight-thirty am check-in, Kennedy, two-day trip.' That was all the information reserves received. What time to report, how many days we'd be gone, and in the case of multiple airport cities, like Washington DC or New York, which airport to show up at. The other details of the trip were only guesses until we arrived at the crew desk and picked up our little printouts—'meters,' that listed all the information. If lucky, we'd get a regular spot replacing a sick or vacationing lineholder. What I usually got were extra-stew trips which mixed up my planes, mixed up the crews I worked with, mixed up my life.

Like an obedient schoolgirl, I'd called the confirmation number before midnight to recite back my assignment; that way the crew desk could be sure I was informed. 'This is Sherri Van Ness. I have an 8:30 A.M. check-in tomorrow at Kennedy.'

I was into my fourth month of flying, and had worked many jam-packed 747 and DC-10 jumbo jet trips. Mostly non-stops to

West Coast cities: LA, San Fran, Seattle. Eight flight attendants were assigned to a regular 747 line with the number increasing depending on the projected load. All summer and into fall, with oversold flights each way, Gateway staffed its 'Sea to Shining Sea' trips with a crew of fifteen. New hire reserves like me were assigned those extra spots and we loved them. *Easy money.* One leg from NYC to the West Coast, layover for eighteen to thirty hours, then work one leg home. Regular lineholders flew six or seven of them in a thirty-day period—fourteen days of flying a month, twenty-eight legs and nice layovers. *Sweet!* Per our union contract, which I prided myself in knowing well, any layover of sixteen plus hours guaranteed us nicer hotels near shopping and restaurants. For convenience and sleep, we were put up in airport hotels/motels when our layovers were short. I'd learned however that shut-eye was a tough thing to get when your motel window faced the runway—it was difficult to drown out noisy takeoffs and landings.

Much as I liked the big-birds, many Gateway attendants preferred narrow-body trips. Louise, the gal I'd worked with when I reported to duty, and Charlie from Cleveland were two. They usually had three or more legs a day, but they didn't mind all the setting up and closing down of galleys—there were lots of choices flying, once one was senior enough to bid regular lines. Anderson must have preferred them too. His mailbox had been at LaGuardia instead of Kennedy; that told me he flew out of the smaller airport more often. I'd thought about Anderson Jeffries a lot. I'd even slipped into LaGuardia very late one night when no one was around, adjusted the scale, then I'd shown up bright and early the next morning to weigh in. I 'pretended' I was jumpseating home so they wouldn't think it was weird that I'd just 'appeared' in uniform, first thing in the morning dressed to go. When we rode jumpseats, we had to be in uniform, so that wouldn't alert anyone.

Anderson grinned at me with his drop-dead killer smile while rolling up his shirtsleeves. His face was tilted to one side as he watched me...

I heard tires and stopped daydreaming. *I need a taxi.* A dark limo glided up to the curb and stopped in front of me. The driver hustled out and ran around to the rear passenger door, opening it and stepping aside like the Queen's guard. At first all I could see was the profile of a handsome woman. She laughed as a slender leg slid out; her foot barely tapped the pavement before the person beside her pulled her back. Her foot lifted into the air briefly and she laughed again. She threw her head back, taking kisses on her throat and mouth from what looked like a strong, virile man. Though she struggled to break free, she looked like she was having a wonderful time. *No wonder—with those looks.* She stood, slowly, gracefully. *The other leg was just as long.* She grabbed the chauffeur's arm for support. He liked it too, leaning into her, enjoying her closeness.

She was dressed in a perfect shade of pale pink from her neckline to her ankles. Silky delicate-thin slacks below a sheer blouse that hugged her lean figure underneath a classic pale-pink scrumptious coat. I'd seen that coat. It was from Oscar de la Renta. The only reason I knew that, was because Jeanna had wanted to buy it; she liked dragging me off on her shopping sprees. The stranger's soft blonde curls were short. The color looked authentic, as did the perfect pearls that danced at her neckline, slipping in and out of the top of her blouse. The man in the car reached out and grabbed her hand but she pulled away.

"Don't walk away," he said, with mischief in his voice. He was as elegant as she was. *This is New York. The beautiful people are definitely here.*

She shook her head, tossing her curls while slipping both hands into the deep pockets of her wonderful coat. I remembered it well; perfect lines, smashing fit, light and gorgeous but long, falling between the knees and ankles. *Must be a model.* But then, maybe she was one of those… expensive women… she stepped away. Her date got out of the car on the driver's side. He was the tallest man I'd seen in a long time. He folded his arms and with ease, leaned across the top of the limo. The top buttons of his tuxedo shirt were undone; the bow tie was missing. Then he smiled.

"Oh God," I muttered under my breath. "It's Matt Lincoln!" He was a powerful defensive lineman for the Chicago Bears. He always looked great on television and spoke well with a quick-wit; the media loved him. Seeing him in person made it easy to understand why he was considered one of the sports world's most eligible bachelors.

I caught his soft southern accent when he spoke to her. "You have a nice day now."

"Already did," she teased.

He stared as she walked away. The limo driver closed her door and raced around to the side of the big football player, waiting for him to duck inside. *"Stop awhile;* turn around girl," he teased, but she didn't. "Call soon," Lincoln said. "Leave a number where I can reach you."

She caught my eye then turned to face him. "Did you give me yours?" There was much playfulness in her voice; it was obvious he had, and obvious that he wanted her to call. She pulled a business card out of her coat pocket, feigned surprise when she looked at it, then held it up to him. In one movement she whirled back around and breezed past me as she pocketed the card. She looked at me again and gave me a brilliant smile. "Hi doll," she said.

I stared at her too as she headed into my aunt's apartment building, using the revolving door. "Hi," I said to her back. I looked back at the polished car.

"Kennedy please," Lincoln said before folding his large frame into the back seat. The chauffeur shut his door and jumped into the driver's spot.

I blurted out, "You're going to the airport?" But it was too late. I stood there feeling stupid and ordinary, as the luxury limo carrying the superstar slid down the street quietly. "Oh… *don't make me cry."*

Would Matt Lincoln have given me a ride if he'd heard me? Maybe I wasn't a tall thin beautiful blonde, in Linda Evan's league, but I was… nice! I knew more about football then that hot hussy—surely he'd appreciate that!

Watching football was a religion in our home. It was like church but with more hamstring pulls. Sunday mornings and Monday nights, whenever dad was home, all fall and winter the games blared from our living room TV set. I knew Lincoln was All-Pro, which was saying a lot since he played for such a struggling team. *Now how many women understood that?* He'd sacked most of the NFL's quarterbacks and blocked many field goal attempts while playing special teams. Why, he'd be fascinated with all I knew! And if I were lucky enough to go out with him… at least I'd wear a dress! It wouldn't be from the junior department at Sears either—like much of my wardrobe. As I stroked my own ego, assuring myself that I was a much better catch than the beauty he'd just been with, I heard footsteps behind me.

She, who had called me 'doll,' who had just had all of Matt Lincoln's attention, was walking back toward me.

"No cabs?" she asked, stopping to light a cigarette.

"Not yet." I took a moment to really study her face in the day's breaking light. She was exquisite; it did not show that she'd been up all night. *What a pretty woman.* No purse either—there was a carefree wildness about her that I liked. She produced a pair of sunglasses from an inside pocket and put them on. How does a woman look that good after partying for hours without a purse full of makeup? How'd she know she'd need sunglasses when she went out last night? Was she *the truth?*

"Where you flying off to?" she asked.

"Don't know. Probably LA or San Francisco. I'm still on what's called reserve…"

"I know," she said, blowing out smoke. She nodded toward the street. From the corner of my eye, I saw a taxi pull up in front of her, passing me. "Take this one," she said. "You were here first."

"Do you need a ride too?" I asked. "We could share…"

"No go ahead. I'm going across town." She waved down another cab. His light had not been on but when she raised her hand, the top light blipped 'Vacant.' She opened the door and looked over at me, flashing that sensational smile again. "What's your name doll?"

"Sherri. Sherri Van Ness," I remembered Louise's warning about not giving out my last name. *Too late.*

She tossed her cigarette into the street. "See you around Sherri."

"Hey *Lady!*" My cab driver hollered at me. "While we're young already; *Christ.* I haven't got all day!"

Chapter 12:

Say You

"SORRY." I FUMBLED WITH MY GEAR, trying to get inside quickly and smiled apologetically at the annoyed driver. "East side terminal please." He took off before I'd settled in, sending me and my suitcase flying into the back seat cushion. Taxi rides were always a reminder that what they'd taught us in emergency training was true: 'The most dangerous parts of any airline journey are the car rides to and from the airport.'

"Hi Vic," I said cheerfully, reporting to the crew desk at Kennedy. "It's Sherri Van Ness and I have an 8:30 A.M. check-in."

"I know who you are now Sherri; the one who's always smiling," he spoke as he looked down at his papers for my trip printout. "Finally got a regular trip to LA with the same crew out and back; same layover hotel—everything. Flight five, briefing room three at the terminal."

"Really…" I admired the printout and caught sight of Jeanna coming in. "Jeanna look, flight five out and flight six back tomorrow with the same crew!"

"Me too," she said. "Paychecks are out. Here, I picked yours up."

Jeanna watched as I tore open the envelope. My face lit up. "Wow again!"

"I know," she said. "It just keeps coming: I can't *Believe* how much money we're making."

I couldn't either. Gateway's pay system gave us half of our base pay on the first of the month. As new-hires, that check was always $350. There were no additions or deductions on that check. On the sixteenth, we received the rest of our pay with additions and deductions. Since our base pay was for seventy-four hours, any additional hours appeared as well as did other add-ons, of which the biggest was meal expenses. For every hour we were on duty, we received a dollar and five cents—none of it was taxed. The trip Jeanna and I were on would give us an additional thirty-three dollars and change—we were clearing $300 a month in tax-free meal money. Since Gateway was busy, we were flying our max of eighty-five hours—our second checks each month were at least $800; in total, we were clearing $1200 plus monthly.

"I'm making more than double what I made at the bank," I said. On my layover, I would take out my pretty little red log-book—the 'real' one, and check the math on my paystub—it was something I looked forward to each month—I felt rich.

At the terminal, Jeanna and I entered briefing room three.

"You are?" The flight attendant at the left side of the room with piles of paperwork on the conference table asked. She was clearly the First Flight Attendant.

"Hi, I'm Sherri Van Ness."

"Jeanna Campion."

"I'm Mitzi, have a seat," she said as she checked off our names. She looked closely at her crew list. "Are you on the whole ID with us?"

"We are," I said.

"Ohhh good," she said, pushing her reading glasses up onto her nose. "It's so much easier that way. Let's get started." She spoke loudly—everyone in the room was talking in small groups. It was cramped—one small table with twenty scattered chairs. There were fifteen attendants and fifteen Gateway suitcases.

One flight attendant seemed especially friendly. She made eye contact as she brushed her long blonde hair. She was starting to put it up into a regulation bun. "Hi," she said to us both. "I'm Marjorie."

One of the males raised his hand. "Hello ladies," he said. "We meet again."

It was the funny steward from our after-training flight into LaGuardia. "Hi Darryl," I said with a happy grin.

"Good memory," he said.

"We are full," Mitzi said. There were groans. "What's the surprise? We've been full all summer. Oversold in coach today by forty-three, so whoever pulls tickets—be careful. And during boarding—stay on top of the double seat assignments. Is everyone working their normal position?"

"Who's working with me," a bearded attendant with a deep scar on his left cheek asked. He wasn't wearing our uniform; he had on a more stylish one in a rich navy-blue. He had to be one of us though; he had on all the same pins. "Donna's not here today," he added.

Mitzi looked at us. "Have either one of you ever worked coast to coast on a jumbo up front?"

Jeanna and I shook our heads.

"Either of you want to?"

We both nodded yes.

She peered down at her papers. "Sherri, you're senior so it's yours unless anyone on my crew wants it?" She looked around.

"You fucking kidding?" Darryl said. "Work with Maurice? He doesn't even speak *English* most the time."

"Lucky you sweetheart," the navy-blue donned steward said to me. "Get to work with a real pro. Ignore that bilious bloke over there; he has no couth—I pray for him on Sundays."

"Everyone—do your safety checks," Mitzi said. "Report any discrepancies to me immediately and *Please People*, all calls to the cockpit go through *Me* only! I have to hear about it later when four of you call to warm up the cabin, while three others call to cool it off."

"I have new pilot jokes to share with them," Maurice teased.

"Fine Mo," Mitzi said. "Go upstairs and snuggle up in person, just stay off the damn phone, you dumb Polack. All you coach-roach people! Carol's the B; I'm going to let her take over the briefing. By the way—if any of you come into my first-class galley for coffees, it's 'Take a Pot, Make a Pot.' Last week we went to start first-class coffees and there was nothing there but empty hot plates and empty pots on the counter."

"Same as last week," Carol said. "We're fully staffed with a crew of fifteen, so we have nine coach aisle people, thank God! I need two to sell headsets for the movie."

Darryl and another gal raised their hands. While Carol continued, Maurice rose and motioned for me to follow. "We can go," he said. "We don't have to listen to how they will handle the hoi polloi today."

"I wanted to work up front," Jeanna pouted.

I hesitated but Maurice tugged my sleeve. "Who are *You?*" he said to Jeanna a bit sharply while pulling me toward the door. "She's senior."

We approached the large 747 parked at gate seven. Passengers were checking in—the boarding area was alive with people. "Don't ever feel bad about being senior sweetheart; that's all we've got. Besides, I can tell she's one of those drama types—don't want that in my first-class cabin," he said. "Nothing worse than a new hire whose already got an attitude." The gate-agent let us in and we walked down the empty jetway; I felt weird getting on the plane without the rest of the crew. "What made you decide to come be a sky-slut?" he asked.

"I don't… I mean…"

"Not yet," said Maurice. "You will. If you're not completely familiar with the first-class cabin on the 47, take a few minutes to get acquainted with it after you do your safety check."

I stowed my things and whipped through my check at door 1Right: Oxygen—safety kit—jumpseat—megaphone—fire extinguisher—exit—check! The nose of the plane had a closet; we would use it for first-class coats, jackets, and extra carry-on luggage. There was only one aisle in first since the nose of the plane was narrow, then right behind the first-class bluerooms, the plane broke off into two aisles. However, there were two seats in the back of first that were centered with a wide console in front of them. We used the console to display magazines before takeoff, and as a table for wine bottles inflight. In front of the first-class bluerooms was the spiral staircase leading upstairs into the first-class lounge and the cockpit. There was an additional bathroom upstairs, as well as a dumb waiter to hoist trays and supplies from the main deck to the lounge.

The first-class galley was behind row eighteen between doors 2Left and 2Right. There was another full galley for coach between doors 4Left and 4Right; each galley had a pit, so two attendants worked downstairs on the 747—one handled all the first-class items and a few extra coach carts; the other handled coach supplies only. Mitzi, the A, would set up and work the first-class galley and Carol, the B, would set up and work the coach galley. I had been downstairs in the back several times, but I had not been downstairs in the first-class pit.

"Can I go down and take a look?" I asked Maurice.

"Of course," he said. "When you get back, I want to show you where we keep the movies. You're going to be in charge of that today."

The first-class pit was similar but backwards—the elevators faced forward rather than backward. Back on the main deck, Maurice opened a small compartment beside the spiral staircase wall. "Here they are," he said, pulling out several VHS tapes. "If you're not sure which one to show, you can always look in 'Gateways to the World' Magazine. Today we're showing *Foul Play*. It's fabulous. If the passengers ask your opinion, tell them you recommend it. Here's the boarding music dial." He turned it on and cranked up the volume.

I laughed out loud as "Green River" blared.

He kept turning it up. "Three Dog Night," he said.

"Credence Clearwater," I corrected, with a knowing smile.

"You sure?"

"Yep. This is one of my favs," I said. "Always wanted to be a barefoot girl dancing in the moonlight."

"What are you waiting for," he asked. "An invitation?" He took my hands and whirled me around the cabin. I laughed. It was tight, trying not to knock into seats and consoles. *I love this guy!*

"Maurice," I said, as we slowed down. "Why are you wearing a different uniform?"

"This is a tester," he told me. "Gateway's getting ready to change uniforms soon; they asked some of us from different domiciles to wear the new prototypes and report back," he touched his uniform and modeled it for me. "I will be recommending this one; it's sublime. Just what I'd expect from Ralph Lauren."

"Now you're talking Jeanna's language," I said. "I don't know one designer from another."

"She your friend?"

"Yes," I said.

"Seems atrabilious; is she always like that?"

"I have no idea what that means." *Note to self: who cares?*

We heard the rest of the crew heading down the jetway; Mitzi was at door 2Left in no time. "Turn that down!" she hollered. "We could hear it from the top of the jetway."

During boarding, I handled pre-departure champagne and orange juice while Maurice started meal and drink orders, stowed items and hung coats. I was at the third row when Matt Lincoln walked onto our plane. *I realize it's you.* He looked at his boarding ticket and took the aisle seat right in front of me: 4C. "Morning," he said.

"Good morning Mr. Lincoln," I said, trying not to sound too excited. *Want to blitz me?* He cracked a smile. Making my way to the queen cart behind the last row of first class, I pointed him out to Maurice. "That's Matt Lincoln," I said with pride. *I should have known he'd be on this flight. This is great!* My first time working first class on a wide-body and I already had a celebrity flying 'coast to coast,'—the route so many of them flew.

"Who is Matt Lincoln?" Maurice asked.

"A football player with the Chicago Bears; they call him 'Lake Effect…'" I could see nothing was registering with him. "Really Maurice?"

"Don't watch football," he explained. "It's pugilistic and interferes with my sense of…"

"Ah," I said. "That may be, but you strike me as a man who admires greatness and I assure you, you're looking at a legend," I flashed him a wicked smile. "He may be as fine a football player as *You* are a flight attendant."

"That good?" He flashed the same smile back.

After takeoff, I went into the first-class galley where Mitzi was already bustling around in her apron and removed the first-class manifest from the galley wall. Mitzi, like many first flight attendants, had taped it up with 'Occupied' seat stickers. Gateway had rolls of them on all its airplanes and we were supposed to use them on 'through' flights to mark seats for customers who wanted to get off the plane between legs. She pointed to Matt's name. "Your first celebrity?" she asked.

"That I recognized," I said.

"We get a lot of them on this route. Most are fine. Just want to be left alone. Some are idiots. Though—some of our non-celebs are idiots too; that's the point," she said, yanking open a steel drawer in her galley and removing several orange juice cartons. "They're just people. Treat them the same as you would anyone. If they're screaming for attention give it to them; if they're showing you the sign of the cross—leave 'em alone."

Maurice set up our first-class liquor cart at door 1Right. I kept staring at Lake Effect; I couldn't help it. He was on Maurice's side for the cocktail service; I worked the AB side. Each time I'd set drinks down I'd catch his eye; he knew I was looking at him. *You've caught my eye. Now sack me!* During the meal service, Maurice set up the entrees while I ran them out. When I got to Matt, he pulled his headset off. "What are you staring at darlin?"

"Hoping to take a few, you know, *to really meet you.* My kid brother's a big fan of yours," I stammered, setting down his Duck Montmorency entrée.

"How old is he?" Lincoln asked.

"Fifteen," I said.

"Does he play?"

"Yes," I said with a big smile. "Going into his sophomore year. He might start this fall."

"Would he like an autograph?" he offered.

Give me the key to your heart! I looked over at Maurice. "Oh no… don't want to bother you; you're eating…" but as I spoke, the look on his face let me know he was reading me completely. "I'd love one," I confessed.

"Hand me my briefcase," he said. It was beneath the seat in front of him.

I looked around again, trying to give Matt his case without toppling over any of the first-class linen or china on his tray table. He was ready for fans. He had 8 x 10 black & white glossies sitting on the outside pocket of the case and a permanent marker. "Who should I make this out to?"

When he handed me back the autographed photo for Shane, he grabbed my hand. "That's an unusual piece," he said, sliding his thumb across the flat surface of my special ring. "May I see it?" He pulled my hand closer and scrutinized the pattern; I loved every moment of him holding my hand. "Ebony, tiger's eye, lapis and?"

"Malachite," I said. "Very good!"

"I like this very much," he said, shaking my hand a bit but still holding it as if he were going to kiss it; "very unusual." He looked right through me with a warm smile. "Nice watch too; you've got good taste."

Forget your pride! I'm going to die. Tackle me! Hit me high, hit me low!

I could tell when the coach attendants had finished most of their service, as some of them were making their way up toward the front to stretch, see what might be available to nibble on up front and just get away from the aft cabins. I had slipped off my shoe and was rubbing my foot. Jeanna and Darryl came toward Maurice and me at our liquor cart.

"Which one's the famous football player?" Jeanna asked.

"Don't you recognize him?" Maurice asked with an arrogant tone—giving me a haughty smile.

"He's the *Big one,*" Darryl said. "Look at those shoulders."

Jeanna started into the first class but Maurice pulled her back. "Where are *You* going?" he asked.

"To get his autograph."

"No, uh uh," Maurice shook his head. "For starters, it's unprofessional. Didn't they tell you that in training? He didn't pay big bucks to sit up here and be hounded by riff-raff. All passengers in my first-class cabins can rely on the aegis of Maurice. And further," he added, "he's got his headsets on—he's enjoying the movie. I'll not permit anyone to come between 'Lake Effect' and Goldie Hawn."

Darryl pulled the white plastic mesh off one of our champagne bottles. "Know what this is?" he asked, holding up the long limp object.

We shook our heads.

"A Polish rubber," he put a finger through one of mesh holes.

"It's not big enough," Maurice shot back without missing a beat. "I'm going to get more first-class vino. When I get back, take a break Sherri; go downstairs and get something to eat."

"Have you found a place to stay yet?" Jeanna asked me.

"No. It's been so frustrating. I know my aunt doesn't really want me there, but I'm family, so she thinks it's something she's called to do."

"Move in with us," Jeanna gushed. "Come on Sherri, I've been asking you forever. We could use another roommate; rent's high."

"And tell my parents I have *Male* roommates? Are you kidding?"

"Mostly they're harmless," she said. "Like your friend up here; Maurice."

"What do you mean?"

"You know," she said, wagging her head.

"No, I don't."

"*Gay* Sherri; they're gay."

"Maurice is gay?"

Jeanna and Darryl laughed like hell.

"Why are gay men always so handsome," Jeanna asked, still laughing. "That scar even makes him better looking," she added. "How'd he get that?"

"No one knows," Darryl sniggered. "Never talks about it."

Maurice returned with four wine bottles. "What's funny?" he asked.

"I… need a place to stay," I said. "Jeanna wants me to move in with her and half our class, but I'm not comfortable with that."

"One of my best friends is looking for a roommate." Maurice studied me for a moment. "I wouldn't suggest anyone to Alex, but you two together—that seems strikingly apposite!"

"Opposite? You're right about that. I can't room with a guy, no way!"

"Alex is a girl. She's perfectly pulchritudinous. You'll *Love* her! I'll give her a call when we get into LA. And I said *Apposite* not opposite."

Note to self: buy thesaurus.

"Told you *Her Majesty* doesn't speak English," Darryl said.

"Her Majesty?" I looked at Darryl quizzically.

"Polack's last name is Majeski. Plus, he's a queen," Darryl said, pointing to Maurice.

"That's why you love me," Maurice retorted.

"Hi," Marjorie joined us. She had such a wonderful smile. "Darryl?" She held out some three by fives photos. "Here are the pictures."

Instinctively we all gathered around to look. They were pictures of an adorable black baby girl. "Ahhh," Darryl cooed. "She's so cute!"

"Who is that?" Jeanna asked.

"My daughter… our daughter Anita," Marjorie beamed. "We just adopted her."

Jeanna and I looked at each other in amazement. I'd never heard of a white couple adopting a black baby; Jeanna seemed as surprised as I.

"Congratulations!" Maurice gave her a hug. "Look at you—you're glowing with refulgent energy."

Marjorie let go. She frowned at me. "You need flat shoes." Then she glanced down at Jeanna's feet. "You too," she added.

"We're still on probation," Jeanna moaned. "We have to wear at least a three-inch heel at all times; that's the rule."

"I don't care," Marjorie tskd. "That's absurd. You can do terrible damage to your legs pushing carts up and down aisles with this cabin pressure. Wear high-heels in the terminal then switch to flat shoes for the service; that's what the rest of us do. No supervisor is going to mark you down for that; they know it's not right," she said. "This isn't the 60s."

"Show them the high-heels you wear in the terminal Maurice," Darryl said.

"The ones I bought to please you?" Maurice said.

After the movie, I moved over to Maurice's side to collect Matt Lincoln's empty glass and clear his table. "Mr. Lincoln?"

"Call me Matt."

"I'd like to thank you again for the autograph. Shane will be thrilled to have it and I want to wish you much luck this season."

"Thank you," he said. "You're a really nice stewardess. I mean… flight attendant. Isn't that what we're supposed to call you now?"

You can call me Anything baby 'cause I like what I see! I nodded and smiled.

"You were wonderful; very attentive and pleasant. Seems like you like what you do," he said. It sounded so nice and genuine. "Same as the guy you work with. You two make an excellent team. Hope to see you again."

You're perfect for me. "Well, it was twice today," I knew it sounded weird; I could feel my face warm; I stroked my collarbone.

"What do you mean?" he asked.

"I saw you this morning," I confessed. "Outside my building. You were dropping off…"

He moved forward in his seat and sat up. He took my hand again. "You know that girl? Leigh? She live in your building?"

I looked up and saw Maurice staring at me. He started making hilarious faces and rubbed his two forefingers together, signifying a 'naughty' sign. I tried not to laugh. "No… I don't know her," I said, trying to pull away.

"Come on," Matt said.

"Honestly, I *Don't.*" He stared at me hard. "Really; I'd tell you if I did. I'm a fan of yours too you know." *What if I flash my pompoms?*

He must have believed me because he let go. "If you *Ever* find out who she is," he said. "You call me. Collect, got it? I like her; I don't mean any…"

"Got it," I said.

"I'll get your kid brother tickets to a game," he offered. "I mean that. Deal?"

"Deal, sure." I said laughing; this was silly. Who was she? *Who do you belong to? Where can I purchase a gun?*

I joined Maurice behind row six—high on one hand for getting so much praise and attention from Matt, yet foolishly a little sad about his obsession with that stranger.

"What did I tell you?" he said with a cocky smile. "Didn't take you but a New York minute, skyslut!" He grabbed Matt Lincoln's business card out of my hand and looked at it.

"He wanted to know about some girl in my building," I tried.

"Yeah, sure," he said, dropping his voice low. "And I'm Joe Namath."

Mitzi hustled up beside us and dragged several large bags out of the closet under the stairwell. "Can you two lend a hand picking up coach headsets?" she asked. "The others are busy handing out mints and hot towels." She grabbed the phone at 2Left and hit the intercom button. "Ladies and gentlemen, this does conclude the audio portion of our trip today. Flight attendants will be coming through the aisles…"

Maurice was grabbing headsets from coach passengers in no time. I beat him back to a bag and stuffed the ones I'd collected inside. He'd collected twice as many as I had. I held the bag open for him. "A little wider please Sherri…" he said.

I didn't look up. Would he really? In front of all these customers?

"Sherri," he said. "Wider dear, wider."

He would.

"You're turning incarnadine Sherri."

Maurice shoved the headsets down into the bag, deep. "How is that for you dear; is that good for you?" Passengers paying attention started snickering in surprise by his boldness.

* * *

When I entered my room at the Amfac Hotel, I kicked off my shoes and groaned out loud. I was so glad we were at the Amfac; it wasn't that close to anything too special so I used that as an excuse not to join anyone. I was beat! I didn't feel like doing anything or going anywhere. After I filled the toilet with ice—yes, ice, I lay down on the bathroom floor and put my feet inside. It was gross but effective. My feet *Really* hurt. When I couldn't stand the cold anymore, I made my way to the bed, already in my PJs and propped my head up on a few pillows while propping my feet up on several more pillows. When I had the strength, I would grab each foot one at a time and rub, groan, rub, groan. Jeanna was beat too; I knew she was napping so when I heard a banging on the door, I was taken by surprise.

"Who is it?" I called.

"Room service."

"I didn't order room service," I called.

"Open this door." I recognized Maurice's voice. "Heard there was some great pussy in there."

I couldn't get to the door fast enough; I did not want him saying anything else that inappropriate in the hallway; *My God!* What was he thinking? "Maurice?"

He pushed his way into my room carrying three containers of Chinese carryout. "You look dreadful," he said. "Did you check under your bed and behind the shower curtain?" When he saw the look on my face, he doubled over laughing—he could tell that I had.

The food was good; the little of it I could get—Maurice could not believe that I did not know how to use chopsticks.

"You're a New Yorker now," he explained. "Time to turn you into a soigné sophisticate; it won't take long. I've been watching you. Come to my place next week. We'll make popcorn; that's the best food for learning how to use chopsticks," he masterfully put food into his mouth as mine dropped all over. "By the way," he sat up straight. "I've already talked to Alex; she said she knows you."

"I'm sure I haven't flown with her," I frowned. "A female New

York crew member named Alex? I'd remember; unlike everyone else, I'm good with names."

"Tall, beautiful, blonde, slender, French slips off her tongue like honey though she rarely shows it off; quite poppysmic by any man's standards, always carries herself with aplomb…"

"I'd remember that Maurice, GEEZ! She sounds like a *Nightmare!*"

"Here's her number," he ignored my remark and handed over a slip of paper from one of the Amfac Hotel scratch pads. "I wrote down her address and my phone number too. Told her you were the *Best* new hire I'd worked with in a long time, so alacritous, charming and mellifluous and that I liked you; she trusts me. She's going to leave a key for you with her doorman. She said you can move in whenever you like, but she'd like to meet you tomorrow night. Just go by for a little bit and say hi. See? I told you she was a winner; it was serendipitous that we worked together today." As he settled back onto the bed, his leg hit my logs. "What's this?" he asked. "You have two logbooks?" He picked up *FlightLog.*

"Nothing." I tried grabbing it, but he pulled away.

"*FlightLog?* You really record all that inconsequential rubbish they tell you to? How tedious Sherri."

"Course I do," I said. "Don't you?"

"Hell no, sweetheart." Maurice flipped through my pages. "But," he said, "this does not appear to be your airplane block times or the number of hours you've flown. This looks like a soliloquy of sorts." I slipped under the covers and buried my head; I knew if I tried to snatch it away, he wouldn't let me have it, and I knew he'd win a tug-a-war. *Let's get this over with.* "Love the majuscular F & L," he crooned. "Reminds me of reading the old classics; quite tasteful Sherri. 'Dear *FlightLog,*'" he read aloud. "'I couldn't possibly tell you how wretched today was. Suffice it to say that it was the most disgusting day since I've arrived.' Great hook," he interjected. "This could sell. I'll be on the lookout for a good agent."

"Maurice, please?"

"Oh listen!" he shouted. "'*I'm an adulterous—let's just say it: I'm a whore.*' I knew I loved you Sherri! You didn't fool me with that innocent 'I'm-from-Kansas-and-I-ain't-never-been-off-the-farm' act."

"Why would I act that way? I've never even *Been* on a farm!"

"Wait! It gets better; *'I'm a murderess!*'" He put *FlightLog* down and looked at me with a hilarious look of phony fear. "Am I safe? Are you a serial type? Secret Man-Hater?"

"Shut up; please?"

"Do whores and murderesses say 'please?' I'm getting such an education here! I can't wait to read this later and see what you've written about me!"

"*That,*" I said, "I could sell for sure."

- *Dear FlightLog; guess who gave me his business card today and begged me to call him – collect? MATT LINCOLN! He's so gorgeous. He touched my hand and held it for a long time – I'm madly in love with him and I'm sure I would be even if he wasn't rich and famous. GEEZ! who wouldn't be? He's a great dresser too – Jeanna was impressed and that's as high a standard as any. Why does everyone think I grew up on a farm? Is Wichita really that hokey? I'm going to start telling people I'm from – well, I'll have to think about it. Also, why do so many of my flying partners swear like sailors and truck drivers? Is it something about* the transportation industry in general? I'm not even going to write down what Maurice shouted in the hallway. He's really fun, but he's exhausting! I had to hide in one of the lavatories for a few minutes just to get away from him during the service. He had me flying up and down that first-class aisle, phew! We have so much work to do, yet he still INVENTS other things to do! No wonder no one wants to work with him. He does it too though; he didn't ask me to work any harder than he does. When he isn't making me laugh or shocking everyone in earshot, he sounds as if he's swallowed all twenty volumes of the Oxford English Dictionary. There, if he finds this, he'll be able to handle these comments; although they might 'disappoint' him. I'm probably supposed to say that he's handsome, smart, funny, that he's the finest flight attendant I've ever seen and that I learned a lot from him. All true; ok, that'll make him feel better. Oh, and I'm probably supposed to say I wish he weren't gay but that's not true. I love that he's gay; I can wear my pajamas around him.

Ps: Look up: Swan-yeah; I think that's what he said I needed to be, a 'swan-yeah sophisticate.'

Chapter 13:

Chain Gang

JEANNA AND I WERE THRILLED TO be regular crew members. We bopped through the LA terminal springing off and on the moving walkways with Maurice, Marjorie, Carol and Darryl. It was going to be a fun trip home; I couldn't wait to work up front with Maurice again, as he'd let me get a good night's sleep, and Jeanna was getting along fine with the coach gang. As an overly officious first, Mitzi had reported to the LA crew desk earlier to get a head start and to collect her paperwork. Fifteen of us breezed past security, flashing our badges and made our way over to Gateway's jumbo jet at gate number sixty-eight. Mitzi was speaking to the agent.

"Sherri?" Looking out at the passengers, I saw him stand up.

"Wow," I said. It was that aggressive passenger, Roman.

"How you doing?" he asked, quickly walking over. "Are you working this flight today?"

Maurice leaned into my arm.

"Yes," I said.

Mitzi came up behind him. "Sherri and Jeanna." She held out two trip printouts. "You've been reassigned."

"No way," said Maurice. "We need them, I'm sure we're full."

"We are," she said. "We're going home understaffed. They're needed on the flight to Chicago to meet the FAA minimum. Plane's waiting for you. You'll have to hurry."

"You go into ops and refuse this trip right now," Maurice instructed. "They can't reassign you once you've been made a part of the regular crew on a regular ID."

"They're on probation," Mitzi said. "They can do whatever they want to them."

"Guess I'm not," I said to Roman.

"You two have to go," Mitzi said. "Plane can't take off without you."

"You're always running away," Roman said, shrugging his shoulders. "One of these days, I'm going to catch you."

Jeanna and I raced through the terminal to the DC-10 aircraft headed for Chicago. We were now scheduled to work a flight to O'Hare, then make a fast connection to another DC-10 flight into Kennedy. As soon as we stepped aboard, the agent shut the door. The first flight attendant told us we were positions seven and eight, one assigned to door 3Right over the wing, and one at door 4Right in the back. We would be working in coach together and wow, work we did! A full DC-10 was usually staffed with ten; we had eight. Strong tailwinds would get us there thirty-eight minutes early. We had three hours once we leveled off to complete a 'Four Star' service, understaffed by two. No one got a break. As soon as we pulled up to the gate, the agent asked the passengers to stand by so that Jeanna and I could get off first because again—our flight to New York was delayed and waiting for us to make up the FAA minimum.

"Jesus!" Jeanna said as we dodged around passengers at O'Hare. "I'm starving, my feet are killing me, and we get to do this all over! I haven't had a smoke since we left the hotel this morning."

"Don't talk about feet; mine hurt so badly I'm ready to cut them off."

We practically jogged aboard the DC-10, took a quick turn left into first class and came face to face with six angry flight attendants. One of them was Anderson Jeffries. At least the gate agent had not yet let the passengers onboard.

"Which one of you's the A?" Jeanna asked.

"You are," snapped one of the frowning females. She handed us the paperwork. "You two are junior and none of us want it, so one of you can be the lead and the other one can work downstairs. I'm Teresa and I'll be number four at door 4Left. I'm not working upfront."

"We're not qualified," Jeanna snapped back at her. "We haven't been trained for jumbo premium positions."

"Tough," she said. "That's not a contractual item. When no one volunteers, the junior man gets it—*That's* the wording."

Anderson must have seen our terror. His face softened. "I'll take the lead," he said. "As long as someone else handles the cockpit—I'll talk to them when they get on but I'm not going up there inflight. And one of you will have to work pit," he said to me and to Jeanna. "I think it will be easier than working the A position; I can help you out a lot."

Jeanna turned to me with a pleading look, "Please don't junior-man me Sherri! Please don't make me do it—you've worked more jumbo flights than I have."

Anderson put a hand on my shoulder. "I'll call down and tell you everything; what to send and where to find it."

"Alright I'll do it," I said. My voice cracked; I was terrified. "But if they reassign me again when we land, I quit. Where the hell does the pit person sit on this airplane anyway?"

Anderson put his inflight smock on. "Soon as you can, get down there," he said. "I need a trash cart first. You can send up two coach and the first-class liquor carts too. All four are on the captain's left."

I raced through my safety check. Grabbing my apron, I headed down the personnel elevator. My heart was racing. I breathed in and out deeply, trying to calm myself. Before checking the safety equipment, I kicked off my shoes. It was against regulations to work without shoes on but I didn't give a rat's ass at that point. I was furious with the crew for making me do this. When I found the carts Anderson wanted, I sent two up. Next, I opened the top compartments and grabbed steel bins full of supplies. *Ice, coffee packets, where were they?* I heard both lifts start back down. When I opened the personnel lift, I pulled the folding shelf down, pushed another liquor cart in and placed as many supplies as I could on top and sent that up too.

Anderson's voice came over the loudspeaker system that only I could hear. "Sherri, I'm ready for the ice. Captain's right, facing the ovens. It's in a low drawer. *Please* break it up before sending. Thanks."

I raced over and pulled out eight bags of ice and threw them to the floor—they were frozen solid. Then I began beating them with the bottom of one of the steel coffee pots and noticed my chipped manicured nails. *Damn.*

"They still haven't started boarding," Anderson said. "Go ahead and send me carts for the back of the plane. The snacks will be under the ovens where the entrée carts normally are. This is a simple service in coach. You won't have to load racks of frozen entrees, cook meals or do any fancy stuff for first class. The first-class meals should already be loaded. You need to plug them in so they stay warm. Say… 250 degrees."

I picked up the galley/pit phone and heard it ring above me.

"Yes?" Anderson said.

"Don't you want me to fix a pre-departure Champagne and orange juice cart for first class Mimosas?"

"We don't have time. If anyone up front wants a drink, we've got their liquor up here; we'll give them a real cocktail," he said with a little laugh in his voice. "Need that ice Sherri; whenever you can."

One less worry. I didn't even know where the collapsible queen carts were, never mind the linen I would need to line them with, flowers, first-class wine glasses… *oh man!*

"That's the sound of the men, working on the chain… gaaang," Anderson sang into my speaker.

"Very funny," I said to no one.

"Need four more bins of soft drinks," Anderson said. "There's usually extra soda on the left side *Behind* the cart elevator. Find the round red dial in the lift; it collapses the wall to one side. You'll have to do that in order to get access. Be *Careful!* Make sure you lock that elevator down because if someone up here calls for the lift, you can get crushed."

"Oh, My, God!" I checked the panel and locked both elevators in the down position. The red dial was easy to find. When I turned it, the right side of the small lift fell in like an accordion. I could see the cart he was talking about and I could see further back into the cargo area of the plane. Luggage was everywhere. *Cool!*

"If there are any bins with extra first-class glasses," Anderson said, "send those up too. We've got forty up front tonight; I've worked this flight before—they drink from takeoff to landing. It's happy hour done-with-work-time."

I retrieved all the extra first-class cocktail and wine glasses I could find and sent them up. We were taxiing. I wasn't sure what to do next, so I opened everything and guessed what Anderson might need. Black second coffee trays. Water pitchers for the top of the drink carts. Sanka packets, tea. Orange juice cartons, more ice.

Before I was ready, I heard the cockpit announce that we were number one for takeoff.

Anderson picked up the phone; I could always hear a 'click' when he lifted it out of its cradle in the galley. "Get up here," he said.

After locking all the compartments, I put my shoes on, hobbled over to the elevator and went upstairs. Anderson was already in his 2Left jumpseat.

On the other side, Jeanna was strapped in the 2Right jumpseat, which meant she was working first class aisle. "Run!" she said.

The plane picked up speed. I ran through first class, my apron still on, and buckled into my jumpseat at 1Left seconds before lift-off. The passenger in 1C smiled as I gave her a thumbs up sign, even though my arms were folded in the 'brace' position. Two minutes later, I was out of my seat and practically slid into the galley past the first-class passengers because of the plane's ascending angle.

"I'm coming with you," Jeanna said. "I *Need* a cigarette!" She grabbed her purse and followed me into the personnel lift.

"No," Anderson said, pulling her back. "One person at a time only." He pushed the button, sending me down, and when I got out, I sent it back up and kicked off my shoes.

"How's it going so far?" Jeanna asked as soon as she opened the door and stepped into my pit. She already had a cigarette out and was lighting it, holding out another one for me.

I was fighting coach tray carts and pushing one of them toward the elevator. "Take a look at my underarms and you'll know." All the pushing and pulling was hard, especially when you were doing it on ascent or descent.

* * *

After I sent up everything else needed for the service, I heard the captain welcoming everyone aboard. Again, we were going to have strong tail winds so our flight was going to be speedy.

"Sherri, when you're ready, we could use you up here," Anderson said.

Up I went. Now I was singing: *"My work is so hard."* When I opened the elevator all the coach attendants were in the aisles, halfway through the first section. Anderson was plating first-class entrees onto china plates and running the meals out from the galley. Jeanna was at the first bulkhead behind the cockpit mixing drinks for first class.

"Where do you need me the most?" I asked.

"Take your pick," Anderson offered. "You can help Jeanna get caught up with drinks, offer first-class rolls, or pick up coach trays; some passengers in the back are already finished."

Examining my wretched manicure I said, "I'll be in coach."

When I'd filled up two empty tray carts at door three, I pulled them off their bolts, stepped down on the bolts flattening them so no one would trip, and took them back to the galley. There was nowhere to put them; every possible storage spot was taken.

"Can you go down for a few minutes?" Anderson asked. "Got to send some of this stuff down, but then I'm going to need you back up here for second coffees," he added.

Jeanna came into the galley. "People upfront drink like fish!" She rifled through the drawers and retrieved two wine bottles. "Can one of you help me?"

"That's the sound of the men, working on the chain… gaaang," Anderson sang.

"Has anyone offered drinks to the cockpit?" Jeanna asked.

"Let me get some of these carts stowed." I opened my elevator door. "I'll be right back to take care of them, then I'll start second coffees in the main cabin."

"Sherri," Jeanna said. "Could you *waft* my first-class glasses?"

Even though I wanted to cry, I laughed. Coach passengers had to wait extra-long to get everything cleaned up and off their tray tables, but they didn't complain. First class however had kicked into party mode. There were six businessmen who all knew each other sitting in the back three rows on one side. They were drinking to excess and taking too long to eat.

"We still need to get more of this stuff downstairs," Anderson said. "We're in our descent, the carts are hard to secure at an angle, especially when the ones beside them slide over and make the slot smaller." He turned to Jeanna. "Can you get your passengers to speed it up?"

"I'll talk to them," she said.

Anderson's phone at 2Left went off. He picked it up and rolled his eyes. "Thanks," he said, putting it back down. "We've got ten minutes left," he said.

As soon as I got back downstairs, Anderson started sending me everything from his galley. The nose of the plane kept diving; it was getting harder to open and close the compartment doors. I looked at my watch. *Five minutes.* Where had the time gone? Sweat poured off my face. I was using my legs to position the carts in place because the plane's angle was making it impossible for me to use just my arms. I ripped my pantyhose in two places. *Rats!* The holes opened up into long runs. I still hadn't received first class supplies. Finally, their liquor cart came down. It nearly ran over me when I pulled it off the bolt. *"Crap!"* I was able to stop it, but then I couldn't get it secured into its spot—we were too far into our descent.

"Sherri! You good?"

"Anderson?" My voice was weak when I picked up the phone. "I can't stow this liquor cart; it's too heavy."

"I'm coming down." I watched his shoes, shins, knees and torso descend through the glass pane of the personnel elevator. Because we were so pressed for time, it seemed like an endless ride. He opened the door and slid over. "Send the elevator back up," he said. "Jeanna's going to send down what's left."

It took both of us to wrestle the liquor cart into its slot. Anderson was strong; I could not have done it without him. When I saw how sweaty he looked, I checked my armpits again. *Gross!* Foolishly, I looked at myself in the mirror above the sink. Loose hairs stuck out of my bun which was falling out; I'd lost several bobby pins and my eye makeup was badly smeared.

Jeanna picked up the phone. "The last of everything is coming down now. You guys, we're getting close!"

The last bins she sent practically fell off the shelf into our arms. One of the pilots made his last announcement telling the crew to be seated.

We shoved everything into the compartments, did a few 'pull' checks on the latches and climbed toward the elevator. Anderson got in and pulled me in too. Raising his hand, he pushed the 'up' button. We were against each other in the tight space, face to face. He didn't even have enough room to bring his arm down and he started to laugh; I was fighting back tears but I smiled anyway. I was pretty sure we were going to land in that elevator. I opened the door once we stopped and saw treetops. Running, I tore up into first class and sat down but never got my belt on. We landed. The woman in 1C opened her mouth. "Close call!" she said.

As Anderson welcomed everyone to New York, Jeanna handed out jackets in first class. I rose and went to the closet by her jumpseat. My feet were so swollen I was surprised I'd been able to get my heels back on. "Let me take them down and hand them to you," I said. "I know your feet hurt too but I'm completely pitted out."

She nodded and took off with 5A's suit jacket. "You do look beat up," she admitted.

As the last passengers deplaned, I tried to pull my suitcase out of one of the first-class smaller closets. It was stuck. Yanking hard, I pulled it free but heard a crack; I'd broken the handle completely off.

Since Jeanna, Anderson, and I were at the front, we were the first crew members to leave the plane; none of us felt as if we had to wait for the others. I wiped a tear away. Breaking the handle of my suitcase had been the last straw. I looked like *Shit*, my hair and makeup were a disaster, I had terrible BO, wet spots under my arms, runs in my stockings, my manicure looked like I was going to a Halloween party as a zombie and I had to carry my suitcase like a box since I didn't have wheelies.

"That flight *Sucked*," Jeanna said.

"You two were troupers," Anderson said with praise. "Both did outstanding jobs, as if you'd been doing it for years. When you want to girl," he said to Jeanna, "you *Handle* rowdy first-class passengers. And *You* Sherri, you really stepped up to the plate. That's a tough gig even when you're trained."

"Can hardly wait to do it again," I stared straight ahead of me. I'd come this far; I didn't want to lose it now.

Teresa, who had greeted us so graciously, passed us without even giving us a sidelong glance. She slid by, her hair perfectly in place, pulling her suitcase easily behind her on a set of wheelies. She had definitely reapplied her 'lipstick and blusher.'

"Bitch," Jeanna said, just loud enough for 1) the bitch to hear it and 2) just quietly enough to pretend the bitch wasn't supposed to hear it.

Anderson didn't even fight back his guffaws.

"Know what she was doing?" Jeanna ratted. "Whining about the contract! Passengers are watching her do almost nothing but hearing her complain about how little she makes. If I'd paid for a seat and had to listen to that garbage, I'd have strangled her," Jeanna said.

We were quiet until we got downstairs into the baggage claim area. Through the windows, we could see the crew bus that would head back to the offices.

"Sherri, listen," Anderson broke the silence. "Want to apologize."

"It's not your fault, we're junior…"

"About the day we met… I was rude and assuming."

"Forget it. I'm getting used to everyone hating pilots. I should be thanking you anyway—I could not have done this today if you hadn't guided me." My voice cracked again and I could feel tears trying to force their way out. "Never mind the help you gave with that other thing…"

"Easy," he said. We were outside now. The crew bus was waiting but it wouldn't wait long. "Listen," he said. "I don't have my car, it's over at LaGuardia; we got reassigned too. Otherwise, I'd offer you a ride home. But I'd like to talk to you sometime. We got off on the wrong foot; shouldn't be like that."

"Agreed," I said. "I'd like to talk too. Why don't you call me?"

"Ok…" he said hesitantly, "I… could do that."

A limo pulled up in front of us. If Matt Lincoln was in it, I was going to dive in front of the next fast-moving car and kill myself.

"Sherri, you and your friends need a ride?"

The three of us peered into the open window. It was Roman— again. *Oh no.*

"Hey," Jeanna said, turning to me. "Isn't that the guy…" I nodded. "*Yes!* We do," she shouted. "Sherri this time I'm not letting you say no. Get in." She pulled my jacket sleeve as I shot Anderson a bewildered look.

"Let me guess," he said with a resigned smile. "He's your uncle." As we pulled away, I heard him sing, *"All day long they're singing… Hooh! Ah! Hooh! Ah!"*

Chapter 14:

I Love the Nightlife

THERE I WAS, EXPERIENCING THE first limousine ride I didn't have to pay for, but I didn't look or feel like a star. I was with an exciting man—and—my girlfriend, who did look the part, with her picture-postcard polished attire and makeup. It would have been a comical contrast: her and me, with my shredded nylons, puffy ankles, sweaty face, cat-wacked hair, broken nails, chipped polish, black tarry smudges from oily pit racks—not to mention my stench, if it hadn't been me.

"So," Roman said, taking a long look.

"So," I said back.

He glanced at Jeanna then back at me.

"I don't always look this good," I said, trying to sound as if this was terribly amusing.

"Does seem as if you…"

"I filled in for a mechanic," I said, pointing to a black grease spot on my calf. "Loaded luggage today. Gonna be a ramp-rat. Tomorrow I'll be fixing engines and repainting runways."

"She got screwed," Jean explained. "It wasn't right—what they did to her."

"Why are you here?" I asked Roman. "Didn't you take the non-stop from LA that landed hours ago? With the crew we were supposed to work home with?"

"I did," Roman said. "Had a business meeting at the airport. Just finished. I called a car to take me downtown and there you were. It's wonderful to see you. Glad we ran into each other."

Jeanna studied him hard. She was seated across from us in the spacious car. "You can drop me at East 83rd," she said. "By the way," she extended her hand. "We haven't been introduced. I'm Jeanna Campion."

The two of them did most of the talking; they were both Californians. Roman owned several travel agencies. He was expanding—branching out all over; he sounded very excited about his work. After Jeanna got out, he moved over. "We're finally alone," he said.

"At the moment, I don't feel like great company for anyone to be with; unless you're a swamp lizard." I was self-conscious; it was uncomfortable having him so close. "I'm sorry about the way I acted when we met."

"Don't apologize, I was forward," he admitted. "Too forward. Let's not *talk about all the plans I had.* You're here now and I'd like to treat you. Let me take you to dinner."

"Not tonight…"

"At *Least* a drink." He cut me off. "Come on. I'm only in town a couple of nights."

"I'm supposed to meet my new roommate," I said.

"Found a new place? Not going to live with your aunt anymore?"

We both laughed.

"Bring her along," he offered. "She's welcome to join us… or him," he said. He looked at me quizzically and cleared his throat. "Is it a him?"

We both laughed again. "No," I said. "But I don't know her. She knows me but…"

"Tell her it's my treat. This can be a lonely town. The company would be wonderful. There must be a reason we keep running into each other… what harm can a drink do? Please let me see you. You can take as long as you'd like, take a nap. I'll pick you up whenever you're ready. This city never sleeps; there's no such thing as too late. Or," he said. "I'll send a car if that makes it easier and if that feels like less pressure. You won't have to introduce me to anyone—anything that makes you comfortable. You name it."

I looked up into his bright eyes, loving the way his laugh lines crinkled up together; he was handsome. "Ok," I said. "Might be up for that."

"Ok maybe dinner?"

"A drink," I said. "But I need time. Look at me; it's going to be late."

"That's fine, *I love the nightlife!* What time can I pick you up?"

"I'll meet you," I said. "I need a long hot bath! Where will you be?"

"Meet me at Maxwell Plums," he said. "Sure I can't pick you up?"

"I'm sure," I said.

"I really hope you'll come," he said, carrying my suitcase into the lobby. The doorman hustled over and awkwardly took the broken bag out of his hands. "And I meant what I said," Roman continued, "your roommate's welcome. See you around nine."

"It'll be more like ten." I leaned over the lobby's desk. "Hello there… Claudio." I said, reading the doorman's nametag. "Think you're holding a key for me."

It was a pretty two-bedroom apartment. Parquet floors like Jeanna's, large floor-to-ceiling windows on two sides—a corner unit on the twenty-second floor. From the entrance I could see the back of a camel-back couch. It seemed old-fashioned compared to the other furnishings, but looked luxuriously large and comfortable. It faced the windows so I had to walk around it into the living area to get to the front and sit down. *Smart.* It felt as if I was flying through the skyline when I admired the view. The hallway was small; it led to a vacant room with a stripped full-size bed and nothing else. I dropped my broken suitcase onto the mattress and kicked off my shoes. Across the hall was an adequate bathroom; clean, nice, roomy enough. And just a stone-toss from that was Alex's room. The master had a walk-in closet. It was tidy but not immaculate; well-read books, candles and trinkets on the nightstands. The bed was made with an inviting array of pillows and a down comforter. She had a rich oriental rug, amazing lamps and beautifully framed gorgeous photos, taken from all over, but I didn't see any of her. The room was cozy, interesting, *yummy.*

The place was bigger than Jeanna's but since she had lived there for years, Alex's rent was only $1250. That was a steal for a nice two bedroom in New York. Maurice said I would pay $575; Alex paid $675 because she had the master. *Expensive but affordable.* It was time for *Freedom.* I had not experienced nearly as much as I'd hoped to in my first few months of living in the Big Apple. Being under my aunt's thumb, I was accountable to her for everything. When I came home late, she stayed up—it was unbearable. But now I had my own place! And, I had a single, female, flight attendant roommate in a contemporary high rise on the Westside—not a walkup studio with roaches. And *I have a date.* I called my aunt and told her I was staying with my new roommate, (who was nowhere to be found) set my alarm, and took a blissful nap across the unmade bed without taking off anything other than the shoes I'd already shed.

* * *

I saw Roman at the bar, fidgety, looking toward the door. He squinted when I entered then his mouth dropped. "Sherri!" he called for no reason—it was obvious we had both seen each other. "Nice," he said, slipping his arm loosely around my waist and guiding me to the bar. I had changed into flatter shoes but they were still heels, so I was hobbling.

"If you want to go where the *people dance,*" I said, "I'll wave to you from a barstool."

"You look different with your hair down. I barely recognized you with your clothes on. I mean out of uniform..." he stammered then laughed. "You know what I mean."

"Good different or bad different?" Quickly I was appreciating being appreciated. Men always responded that way the first time they saw me with my hair down. And after today, feeling so ludicrously unattractive by the time we landed, I was going to enjoy Roman's fawning—he was good at it. *I want to live.*

"Marvelous," he said, reaching up and putting his left hand on mine. "You look spectacular. Thanks for coming. I... didn't think you were going to." He motioned for the bartender. "Why did you come? Was it because you couldn't resist me?"

"Because I couldn't let your last impression of me be of the way I looked earlier," I said. "That's done; I'll be heading home now..." I started to stand.

He put a hand on my shoulder and gently pushed me down. I was wearing a thin strapped dress; his fingers on my shoulder *Did* something.

"What can I get you here?" the bartender asked.

"I'll have another," Roman said, "and the lady..."

This always took too long. I wasn't much of a drinker and in many of the cities I flew into, I wasn't old enough to drink anyway. I didn't have a regular drink yet. "May I have a tequila sunrise?"

"Can I see some ID?"

Fumbling through my purse, I unburied my wallet and displayed my Kansas license.

"Well, that's a relief." Roman playfully wiped his brow.

"Do I really look that young?"

"You do," he said, raising his martini. "Here's to you. A lovely young lady who's as beautiful on the inside as she is on the outside."

"You don't know that," I said.

"I'm a *Great* judge of character, and you've got it all kid," he tipped his glass and clinked it on my mine then took a swig; he was happy.

I decided I was done dodging, fearing and worrying about him being too old, too suave, and living too far away. "Here's to fun tonight," I said.

"Cheers."

When we stepped outside after drinks, Roman hailed a cab. "Dinner?"

"I'm not hungry," I lied.

"Let's find some live music."

I had never gone anywhere to listen to jazz. It was dark and smoky in the joint; just like in the movies. I wasn't terribly fond of the sound.

"What are you having here," our waiter asked.

"We're celebrating tonight," Roman said. "Do you have a nice bottle of champagne?"

"What are we celebrating?" I asked after the waiter left.

He leaned across the table and took both of my hands. "It's a beautiful night, I'm with a charming lady who couldn't be nicer to look at..." he pulled back. "There, right there. It's that smile. I haven't stopped thinking about it since the first time I saw it. I am in *Love* with that smile. I'm in love with a lot of things about you."

"Thank you," I didn't know what else to say. *Please don't talk about love tonight.*

"What kind of music do you like," he asked.

"Mostly rock," I looked at him and decided to just be honest. "Listen to a lot of pop—I still like Donnie and Marie," I said.

"What an admission," he laughed.

"Disco's growing on me. It's gotten better in the last few years. When I was little though, my favorite was Soul Music."

"No kidding."

"Absolutely, Gordy Records, which became Motown—loved it. I had every Supremes and every Temptations album. Loved Ray Charles, Stevie Wonder—that was as close to Black Americans as I ever got," I told him. "My parents were worried about me," I chortled, remembering. "Sounds so innocent now." And *borderline racist.* "Comparatively speaking."

"Where would you have gone tonight if I hadn't agreed to meet you," he asked. "You were so forceful—dragging me out of my hotel room when all I wanted to do was sleep."

"Nowhere," I told him. "I would have curled up with my… I would have recorded things, about yesterday's flight—I had Matt Lincoln in first class—and about today's awful trip."

"You a journalist?"

I frowned.

"I mean, do you journal?" he asked. "Hear it's very therapeutic."

"I do. And it is. That's what I'd be doing—or waiting up for my new roommate who never showed up."

"You a Bears fan?"

"Chiefs," I said, "but I love football so I know a lot of the players. Lincoln gave me an autographed picture for my brother." I was on my third glass of champagne. No dinner. The dark room started to pitch. I closed my eyes.

"Ready to leave?"

Walking the sidewalks of New York on the arm of a hand-some man who was crazy about me in sweet-breezy weather seemed like the *Best* way to experience the city. "What have I been waiting for?" I said aloud. *"I've got to boogie!"*

"On the disco 'round?" Roman tightened his hold. I sucked in, feeling self-conscious about my weight. "Come on," he said, as if understanding I felt behind in enjoying New York. *I think he just felt my behind!* "Let's take a carriage ride!"

Ahhh, it felt so good. The ride, I mean. Relaxing in the back of the carriage, I listened to the soft padding of the horse's hooves on the pavement, and the jingle-sounds from tiny bells on the reigns. It was like being in a movie.

"You know," Roman said, leaning in, "you're really nice."

"You know, thanks to you, I've had my first carriage ride in Central Park." I smiled back. His face started to whirl.

"I mean you're... really nice." He leaned forward to kiss me.

I sat up and pushed him away. "Could you," I was hoping the driver could hear me. "Could you stop?"

"What's wrong?" Roman look worried.

"Not feeling well," I said, holding my head down while rub-bing my stomach. If I was going to be ill, I couldn't let him see that—no way, not after my complete humiliation in front of my whole class in training. Vomit can be so unattractive.

"Please stop!" As soon as we did, I jumped down and ran toward the park's entrance. I could see the street in the front of the Plaza hotel; there were cabs everywhere. It took Roman awhile to catch me—I assumed he'd stopped to pay the carriage guy, but it was too late—I was in my own cab and the door was closed.

Roman banged on the window. "Let me take you home."

"I'm fine," I said. "Go," I told the driver.

* * *

The sun beating into my bedroom windows did not wake me until almost ten. As soon as I lifted my head, I was aware of my hangover. *Ouch!* It felt as if my skull had been crushed on the cart lift after all. My memories were mixed up—the two flights home, Anderson Jeffries, working the pit, coming here to Alex's, a fabulous evening with Roman… how had that ended?

When I shuffled into the living/dining room, she was there in a long white terrycloth robe having a cup of coffee and smoking a cigarette. "It's you!" I exclaimed.

"Good morning," she moved the *New York Times* away from a spot at the small glass table, inviting me to take a seat. "Would you like some coffee?"

"I thought your name was Leigh!" None of this made sense. It was the woman I'd seen outside my aunt's apartment—the one Lake Effect had dropped off.

"Leigh?" she asked.

"Matt Lincoln… he was on my flight two days ago—he asked about you—said that was your name."

"Who's Matt Lincoln?"

I must still be drunk. I sat down, staring at her. *Was she teasing?* "Am I still on Earth?"

She laughed.

"The *Football* player—you were with him in the limo when we saw each other."

"Oh, oh. Matty," she said, smiling and taking a sip of her coffee. "He plays football?"

"Didn't you know that? He's one of the best players in the NFL!"

"I ran into him at a party," she said. "Don't always use my real name."

"He said to call him collect if I ever found out who you were; this is incredible!" I knew I sounded like I was arguing, but I couldn't understand her response. She didn't even care!

One side of her lip curled up in amusement. "That's why I didn't let him drop me off here; don't want strangers to know where I live."

"Stranger? He could be your *Boyfriend;* and, he's handsome; he's famous!"

"Don't have time for that," she said. "I do a lot of union work."

"But he promised me tickets to a game if I found you and called him." I was in disbelief.

She just shook her head. A buzzer sounded beside the front door. Alex stood and went over to the intercom. "Yes?" she asked, holding down the button. "Fine, send them up." She glided into the kitchen. "Flowers are here for you." The sunlight glowing into our East-facing kitchen window kissed the slight overbite of her gorgeous smile. "Coffee yet?"

Flowers? From Roman?

When they arrived, Alex retrieved a vase from above the refrigerator and arranged the long-stemmed roses, baby's breath and green ferns.

"Roman was here? Last night?" I was still having trouble focusing on the events from the previous two days—seeing her with Matt seemed long ago; the end of last night was blurry.

"You were out cold. He came to the building because that's where he had dropped you off," she said. "The door man would not give him my phone number. Claudio called up here himself and explained everything, so I let him in and calmed him down. He was worried about you. Said you weren't feeling well."

"I can't believe I slept through all of that," I picked up the note attached to the flowers. 'Thank you for such a wonderful evening; looking forward to many more; love Roman.' It brought a smile to my face. I'd really had *Fun* last night. And Roman was doting and had shown me a good time in this fabulous city.

The phone rang. Alex said a quick hello and handed it to me, grinning widely. Seems she'd given him our number after all; I knew it was him.

"How are you feeling?" he laughed. "Better?"

"Umm, thank you for the roses; they're gorgeous, really."

"Pretty flowers for a pretty lady."

"They did perk me up. Alex did a great job of arranging them," I said.

"Better get her to show you how," he said. "You're going to be getting a lot more. How about lunch? I could pick you up in an hour."

"Oh, boy," I said. "Think I'm going to skip eating today."

"Let's take a stroll down 5th Avenue," he suggested. "Fresh air will do you good; I love to shop," he said. "Is there anything you need?"

I started to say no.

"Please don't say no," he said quickly.

I looked at Alex, who was now taking pictures of my flowers with a nice camera, and whispering to them in what sounded like French. What would she say to Roman's question? I thought about Jeanna—she'd ask for the moon on a gold string. "Some flat shoes in mauve or beige… a set of wheelies… a dictionary… and chopsticks."

• *Dear FlightLog. I'm writing from my new home where I live with Alex. It's even better than I could have hoped – I feel like I've finally 'landed' in New York. Turns out Alex is the girl that Matt Lincoln liked and called*

'Leigh.' She gave him a false name; got to be a good story there — she wouldn't even let him drop her off at her own building. Can you imagine? NOT wanting a guy like that to call you again? Takes all kinds, right? So... I had the flight from hell — I was forced into working pit and it was horrible. Anderson, the steward who thought Sean was a guy hitting on me before I could explain that he was my dad, worked the A position and helped me through it. Turns out he really is nice, he just jumped to conclusions. I was angry about what he said, but many FAs don't like pilots. I like Anderson; I feel conflicted about that — as Jeanna says, he's 'just a black steward' — not sure which of those is least attractive to her — lack of money or lack of sameness, but I do admit, I don't think I could march him into my parent's living room all bubbly-like and announce: 'Here's my new boyfriend' because deep-down I know Mom & Dad wouldn't feel the same way I do — I know I would be defensive. Is that wrong? I'm pretty sure he likes me too, after all, why would he be bothered about a pilot trying to pick me up? And he's offered me a ride twice now — though that could have been an attempt at apologizing. He said he wanted to talk to me, so I told him to call. Is that promiscuous? I don't know how to behave around him. Anyway, I had another limo ride! This one was so much bigger, it had two seats facing each other, a bar, which none of us touched — I had just finished that wretched trip so I was distracted… but then I went out for 'an evening on the town' with the smashing guy I met months ago — Roman — the one who unnerved me; how dreamy is that name? He LOVES to spend money, My God! I can't buy anything! We take cabs, limos and horse-drawn carriage rides; he orders expensive champagne and even if I'm picking out a cheap set of chopsticks, he won't let me pay. I got irritated but he told me I wasn't going to win. It surprised me how easy it was to find them; I've never seen chopsticks sold anywhere in Wichita. The Chinese restaurants there don't even offer them to diners. I didn't go out with him last night; he had to get up early today, but I did let him kiss me. I knew it was going to be good and it was! But that's all that happened. After Sheldon, I'm going slow. REAL slow. I feel as if I've lost something by waiting so long to write, but sometimes I'm just too busy, tired — or in the case of the other night — drunk, to pick you up and tell all.

Chapter 15:

. . . .

Windy

LONG AFTER WORKING THE PIT, I was assigned to 'Jumbo Aircraft Premium Positions Training' with Jeanna. We rode the Carey Bus out to Gateway's offices. Though the subway was under a dollar and often faster, you had to switch trains, hustle through the underground tunnels with luggage and connect to a commuter bus where there was usually standing room only. The Carey Bus gave airline personal discounted rates; it was about four dollars each way.

We stopped at the crew desk to say hi to the hard-working schedulers, checked our mailboxes, picked up our latest revisions, then made our way into a conference room where several other newer attendants were seated.

"Sherri and Jeanna?"

"Reporting," Jeanna said.

Our domicile manager stared straight into Jeanna's stormy eyes then checked her out up and down. They smiled at each other. "I apologize if I haven't already had the opportunity to welcome each of you individually," he said. "If we haven't said hello yet, my name is Alonso Moretti. I've been with Gateway Airlines for seventeen years…"

Whenever anyone from the company spoke—trainers, supervisors, management, and even flight attendants—the first thing they always told us was how long they'd worked for the airlines. Guess we were supposed to 'ooh and aah' with admiration.

Alonso was pleasant. He had on a gorgeous jacket and was keenly aware of Jeanna. He seemed jovial and had a bit of a receding hairline—I guessed fortyish. When we met our instructor, Brenda, she had already heard about me being forced to work in the pit and nodded at me with a look of apology.

"We have fallen behind in our training," she said, "but we're forging ahead and the next classes coming into the domicile will not have to wait as long as you did." She was still looking at me. "We don't want others facing what Sherri did."

"We were told in training," Jeanna said right away, "that we could *Not* be forced into working any premium positions until we were qualified."

"Well," Brenda admitted, "that's not technically correct. We're trying to get the language changed—since as you witnessed, the honor system doesn't always work."

"No shit," said Jeanna.

Since we only had an hour for lunch, it wasn't feasible to go all the way over to the terminal to grab something to eat. There were a few vending machines for the staff but nothing else. Looked as if it was going to be soda and pretzels for chow.

"Here he comes," Brenda announced.

Alonso entered with tubs of KFC. "It's the least I can do," he said. "Offer lunch to my new attendants." He sat down, positioning himself as close to Jeanna as he could.

I spent the time talking to Brenda. She'd been flying for ten years—I still couldn't get over how long some of my peers had flown. Brenda had won $15,000 on "The Price is Right." She said the first thing she'd done was buy a full-fare ticket home—it was so nice not to go standby.

"Lots of flight attendants get on game shows," she said. "We can travel, we get plenty of days off and demographically, we're a well-educated group so we interview well."

"Not sure I'm ready for a game show," I said. *My life is a sit-com already.*

"You'll be ready soon if it's something you'd like to do," she said. "You're going to be a great pit-person. You're eager, focused—and based on your comments and questions, I can tell that you care about good service."

It was a fascinating training unit; I was interested in everything. Brenda knew her positions, worked them regularly and gave us great pointers. What was really nice was that at five o'clock, we got to go home. Jeanna and I were scheduled to fly in the morning—we wouldn't know any details until we heard the tape after 8 P.M. so we said adios and planned an evening out for several nights later.

* * *

Since I'd moved out of my aunt's apartment and met Roman, I had come into a real life of being a New Yorker. Roman was always up for theatre, museums, and fabulous dinners. Alex was great at helping me with the *New York Times* crossword puzzle, going for walks, talking about life, the world, flying, union conflicts, families, love, anything, and Jeanna was always up for being 'seen' and having fun; she wasn't into going to the library or checking out bookstores. Lunch and brunch were her daytime favorites; nightclubbing into the wee hours was her evening staple. We'd find plenty of fellows willing to buy us drinks—it was almost embarrassing. I never said yes or no; I let Jeanna do the deciding because she was the one doing the looking for hooking up. I'd let her know if I thought 'this one' was a catch or not, based on far too little information, but it didn't matter anyway; she did what she wanted. It didn't take long to figure out that she favored men who spent a lot of money and who had their own apartments. She always had the name of a different bar or club she wanted to try; I'd nod, and meet her. She was never on time, but there was usually someone interesting to talk to while I waited, and I did enjoy meeting just about anyone.

Tonight, it was Ice Palace 57; close to where I lived. The cover charge included two drinks, and even I could down two. It was all splash—divided dance floor and dining levels, mirrors and glass everywhere—worlds away from anything in my Kansas suburb.

I hadn't even finished my first Sombrero when Jeanna showed up. "You're early," I said.

"Guess who called me?" She practically skipped over.

"Does he work for Gateway?"

"You're no fun," she said. "We went out on Saturday—he took me all over the Island. It was amazing! He's *So* romantic," she said. "Sherri, I think I'm in love!"

I had to admit: Jeanna's interest in the eligible bachelors that night waned. She was positively effervescent with the anticipation of seeing Alonso again.

"First," she said. "He picked me up and took me to Rockefeller Center to see the tree. Then we saw that movie—*The New York Experience*—have you seen it?"

I shook my head.

"You've *Got* to go," she said. "Have Roman take you the next time he's in town. Then we grabbed a quick bite and went down to Battery Park to ride the ferry over to Ellis Island and saw the Statue of Liberty," she squealed. "We didn't come back until it was dark and while we were riding back, the lights came on and shined right on her—she was so beautiful," she beamed. "Proud and glowing as our boat slipped away." She grabbed my wrist. "And *Then* he kissed me," she said with a big grin. "As *You* would say, it was just like being in a movie!"

I enjoyed seeing her so happy. "Sounds like a perfect date for someone new to this town."

"He called yesterday. I saw him last night too."

"You two are an item," I nodded.

"We are! I feel like I'm on a magic carpet ride when I'm with him."

We left early. Jeanna wanted to make sure she was home in time for Alonso's regular evening phone call. I made sure to push my coaster toward her; she was collecting them now; she already had scores of them from various clubs and bars.

*   *   *

"Baby it's cold outside. And *windy!*" Claudio hugged himself when he saw Alex and me exiting the elevator. "Love that coat," he said. Alex flashed her smile. "Give them a thrill," he shouted as we neared the doors. "The only thing better than being outside today watching you two *tripping down the streets of this city,* is being in here and experiencing it close up."

Claudio was in love with my roommate. And she did look sensational in her Oscar outerwear.

We were headed uptown to the condo Maurice shared with his boyfriend, Sergio, for a get-together. Their parties were wonderful; interesting, different adults of all ages and from all walks of live—which pretty much described most of the flight attendants based in New York City. Even though I still didn't feel like I was one of them, I wanted to be. I loved being with them. They made me… better, I thought and pushed me in a good way.

"Alex, do you have a will?"

"No," she gave me a questioning look. "Why?"

"I want you to leave me that coat." Alex always made us walk, unless it was raining, because she wouldn't carry an umbrella. When wind or cold sent others racing for cabs, she stepped outside and said, 'Can't get enough of the air in my hair.'

We approached a construction site where several workers stood on an exposed second story; they stared. I squirmed; they watched every step we took, glaring at us as if they'd been in solitary confinement and we were the first females they'd seen in years. I tucked my head into the collar of my uniform coat.

Alex met their gaze. "Hey guys," she called out in a friendly tone. "Looks like you're working hard today."

"Not too hard to notice you two," one of them returned. Couple of the others whistled. I cringed.

"Why don't you ladies join us?" another offered.

"Maybe next time," Alex, who *smiled at everybody she saw,* waved and looked at me rolling my eyes. It made her laugh.

We reached the four-story white building on the west side, rang the bell and headed up. Our friends' condo consisted of the entire third and fourth floors. *This* building had an elevator. The first time I'd been there, I'd been stunned to learn that two gay men openly lived together. This sure wasn't Kansas; there, two gay men or women living together who didn't keep their relationship a secret would be taking huge risks. *Life threatening risks.*

Maurice threw his arms around Alex. "Welcome to S & M's," he said, giving us his 'go-to' greeting. "Sherriii," he cooed as he took the aluminum-foil topped pan out of my hands. "You shouldn't have!"

I glanced at the banquet table near the long galley-style kitchen. *Exotic as usual.* There were dishes I'd never seen before moving to New York: stuffed grape leaves, empanadas, curried foods, pomegranates, pesto something-or-others; *Sushi*. My mother had never served any of it. And when Toby took me out to dinner, I always had steak and potatoes. Unless I was feeling adventurous—then I'd have a beef kabob, which usually came with rice.

"Looks just like what you'd eat in Wichita, right?" Maurice said dryly.

"Wichita is renowned for being hometown to one of the most elegant foreign food chains in the nation," I said defensively.

"Which one?" he asked.

"Pizza Hut."

Maurice chuckled. He whirled, set my pan down and lifted the foil cover. "You brought… Rice Krispy Treats?" he howled. "You are too funny girl." He wrapped me in his arms, teetering me left, right, left, right. "Such a facetious little wit you are. They'll probably disappear before anything else." Swinging to my side, he put his arm around me. "Has everyone heard that Sherri successfully pulled off working the DC-10 pit on an understaffed speedy flight from Chicago to New York *before* being officially trained?"

"How did you handle that?" Danielle, a flight attendant originally from Jamaica, asked me. She was so thin, it was hard to picture how she didn't fall forward from the weight of her ample bosom. I tried not to stare.

"I did what any mature-professional would do," I said. "I cried first."

"Let me take your coat," Maurice said to Alex. "I may even give it back."

I made my way over to Sergio and Danielle. I loved listening to Danielle because of her accent. She had changed her hair since I'd seen her last. "We are going back to Helsinki and Reykjavik in the spring," Danielle was telling Sergio. "I have not been there in so long."

"Where are they?" I asked. "Minnesota?"

Danielle chuckled. "I'm looking forward to getting a couple more stems," she said. "The selections are getting better and better all the time."

"Stems?" I asked as Sergio grinned and took a sip of his beer.

"Jim and I collect wine glasses; we get them from each place we visit," she explained. "I must have you over to take a look; I think that you'll like them very much."

Sergio was excited about his next gig which was working for Toyota. "In February I demoed their new prototype for five days in Chicago," he said to both of us now. "They're sending me their convention list for next year; I've been invited to accept any of the cities and dates I want."

Danielle pinched his cheek. "Ahhh!" she exclaimed. "I can see why they would want you back—I would buy any car after listening to you," she said.

Sergio had a successful acting career. Not so much in theatre or movies, but doing demonstrations and commercials—mostly radio ads and conventions.

"Sherri?" Danielle pulled me toward a mustached man whom I had never seen before. "Have you met my husband, Jim?"

"How do you do," I said, immediately regretting the formality. Jim was white; meeting my first interracial couple made me feel awkward. I was afraid I'd say something stupid. *If Anderson Jeffries and I became a couple, is that the reaction we would get?*

Jim had been talking but I wasn't paying attention. "Beg your pardon?" I asked.

"I said, Danielle says that you're new to these parts," he was loud and friendly and spoke with his hands. "Nice to meet you; Jim Goldman." His wine glass did circles as he pantomimed. "If you haven't been down to Wall Street, come by our offices and I'll show you around; I love introducing people to the chaos. It's one of the most important parts of New York and it makes this town tick."

"Did you say Wall Street?" A familiar voice asked from behind me.

"Jeanna!" I exclaimed; I hadn't seen her in a while. "You came!"

Maurice had reluctantly agreed to invite her. 'Alright Sherri,' he'd said. 'If she's really that much of a friend, I'll acquiesce.'

Most of us sat on floor pillows near the fireplace which everyone helped stoke as needed. Sergio passed around a joint but I didn't partake. The phonograph blared Dolly Parton's "Here You Come Again."

"This put her on the crossover charts," Maurice said boastfully. "I loved Dolly from way back." He was admiring her album cover. "She's just… salaciously adorable; agreed?"

Later in the kitchen, I found Alex and Maurice talking quietly. Alex was holding up a near-empty wine bottle. "What did you do?" she asked him. "Take this off the plane?" Tipping the bottle back, she swallowed the last drops.

"What was your first clue," Maurice asked.

"The screw top," she said.

"Jeanna brought it," he said in a whisper. The three of us looked at each other.

"Shouldn't have bothered," Alex laughed. "Would you risk your job for this?"

I stared. I couldn't believe Jeanna would do something so dangerous; we weren't even off probation yet.

"Speaking of work and risks…" Alex said.

"I'm going back into the living room." Maurice exited quickly.

"What's going on?" I asked.

Alex shook her head and followed him. Jeanna slipped into the kitchen and grabbed me. "I have to talk to you about Alonso," she said all glowing. "He could be the one. I really think I could marry him," she said.

"What? Jeanna, that's kind of sudden."

"I mean, eventually. I realize how much he means to me now, because we haven't been able to see as much of each other," she said. "He's been so busy with the holidays. I miss him!"

Hours later, everyone was still present. The atmosphere at S & M's just *worked*—no one was in a hurry to leave. The shop-talk began. Our gatherings always included shop-gossip, opinions, and declarations, such as:

TWA had the best uniforms. Abandoning the trendy colorful splashy uniforms of the 70s, they had returned to the 50s/60s sleek, dark-blue, military uniforms that the rest of us longed for. Delta attendants were the highest paid. Braniff attendants had to share rooms—gross, but theirs was the only US carrier to officially allow its female flight attendants to wear flat shoes in the cabin. United was the friendliest—but only on their flights to and from Hawaii. Air France was formal, American had the cleanest US airplanes and Singapore Air was best all around—it stood for: service, service, service. They staffed their 747s with twenty-two attendants to our fifteen, yet their configuration held fewer passengers than ours. If Maurice said it was so, it was Gospel. And, if anyone mentioned having a male celebrity onboard, Maurice *Knew* he was gay.

I'd finally been able to brag about a celebrity—Mr. Matt Lincoln of course; Maurice had been there, so he knew that too. 'Please don't try to tell me he's gay,' I'd said before he'd opened his mouth. 'Maybe not *That* one,' Maurice admitted.

Bonnie was a new hire who had been in New York for three weeks. "Is this going to be your first winter in New York too?" she asked me.

"Yes," I said.

"I'm looking forward to ice skating at Rockefeller Center," she told me. "It's so pretty down there."

I nodded. "Have you seen it?"

"Oh yes! I never expected to like this city so much," she said. "Can't get enough of it—I go out every day and look all around, trying to *capture every special moment* I can. Do you go to Central Park?"

"I do," I said with a smile. "Alex and I take long walks there. Your enthusiasm is infectious. I can see why Maurice invited you; he absolutely *Loves* people who are joy-struck." Bonnie was cute. She was from a small town south of Tucson which she described as: 'bleary, weary and dreary.' She was anything but. Her dimples were perfect, but I didn't mention them, because most people who had them loathed them. The way her white teeth set reminded me of Mara. I got a quick pang of sorrow and wondered how Mara was doing.

"Yes, that is what I'm telling you!" Danielle said loudly to Mitzi, who had arrived late. The rest of us tuned in. "I was working an extra stew line with an LA crew and they told me they knew her."

"Who, what?" Jeanna asked.

"One of the senior coach aisle attendants said she knows the flight attendant who has the personal license plate that reads, 'Headsets 1.'"

The latest scandalous airline story was that a flight attendant had made so much money siphoning off headset money from coach movie sales, she had bought a car with the cash and ordered vanity plates that read: 'Headsets 1.'

"Well I heard from a *United* flight attendant on the Carey bus that is was one of *their* crew members," Jeanna said. "She did say that she was based in LA."

"Maybe every airline's got one," Maurice said. "Fitting, they're all rumored to be from LA—home of Hollywood puffs," he sniffed. "If the companies are hebetudinous enough not to provide receipts, there will be theft."

I nodded in agreement. I had no idea what he'd just said.

Ellen, the oldest flight attendant I'd ever met, was looped. She had flown for twenty-three years! She was the most senior attendant at Kennedy—which meant that she only had to bid once. *One Time!* She had already told us that Lucille Ball was the rudest celebrity the skies had ever seen, but I'd already heard that one. And, that once she'd opened a lavatory door to find a woman combing her wig—which she had taken off—between her legs while seated on the toilet, so it looked as if she were combing pubic hair. I'd heard that one too.

I'd written both stories off as more silly, oft-repeated claims, the same way I'd doubted Captain Nichols when he told me, 'I let the first flight attendant land the airplane.' Airline personnel had great stories, but I was beginning to suspect that for each event worth telling, dozens of others claimed to have been there. I challenged Ellen, just as I had challenged Captain Nichols.

"You had Lucille Ball on a flight and she refused to talk to you?"

"That's right," she said.

"When was that?" I asked.

"Honey it was years ago," she said, waving her cigarette through the air.

"Who did the talking for her if she wouldn't say anything? Did she refuse drinks and a meal? Was she with the guy she married after Desi Arnaz? What's his name…"

Maurice shot me a 'shut-the-hell-up' look.

Now, several hours later, when she talked, she was louder than ever. "I was near the union office and heard Alex talking to Alonso about the results from a formal hearing for a steward—I mean, *Male Flight Attendant*, caught wearing a phony tester uniform…" she laughed hard. Her hysterics developed into full-blown cackling after several people around the room gasped. Everyone stared at Maurice.

"He was carrying a forged letter on company stationery," Ellen said, wiping her tears.

Danielle, who was sitting beside Maurice, grabbed a pillow and slugged him with it.

"Someone had to take a stand against the incondite clothing we suffer in," Maurice said.

Jeanna burst out loud. "You tell 'em Mo!"

Apparently, this was *Not* one of those oft-repeated 'stories.' But soon enough, I knew it was going to be.

"It's criminal, making us walk around in those mephitic rags. Why can't we drop the clown-like uniforms and return to the sharp military ensembles like TWA did?"

"Agreed," I said.

"Passengers would be less-questioning if we had a more professional appearance," Maurice continued. "We look like court jesters."

"I told Jim to tear that damn thing off me the last time I have to wear it," Danielle said. "It is time to replace it."

"And I can't wait," Jim said. "Bring it on Gateway."

Jeanna turned to Alex. "Did he get fired?"

"Thirty-day suspension," Alex said, turning toward Maurice.

"What?" Maurice asked her. "The way you're looking at me…"

"Flash at the sound of lies," she said quietly.

"I didn't lie to you," he said, "I just didn't *Tell* you."

"Beguilement is dishonesty; it's the same as a lie," she said.

"This union work is making you humorless Miss *Stormy eyes,"* Maurice said. "You used to be fun before you volunteered for that laborious rot." He looked around hopefully. "What do you call a crew of pilots tipping the layover hotel van driver? The March of

Dimes." His attempt at humor was followed by an uncomfortable silence. "Who wants Crème Brule?" He leapt to his feet. "I bought the cutest kitchen torch last week."

"Your hair is so beautiful," Danielle said, reaching out to stroke my locks.

"Yours is too; you changed it."

"Darling, this is a wig," she laughed. "Let me show you what I can do with yours. Have you ever French braided it?" Within minutes, I was seated with my back to Danielle as she twisted and plaited; we talked about Roman. "How long have you been sleeping with him," she asked me.

I swallowed. "People in New York are so… forward," I said.

"Why do you say this?" she spoke softly, gently.

"I don't mean anything bad by that, but I would never ask anyone that."

"How old are you Sherri?"

"Twenty."

"So young," she said, pulling my head back toward her and sweetly tapping my forehead with hers. "You have your whole life ahead of you."

Maurice and Sergio kept a large flat copper bowl on the floor filled with matchbooks and matchboxes from restaurants and hotels they'd visited. It was interesting—to sort through their collection, as I did now. Some were in languages I couldn't even guess. "Can I ask you a personal question?"

Danielle laughed. "You can ask me anything you like; I do all the time," she said.

"Is it… sometimes hard? Being a biracial couple?"

"Certainly," she said. "Not only is he white, but he's Jewish. Makes some of my people hot with fire inside. I have been sworn at and threatened, spit at, but… I cannot tell my heart what to do. True love can conquer lots—maybe not all, but we try, eh?"

190

Jeanna plopped down beside us. "That braiding is beautiful," she said. "Let me see how you do that."

"Me too," said Bonnie.

"Are you enjoying New York?" Danielle asked Bonnie, as the new-hire settled in beside us. "You've only been here a little while, eh?"

"It's fabulous," Bonnie said. "I'm so happy Gateway gave me wings to fly, but frankly nothing I've seen tops *This city!* The best part so far was seeing the Statue of Liberty."

I heard Jeanna suck in her breath. "The Statue of Liberty?" Jeanna asked. "When did you go there?"

"Last weekend." Bonnie talked with animation and smiled wide. "A date took me there; it was a surprise. We took the ferry…"

"Let me guess," Danielle interrupted. "You had your pit training, and Alonso asked you out?"

Bonnie sat back; I saw the expression of surprise on her face. "Did he tell you?" she asked Danielle. "He told me not to broadcast it around the base."

"That's what he always does," Danielle said. "Every time he welcomes a new training class he brings lunch, checks it out, and picks one of the girls. He takes them to Rockefeller Center then to see the film, *The New York Experience* at the McGraw Hill building—and finally onto the ferry to see the Statue of Liberty. When they sail back, he sets her where she can see the lights hit the statue to make a big impression, then he kisses her."

Bonnie gasped and then she laughed. "That's exactly what he did."

It was Jeanna's turn to race for the door and make a fast exit.

• *Dear FlightLog. WHAT is the matter with the men who work for this company? So far, Jeanna and I have met with terrible disappointment on both fronts – Cleveland and*

New York. Oddly enough, it hasn't been PILOTS like everyone warned us about! Although we haven't been out with any pilots yet – could they be any worse? On the jumbos, they're so senior – all about a hundred years old, so it's not like I've been tempted. Actually FlightLog, some of the flight attendants are old too! There's one who always goes to S & M's and she's 45; as old as my parents! She's been flying longer than I've been alive. Never been married. Maurice said that when he started eight years ago, the average seniority of a Gateway flight attendant was three years – he started two years after the government forbid the airlines for firing 'stewardesses' who got married. Now, eight years later, the average seniority is almost ten years. He says that since no one quits, the average goes up every year. It doesn't look like Jeanna and I will ever be off reserve – unless we want to transfer to Cleveland, where it's really junior.

On a happier note, everyone at Maurice's tonight made me feel good all over about the Pit. I loved hearing Maurice brag about me. I still feel as if I haven't had enough celebrities. Maurice and Alex have had 'repeats' – meaning they've had the same hot-shots twice or more. Alex has had Robert Redford on a flight four times. He's always going to Salt Lake City, she said. And Maurice has had

Richard Chamberlain twice – another one of my heart throbs. Of course, you know what Maurice has to say about him – yeah, right. Ok, so, I'd like a celebrity to recognize me. Like maybe... the Pope.

'Hey, Popey,' I'd say. 'How ya doing?' He'd give me a high-five.

'Yo, Sherri,' the Pope would say back, since we'd flown together so many times. 'What's up girlfriend?' Another high-five. The rest of the crew would look at me with awe and envy. 'She's so cool!' they'd think.

Chapter 16:

Take a Chance on Me

I WAS STRUGGLING TO LOOK PERKY, as I made my way down the terminal concourse at LaGuardia for an early 6 A.M. check in. It was cold outside. Wearing the uniform skirt was a terrible choice. I made a conscious decision that from now on, I would don my uniform slacks anytime it was twenty-five degrees or colder outside.

"Looking for operations?"

My heart raced; I turned and saw that impossibly breath-taking smile. And I saw him skip a step too. *He's glad to see me.* "Anderson Jeffries!" Suddenly, being perky was easy.

"Sherri Van Ness. Where you headed this morning?"

"Denver," I laughed. "That's all I know." We picked up speed. Just like the first time we'd met. Anderson held the gate at the front of the staircase leading to operations for me as I stepped down. And just like the first time we met, I popped out my retainer and pocketed it.

"You're flying with us girl," he said with a broad grin.

"Where are you laying over?" I asked him.

"Vegas."

Out of LaGuardia, Gateway flew the long, skinny, stretch-8 airplanes to Vegas—Jeanna had worked a lot of those flights and they usually stopped in Denver. This would be my first time there, if I was lucky enough to stay with the crew and not change in Denver for something else. Skip was at his desk when we opened the door to operations.

I practically ran to him. "Sherri Van Ness?"

He picked up my trip ID. "Laying over in Las Vegas," he said. "Thirty-two hours," he grinned. "Three-day trip with only two duty periods. Great trip for a reserve."

I clapped my hands together and spun around. My face said it all. Anderson gave me a wink. Then I saw Suzanne, the first flight attendant whom I had observed in training when I flew with Danny, the one I'd nicknamed, 'The Happy Hooker.'

"Well, hello there," she said. She remembered me too. "Looks like we're going to have an excellent crew today."

Narrow-body briefings at LaGuardia were nothing compared to what we went through at Kennedy. Suzanne told me I'd be filling in at the number five spot, working with *And* in the third galley, serving the second half of a long coach cabin, and our briefing was done. She had a helper up front—Patty, and two other flight attendants were working in the first half of coach—Nate and Ilsa. I would be with them for the whole three-day/two-duty period trip: La Guardia to Denver and Vegas, returning early the third morning, backtracking our route.

Anderson and I boarded together. I poked my head into the cockpit and said hello, promised to visit, passed the eight rows in first, the first-class galley, the first of the coach galleys, then took the long walk to the aft jumpseats. "Man, this airplane is long," I said.

"It's longer than the 10," Anderson said.

The rear of the plane had all kinds of closets. Passengers familiar with the configuration came straight back to hang their heavy garment bags and toss their suitcases onto one of the many shelves; they didn't even bother fighting the small spaces under the seats in front of them or in the overheads.

"Morning," many of them said.

Anderson was setting up the galley and the freshly brewed coffee smelled delicious. He moved fast as I gathered up a few magazines to pass out along with the coach menus. "Can you call up front and tell them we have seventy-eight meals back here?" he asked. "No specials."

"No specials?" I laughed with surprise. "We had twenty-six Kosher meals coming home from LA last week," I told him. "Plus five kid meals, one diabetic and three fruit plates."

Like the small 737s, the DC-8s did not have pre-set liquor carts; we had to set up a queen cart for drinks. For the first time in a long while, I wasn't in any hurry to get off the back jumpseat. *I'm here if you're all alone.* I felt giddy sitting so close to him; we relaxed from our brace positions just moments after takeoff, and grinned at each other.

"If you set up," he said, "I'll run." *Hopefully to me.*

I popped the insulated doors off the warming ovens that held our hot entrees. French toast and quiche. Each drawer held twelve entrees—like the 27s. Turning to the other side, I popped off two large doors that held the trays. Using my long hot pad, I stacked French toast entrees on the left trays, and quiche entrées on the right ones. Then I set two on the counter. Once we finished setting up the drink cart, Anderson took off for the middle of coach—row twenty-two. Nate and Ilsa would work from row twenty-one to the front of coach. Anderson would serve six rows, then I would take the cart up and start drinks in the same direction. When he finished running the meals, he would join me on the cart.

Each time Anderson rounded the corner into my galley, our eyes met. 'Two French toast and a quiche,' he'd say. I'd smile and set up some more trays. After ten trips, it was time for me to get the cart started. I grabbed a full coffee pot, started another one brewing and stepped back—right into Anderson who was racing into the galley. He put his hands out to steady my shoulders.

"I'm sorry," I said, my eyes wide with relief that hot coffee hadn't spilled all over.

Anderson waited an extra moment before releasing me. "You don't *Ever* have to be sorry for that," he said. *Thump thump.* Then he helped me take the drink cart forward.

"Scuse me Miss," a passenger said, waving me down. He frowned at the coach menu. "What's kwi-shee?" *Maurice would've had a field day with this guy.*

"It's quiche," I said with a grin. "It's good. Eggs and cheese baked in a pie crust. Today it's made with sausage and peppers." At row thirty, we ran out of the quiche; the passengers had liked my recommendation. It was absolutely a drag to run out of meal choices; there was usually at least one customer who would scowl and sulk; occasionally one would throw a fit—they were all suddenly allergic to the remaining choice—or had just as equally a valid complaint for the horrendous situation of being deprived of a choice.

"Here's what I did," Anderson told the people in the remaining rows. "I *Saved* you guys the French toast. I cooked it, and I know how to do breakfast. See my flying partner, there?" he pointed to me. "She burnt the quiche; thank goodness it's all gone." In my months of flying, I'd seen that passengers reacted with fewer outcries when male stewards were around, especially funny ones; therefore I appreciated when one or more were part of my crew. Anderson finished running the meals, then jumped on the aft side of our beverage cart to assist me.

"Could you hand me a ginger ale?" I asked him. "I'm out over here."

He handed me the can. I grabbed it, but he held on. "I can't let go," he said, winking again. *Thump thump. Thump thump.*

Fun. This trip felt so different than the last one I'd worked with him! In the last row, we encountered a young Marine, dressed up in his sharp uniform. "What can I get you to drink this morning?" I asked him.

"Could I get a beer ma'am?"

"Uh… are you… twenty-one?" It felt awful asking, not only because I wasn't twenty-one either, but I had a soft spot for military personnel; my father had flown for the Air Force. He started to shake his head, but Anderson put up his hand to quiet him.

"I'll get this one," Anderson said loudly, handing the marine a beer. "Cheers." As our passenger reached for his wallet, he added, "No charge sir."

Our ride was quiet and easy. After breakfast most of our passengers slept; we had time left over after cleaning everything up. "And," I asked, "should we head up front to help out?"

"What's this 'And' stuff?" he asked.

"I heard Suzanne call you that," I said.

"She's the only person who can," he feigned anger.

I felt a creep of jealousy rise. "Why so?"

"She's a special friend."

"Well so am I," I said boldly. "I'm going up front to help."

He was right behind me.

In Suzanne's galley, Anderson picked up a platter with sausages and steak pieces. He grabbed tongs and headed up to offer the meat asides.

"Have you started rolls?" I asked. Suzanne shook her head; she was running out trays and hot entrees. I grabbed the bread basket and headed up to row one. Patty followed with coffees. Unlike our customers in coach, this group was wide awake. They had a choice of cheese blintz or mushroom omelets. Each tray also had a beautiful bowl of sliced strawberries, served with sour cream and brown sugar. The first time I'd seen it, it seemed weird—until I'd tasted it. *Yum.* Once the trays were delivered, we went through with all the accompaniments of rolls, meat asides, more cocktails, mimosas, and more coffee.

"Could we get two more Bloody Marys here?" the man in 5C asked. With four of us up front, we got Suzanne's service completed in record time.

"Thanks you two," Suzanne said to us. "Could you do one more thing for me and call the cockpit?"

"I'll do it," I volunteered.

"Wonderful," Suzanne said. "And doesn't like…"

"I know," I said, picking up the phone at door 2Left.

"Tell them I have crew meals—Eggs Benedict, but I also have an omelet and a blintz left over if they'd rather have either of those."

"They'd like one Eggs Benedict with black coffee and an OJ; an omelet with tea—sweet and low and lemon, and apple juice if you've got it for now." The captain and the co-pilot never ate at the same time; we never delivered all three meals at once.

Suzanne threw away the cold rolls from the crew meal trays, and carefully replaced them with warm first-class bread from the oven. She added strawberry bowls with sour cream and brown sugar as well, so that it was just as nice as any leftover first-class meal.

"Will you take a few to go up and say hello?" she asked me. I nodded yes. "I know it seems old-fashioned," she said, "but be gracious—like them or not, our lives are in their hands and they are very good at what they do. I for one do my best to treat them respectfully because then I get it back."

"I remember," I told her. "I had an OB flight with you. My father flies for American; he's a captain," I said. "Kept that a secret."

"Then you know; hope he's one of the classy ones." She handed me a tray and carried another. First-class trays were bigger than coach ones; carrying one was enough. She kicked the bottom of the door twice, and I was in.

"Hot rolls," the copilot exclaimed gleefully. "Love flying with Suzanne! She takes such good care of us."

Walking back through first, I checked to see if anyone else needed their drinks refreshed, then slid into the first galley to get more Bloody Marys for the couple in row five.

"Sherri," Suzanne said as I mixed the cocktails. "Patty and I are going to catch a show tonight. We usually get in for free if we take our airline IDs," she said. "Wanna come?"

"Is Anderson going?"

"And?" Suzanne rolled her eyes. "He never goes," she said. "He goes *Jogging.*"

"You call him 'And'" I said. "I like that."

"Oh, we go *Way* back," she turned away, but not before I caught a thin smile.

I did *Not* like that.

"If Rich Little's in town, we'll try to see him," she said. "Just let me know; *gonna be around.*"

* * *

In Denver, a capacity crowd boarded our flight. It was easy to get a 'head' count when all the seats were taken. Full stretch-8: twenty-six passengers up front, 160 in the back, no laps, six attendants, three pilots. *'One hundred ninety-five souls aboard sir.'*

Suzanne grabbed the PA after the gate agent wished everyone a good flight. She played up her smoky voice. "Hello everyone, we'd like to make a destination check before we leave Denver this morning. Flight 711 is going to the city of—Lost… Wages…"

We were airborne. Time to: set up the queen cart, race through the cabin with drinks, strip the cart, figure the liquor sales, do the paperwork and the cash math, then start our descent. *Phew!* I did find a moment to hand out all the decks of cards onboard. These customers were ready. *To lose their shirts.* As for me—I didn't know what I was ready for.

"You can't go to Vegas and not gamble," And said as I stripped off my apron and stashed it near my new wheelies. I'd broken down and let Roman buy me a set.

"I'm not twenty-one," I told him. "I won't be able to."

"They won't card you if you're with me," he said. "You're a crew member so they'll assume you're old enough. Carry your uniform purse."

"I didn't bring a lot of money…"

"I'll ante up for you a couple of times. If you win, stay and play awhile. If not, then you can go. Fair enough?"

*   *   *

My room at the Flamingo Hilton was a mess. My suitcase seemed to have exploded; I didn't know what to wear. I'd tried on the cute skirt twice with two different tops, then decided it looked like I was trying too hard, so I'd put slacks on instead. I opted for a black Hawaiian top with bright red flowers. Above the black slacks with my dark hair, it looked smashing. Heels or flats? I ran in and out of the bathroom touching up my makeup while trying on my shoes. I wanted to look absolutely fantastic without looking like I'd *Tried* to. You know, like when And might say, 'you look fantastic,' I could feign complete surprise and say, 'these old things?'

As soon as the elevator door opened, I caught his eye. He stood up from a sofa in the lobby and touched his heart. "Oh girl," he shook his head. *Thumpie thump thump.*

I beamed; it was impossible not to. When he stepped beside me, he offered his arm and I took it. *It felt like a date. Take a chance on me boy.* We stepped out into the mild, pleasant breeze, and headed across the street toward Caesars Palace.

"This is where I come to bet games," And explained. "You like football, right?" At the counter, Anderson grabbed some strip cards.

"In this game, Dallas is favored by fourteen points," he explained. "If you bet Dallas, they must win by at least that," if you bet on this team they don't have to win," he said. "As long as they lose by thirteen points or less, you're covered."

"So, if I think they're going to lose, but just by just a few points…"

"You bet on them. Now, if you want to bet another game or two, you can bet each one separately or you can parley your bets. If they all win, you take home substantially more; if only one loses however, you lose all the money you've put down."

"Like the trifecta!" I exclaimed, remembering Checker's bets at Belmont.

The possibilities for betting games were endless. I made some selections for games that weekend, placed my bets and collected my receipt stubs.

"I'm ready for the weekend," I said. "It'll be different watching now." And made several bets; many were based on what he believed Walter Payton's performance would be; total yards rushing, receiving, number of touchdowns. He looked pleased.

"You're a 'Sweetness' fan," I stated with approval.

"You do know football," he grinned. "He's my favorite. Love the Bears. I practically grew up in Chicago…"

"Yes," I said. "Finally! Someone I can brag to who will be impressed!"

"What?"

"I had 'Lake Effect' on a flight to the West Coast!"

"What was he like?"

"Perfectly perfect." We talked football until Anderson dragged me into another casino.

"Now," he started. "Would you like to begin your gambling education with Blackjack or with Craps?"

We passed a small lounge. A trio of singers impersonated Diana Ross and the Supremes.

I sang along. "From this old world, I try to hide my face, but from this loneliness, there's no hiding place."

And arched an eyebrow. "Didn't know folks listened to Soul music in Nebraska," he said. "You must have loved the Supremes; that wasn't one of their biggest hits."

"Kansas, and I did. Loved Dianna Ross; still do."

"Football and Motown."

"We *All* grew up listening to the Supremes. I'm not just some dumb white girl you know."

That one made him double over. "You sure?"

"Shut up."

"Can I ask you a personal question?"

"You can…" I said, "don't know if I'll answer."

"You ever date a brother?"

I placed my hands back around his arm and asked, "Have you?"

"Ouch! Take back what I said about being sweet."

Blackjack at the Stardust. The dealer kindly tolerated my naiveté. I asked And what to do on every hand. The dealer showed a seven. I had a King and a three. It was my turn.

"Always assume the dealer has a ten," And said. "You should hit."

"Hit!" I shouted. The dealer gave me a six. *Nineteen.* And was right; the dealer had seventeen and I won. "I've won thirteen dollars," I bragged. Behind us was a big commotion at what looked like a pool table. Many people surrounded it; I could see that they were shooting dice. "I want to play that," I told And.

"You in?" the blackjack dealer asked.

"We're out." Anderson collected our chips. He put three into the dealer's tip jar. "Thank you," he said, before racing up beside me.

"You like Billie Holliday?" And asked out of nowhere.

"Don't appreciate jazz; I don't get it."

"Good enough that you knew that much."

"She always wore a gardenia in her hair," I looked at him with wide eyes. "I liked that. Pretty lady. I know *That* because Diana Ross played her in *Lady Sings the Blues.*"

And pointed to the sign on the table and read aloud: "'Five dollar minimum.' High stakes here. We can play cautiously or go downtown where they have fifty cent tables. It's a lot more fun." He looped his arm into mine again and dragged me away.

In the cab, I asked. "What if I win my strip cards? How will I collect my money?"

"I'm flying here all month," he said. "I could pick up your winnings… or… you could fly out. You're with the airlines now; ride the jump seat or take a pass. Could come out with us on one of our trips."

I took a deep breath. *When I dream I'm alone with you it's magic.* I blushed but looked into his eyes anyway. He smiled so pretty.

"Always blush so easily?"

I nodded. This time I looked away and stroked my collarbone.

"Sensitive about it?"

"Yep."

"Sensitive about how you rub your collarbones when you get nervous too?"

I stopped. No one had ever asked me that. I didn't even know I'd done it. "I wasn't before, but I am now!"

He laughed and that made me laugh too. *Geez!* I had a nervous tic now; one more thing to brood about.

*   *   *

"The basics in Craps are simple," he yelled above the boisterous Golden Nugget Casino crowd. "You can make the game harder with other wagers but basically, a player throws the dice to establish a number. They continue to roll until they hit that same number. That's a win. Or they crap out by throwing a seven. If the thrower wins a round, he throws again until he loses the dice."

A new player was set to go. People all around the table put chips on the 'Come' line. He threw a seven and most of them cheered wildly.

"Wait," I said. "I thought seven was bad."

"Unless you throw a seven *First;* then it's an automatic win," he explained.

"So he won? Just like that?"

"Yep, so did we."

The roller threw an eight. He directed one of the pit guys to put money on the 'Hard' eight.

"What's that?" I asked.

"The hard eight," And said. "He's betting that the dice will come up with two fours before it comes up with a seven and a one, a six and a two, or a five and a three. He can lose that bet, but it won't affect his main bet."

"What are the odds?" I asked.

"Pays eight to one. It's not a good bet really…"

"Two on the hard eight," I shouted, handing over four fifty cent chips.

And just like that, two fours came up.

"I just won sixteen bucks!"

And laughed and shook his head.

I got the dice, threw a nine, looked at And.

"Now, just throw a nine again, before you-know-what," he said. "Ok, doll?"

I threw a ten. "My roommate calls me that," I said.

"Who's your roommate?"

"Alex Albright."

I threw a six as Anderson whistled.

"You know her?"

"We only have three hundred flight attendants in New York Sherri," he said. "Course I know her."

After several more tosses, I hit the nine and couldn't contain myself; I gave Anderson a happy hug. We locked eyes just a little too long.

"Save it for later you two," a scruffy old gambler on the other side of the table said. "Lady's lucky; let her throw."

And had some luck with the dice as well. He was looking for a five.

"Two on the hard eight!" I cried out. "No—the hard six! I mean the hard ten!"

The dealer gave me an unpleasant look.

"Ok really," I blurted out. "The hard six; sorry."

Anderson threw two threes, and I went ballistic.

"Wanna *just talk* for a bit," he asked after we'd left the casino. We were walking in the direction of our hotel; it was far, but we didn't care. *"We can listen to some music, go dancing...* what do you want to do?"

We'd made our way into a restaurant; I'd admitted to Anderson that I was hungry. Leaning back in the red plastic booth, I thought about how much fun we were having. Anderson excused himself. I was counting my winnings with relish. *Over fifty dollars!* When he returned, he held out a white gardenia.

"Ah," I held it close and inhaled its wonderful aroma. "Beautiful," I cooed, as he sat down. "Thank you, And."

"Sure don't need anything to make you look finer," he said. "Thought you'd like it."

Holding it up to my right ear I asked, "So Mr. Hawaii; is this the right side? To let 'em know I'm available?"

"How do you know about that?" he asked.

"I read!" He really did think I was just a dumb girl. "And?" My thoughts were wandering. *Get to know you better.* "Did you mean what you said earlier?"

"What'd I say?"

"About me coming out here later? With your crew... you know you never called me..."

The waitress appeared abruptly and practically threw two menus at us. I looked up at her with surprise.

"Water?" she asked, but her tone was stern.

"Yes please, and can I..."

Before I finished, she turned away. Anderson watched her closely. When she returned, she slammed down two plastic water cups; mine spilled a little. "Ready to order?" Her face was rigid; cold.

"We're leaving," Anderson said, standing up.

"What's wrong?" I fumbled for my purse. He waited, took my arm, and led me out. I could tell he was breathing hard. Outside, I pulled my arm away. "What is it?"

"She's mad," he said, gesturing with his head toward the restaurant—toward the waitress. "Cause we're together."

"What do you mean?" I asked.

"Come on Sherri; do I have to spell it out?" He put his hands in his pockets and turned away for a moment. Then he turned back around. "I'm black," he said quietly, but I could see he wanted to yell. "With a white girl."

I froze and looked into the glass front of the restaurant's large window. The waitress was glaring at us. "Oh my God; I never thought… We're friends…"

"You want to go back and explain that to her? Apologize for letting her think there might be something more?" This time, he couldn't hide his anger.

I wanted to cry. *Dumb white girl Sherri.* "No," I whispered. "It's none of her business. I'm sorry I'm really sorry. I'm not used to…"

"People hating you because of your color?"

"Let's go somewhere else," I said.

"I'm done," he said. "Going back to the hotel."

"No, come on; you said you were hungry too! Don't let her ruin it," I pleaded.

"Ruin what?"

"I've never had so much fun on a layover. Please? I know you fly here a lot, but haven't you had a wonderful time? With me? Let's get a bite at least before we go back."

We walked in silence. *You want me to leave it there, afraid of a love affair, but I think you know…*

"You two seem so different," Anderson suddenly said out of nowhere. "Heard Alex was a fag-hag."

"What is a *fag-hag?*" I asked.

"Chick who hangs with gay dudes."

"Then I'm one too," I said defensively. "You just got mad about hateful behavior, now you're using ugly words. *Fag?* Come on! I love Maurice; I know you know who he is."

"Everyone knows Maurice," he admitted.

"Why would you care who she hangs out with," I said. "I'm sure you think she's just as gorgeous as everyone else does anyway."

"I do," he said. "Not my type, but she's a looker all right."

"What is your type?"

He stopped. "You're close," he teased.

I bent over and laughed. "Guess I walked into that one."

"I did call you."

"When?" I was surprised, and felt myself flush.

"I don't know, you never picked up," he said.

"You mean, *we* never picked up? Alex would have told me if you'd called; she's not the forgetful, scatter-brained type."

"Right, yeah," he agreed. "Neither one of you ever picked up."

We stepped inside the Flamingo Hilton's doors.

"Are you off Sunday? Gonna watch football?" I asked. *I'm the first in line.*

"Of course; and I am off. Go to a neighborhood bar called 'Nicks.' Fun crowd."

"If I fly and get home early enough, could I watch the games with you?"

"You could," he said slowly. "There aren't a whole lot of white people there."

"I don't care," I said. "Uh… is it dangerous?"

He laughed out loud. I could tell it felt good for him to release the tension. "Ain't Harlem if that's what you mean."

"Hey, you guys," Suzanne and Patty had just entered the lobby as well. "Have fun?"

"Yes!" I exclaimed. "I won fifty dollars!"

Suzanne held out a folded piece of paper for me. "Someone's looking for you," she said. "I think his name is Roman?"

"Roman's… *Here?" Thump… no, gulp!*

"We were getting ready to leave and I heard him ask for you at the front desk," she said. "Think he was trying to surprise you; they wouldn't give him your room number of course, but I told him I could probably get a message to you before you got back."

210

From the look on her face, I could see that she knew I was upset.

Anderson backed up toward the elevators. "Well ladies; it's time for me to retire." He pursed his lips, gave a short wave and left.

"Sherri?" Suzanne started, "I'm sorry; is this a problem?"

"No, *No!* It's fine… I'm fine. Did he tell you where he was?"

"The Desert Inn," she said. "Number's on the note."

Upstairs, I stared at the red roses from Roman on the desk, and listened to him on the other end of the phone. "I wanted to surprise you," he said.

I pulled the coiling white telephone cord as far as I possibly could while pacing around the bed. "I didn't even know I'd be in Vegas tonight! How the hell did *You* find out? How did you know what our layover hotel was?" I was fire-engine red and mad as a hornet.

"You sound angry," he said. "I don't think I've ever heard you swear before. You alright? Let me come over and pick you up."

"Answer me! *How* did you know?"

"I'll tell you all about it when I get…"

"*What* happened Roman?"

"I made some phone calls, that's all. Now, you tell me; who's Anderson?"

Silence.

"Sherri?"

"He's a steward…" I said. "Probably gay."

In the bathroom I looked at myself in the mirror for a long time. My face was still crimson. Picking up my sweater, I started out. Then I turned back, took the flower out of my hair and tossed it into the waste basket. That hadn't helped; it made me feel worse. I retrieved it and set it in one of the bathroom drinking glasses filled with water before leaving my room.

Chapter 17:

Viva Las Vegas

Roman and I stayed up late and witnessed the night turn into daybreak. We grabbed a quick nap at his hotel before heading down for a late breakfast. "I have all day," I told him, still hung-over from all my free drinks the night before. "What's your schedule?"

"I'm taking most of the day off," he said. "Have an afternoon meeting with an agency here. No rush. I'll fly back to LA tomorrow after you leave."

"Let's go back to my hotel," I said. "I need a change of clothes."

Roman packed a day-bag and we headed over to the Flamingo. He pulled me toward the Casino area. "Let's see what you learned." Picking up two dice at an empty table, he asked for change then put two five-dollar chips on the Pass Line and threw a twelve. *Crap out.*

"Sorry," I said, taking a twenty dollar bill out of my purse to exchange for chips. I let Roman throw again; he tossed a six.

"Two on the Come Line," I said, putting a couple of one-dollar chips down. Roman threw a nine. "I'll take odds on that," I told the dealer, tossing down six more chips. "Three-to-one odds here," I said. "Nice."

"See you've got the hang of it a bit," Roman said; he sounded irritated. "You don't have to announce you're putting money on the Come Line. They'll figure it out Sherri."

"We found a place last night with a fifty cent minimum," I told him, ignoring his tone. "It was easy to learn that way; it's all about the odds."

Roman glowered at me. "What's your max?" he asked the pit boss.

"One hundred."

He took out a wad of cash and threw several C notes down. "Two of those on the Come Line."

"Strong heart, nerves of steel," I said, leaning over the table. *Gotta whole lot of money that's ready to burn.* "You don't have to announce your bet Roman; they'll figure it out."

His throws were marvelous; people gathered; within a few minutes, he was up a grand; the chips were stacking up.

"Lady Luck," Roman sang a bit, *"please let the dice stay hot."*

He won $4000 in twenty minutes. By the time he gathered up his winnings, a crowd had packed around the table. The pit boss and croupiers pushed others trying to nudge themselves tableside away. Those lucky enough to get in early cheered, high-fived, laughed, ordered free drinks, tossed chips on the Pass Line, the Come Line, all the other bets, and enjoyed themselves. This was what novices dreamed Vegas would be like—throw well, win money, look like a movie star, be a beautiful couple and be a hero for everyone at the table—and—take money from the too-serious, rumored-to-be-mob-affiliated casinos. *So… why am I not having fun?*

Roman grabbed my face and kissed me hard on the mouth. *"Gonna set my soul on fire.* What luck you brought me. We're done here," he said, giving the crowd an appreciative 'I did it' smile. "Good luck everyone." He slipped his arm around my shoulder.

"What's my girl want to do now?" He snuggled close to me. *Winner. He feels like a big-shot. He was breathing hard and keeping me close. I could feel his excitement. Let him have this moment,* I thought.

"Let's go for a swim," I said, giving him my best 'I adore you' look. It was unseasonably warm that day. "That will cool us off."

The cocktail waitress, who was as good looking as anyone ever—handed me my gratis screwdriver and a free pack of Merits—my new brand—with a splashy display of pearly-whites. *A thousand pretty women here.* 'Smile for the customers,' I could imagine her bosses saying. I took a ten-dollar chip from Roman's stash and put in on her tray. She gave me a sweet nod and set off delivering the rest of her drinks. I watched her wiggle away in her oh-so high heels and hot pants. *You need flat shoes.* Like that would be a fight these servers could ever win. I bet she had to 'weigh in' once a month like I did; maybe once a week. *That wager would be good odds.*

I wasn't a great swimmer; I didn't glide along the surface like Mark Spitz, breathing in graceful tempo with barely a lift of the chin—but I cherished swimming under water and pretending to be a mermaid. The pools in Vegas didn't require bathing caps like the ones back home, so deep I went, with my tresses dancing behind me. What a release! And even though I wasn't exactly thrilled that I was wearing a size eight instead of a size four or six, I certainly felt attractive enough in my sexy cut-outs-everywhere one-piece. Roman had plopped himself down on a chaise beside Suzanne and Patty. I'd brought up his hot streak at the tables and they'd reacted with appreciative enthusiasm. I dove in as he offered them a round of drinks.

Suzanne was the best, recognizing that I just wanted to get away. She patted the empty chaise beside her and said to Roman, "Hey big spender; why don't you sit down and spend a little dime on me?"

I crisscrossed the bottom of the pool only coming up for air as needed. Taking deep gulps, I held my breath and sank into the depths as if pearl diving. At each resurfacing, I checked to make sure Roman's ego was still being adequately stroked. Before my next plunge, I saw a fit, dark-skinned man in loose swimming trunks and metallic sunglasses, walking toward the pool. *Anderson Jeffries*. He carried his towel and shirt with an air of confidence.

"Well look who's here?" Patty called from her lounge chair. "Never seen *You* poolside before."

Anderson grinned. He could hear her from across the deck. Two long-limbed beauties passed him, going in the opposite direction. Their bathing suits couldn't have been more than twenty square inches of fabric; each wore heels and had gold chains around their waists. They looked like they were getting ready for a magazine shoot, or off to service Hugh Hefner. Anderson did a double take, acting as if he was discombobulated with distraction, and had lost his balance from watching. He let his shirt and towel drop to the ground and then he fell into the pool. The girls, turning, laughed and smiled. They even waved at him. *Bitches.*

He swam over to me. Sputtering and wiping water off his face, he said, "Show girls always liven up the pool."

I splashed him and giggled. I got it; he'd done it on purpose to get near me in the water. "You look like you're a good swimmer," I said with relief. The disappointment I'd felt from him last night seem to have dissipated. In no time, he was giving me pointers. I gauged Roman's reactions from quick sideway glances. His eyes were glued on us.

"Your face is tilted too high," Anderson said. "Look down so you can see the bottom of the pool. It'll increase your speed."

I swam in small circles, practicing.

"Ready for a drink yet?" Roman called out.

"No," I told him. "Come on in; the water feels great!"

He surprised me by diving in. After a quick introduction, we watched Anderson take off in a smooth front crawl. Roman followed—suddenly they were swimming laps together. They picked up speed. I got out and dried off beside Patty and Suzanne. We watched the two of them compete while trying to pretend they weren't competing.

"And is training for some extreme athletic event," Suzanne said. "Don't think Roman's got a chance of keeping up with him," she said.

"He's from LA; thinks he's a great swimmer," I said.

"Anderson spent half his childhood in Hawaii; he's headed back there for that race."

"What race?" I asked.

"It's called the Ironman. You swim in the ocean—I don't know how far, then you bike a hundred miles, and then, you run a full marathon—whatever that is. It's crazy."

"It's in Hawaii?" I asked.

"Yes, they held it in Kona at the first of the year and they're going to do it annually. That's why we never see him," Suzanne said. "He's always training."

"Interesting guy," Patty said. "He visits ruins, goes to the Galapagos or Tibet," she said. "Everyone else goes to London, Paris or Munich."

"Or nowhere at all," Suzanne countered.

Yes, an interesting guy. Whom I'm interested in.

Anderson executed a perfect flip turn, passing Roman going in the other direction. He finished easily in the lead and stood up at the shallow end. Roman gasped when he got back beside him. He was panting.

"Let me know when you're warmed up," Anderson said. "We can pace each other." He dove forward and swam away effortlessly.

Roman got out. "I thought blacks were lousy swimmers," he mumbled.

"He's Hawaiian," I said. Suzanne gave me an amused look. I picked up a magazine.

"Most macho gay dude I've ever seen," Roman added.

"He's not gay," Suzanne tskd. "Trust me, you can take my word for it."

We all looked at her; Suzanne grinned and took a sip of her fancy cocktail. Patty laughed.

"I can tell you two are flight attendants," said a young man walking past us making his way over to a group nearby. My guess was that they were flight attendants too—probably from another carrier. "You're probably not," he said to me.

"How can you tell?" Suzanne asked.

"By the bruises you have on your right thighs from your wheelies," he said.

We all laughed—it was true. Our metal wheelies had hard edges when we hooked them up to our suitcases. The cases were too big to roll down the aisles so we carried them beside us getting on and off planes. The wheelie's hard edges banged into the sides of our legs. My bruises weren't pronounced yet, because I hadn't been using wheelies that long.

The group grew loud. I strained to hear the discussion; something was terribly wrong all of a sudden. "What did he say?" I asked Patty, who was seated closest to the group.

"The Mayor of San Francisco was shot," she said. "Someone else was killed too."

*   *   *

Early the next morning, in the hotel van taking us to the airport, we met the pilots who were flying us to Denver. Based in San Francisco, they were going to sit for three hours before heading home.

Suzanne was chatty and friendly, telling them we only had thirty minutes before our flight continued on to LaGuardia. "I'm sorry gentlemen," she said. "We're always oversold and since the flight is so short, no one sleeps—especially up front. It's a beverage-only service—thank goodness. I'll get you drinks before take-off, but once we're airborne, I won't have time to check back on you."

"We understand," said the second officer. "Coffee before takeoff would be perfect. It's all we need; plenty of time in Denver to grab a bite. Did you guys see the news? The mayor of San Francisco was shot and killed yesterday," he told us.

"Along with that fruitcake supervisor, 'Milk,'" said the captain.

"Fruitcake?" Patty repeated in a disapproving tone.

"Yeah, Fruitcake," the captain said again, turning around from the front seat of the van to glare at Patty. "He was a Queer!" He turned back away. "What did they expect? They elect an open homosexual who campaigned on *Gay Rights*—no wonder he got shot."

"Actually," Suzanne said. "Supervisor Harvey Milks' campaign was more about advancing childcare, providing more low-rent housing in a city that probably has higher rents than New York, and opening a civilian police review board. I followed it in the Times."

"He got elected because he was a fag in a fag-loving town," the captain said.

The rest of the ride to the airport was quiet.

We boarded the plane and the agent sent the first few passengers down. Ilsa made her way to the door and collected tickets while Nate set up their galley. 'I'd rather not take tickets and be near that captain,' I'd heard him say.

Anderson stayed quiet. When I spoke, he'd respond with an 'um' or a half-smile, then quickly look away or busy himself with something else. He'd been so nice at the pool but this... this was different than two days ago when we'd flirted like hell, enjoying the moments when our arms and legs touched on the jumpseat. Trying to get reactions from him, I talked too much. My discomfort grew.

We landed quickly. Per our contract, on 'through' flights we tidied the cabin. I began collecting voluminous piles of newspapers as soon as the last of passengers started up the aisle. The assassination in San Francisco was front-page news. Up front, I plopped down into 5B, across from Suzanne's galley.

"You know, I noticed a smell," Suzanne said, opening one of the warming ovens. She pulled out a foil packet and discovered sweet rolls inside. "I didn't know these were here," she said. "Usually, they change my galley in Vegas—must have forgotten to unload the oven drawers." She held out the packet so that I could grab a roll. She offered some to Ilsa, Nate, and Patty just as the cockpit crew exited the cockpit. Anderson had made his way into first class as well and looked as if he was going to take a seat in the row behind me.

"Thanks for the coffees," the deplaning captain said. I could see his eyes take everything in. Suzanne holding sweet rolls and the rest of us eating or reaching for them. "Thought you said there wasn't anything to eat on this flight," he said abruptly.

Suzanne put up her free hand. "I did not know these were here. Must be leftovers from a previous flight…"

Anderson pushed his way in front of her. "If she told you there wasn't anything, then that's what she thought," he said.

Silence.

"Ain't her job to check the ovens on a flight with no meal service," Anderson said, louder than before. "Thought you had three hours here; what's the matter, can't afford breakfast?"

Suzanne stepped in front of Anderson. "We had a full, quick flight. I did not have time for anything but my service." She was covering the rolls with the foil as she spoke. "If you want these," she held out the packet, "they're yours."

The captain glared at her. "Just asking for a little courtesy," he said.

"She's given you that pal," Anderson said. "She's not getting it back."

The gate agent stepped on. "Ready for boarding?"

Fortunately, we had a wonderful cockpit crew taking us back to LaGuardia. Since Anderson wasn't talking to me, I headed into the cockpit with drinks after the meal service, had a few cigarettes and chatted. The second officer was young, probably the youngest pilot I'd flown with. Our pilots all had similar backgrounds. They'd flown for the Navy, Marine Corps or the Air Force, then had come to work for the airlines. They couldn't be older than thirty-five at hiring, and they were almost always white males.

"What's your name?" I asked the cute engineer/second officer.

He beamed. "Eric."

"How long have you been flying?" I asked. "Everybody always asks me that first."

"Four months."

"You're junior to me," I teased.

The captain and the co-pilot/first officer were friends. They told me that no matter what I'd heard, pilots believed in UFOs. "When you sit in this chair," the captain said, "year after year, and see unexplainable things in those skies that aren't on the radar, you become a believer."

I made a mental note to ask Sean about it. He'd never said anything about that.

The co-pilot nodded. He had eaten, and now the captain and Eric were hungry, so I went back into Suzanne's galley to get their meals. "You ok?" I asked her.

"Sure, go back," she said.

"Wonder how And's doing," I asked.

"He's fine," she said. "I just took him a salad; he's eating. Your passengers are resting. They're tired and hungover. Go."

Eric and I talked about relationships and the strain of airline work as junior employees. His girlfriend was having a hard time dealing with him being on reserve, having to go at a moment's notice and never having weekends off. "Now I get why so many airline people date airline people," he said. "They understand; others don't."

I talked about Roman, my likes, dislikes and doubts—such as his age.

"Does anyone ever tell you that you look like Marie Osmond?"

I smiled, nodded. "Heard that a couple of times since I started flying. Wish I could sing like she does." *Not sure I want to be a Mormon, though.*

"Would you like to go get a cup of coffee or a drink sometime?" he asked.

"I would," I said honestly, "but I'm…"

"Me too," he said. "Didn't mean a date, just to talk. You're so nice and easy to talk to." His number had a 303 area code; he was in Denver. I promised to call if I was ever in town.

"What about tonight?" he asked, his eyes were hopeful.

"I don't know…" I started.

"When you're ready," he smiled. "Don't forget me."

Back in the cabin, I walked into a lively debate about male sex symbols. Ilsa and Nate had joined the first-class girls; And was still alone in the back.

"I don't flip for celebrities anymore," Suzanne said. "But if I had *Him* on a flight—he would not be safe."

"Who?" I asked.

"The one they *Almost* picked for the next James Bond," she said. "Ray Rawls Paxton."

"No one beats Sean Connery," Patty said.

"Every girl in the world loves him," Nate complained.

We nodded; it was true.

Passengers were starting to stir; I grabbed some magazines. Finding plenty of game kits and toy wings, I handed them out too. A cute girl of about eight pulled on my skirt hem.

I bent down so I could look her in the eye; passengers liked that—it was more personable and gave us a modicum of privacy. "Yes?" I asked her.

Anderson was approaching, checking on the cabin. He stopped when he got to us.

"I want to be a stewardess when I grow up," she told me.

"When I was your age, I wanted the same thing," I told her. "We're called Flight Attendants now," I said, pointing to Anderson. "And I know that you're going to be a very good one. Would you like to hand out some pillows? I think some of the other passengers would really like to sleep."

Her eyes went wide; she looked at her mother who gave her a smile and a nod of permission.

"Put your wings on first," Anderson said, taking her pin and putting it above her heart. "What's your name little helper?"

Later in the galley, Anderson commended me. "That was cute, letting that little girl help. You're a good flight attendant. Not just a sweet thing but a worker; I've noticed. If you're in front you think about coach, if you're in coach you think about the front. Take care of your passengers, co-workers and the cockpit," he said, rolling his eyes with a grin.

"Thank you And," I said. "Means a lot to me."

"I'm a pretty good judge of character," he said. "Think I've got you pegged—except for one thing."

"Men always think they're such good judges of character," I teased. "Especially mine."

"Like Roman?" he asked.

I looked at him and waited.

"Not sure about him," he said. "Roman. I can tell you're not sure either; are you? I know I should be careful, after I jumped to conclusions about your dad. I'm still sorry about that, but I like you; are you two serious?"

"Don't know him that well yet," I said. "He lives in LA. I don't see him very often."

Things got quiet again. Too quiet. I stood and stared out the exit door at 3Left for a long, long, time. The dark sky was still; it didn't seem as if we were moving or as if anything else was out there, except for a clear white light. I watched it for minutes; it was right there—it wasn't anything on the ground, and it wasn't a plane. Blinking to make sure my vision was clear, I kept staring; there was something out there! My face dropped. Chills went through me; I could just imagine some kind of higher power watching us and sensing my distress.

"And?" I whispered, not daring to take my eyes off the light. "What's up?"

"What… is that?" I pointed to it but I didn't move. My stomach felt queer, I could hear my breathing.

He put his face to the window. I saw him frown, look, and study the object hard. "That," he said. "Is the light at the end of the wing."

We burst out laughing. "I thought…"

"I know you did," he laughed. "When it's this dark and you can't make out the wing's edges, it's easy to think it's something else."

After landing, we stood up and handed out the luggage and coats passengers had stored in the back closets. I didn't have much time left. The mood was still light from my non-UFO sighting;

I went for it. "Want to watch the games together on Sunday? It would be fun, since we both have bets on the game."

"Aren't a lot of white people in my neighborhood," he said. "You might be nervous getting yourself there."

"You have a car," I said boldly. "You could… pick me up? You've offered me rides before." *Did I just say that?* I did a quick head bob for laughs.

"Roman wouldn't like that." Anderson smiled back—like this was such a fun joke. "See, I don't pick up *Friends* in the city to drive them to Queens," he said. "I pick up dates." He stopped what he was doing and looked right at me. "Is this a date?"

- *Dear FlightLog; I had my first layover in Las Vegas. 'Lost Wages' as Suzanne says. And, I was with Anderson Jeffries – the guy who helped me with the scale and helped me when I worked in the pit. We had such a good time working together and then again on our layover. He taught me how to play Blackjack, Craps and how to bet strip cards, which I'd never heard of before. I was ready to marry him then Roman showed up. I didn't even know I was going to be there – he's got a friend at Gateway that's feeding him information. That's private, isn't it? That person could get fired; when I tell Alex, she's going to have a fit. Anyway, Roman and I did have a good time but I was cross with him for a while. Said he'd call early tonight but he hasn't. He was aggressive at the Crap tables. Dropped several hundred, the dice*

were hot, he kept a lot of money on the table and he won
like $4000.00. Like a movie; I know, I say that a lot.
When I mentioned that And and I had found a low-minimum
table, Roman had to bet the max — that's why he won so
much — he had to make the point: that he's got bucks but
And is just a flight attendant. Mean, huh? I threw a few
times but the dice were hotter in his hands. I felt weird,
being there with him when my flight crew was around.
Not sure why. Then he tried to act all macho in the pool,
tried to outswim Anderson, which was laughable. We had
a two-night layover. The second night we saw Rich Little
at Suzanne's (aka the Happy Hooker's) urging. Danny
and I flew with her in training. Rich was fantastic. His
impersonation of Richard Nixon was hilarious. That was
fun... today we were tired. We started early and a stupid
cockpit crew ruined our morning — the captain made awful
remarks about the shooting and the mayor of SFO getting
killed — then he was mad that Suzanne didn't find out
there were leftover sweet rolls in the galley. I do get
why so many flight attendants can't stand pilots. Some are
arrogant sons-of-bitches who think they're God; so, when
I'm flying with someone like Anderson who really hates
them, it infuriates me when they're rude and obnoxious and
live up to their bad reputations. Then there are nice ones,
like Eric. I met him today; he's based in Denver, and you

know what? I almost stepped out on Roman again tonight by going out with him! Eric stays in the cockpit and does his job – he doesn't come into the cabin and strut or hang out in the galley trying to pick up flight attendants. He's smart, attractive, hard-working and he isn't looking around the corner to see if he can pick up some new-hire or some pilot-infatuated passenger. I really liked him. He's at the Sheraton right now and I've half a mind to call him and meet him for a drink. Alex isn't home, I haven't heard from Jeanna or Maurice, and Anderson doesn't want to see me. I practically threw myself at him by ASKING him to pick me up this weekend to watch football; why can't we just be 'friends?' Why does it have to be a 'date?' You know what FlightLog? I'm calling Eric. After all the fun in Vegas, I'm charged up for more. I live in New York now; I'm NOT putting on slippers and curling up with a magazine and a lousy cup of tepid tea. Why shouldn't I have a world of casual friends and acquaintances like everyone else? I need to go and enjoy some more of his company. I am going to make his night by calling his hotel room right now, and saying: 'you still up for getting that drink?' He will jump for joy. I will wear my hair down, he'll flip – they always do, and if nothing else, we will catch peoples' eyes as a good-looking couple and we will LAUGH!! Good night FlightLog! Don't wait up for me!

But when the hotel operator rang his room, he didn't answer. I didn't leave a message. I headed out into the cold New York night alone.

Chapter 18

What Are You Doing New Year's Eve?

"BOB KEESHAN IS ON OUR flight today," I exclaimed with delight. This was my first 'official' briefing as a first flight attendant. I'd flown 'A' several times, but only on a miscellaneous leg here and there—never on an entire trip with the same crew. Today that would change. The 'A' was on sick list; it was a three-day trip out of LaGuardia with layovers in Atlanta and Boise. Four legs the first day, five the second, and three the last; I would be the 'First' on every leg. This time, I was ready, unlike my first occurrence working in the pit.

"Who's Bob Keeshan?" Tabatha, one of the junior girls asked me. We were working a standard-8; I had a regular crew of three others with me. The aircraft was cute. There were booths in front and in back—the front booth was a lounge for first class; the back booth was a lounge for coach. As crew members, they were where we plopped ourselves down to eat and strew out all of our stuff.

"Captain Kangaroo," I said.

"I love him!" Tabatha said.

"Me too," I said. *Maybe I'm loving too many guys right now.*

I continued my spiel. "Please direct all calls to the cockpit through me. It's a small plane but they get frustrated if they receive calls asking for something they just answered to. I appreciate your cooperation on this in advance. We have two unaccompanied minors going to Atlanta," I said. "Anyone interested in handling them?"

"I'll do it," Kurt said. "I'll pass out all the stuff, check their parents' ID's... I know the drill. I was a child of divorce," he explained. "I flew back and forth every summer and Christmas holiday between Mom and Dad; I know what it's like."

"Thanks; ask for help if you need it," I said. "We're not doing a full meal service in coach—just snack trays and cocktails on this first leg, but I am doing a full service up front. If one of you will help me get the entrées out, I can do the rest and I'll start second coffees in back as soon as everyone in first is eating."

"I'm sitting up there with you," Tabatha said. "I'll take care of the cockpit."

"Perfect. Let them know we'll offer them leftover meals if we have any."

*   *   *

"Mr. Keeshan? Captain?" I said, as our celebrity passenger took his seat in the first row. He grinned and handed me his coat, which I wrapped around a hangar. "I'm a big fan. I watched your show for years! Thanks for the memories."

"Very kind of you to say so," he said.

"I'd do a song and dance to reciprocate," I said, "but that's not my strength, so... instead, what can I offer you to drink after takeoff?"

Everything had gone well; my crew was eager, friendly, hard-working and we all got along. Our first flight was on time. The temperature on the plane was comfortable, we had enough supplies, the gate agents had been wonderful, the cockpit crew was nice, professional, undemanding, and now, all I had to do was invite my passengers to sit back, relax, and enjoy their flight to Atlanta: the first of twelve legs on a three-day journey where I would man the helm and I was going to be great!

We picked up speed and took off; we were airborne. Ten seconds later, the cockpit crew turned off the No Smoking sign—I picked up the PA. "Ladies and Gentlemen, Captain Donovan has turned off the no smoking sign and you are free to light up. Our cabins are divided into smoking and non-smoking sections, so if you are seated in rows three and four upfront, or in rows fourteen through nineteen in coach, you may smoke at this time. Please understand that Gateway only permits cigarettes; pipes and cigars are not allowed. If you wish to smoke and are not seating in one of our designated smoking rows, let one of the crew members know and we will make every effort to reseat you once the 'Fasten Seat Belt' sign has been turned off. Once we are airborne, flight attendants will be coming through the aisle…"

I hesitated and glanced at Kurt; his jumpseat faced mine. I was confused about what to say. I had a full meal service with a choice of entrees in first, but coach only had snacks and a drink service. "We will be coming through the aisle with cock… sn." *Damn. Stop thinking about men.* I'd started to say snacks, before I'd finished saying cocktails, pronouncing the 'SN' a few seconds after my first syllable, which sounded awful. I stopped to compose myself. Kurt leaned forward on the jumpseat, sniggering. *Did I really just say that?* I tried again. "We will be coming through the aisle with cocks and snacktails…"

I saw all of the first-class passengers faces from my seat. Their eyes were wide open. "In coach only…" I added, feeling a rush of heat on my hairline. I rubbed my collarbones; even my neck was hot.

"Too bad," the first-class passenger in 2B said. "Think I want to sit in coach!"

After takeoff I hid in the galley. Taking advantage of Tabatha's kindness, I let her run everything out while I set up. I couldn't face my customers. When a call light went off and I saw a coach passenger get sick, I had to help. "You're going to feel much better," I told the teenage boy. He'd missed the airsick bag, so when Kurt appeared, I asked him to get coffee to douse the mess.

Apparently, Kurt didn't have the same instructors in training than I'd had; he returned with two small packets of Sanka and offered them to me. It was my turn to snigger.

Customers stared; not only did I talk filth on the PA, I was now laughing at a young boy being ill and attempting to cover it up with… two teaspoons of dry Sanka? "Kurt," I said slowly. "Please get two cans of *used, wet* coffee grounds; I have something to show you."

When I returned up front, Bob Keeshan came into my galley. "You all right," he asked.

"I am now," I lied. "Still embarrassed, that's for sure."

"Don't ever let them see you sweat," he said. "Bloopers are a big part of my business. Act as if you may have said it on purpose. Hold your head high and let it go. You didn't mean anything. If anyone's offended it's their problem, not yours," he said.

"I doubt if on a kid's show you ever made a blooper like that," I said. *Like saying Mister Greencocks… jeans!* "I've even *heard* a story of someone saying that before! Thought it was one of those rumors flight attendants brag about. Guess everyone on this plane now knows it's true."

"All the more reason it's funny," he said. "Forgive yourself. There are worse crimes."

But I couldn't. Even by the third day—the last leg, I was still mortified about my slip. I pictured *FlightLog* leaping out of my lap with laughter if I dared write down the details.

- *Dear FlightLog; so... maybe it was a Freudian slip but that's tough for me to swallow, (oh God! Another Freudian slip?) because everyone on the airplane had been so pleasant; the cockpit had been wonderful... so why was I thinking 'cocks and snacktails' instead of 'snacks and cocktails' a story I'd heard in training – before I said it myself? I did qualify this rare and unusual offer by clarifying that it was 'only in coach.' Thank goodness Maurice wasn't there. Next week is New Year's. I've been flying for seven months. Roman was going to spend three days in town and show me a great time but that's cancelled. I'm shattered. This isn't some little thing that we've talked about once; this has been an ongoing discussion. He has to be in LA for Christmas now and I'm surely flying, so that's not going down. But he promised me New Year's Eve or day, whatever my schedule allowed. Now that's off. Know what? I don't care what city I end up in... I'm going out. Even if I'm alone. I'll be damned if I'm going to sulk around a hotel room or here in the city when the New Year rings in. I'm going to kiss the first good-looking guy who smiles at me after midnight, and it's going to be a kiss he's never, ever, going to forget. SCREW Roman!*

Sitting on the couch with my feet up on the coffee table, I was watching two things: the night lights in the city and a lousy TV show that I was hooked on anyway, called "Flying High." It was so fake! The actresses playing the flight attendants were all worthy of Glamour Magazine covers. It was a "Charlie's Angels" rip-off. The three attendants always flew with the same pilots, (yeah, right) they had fifty different uniforms with dozens of color and style combinations. For their emergency training, they had gone up in a real plane full of employees posing as passengers and did drills while the pilots pitched and banked the plane. *Sure.* With the cost of fuel, the airlines had given that up eons ago. Nevertheless, I always tuned in when I could, even though I would roll my eyes while watching. The phone rang; I put my popcorn down, got up and answered.

"Hey," Jeanna said on the other end. "What are you doing?"

"Watching that new show, 'Flying High.'"

"On a Friday night?"

"That's when it comes on. You've gotta see it; it's hysterical. They have three-day long layovers in Miami even though they're based in the US. They wear a different uniform in every episode and one of the uniforms is a sleeveless, low-cut number…"

"Sherri, I don't care," Jeanna said, cutting me off. *"Here comes the jackpot question: what are you doing New Year's Eve?"*

I perked up and looked at the calendar; it was December 29. "I don't know," I said. "I'm almost at eighty-five hours. They can fly me tomorrow and part of the next day, but they'll have to get me back by midnight. Pretty sure I'll be ringing in the New Year right here. Probably go to Times Square. Alex is in London with Maurice and Sergio. What about you?"

"I'm already maxed out," she cried with glee. "Now that's 'wow, gee, real neat' as you would say! I'm off until January second. And… I met someone hot. He works at Studio 54; so guess *What?* We are going to *Studio 54* for New Year's *Eve!*"

Nobody in the world didn't know how cool Studio 54 was. People lined up for hours trying to get in—it was a legend in its own time; it sounded exactly like the kind of place where Jeanna would fit in—but I wasn't Jeanna…

"I don't have anything to wear," I said.

"The less you wear the better," she said.

"Jeanna, I won't be comfortable." But even as I was saying it, I was taken over with excitement.

"Shut up Sherri. We're going! I'll pick you up at nine. It's a little early but I want to get there before it's insane. Actually… *You* pick me up. That way if I have to modify your wardrobe, I can do it here. Got it?"

* * *

Jeanna approved of my outfit. I had on a see-through turquoise long blouse, cinched at the waist with a busy beaded belt worn over a gauzy, sheer full white skirt, very high heels and a shiny gold coat.

"Cool coat," she said. "You're learning from Alex." Jeanna, after only six months of flying, had already bought lots of fur-lined and leather items. Hats, gloves, jackets, scarves, and even a $250 palomino belt. She was dressed head to toe in black leather and fur; she looked marvelous. Her doorbell beeped. "We're outta here," she said.

Downstairs, I met Brad for the first time. Behind him was a quieter guy—Wayne.

"Hi," I said to my blind date told-I-had-a-boyfriend-already companion.

Brad pulled Jeanna into his arms and practically made love to her right there on the sidewalk.

"Hi," Wayne said, stepping forward and offering his hand. "I'm Wayne."

"Sherri."

And I will admit, it was damn cool when we exited the cab, approached the long, hopeful line of folks trying to get in, and were ushered immediately through the door like celebrities. But I did find the whole experience degrading—for the others. We were inside, staring at the wildly-costumed clientele, the blinking blazing light-show dance floor, and… the balcony seats above where couples… and threesomes or more were clearly doing any-thing—*Anything* they wanted to.

Jeanna and Brad disappeared fast. Wayne took my arm and whispered, "Don't plan on going to bed early; we've got plenty of coke." He held out his hand for me to take something.

"Uhhh… keep it," I said. "I don't do that." *Just Diet Coke, Wayne!*

He laughed. "Ok, let's dance."

Two hours later, following two trips to the washroom where I witnessed coked-out women sharing stories, and Jeanna in tears because Brad was suddenly a 'bastard,' I decided I'd had enough.

"Thanks Jeanna, for everything. It was great being here," I said. "But I'm going to go."

"You can't leave now; it's not even midnight!"

"This isn't my scene. I really want to see the ball drop at Times Square. There's still time. Why don't you come with me?"

She hesitated, but said no.

"Have fun Jeanna. Tell Wayne I said good night and that I had a good time; I can't find him anywhere."

"Ok." She pulled me to her and gave me a long hug. "Happy New Year Sherri. You know I love you, right?"

I walked for blocks, getting turned around once as I was unsure where I was, but enjoyed the cold fresh air after all the dancing. I could see the Sheraton Hotel and got a pang of excitement. Eric said he was going to be in New York for New Year's. I'd called him the night we'd met, but he hadn't been there. *Should have left him my number.* Wouldn't it be fun now if… I picked up speed, waltzed into the lobby and made my way over to the front desk.

"I'll connect you now," the clerk behind the counter said. I could hear the phone ring, ring, ring, and ring. "There's no answer," he said. "Would you like to leave a message?"

"No thank you." I chickened out again. Then I headed south, this time, knowing it was in the right direction. I sensed the crowd and heard the noise. It cheered me. Finding an empty street light, I leaned up against the pole and settled in, waiting for the midnight hour.

"Sherri?" He was only three steps away from me.

"I just stopped by your hotel to pick you up," I said, smiling broadly, suddenly so happy.

"I can't believe you're here," he hollered. "Are you really all alone?"

"No, Eric," I said. "I'm not; I'm with you!"

"When I asked, *'What are you doing New Year's Eve?'* I wasn't *crazy enough to suppose* we'd actually end up in Times Square together."

After the countdown was done, the ball had dropped, and the New Year had officially hit, I planted the best kiss on him ever; it was my *FlightLog* promise and I wanted to do it. It was maddeningly good. He wanted more. I did too. I happily gave it to him. He hungrily took it.

"Of all the *thousands of invites* you must have had," Eric said, wrapping me up in an altar-like embrace. "We know *whose arms will hold you good and tight,*" he said. "All night. And all morning as long as I can keep you. Don't make any plans," he said, making me laugh and turn red. At least out here, no one could tell. I threw my arms around him and we headed back to the Sheraton, chatting, teasing, skipping, and smooching all the way.

*   *   *

"Morning," Eric said when I opened my eyes. "What an amazing, perfect way to be *welcoming in the New Year*. Best surprise of my life." He was smiling beautifully, looking over my naked body curled up in his sheets. It was that lovely, appreciative look one gets in the morning after a night of intimacy with a man who adores you. Why can't they always look at you like that? Forever? Why did it have to become so… familiar?

"God you're so beautiful," he said, nuzzling his face into the back of my neck and pulling my hair over his face playfully. "I love your hair," he added, as he started tickling me.

Teasing, laughter-filled fun. We kept at it for hours. I donned his flight shirt with his wings and his pilot hat; he loved it, and called me sexy. Eventually we succumbed to hunger and went out for food. We sat across from each other at a booth inside the first eatery that was open and just kept grinning at each other; remembering, looking up, looking down a bit shy, giggling, and holding hands across the tabletop.

"I feel like the luckiest man alive," Eric said. "Never thought you'd stay last night."

"I didn't either," I admitted. "But after we had that champagne at the hotel, and you practically carried me upstairs for 'one more drink'—and you were *So yummy*… I mean… it was hard to fight you. I surprised myself too, this fast stuff is scary to me. I got stung bad once, letting a one-nighter sneak up on me."

"We've all been burned that way," Eric said. "But… I promise I won't hurt you. Do you promise you won't hurt me?"

My eyebrow went up; I could feel my bottom lip drop slightly.

"Uh oh." He sat up and took on a more-serious expression. "Come on Sherri. You are going to let me see you again, aren't you?"

"I… I don't know." He frowned. "Eric, I'm trying to be *Honest*. I really don't know. My, God, you're terrific; you're wonderful! You're fun, smart, handsome, sweet… but you have a girlfriend! And you know I have a boyfriend. I assumed last night was a 'nuzzle, feel-good-all-over' cuddle thing that happened because we ran into each other on a super-special night—you know, you talked about your girl not understanding certain things, and said she accused you of cheating anyway. As for me, Roman was *Supposed* to be here last night, then he cancelled. I thought we were—I thought you and I were two lonely people with a strong attraction who had… committed to sharing a secret we could trust each other with… an understanding. God, I'm not good at this. Trying to talk myself into not feeling guilty, but this *Is* the first time I've been unfaithful; ever, with anyone. Oh, wow I'm babbling. Can we change the subject?"

Eric came over to my side of the booth, slid in and hugged me. "We won't talk seriously; it's *too early in the game*. But this conversation isn't over. You mean a lot to me. I was dying for you. I wanted you to stay all night and I'm glad you did. Let me squeeze you again. Our limo picks us up at four. What would you like to do until I have to leave?"

• *Dear FlightLog; Is it ok to make a New Year's resolution after the New Year starts – even if you already broke* that resolution after midnight? If I resolve not to be dishonest and unfaithful in my relationship w/ Roman, can I get a pass? I'm finding out all kinds of surprising, alarming things about myself that I never dreamed I'd do before I started flying. First, I went to bed w/ a guy on our first date — Sheldon, and he chewed me up and spit me out, and I swore that would never happen again. Fast-forward to last night. Not only was that my first night w/ Eric, but we ran into each other; it wasn't even a date! I was alone with an attractive man in his hotel room all night. Got it? I wasn't an innocent who didn't 'know' (like when Sheldon was married). What does this make me? A liar? A cheater? A TRAMP? A sky-slut as Mo would say? Is this what happens when a squeaky-clean small-town girl moves to the Big City? Not only is this town an icon of such bad, selfish, hedonistic behavior, living in it woos you into thinking that it's alright — since everyone else seems to be doing it. You know what? Maurice would laugh. Jeanna would look at me strange for feeling bad at all and Alex — well she's smart. She would know that it was a mistake for <u>ME</u>, because I try to be a good, honest, person, and I've failed without good reason; I was weak and selfish, and now I feel guilty and ashamed. I can rationalize all I want about Eric that no harm was done, but that's not true. Not only have I let myself and Roman down — I've hurt Eric. That's the worst part. I never, ever, expected that to happen. I wasn't thinking about his feelings when I was accepting his passion. He wasn't just trying to jump in the sack – there are feelings there. I would be devastated if Roman did this to me. Later, I asked Eric to take me to the movie, 'California Suite.' It was all about relationships, drama, funny, sad, we kept looking at each other and elbowing each other... what a strange New Year's Day. Why the hell didn't Gateway send me to Omaha for New Year's Eve? Ok Flightlog, I admit – I'm glad they didn't!

Chapter 19:

· · · · · · · · · ·

Can You Come Out Tonight?

I HAD ANOTHER EARLY CHECK-IN at LaGuardia. I still had to weigh in for the month of February—there were five days left in the month. Despite my self-promises, I couldn't get the extra weight off. In the last few days of each month, I'd scramble. I was two pounds over now. Several times, I'd taken the Carey Bus late to LaGuardia, gone into the quiet office alone and fixed the scale the way Anderson had shown me. I didn't cheat much—just enough to keep me from being 'over.' My check in was at 7 A.M. I had twenty minutes to spare. As I exited the staircase into the hallway, I ran into Quentin—one of the ramp guys who was always there. We were pals now.

"Hi Quentin; how are you?" I asked.

"Great! Flying early? Or are you pass riding off somewhere?"

"Not flying 'til eight but I came in early to get weighed."

"Too bad," he said with a funny grin. "I just balanced the scale; it was registering low."

My blood drained directly into my gut and I froze.

"Sherri?" He walked toward me and grabbed my upper arm. "What's wrong? If you weren't so young, I'd swear you were having a heart attack."

"I, I-I-I… I'm fine. Oh boy…" I set my suitcase down and sat on it, breathing hard. "Not sure; just got dizzy suddenly."

"Need to get over to medical and have them check you out."

"I'll be fine, really."

"Let me get you some juice and a bagel…"

"No! No food! No, I mean," I said, lowering my voice, "I don't think I should eat."

I sat numbly in the hallway for several minutes. After I'd convinced Quentin that I was fine, he'd gone off to service our aircraft. *Five days left in February.* Even if I had a three-day trip and got home late the third day, I'd be able to weigh in on day four or five. But… if I had an early check in at Kennedy on day four for a two or a three-day trip, I wouldn't be able to get back to LaGuardia. I couldn't manipulate the scale at JFK; the office was manned round the clock. There was only one thing to do: go on a crash diet during my trip, and pray it was enough to lose three pounds. I was already hungry. I had planned to grab a muffin at the Host Cafe after my weigh in. The lousy cafeteria was our only dining option at LaGuardia.

Instead, I dragged myself to the office, grateful I'd run into Quentin, checked in for my trip with Skip, then went back upstairs to get a large cup of coffee. In line, I studied my trip ID. Six legs today. Fourteen-hour duty-day. Ten-hour layover in… Milwaukee, *oh boy; wow, real neat…* five legs tomorrow. A nine-hour layover in… Buffalo, followed by six legs back to LaGuardia on day three with a few long sits in between, arriving home at 10 P.M. All legs on old un-refurbished 737s; one hundred and three coach passengers, no first class. Setting up and stripping down the queen cart every leg—this was nuts. *This* was one of those 'dog' trips. It was going to be cold, awful, and full on every leg, no doubt. We'd have to race to get the services done and everything put away, the liquor counted and locked while on a steep descent—I was going to work very hard and… starve… probably to death. *I'd rather starve to death than suffer the humiliation of losing my job because I was too fat.*

"Would you like a sweet roll or a donut with that coffee?" the sales clerk asked.

We served a hot breakfast on the first leg, soup and sandwiches on the fourth leg. I hadn't worked a meal service on the all-coach 737s for a while, so I kept forgetting that the oven drawers were shorter than the ones on the other planes. Most of the time, the drawers held twelve hot entrees but on the old 37s, they only held six.

I volunteered to set up the trays rather than run meals, thinking it would help preserve my strength. Twice, I pulled one of the noisy, steel drawers all the way out and the hot breakfast entrees crashed to the floor; the ceramic dishes broke into pieces. "We just lost six more meals," I told Fanny, the A stew, when she came back into the galley the second time.

"Seem to be having a rough time today," she said. "Why don't you run and I'll set up?"

By leg four, she must have assumed I'd righted everything, as she agreed to let me set up again. The ceramic soup mugs were smaller than the ceramic entrée dishes, so when I pulled the drawer out all the way and sent hot soup crashing, we lost a lot more than six of them. I had to apologize to the last few rows of passengers, begging forgiveness for splashing their soup all over the galley.

"Are you on something?" Fanny asked, eyeing me suspiciously. On our grand Milwaukee layover, I went straight to my room, took a hot bath and tried to fall asleep, though I was ravenous and couldn't think about anything except *food, Food, FOOD!*

By the third leg of day two, I decided I was going to eat in Buffalo. I'd die, I'd really die, if I didn't. Though I'd never heard of them growing up, a few crew members had talked about Buffalo Chicken Wings; you could only get them in... Buffalo; that sounded perfect. Fowl was low in calories and essentially all protein. I could remove the skin, eat a wing or two and that would probably tide me over—get me through the night and day three.

I had no idea whatsoever how Buffalo Chicken Wings were prepared. Were they baked? Fried? However they were cooked, people raved about them. My crew members said we got in too late to eat in the hotel restaurant, but that the bar served the famous wings as appetizers and that they were good. *Done.*

To the bar I raced after washing up and throwing on jeans. I reached out eagerly. "Are these your famous Buffalo Chicken Wings?" I asked the bartender rhetorically, as a platter of wings was the only food on the counter.

"Yes, they..."

The pieces were small. I was so *Starved,* I dismissed removing the skin and hungrily took a bite before he could finish saying:

"Careful there Miss."

It didn't matter that I didn't swallow—the hot sauce had penetrated my lips, gums, and all the soft tissue inside my mouth instantly. "Water please!" I said, making the bartender chortle as my hands went to my mouth. I tried blowing hotness out while sucking in cooler air. I was a 'hot food' virgin—this solved the problem of me wanting to eat.

When I got upstairs after drinking two Tabs, I started to cry. "I'll never get to sleep," I moaned. Then I cried again, because there was hot sauce residue on my hands, which I'd just transferred to my eyes. My mother never used anything as repulsive as hot sauce. What was all the fuss about?

* * *

Ring! Ring! Ring!

Waking up to a blaring phone ringing, I remembered where I was and checked the windows. It was still dark outside. "Hello?" I groaned. The hotel clock by the bed said 4:03 A.M.

"Hi Sherri, it's Fanny. Our flight cancelled; we're snowed in and the airport's closed. You can go back to sleep. Let me know if you leave the hotel because we have not been officially released. Ops is hoping they will open the airport later and maybe we can still get out. Did you have fun last night? Sorry I didn't make it down to the bar; I was too tired. Did you try the wings?"

The call was a *Joy*. I was beat; exhausted from two hard days, short nights, little rest and lack of food. I set the phone down and slept until noon. When I woke, I didn't dare go downstairs. The restaurant would stay open until nine and I'd be too tempted to eat everything on the menu. I would wait until late, go down to the bar, ask the bartender if I could take five or six wings with me back to the room, wash the awful sauce off, and eat the chicken, which was exactly what I did.

The time passed slowly, even though I had two good reads: *The World According to Garp* and *Eye of the Needle*. The airport reopened, but only for an hour. We weren't reassigned. When the phone rang early again the next morning, I just *Knew* we were still grounded.

"Sherri?" Fanny asked, after telling me we'd had more snow and confirming what I thought. She sounded weird. "No one saw you yesterday. You alright?"

"I'm better," I said. "Extra sleep did me wonders. I wasn't feeling well; sorry about all the lost meals."

"Let's pray we get out tomorrow. Hanging around an airport motel in Buffalo is a drag. But the van drivers have been great.

They'll take you anywhere you want as long it's on one of the open roads," she said. "Hope to see you later."

"Thanks Fanny." And as I hung up, it hit me. *Tomorrow is the last day of the month—the last day I can weigh in for February! Oh my God!* Plus, I had to arrive in LaGuardia early because operations closed by six. I drank water all day and chewed dozens of pieces of gum, because I had iguana breath from smoking and starving.

Lying back on the bed, I could feel my hip bones. They were certainly popping out. I knew I'd lost a few pounds in water weight, but flying would bloat me again. One more day working, I'd retain water, so I couldn't let my guard up—I had to keep starving. Roman called. I didn't confess anything—it was too embarrassing. Later, I repeated my actions from the day before—holing myself up, reading, bathing, watching TV mindlessly and avoiding the hotel restaurant. Oddly enough, when I entered the bar to get wings to soak in my sink before eating, I was feeling better. I heard:

"Rejects? Yo, Reej! It is you! It's really you!"

"Danny!"

It was so great to see him; I hugged him and felt tears well up in my eyes.

"Sherri," he asked. "What's wrong? Why are you wearing sunglasses? They're cute; tiger striped frames to advertise what a kitten you are, but it's dark in here."

I burst into tears then I started laughing. "That's only the second time you've called me by my name," I said, climbing onto a barstool after assuring him I was just emotional. He'd been at the hotel last night. His crew had flown in during the one hour the airport had reopened, but then the airport had closed again, so they'd gotten stuck. Of course, he'd gone downtown Buffalo last night in spite of the snow.

"Let me take you downtown," he said with a big smile. "You gotta *come out tonight.*"

How could I go downtown anywhere and not eat or drink? "Danny?"

"What?"

"I have to tell you something," and I told him everything. He was a good listener. I wondered why talking to him was so much easier than talking to Roman. Danny was frowning and shaking his head. "I can't go anywhere tonight unless it's to a sauna or steam room," I said.

"Ooh," he brightened. "Wish we were at a nicer hotel with a spa. I will say this, I don't get it because you look thinner than the last time I saw you. Your cheek bones are starting to stick out. *Mmm, you look so fine* Sherry baby," he sang. *"Girl, you make me lose my mind."*

"I hate that song," I admitted.

"It's cute; just like you are." He began again. *"She—e—rry, can you come out tonight."*

"I wish," I said sadly. "Go and have fun. I've got two great reads."

He laughed loud. "Uh uh, no way. Leave you here? Alone? Not a chance."

It was *So Fun* catching up with him. I told him all about Roman, Alex, filled him in on Jeanna and the latest, and of course, told him about Maurice too. Danny was having a blast flying; said he was now collecting hotel room keys.

"Everyone's collecting something except me," I whined. "What's wrong with me?"

"Not a thing," he lifted his beer as if to toast.

I grinned; it was nice to hear. "Say, do you ever fly with anyone from our class?" I asked.

"Not often," he said. "Cleveland's a big base. But guess what? I'm probably going to be off reserve this year."

"No way!"

"Yep. It's that junior, and so many new-grads in the classes below us ended up there. They're cranking out a bunch more training classes now too; the numbers look good."

"I'll never be off reserve in New York," I said. "Do you ever fly with anyone from some of the other classes?" I asked.

"Why don't you just ask me if I've run into Sheldon, Reej."

"How did you know?"

"There was talk; flowers sent to you in training—I figured it out. He's weird. Doesn't mingle—not sure this is the right job for him. Whatever; I don't care. His wife's a sweetheart! Everyone loves her. Can't believe he treated her like that. Supposedly he steps out on her all the time, and that's the last we're going to say about him."

"I don't carry a torch for him if that's what you think. Probably... I was hoping to hear that his wife had hit him upside the head with a frying pan and dumped him. How are your old roommates? Did Tom come out of the closet yet?"

"Sherri, he's in New York with you! Don't you ever fly with him?"

"No," I said. "It's funny. I can fly with the same people over and over, and then there are others I never see. I forgot he was in New York. Do you talk to him? You two were close."

"I do," he said. "He's not out yet," Danny said. "Feel bad for him. I know he's gay, of course he knows he's gay, but he doesn't understand that the rest of us know. Lots of pressure to appear straight. Even in this industry; it's worse in Cleveland cause its headquarters; more management types around. Least he's in New York. Told me he's dating some girl, but I bet it's just for show. Why don't you call him?"

"I will! It's much better in New York," I said. "I have wonderful gay friends who could help him come to grips with it. Maybe give him some courage."

"I'll bet you do. You're so nice; you know that?"

"Do you ever worry about people thinking you're gay? Since you're a steward?"

"No."

"Really? Not even just a little bit?"

"Maybe at first, but not now. I stay busy, work hard on the planes—probably like you do. Do my job, try to make people feel good, make 'em laugh. Consider myself an entertainer of sorts; want to show 'em I'm glad they chose my airline. No time to worry about macho customers or macho pilots—they're the worst by the way. Stay away from them."

"Just so you know, my dad's a pilot; 727 Captain with American Airlines."

He laughed. "Wow! Why'd you keep it a secret?"

"I was stupid. Thought people would think he got me the job—like an American Airlines pilot would have a say in who Gateway hires; I was so insecure."

"And now you're a pillar of self-assuredness?"

I started to cry again. Danny hugged me; I liked when he hugged me. We stayed up too late and I drank a beer. It didn't taste good so it was easy for me to sip slowly and make it last.

"We're probably drinking illegally," Danny said.

"No doubt," I agreed. There was a good chance we'd be flying within the next twelve hours, but the chances of someone from Gateway management being stuck with us in a small, dumpy, musty, airport motel in Buffalo during a snow storm were slim, so we drank openly at the bar.

Danny pounded several down. "Rejects," he slurred; it was way past midnight. "Do you have any idea how in love with you I was?"

"Danny…"

"No really. Do you? Now I'm seeing you here, the girl of my dreams, all those feelings are coming up again. *I'm gonna make-a you mine.* Will you come to my room?"

"Of course not."

"Ok," he said, "we'll go to yours," he chuckled and threw his arm around my shoulder and got down from his bar stool all at the same time.

"Come on," I said, slipping off my stool and putting his arm more firmly around my shoulder while slipping my arm around his waist. "It's bedtime; I'm dropping you off at your room."

"Are you going to tuck me in? Will you undress me?"

"I should take you outside and toss you in the snow."

"Long as you fall in with me. We can make snow angels *where the bright moon shines.*" He was sweet and as cute as I remembered, and funny, and thank goodness, he didn't try to kiss me when I got him to his room. "Good night Rejects. Funny, isn't it? I'm the one who gave you than nickname, and it's come back to haunt me—you reject all my advances."

"You've never made any advances."

"I asked you to marry me."

"That's *Not* making an advance. Night Danny. See you in the morning. Thanks for listening." I blew him a kiss from the doorway but I think his eyes were already closed.

We all got called at 3 A.M. My crew would combine with Danny's to work a stretch-8 flight to Cleveland, then we would get further assignments from there. We showed up at seven for our eight o'clock flight, but the departure kept being pushed back—it was one of those 'creeping' delays.

Finally, we were confirmed by air traffic control for a 10:45 A.M. departure. Fanny was senior, so she held onto the A spot. Danny and I would work out of the second galley on the long plane. Across from our galley at row nine were two lavatories and a long garment bag rack with a rod that slid out into the aisle. Garment bags were ludicrously popular, and they usually weighed forty or fifty pounds each. Instead of being able to accommodate dozens of bags with one or two items, the closet was full after fifteen or fewer bags. Passengers *Hated* not being able to hang those bags! The rest of them would board and snarl angrily, because they either had to 1) roll up their extra-large bag and stuff it into the overhead, or 2) check it.

Danny set up our galley. I was in charge of the aisle, seating, and that front coach closet. It was *The Worst hands down* boarding assignment on any Gateway plane ever; manning the front coach closet on a stretch-8. The first few customers had boarded; I took their household belongings or whatever they'd stuffed into them, and hung their heavy hanging bags, straining and panting. Then I got to 'smile' as I told the rest of the passengers getting on: 'this closet is full.' It was what I called a self 'test.' I pretended there were secret cameras and that the CEO of Gateway Airlines, Richard Kabella, was watching.

It was a mix that morning of passengers greatly relieved for finally being able to get out of town, and those still mad as hell with the airlines and the airports for closing. And, they'd had to wait after arriving early due to the delay—everyone was tired. No doubt the customers had been called in the wee hours like we had, so I set my shoulders, took deep breaths and *Smiled* through every terse remark, sneer, and hateful look.

Fanny asked me to hand out magazines and newspapers up front. Danny was finished setting up so he followed me with a handful of pillows and blankets.

The gate agent stepped on and made an announcement for 'Mr. Bennett' to come forward. When he did, Mr. Bennett was greeted with the awful news that as a waitlisted passenger, he now had to get off, because someone with a higher boarding priority had shown up. *Oh Boy.* These were tough scenarios. Meanwhile the mechanic came on, handed the cockpit their papers and we were ready to go. Our late arriver stood there nonplused, waiting calmly for Mr. Bennett to leave so he could move past him and take his seat.

"I'm not getting off," Mr. Bennett said firmly. "We were all on standby… this isn't a regularly scheduled flight. There is no priority!"

"Sir, please," the gate agent pleaded. "Everyone's tense after an airport closure of two days; I assure you, you will be the *First* one…"

"I'm *Not* getting *Off!*"

The cockpit door was still open. The captain hollered back. "We're going to miss our slot if we don't push back in thirty seconds. I for one want to get home today, so either shut that door or I'm pulling back with it open."

The agent's eyes widened. "Mr. Bennett," he started…

Danny brazenly took Mr. Bennett's arm. "Sir," he said, loudly. "If you do not get off this *Airplane*… all these passengers here," he swept his arm over the twenty-six passengers in first class then kept his eyes on them, "are going to miss their connections in Denver."

Everyone was still; all eyes were on Danny.

"This plane is going to Denver?" Mr. Bennett asked.

Fanny blurted out, "We are headed for Denver sir, are you on the right airplane?"

He raced off in a panic. The agent gave Danny a thumbs up, made the sign of the cross and pulled back the jetway.

Fanny already had the PA in her hand. Danny shut door 1Right and I closed the cockpit door as Fanny said, "Prepare for departure; everyone, we are… headed for Cleveland." The first-class passengers burst into relieved laughter.

After the service, I found Danny in our galley admiring a picture in *People Magazine* of Lindsay Wagner, star of "The Bionic Woman." He took his pen out of his pocket and wrote across the bottom, 'To Danny with Love, Lindsay,' then tore the page out and stuck it to the front of a galley door with Occupied Stickers.

"What-are-you-doing?" I asked curiously.

"Creating a conversation piece," he said. "My passengers enjoy all the autographed pictures from celebrities I share with them. But don't tell; most of the crew members don't know they're phonies any more than the customers do."

"Another flight attendant who exaggerates his brushes with greatness," I said. "We all have enough celebrity run-ins; why the pretense?"

"People love it! They perk up hearing about famous people; we haven't even flown a year yet Reej, we can't let honesty get in the way of good old-fashioned entertainment, can we? I call it, 'The Bragging Rights.' One of the biggest reasons people gravitate to this job."

"But I even heard a twenty-three-year attendant pretend she had Lucille Ball on a flight; I know it wasn't true. I'd already heard the exact same story from someone who works for Eastern Airlines. Then a pilot told me that back in the day, he let a stewardess land the plane!"

"I hope that one's true," Danny grinned, turning to welcome a passenger coming near us.

Sure enough, several passengers stretching, or using the front lavatories, stopped to admire the picture and listened intently as Danny described what 'she' was like. She was on his last flight—this very plane. Wow, didn't they *Get* that this plane was grounded in Buffalo last night like they were? Which would mean... she flew into Buffalo in February... ah, for what? A film festival? They didn't get it, as he explained, because his stories were fun and they wanted them to be true.

"Ladies and gentleman," we heard from the cockpit PA, "seems as if all that scurrying to get us out of Buffalo on time was for naught. Lots of planes coming into Cleveland this morning, so… we're going to circle for a while." Groans filled the plane. "But don't worry," he continued. "I know you've got a super crew back there, with Fanny in the lead, and they're going to do absolutely everything they can to make it a pleasant trip for you. Tell you what. Long as you're twenty-one, I'm going to tell them to give you each a couple of cocktails on the house, how's that?"

"We better set the queen cart back up," Danny said.

"Let's *Not* break it down until we know for sure we're done circling," I said.

We began a forty-five minute 'hold,' circling the airport, which stretched into two hours. Danny stood at the front of coach. With the PA in his hand, he handed out mini bottles of booze for the most arbitrary of prizes—just like when we'd graduated from training. We didn't have to worry about balancing the liquor sales to our inventory—the captain was signing for all the 'comps,' so we kept giving away prizes.

"I've got a mini bottle of Kahlua here for the first person to walk up this aisle with their dentures in their hand," Danny offered. The woman in 18C jumped up, took her dentures out and raced forward to collect her prize as the cabin applauded. Another gentleman won a beer for coming forward with his toupee on his shoulder. A young sister and brother were gifted a bowl of mints from first class for standing at the front of coach and singing a song, while another family member played the guitar. One customer suggested that Danny make Lindsay Wagner's autographed photo a prize—*he wouldn't… would he?* But he graciously declined, explaining that it was far too valuable for him to part with.

Later, sitting on the back of the jumpseat together, I lit up. Danny frowned. "Smoking a lot; I don't remember you doing that in training."

"You're right; I am. Nervous as a cornered rat. Danny, I've *Got* to get into LaGuardia by six! I've *Got* to weigh in! Remember? They warned us in training, 'don't wait till the end of the month, because if you don't make it back in time from your last trip due to delays, that's no excuse for missing a weigh in.'"

"No telling what they're going to do with us when we land, but I'll probably be released. You'll probably deadhead back to New York and be done. Should be fine."

"Only if I get into La Guardia by six before the office closes."

The plane was still. Many slept peacefully after the early take-off, full from a hot breakfast, followed by a complimentary liquor service and Danny's games. The hard-core drinkers were in the back with us, standing around the queen cart that was now a bar. The two attendants in back were happy to work it as people mingled, chatted. We took turns walking through the cabin every fifteen minutes. The passengers were quiet, though as anxious as we to land. Between our cabin checks, we talked. We had never, ever, talked so much. I was really liking Danny and trusting him; it was comforting. I drank buckets of coffee and smoked.

"When you work in the back on this plane," Danny asked, "do you put a half-filled coffee cup under the jumpseat and your cigarettes under your skirt like all the others?"

I grinned and nodded. "Yep. Soon as that No-Smoking sign goes off, I'm ready."

"It's a wonder you gals don't wear garter belts and tuck your smokes in them."

"That's a good idea. You could recommend that as a uni-form-issue item."

When we landed, I followed Danny into Cleveland operations. Just as he suspected, he was released for the day and could go home. My crew had a three-hour and fifty-nine-minute sit in Cleveland before we would deadhead back to LaGuardia, arriving there at 6:10 P.M. Three hours and fifty-nine minutes was a critical number at Gateway. Per our contract, if we were scheduled anytime between flights for four hours or more, the company was required to get us a hotel room (it was considered a 'layover'). Thus, many trips had scheduled sits for three hours and fifty-some minutes; it was amazing.

"I am… in big trouble," I announced. "Guess I'll have to take a bus over to Kennedy and weigh in there. The supervisors will all be gone though. Do you think they'll let the crew desk weigh me in?"

"Hold on," Danny said, starting down a hallway. "I'll be right back." He poked his head out of an office several minutes later and motioned for me. "Rejects, come here." Danny had talked his supervisor into weighing me and calling my supervisor. It wasn't exactly protocol, but I *Did* have the snowstorm excuse. And, it was clear that Danny had her wrapped around his finger. I weighed in at 120 pounds. Five pounds under my max! It was the lowest I'd weighed in eight months.

"Thanks Danny; so much. I… owe you one."

"Funny you should mention that," he grinned. "Come on. Let me get you something to eat. Gotta get you back to 125."

"Aren't you going home?"

"And leave a ravenous beauty unfed and alone? I'm getting you some food then I'm flying into New York with you for an evening of fun."

"Danny…"

He pulled me toward him, setting his chin. "Listen. I absolutely know, that this was a rare treat and a chance of a lifetime. You're never going to be my girl. I can't compete with guys like Roman, or young pilots on their way to being rich captains. But I want to be a great friend. Who knows when I'll see you again? I'm here, you're in New York, your boyfriend's from LA; you'll probably move out there soon. If he's smart, he'll set that up

ASAP. People always say, 'Oh, we'll have to get together again soon,' but when it's not friends of the same sex or two people dating, it doesn't happen, does it? So… I'm going to enjoy watching you eat a proper meal, then because I'm off tomorrow and you're deadheading into New York on an empty plane—it is empty, I already checked—I'm coming with you. You're going to show me the town and we're going to have a blast. Call Roman and tell him I'm going to be there. You can make me stay in a hotel; but tonight, I'm going to be your guy-pal because I won't get this opportunity again. I'm not going to hit on you either. Just to show you I'm not clowning I'll even call you by your real name— but just for tonight. You'll always be 'Rejects' to me."

"Alex is home tonight," I told him. "You can have the couch; I'd love you to meet her anyway; and Maurice too, if he's around."

He fed me and it was wonderful. We also sat in first class together on the flight into LGA, laughing, drinking, and telling more stories. We'd changed into civvies and since I was feeling so thin and pretty, I'd put a nice silk, long-sleeved rust-colored dress on with high-heeled maroon boots. Danny looked nice too; I was surprised that he'd packed more than jeans.

The gentleman across the aisle kept staring at us. Eventually, he spoke up. "You too make a really cute couple," he said as I giggled. "Do you live in New York?"

After we told him our situation he said, "I belong to a special club in Manhattan; you might want to give it a try. Very exclusive. You have to join at the door but it's absolutely worth it. It's a non-stop party with fascinating people from all over. There's a buffet table that's always full of great food, music, people are dancing…" and he raved so much about the club that Danny was intrigued. "It's called Plato's; I've got a card," he said, reaching into his briefcase and shuffling around before handing it over. "Plato's Retreat. Maybe I'll see you there later tonight."

Since the two of us had already changed out of our uniforms, we took a cab right from the airport to the club. The people on the main floor were friendly. They explained how to sign up and we joined. Danny, of course, wouldn't let me pay for my membership. They let us leave our suitcases upstairs and showed us the staircase leading down into the main room of the club.

At first, all I could see were electric blue walls and hear music. Then I saw the buffet table with a beautiful spread of dishes. *And no chicken wings!* I was still in a food trance, though I'd eaten at the airport and again on the plane. Near it was the largest Jacuzzi I'd ever seen; several people were in it, laughing, smooching, having a great time. Halfway down the stairs, I saw what looked like a ship-sized air mattress. On top of it were several naked couples—copulating.

I practically knocked Danny over as I turned and pushed past him on the stairwell, racing up and out of the club.

"You totally set me up," I said later, after we'd laughed so hard we'd cried, walking around in circles, dazed, and continually cracking up from the event. *Wow I really was young and naïve!* When Danny had exited the club with the same wide eyes I had—and our suitcases in tow—I realized he absolutely had not known what the club was all about either. But I was going to hold it over him forever. Nothing—nothing in my life had ever happened to me that was so hilariously humiliating. "No one back home is *Ever* going to believe this," I said. "I've got big time 'Bragging Rights' on this one!"

"Just my luck," Danny laughed. "The one time I drop big bucks to join a fancy swingers club with a gorgeous gal, she happens to be the woman I *Just* told I wouldn't hit on. Let me ask you; if I was Roman, would you have…"

"No!"

"Is that a—no I can't ask you? Or a—no you wouldn't have stayed with him?"

"I wouldn't have stayed, even if I was with Sean Connery," I said.

"That much of a prude?"

"Yes."

He stopped for a moment, thought about something then howled again. *"Why don't you come out, with your red dress on!"* he sang. "That guy was dreaming about seeing you there and taking that dress off you; that's what he was thinking."

The next day after Danny left our apartment, I sat with Alex and told her all about our trip, how he'd been toward me in training, all he'd said, and how he'd saved me from missing my weigh in. She had already heard all about the night before.

"He's right," she said. "Might run into him every three to four months and coincidentally be at the same hotels, but that's rare. You probably won't see each other for years unless you make a point of it. How do you *Really* feel about him?" she asked me. "How does it compare to how you feel about Roman?"

"I think of Danny as a friend. I had a crush on him for five minutes, but then he hurt my feelings. He was silly, pulled stunts—then I developed a crush on someone else in training and forgot about him. Guess I feel like he could be family; a big brother. I love *Roman*, Alex!"

"You and Danny don't fight. He's crazy mad for you, surely you know that. You two were both up late and had lots to drink after a long trip. There wasn't one disagreement. I hear you and Roman fighting on the phone and in person," she said. "A lot. Maybe Danny isn't the one, but is Roman?"

• *Dear FlightLog. I called Roman tonight and told him I needed some time to think; he fought me but I stood my ground, told him we need a trial separation. Want to figure* out why I was unfaithful. Need to focus on myself; and, I need to go on a 'sensible' diet! I keep putting it off, then starving for the last few days of each month — and it's making me physically and emotionally ill. What a fright I had. Even though I got the weight off, I would have been written up for not making my weigh in if Danny hadn't rescued me. Seems as if stewards are always rescuing me from my weight 'anchor.' Anyway... what I really want to write about is: Danny and Roman. With all Alex pointed out, I think I'm confused. Danny's special; but like Eric, who's also special, and has called a couple of times and spoken to Alex (I haven't returned his calls) I'm not... attracted to Danny 'that' way; or am I? He's so fun and easy to talk to — more so than Roman. Maybe — maybe I should consider it? Unlike with Eric, I didn't do anything stupid. I didn't lead him on. He's put himself out there to be a true friend. But that will never happen, will it? What do you think Roman would say if I said: 'I'm going to Cleveland for three days to kick around with my 'good' buddy Danny, a fantastic looking guy who's straight, but we're just pals.' Yeah, right. It's too bad, isn't it? And even if Roman and I do end up breaking up, Danny will have a girlfriend as soon as he really wants one. Would she go for us visiting each other in our respective cities? I don't think so. I wouldn't go for it if the roles were reversed. I'm glad he came to New

York for the night; he's right. It won't likely ever happen again. And you know what? That makes me sad. And, maybe my feelings for Danny are more complicated than all that – maybe I didn't stay with him because deep-down I want something more serious. See? I'm confused! And I'm sad he's gone! And, this trial separation from Roman is making me sad too. And then there's Eric, and then there's Anderson – Ahhhhhh!!! Neither of those feel resolved either. WHO, and WHAT THE HELL, do I want?

Chapter 20:

Rainy Days and Mondays

"Sherri," Alex called from the living room. "Maurice is on the phone; you up yet?"

I glanced at the clock. It was only nine; I had to work the all-nighter to Portland at 10:15 P.M. I'd hoped to sleep in later. But I slipped my cold feet into slippers, pulled my terrycloth robe from the Hilton over my shoulders, and padded out to take the phone. Alex was dressed. The apartment smelled of coffee; she glanced at her watch. She didn't address me with her usual friendly good morning.

"Hello?" I said into the phone.

"They're striking! Did Alex tell you? Setting up picket lines now; you flying tonight?"

"Yeah, Portland all-nighter."

"You're flying with Danielle," Maurice said. "Good. You'll have someone to hang out with while you're trying to get home."

"Where will you be?"

"In Baltimore," he said. "I'll hop a train; it'll get me home faster; been through this before. Don't want to standby for days at the airport."

I hung up and looked at my roommate. After months of heated negotiations between the company and Gateway's Machinists Union, a still unsettled issue over a paid lunch remained. Both sides had been forced into a thirty-day cooling off period. It was over at midnight, and now the union had the legal right to strike. They were walking off the job. "What's going to happen to me?" I asked Alex.

"You could get stuck for days waiting to get back. The planes takeoff and land all over, picking up and dropping off crew members, but it's disorganized. They won't be able to take regular passengers. Everyone holding Gateway tickets will have to get other airlines to accept their tickets."

"Unlike me, who'll be stuck for… days? Really?"

"You're not at a hub. Try to get to LA, San Fran or even Seattle; you'll get home faster. The bigger the city, the better your chances of getting home sooner."

"Where are you going?"

"To the office. We're officially backing the Machinists; have to help prepare the press release. I gotta go." She gave me a quick hug. "Good luck getting home."

If Roman and I were still dating, he'd be buying me tickets on another airline to fly from Portland to Los Angeles in the morning. I'd bitched at him all the time about being a spend-thrift, now I was missing it. The last letter he'd sent sat on the table. He said this separation has proved to him we were right for each other. Please would I take his calls? *Nice to know somebody loves me.* I couldn't think about that right now—I needed to make sure I had enough clothes for several days. Looked like I was going to get stuck in Oregon.

Jeanna called next. She too had an all-nighter, but her check-in was later than usual; she was laying over in LA. *Ouch.* "Sherri, I think they're *Deadheading* me out there to cover a return trip tomorrow; that's crazy! There's isn't going to *Be* a return trip! The mechanics are going on strike at Midnight; I'm supposed to deadhead out there—just to get stuck?"

"Call them; see if they'll reason with you," I suggested.

"Can't get through; lines are jammed. Everyone else is calling too."

"What time's your check-in?"

"Eight-thirty the tape said. The LA all-nighter leaves at 9:15 P.M. so I'm checking in forty-five minutes prior, which means I'm deadheading. It's got to be that trip. I had this really great classmate who made sure I understood every detail of this stupid contract."

"My trip to Portland leaves at 10:15 P.M. Have to be there at nine. Let's meet at the Carey Bus—take the 8:00 P.M.? You're going to have to show up Jeanna, no matter what."

"You're right," she said. "I'm going to keep calling. If I can't get through or if I find out I'm actually working a trip, I'll meet you for the eight o'clock bus."

Jeanna was indeed scheduled to deadhead to the west coast to cover a non-stop flight back the next day. Like all scheduled Gateway flights, it was going to cancel.

"Why are you doing this to me Vic," she pleaded with the lead scheduler. "You *Know* there's going to be a strike, look out the window!" She pushed past the gate dividing the operations side from the check in side and went to the window. Several Gateway Mechanics were already putting up signs by the road beneath the highway. "You should see how many of them are already outside the terminal."

Vic nodded and looked down. "We have to cover the flights and assume business-as-usual. LA's short-staffed. Need you tomorrow to cover one of their trips. They could settle in the next couple of hours," he looked at his watch. "Stranger things have happened."

Jeanna was shouting now. "Vic, they're going to walk off the job! I grew up near there; LA's old history for me."

"Could always go home," he said.

Jeanna let out a shriek of exasperation. "I can't stand my family," she said as she left the briefing room. "My friends and my life are all here!"

"Been a long day," Vic said to me with his own exasperated look. "Not going to give me a hard time too, are you?"

"No—going to Portland—where it's raining; gee, wow, real neat."

"Make some good meal money if you're stuck there for several days."

"What are you going to do—during the strike?" I asked him.

"Been promising my wife I'd build shelves in her pantry. Looks like I'll have time now."

We took the employee bus over to the terminal; Jeanna was still steaming. When we got out, the Carey bus heading back to the city was right in front of us.

"Jeanna," I said. "Get on."

"Really? Think it'll be ok?"

"*Seems that it's the only thing to do.* After midnight it won't matter. You being here gives them one less person to get back. As for the crew, they're not going to call and say you didn't show up. When was the last time you gave a damn if a deadheading crewmember was onboard? You've already checked in."

"Everyone working the trip has also checked in," she said. "I made sure, so they won't need me."

"Go!" I felt excited for her.

She gave a little hop and grinned. "I love you Sherri," she said, before giving me a hug. "Have a safe trip and get back soon. I'll be waiting for you!" And up the steps she bounded into the bus. She'd be a bar in no time, looking for a great-looking guy to spend the evening with.

My trip was a jumbo of course, DC-10; the pit position was open.

Danielle was our A. "I assume you want to work downstairs?" she asked me.

"Yep." That would make the all-nighter bearable. I found it hard to walk around a dark quiet plane for hours while people slept, looking for someone, *Anyone,* who might want to talk. I refused to sit on a jumpseat; it was against regulations. The options were to find an empty passenger seat, hang out in the galley or in the cockpit. During long all-nighters, I did visit the bar carts so others could go downstairs and take breaks, but since it was my position, it was completely normal for me to stay down there if I wasn't needed.

It was never a surprise to find cigarette butts on the inside of our emergency oxygen masks in the pit. I cleaned them out and threw the butts away. I tripped in the corner; the end of the carpeting was loose and sticking up. "Safety infraction," I said to no-one, making a mental note to write up the loose carpeting in the aircraft maintenance log. I tried to get a big area out of my way; it was inhibiting me from opening the heavy door and removing carts. "Damn!" The carpets were always coming up in the corners. I began counting the meals.

"We've got forty first-class snack trays: twenty-six cold stuffed chicken breasts and fourteen soup/salad combos," I told Danielle from my galley phone. "Soup is clam chowder. Three cockpit meals—two hamburgers and a crab salad. Coach: 220 snack trays. Choice of BLT's or ham and cheese, one low sodium special and two kiddie meals. We're good."

The only thing I had to cook now was the soup; if the cockpit wanted the burgers, I could cook them later. I loaded soup racks into an oven and turned it on. Then I put the first-class rolls for the chicken breast snacks into one of the plugged-in entrée carts and sent up supplies.

After takeoff, I did my usual slide into the galley while the plane was in a deep ascent angle from door 1Left and glanced at the manifest. "Bobby Orr?" I looked over at Danielle; she was still in her jumpseat and wouldn't get up until after the captain had turned off the no smoking sign. "Bobby Orr! His brother's one of my best friends!" I squealed.

"So you've said," she nodded. "He graduated with you, didn't he?"

"Yes! I can't wait to go talk to him; I was feeling blue, but this'll make my day!" I peered into first class and spotted the man in 3D. "I'll be up shortly," I said.

Downstairs I took extra time with the presentation carts for first class. I had a new hop in my step. As soon as all the carts were upstairs, I raced up too. I put the coach special meals at door three, restocked soft drink bins, juice and milk, made sure there was plenty of ice, then hustled up front grabbing two wine bottles on my way.

"Mr. Orr," I cooed with the biggest smile I could muster. "I'm so happy to finally meet you," I burst. "I'm Sherri Van Ness, Danny's friend. The one you got this watch for! Did he give you the thank-you letter I wrote?" I flashed my wrist proudly. "I just saw him! We had a Buffalo layover together." I was so giddy, I couldn't contain my excitement. "If I wasn't holding these wine bottles, I'd give you a big hug," I said.

"Uh…" He was much shyer than Danny—I could see he didn't know what to say. Perhaps I shouldn't have said anything about a hug. "Danny?" he asked me. "A watch?"

"Your brother," I said. "We were in the same training class."

"Sorry," he said, putting his headset down on his lap and looking at the person next to him then back at me. "I don't have a brother named Danny."

My face went white as blood drained straight down to my ankles. I felt as if I might drop the wine bottles. "You… I… is Danny a nickname maybe?" I was stumbling. "You sent this watch…" I tapped it with a wine bottle. "Don't you have a brother who flies for us?"

"No," he said with a funny smile. "I don't."

"Are you *Sure?*" We both laughed together but mine was a nervous, high-pitched desperate laugh. "I… he's from Canada… he played hockey…"

"Gotcha good; didn't he?"

"Not as bad as I'm going to get him," I said. I had to get out of there. "I'm so sorry."

"It's ok," he said.

I offered wine to the rest of the customers up front. Some were giving me sideway looks. I must have appeared completely ridiculous racing up there, gushing all over the sports hero and making a complete fool out of myself. *God DAMN Danny! Wait til Alex hears about this! Danny and I never fight? HAH! Maybe I did have feelings for him? Yeah, I hated his guts! I was going to kill that lying son-of-a-bitch, hang him by his hockey-puck sized balls and rip his face off!*

I choked while telling Danielle what happened. I'd known Danny too long; way too long, for him to have carried this joke this far. I couldn't believe that I'd recently considered giving him a try—I trusted him! He was completely insane and worse, a liar!

Danielle shrugged. "Airline people have the best stories," she said. "They're just not always true," she gave me that 'listen-to-me-I'm-wise' look.

"No shit," I growled between clenched teeth. "Danny's taken this 'bragging rights' thing too far. He's always making up BS!"

"I've never heard you swear before," she laughed.

Later, the passenger sitting in 5C asked me what had happened. "You looked shook up," he said. He wanted to talk. He lived in Portland and had a boat—and of course, I was welcome anytime I was in town to join him. As a matter of fact, what was I doing tomorrow?

I found myself thinking about it. "Let me make sure the service is done in back and I'll come chat some more," I told him. "Would you like some more wine?" I'd already started filling his glass.

Everything was picked up in coach. The tray carts were downstairs and we had our makeshift bars set up at cross aisles three and four. Coach attendants wanted their breaks, so I stayed upstairs. Only two people at a time were ever allowed down in the pit. We checked in with the cockpit to see what they knew. They'd gotten the word; Gateway Airline Mechanics were officially on strike.

"What are you going to do in Portland?" the captain asked me.

"Hang out at the airport and wait for a seat home I guess."

"Like everyone else," he laughed.

Len, my new friend in 5C, sat up in his seat when I came back into the cabin. A few of the other first-class customers had their reading lights on. Some were watching the movie but the rest were sleeping, tucked in with pillows, blankets and wearing the socks, earplugs and eye masks from our complimentary first-class amenity kits.

"Tell me more about your boat," I said. *Just get them talking about something they like. It was so easy.*

"I've got two." He talked excitedly about his sail boat and his schooner. "Just got the sail boat," he said. "She's old and beautiful but I've got my work cut out for me," he said.

"You do all the work yourself?" I asked.

"It's a hobby," he explained. "Boat people are into their boats."

"What do you have to do before you can sail it?"

"She sails now," he said. "But I want to restore her; sand her down and re-do the woodwork. Need to put a rug down in her galley too."

"How big is this boat? How big is the galley?"

"From here to the other side of that aisle," he said. "That's about the floor size of what I want to cover. For now, until I do more work, I'm just looking for used carpeting to put down. Maybe six by eight feet." He swirled the ice cubes in his water glass and looked straight at me. "You didn't tell me yet what you're doing tomorrow. Rumor has it this airline's shutting down."

"They did," I told him. "Cockpit got confirmation from ground control. If you're flying on Gateway in the next few weeks, might want to get over to another carrier when we land to make new arrangements."

"Will the other carriers take my tickets?"

"Absolutely. The major airlines all have reciprocal agreements."

"What will you do?" He studied me, waiting.

"This is my first experience with this," I said. "I'm told we all go to the airport and wait. Gateway planes will pick up stranded crew members. Planes hop from city to city getting as many as they can home."

"Sounds like chaos," he said.

"It is. But they'll have to pay me until I get back. I won't be getting a pay check for a while; New York doesn't pay unemployment to employees of companies on strike, even though we're not the striking party."

"Doesn't sound right," he said.

"It's the only state that doesn't," I said.

"What about tonight?" he said.

"We'll still get our hotel rooms," I said. "They'll have to provide us rooms until we get home. They're booked long in advance."

We left it at that. I would go to the airport the next day when Gateway told me to, if they told me to. If I didn't get out of town, I had a date with Len. He would take me sailing or cruising—I could choose. When I went back downstairs, I stared at the floor for a long time. Did I really want to go out on a boat with this guy? He was nice and all that—but—a boat? What if he was a serial killer who wanted to chop me up into little pieces and throw my remains into the Pacific? "What if?" I said out loud, looking at my serious expression in the tiny mirror over the sink. *Talking to myself and feeling… yeah, feeling a little tired and out of sorts.* What did I want to do? The corner of the carpet caught my eye; it had lifted up higher from the strain of carts rolling over it. I pulled the corner; it came right up. *Oh, wow,* I mused. Rubbing my collarbones, I thought: *Should I?*

Back upstairs, I slid over to Len and bent down beside him. He gave me a charming smile. "Would you mind waiting around a few extra minutes after we land?"

*   *   *

After landing, I hung around upstairs until most of the first-class passengers had deplaned. Bobby Orr stepped into the aisle and I gave him a shy glance.

"Don't hurt him too badly," he said with an amused look.

The front cabin was empty. "Stay here," I told Len. "Stand right… here." I led him over to the covered hatch in the floor which was the pit emergency exit. "Don't let anyone step on this," I said. I raced back downstairs. Then I yanked hard, pulling up all the carpeting—it was heavier than I'd thought it would be, but I managed to roll it into a tube. Struggling, I set it on one end and climbed onto the counter to open the emergency hatch. I pushed. The square cover popped off. Len was looking down at me. "Ready?" I asked, "I'm going to need your strength to pull this out," I said. I angled the carpeting toward the exit—thank goodness it was a low ceiling. "Ok," I said. "Pull!"

When I got back upstairs again, the crew was scrutinizing Len's new boat carpeting. The pilots were talking happily with him. They loved planes—Len loved boats—boys and their toys.

"You're going to need assistance," the first officer said, eyeing the large roll of carpeting.

"I've got an idea," Danielle said. "Since we're looting now," she pulled one of the queen carts out from its opening and set it up. "Here, you can wheel your prize right out to baggage claim."

And off we went: Len with his carpeting on the cart, his bags on the bottom shelf, eight flight attendants and three pilots.

The gate agent looked down at his computer screen as we passed and said, "I know nothing, I know nothing."

Outside, the hotel van was waiting. I glanced behind me at the long lines. Gateway ticket agents were going to have a rough night.

"Sherri?" Len called out as we all moved toward the hotel van with our bags. "Am I going to hear from you tomorrow?"

"You're going to hear from all of us," Danielle said. "Party on Len's boat tomorrow if we don't get out of town."

The crew cheered.

Len shrugged. "All right," he said. "Might be crowded, but you're all invited."

"We have no idea what they'll tell us to do," I said honestly. "They've got to be swamped; thousands of us are stranded. I promise I'll call you either way."

When I climbed into the van I announced, "I don't know about Len's boat, but party in my room! Seems a little bit of the liquor also walked off the airplane tonight."

"I remember when you were horrified about a friend of yours removing one bottle of wine from a plane," Danielle teased. "You're changing Sherri."

"I'll be broke for a while and it's all Gateway's fault," I rationalized out loud. "Besides, management's so busy with this strike, they couldn't possibly have sent anyone to Portland to do suitcase checks."

We partied all night. I'd taken all the beer and wine I could stuff into my bags, purse and suitcase, as well as a full tray of mini bottles—fifty-six in all.

The next day it rained, and rained, and rained. I called Len; he tried to talk me into dinner and a movie instead. "What's wrong?" he asked.

"*Rainy days and Mondays always get me down,*" I said. "Nothing's really wrong; I just feel like *I don't belong* here; I want to go home; I want to get back to New York."

The following day, Gateway told us to get to the airport because they had a DC-10 coming for all the people stuck in their Northwest cities. We didn't get out though. Back to the hotel we went, where Danielle and I drank some more, and played with her wigs. I *wanted to quit;* just call headquarters and tell them I was done. But that wasn't going to help. I'd be at Portland airport stranded with all the other passengers, only I wouldn't be holding a ticket.

• *Dear FlightLog; It's been raining for two days. I have no idea when I'll get home - a nice guy keeps calling me but I don't want to go out with him and start something long-distance in the middle of a strike, GEEZ! Like I need anymore 'maybe' boyfriends! I'm tempted to go to LA. You know — run and find the one who loves me. Would I be doing it just to escape this plight, or to find out once and for all if Roman and I have a chance? Could we work out everything that's messy and unsaid in our relationship? When do I know that if I go back to someone, it isn't just because my life's a disaster at the moment? I can't do that, can I? Go back to him just because I've got the blues and I'm unhappy? I've had the craziest year; I'm overwhelmed! I'm thinking about Roman. Thought about Danny a lot too, then I found out that my first impression of him — being a total dork — was right. He's irritatingly childish and I'm furious! I can't really say that 'what I feel has come and gone before; no need to talk it out; you know what it's all about.' FlightLog, when am I going to KNOW what it's all about, WHEN?*

On day three, Danielle and I got seats on a 747. The gate agent couldn't stop staring at Danielle's chest. "Here you go ladies," he said, not looking into her eyes. "Enjoy your ride."

Danielle pressed her lips together. "Those are not speakers," she said to him matter-of-factly. She was simply letting him know that he should check his body language. I laughed.

We had no idea how many stops we'd make; the many landings and take offs were torture. The poor attendants working the trip were the most junior in the system, and the A did not deviate from the required safety announcements.

"There's no one onboard except crew members!" One very drunk steward hollered. "We *Know* how to fasten our seat belts; we *Know* where the exits are; for *God's Sake* hon, we *Know* how to put on the oxygen masks!"

The junior attendant didn't flinch. "One of you could be an FAA check rider; I'm not taking any risks," she said. "You guys junior-manned me—so you can suffer through all my announcements." We landed in Kansas City. "Welcome to Kansas City, Kansas…" she started.

The whole airplane groaned loudly; some booed.

"It's Missouri," I said to her softly. "Kansas City's in Missouri."

"Are you sure?" she frowned.

"I'm a Kansas girl from Wichita," I told her, lifting my dark glasses so she could see my eyes. "I'm very, very, sure."

And then, something *Good* happened. We landed in Knoxville, and Maurice walked onto the plane. "Maurice!" Danielle and I both screamed. "Could you move over?" I asked the pilot sitting next to us. "Why are you here?" I asked him. "Thought you were in Baltimore?"

"Cute glasses; they new?" He took them off me, examining them as he spoke. "Our flight out of here was delayed. They have noise abatement in Baltimore; what an antiquated city. We would arrive too late; by then, we were on strike. Least we were at the Hyatt; I was marvelously cossetted," he said. "They told us not to go to the airport until today, so I've been exploring. Ready to get home. We're going to have *One Hell* of a Strike Party when we arrive! Sergio, Alex and Jeanna are setting up now waiting for as many of us to get back as possible."

Maurice tested his newest pilot jokes. "Do you know how copper wire was invented," he offered. "Two pilots fighting over a penny!" The pilots near us were not amused. One let Maurice know, so he followed with: "What do pilots use for birth-control?" Pause; no takers. "Their personalities."

I could have kissed the ground when we landed at Kennedy. I'd been gone for six days; it seemed like six months. Within hours, I'd be at my favorite place: on Maurice's living room floor by the fire, telling my damn-Danny story and listening to everyone else's crazy strike stories, and I'd be happy; and I was.

I waited until it was loud and gregarious and I'd had a few, then I went into Maurice's kitchen to call Danny. It was a long-distance call and would probably cost Mo ten bucks, but I didn't care. "Danny! You Mother-Fucking-Lying-Bastard-Piece-of-Shit! How the hell are you?"

Jeanna threw her arm around me and moved close to the mouthpiece. "You are *So Fucked* Danny! Just wait until Sherri gets her claws on you; she's sharpening them now!"

I had to put my finger in my ear, she was so loud.

"Reej?" he said. "What's going on. Where are you? It's really loud there."

"We're having a Strike party," I hollered.

"Of course you are," he said quietly. "New York's partying because a strike means time off to play, while here in Cleveland, employees are behaving as if it's a funeral procession. Everyone's convinced we're closing shop; that we'll never work again and the company's going under—that they'll file for bankruptcy… You should see the long faces, hung heads and drooping shoulders. Remember your old training buddy? Amy? I saw her at the airport when I landed. She was sobbing; lots of people are."

"That's crap Danny," I said, feeling bad for him but getting a pang of pleasure thinking about Amy crying. "This is all going to blow over. Airlines go on strike all the time. Such a typical response for unsophisticated scaredy-cat Midwesterners."

"You're a Midwesterner Rejects. You're from Kansas."

"Not anymore!"

"Hope you guys are right," he said. "Not sure I believe it's going to just 'blow over' as you say. This doom and gloom feeling is contagious."

"Well, if it doesn't—look at it this way. You. Are. Dead. Meat. Either. Way!"

"Why?"

"I had Bobby Orr on a flight," I said. "I told him, 'Oh if I wasn't holding these wine bottles, I'd give you a hug,' showing off my watch like some bimbo-groupie idiot." I'd intended to scream at Danny—but the words just slipped out matter-of-factly.

There was a pause; I wasn't sure he'd heard me, then Danny laughed so hard and for so long, I could hear him gasping, coughing, trying to recover himself, which only led to more fits of howling. "REEJ! That is the funniest thing I've heard all day! Oh God; thanks for that! Just what I needed after seeing all these sad sacks." He couldn't stop laughing. "Did you get me his autograph?" I did not find that amusing, but Danny kept up his choking laughter.

It didn't seem as if he was going to stop anytime soon, so I hung up defeatedly. "Guess I told him," I said to Jeanna as I rubbed my collarbones with one hand.

"*He's* the one who bought you that watch Reej," she said, pointing at my wrist.

"Don't call me that, Jeanna Meana!"

"Lotta money for a new-hire flight attendant. He loves you. Couldn't admit it back then."

"So… he's some kind of modern Cyrano de Bergerac?"

"A lot cuter," she said.

"He's a liar! The only thing he pens are phony autographs."
Oh, Danny boy.

"Maybe you should just *date* him for a while," she said. "Try it out; he is funny."

"What happened to the girlfriend I had who said, 'he's only a *Steward*, Sherri!'"

Chapter 21

Takin' Care of Business

"THIS REALLY IS THE PERFECT SPOT," said Jeanna as she collected a dollar from an eager customer.

We were outdoors on a busy street corner near Maurice's subway stop—working. We'd *get up every morning* and gather there, Monday through Friday, since the strike began, to sell sweet rolls and sticky buns. Alex borrowed two banquet tables from the union office. Jeanna came up with red and white checkerboard tablecloths—we'd had an idea—and we went for it. We bought warm, yummy pastries from the local bakeries who'd sell them to us for three dollars a dozen. Then we'd sell them to the fast-moving *'people pushin' people shovin'* crowds, right there on the sidewalk, for a buck each. We provided smiles, *(us girls—we tried to look pretty)* and napkins. No need to stop, get in line, no tax, no receipts, we even provided run-beside-you service so they could *get to work by nine*—it was a success! Danielle's husband, Jim, perfected the idea when we were at one of Maurice's gatherings brainstorming ways to make money. He'd also learned that the beat cop regularly came by at 10 A.M.—so we had to be packed up and on our way by that hour which was perfect, because by then, the rush hour crowds had thinned.

In a few days, the business had grown. Returning customers looked forward to seeing us. Their mouths watered for our hot, warm, pastries, delivered in Jeanna's origami-folded napkins. Alex went back to the union office and found coffee carafes. Now we also offered to-go cups of coffee for fifty cents; more business! It was week two, day four. We were making hundreds of dollars a day. It wasn't bad, and it helped make up for not being able to collect unemployment.

"Ugh," Jeanna complained. "Not sure I can handle this five days a week stuff."

"Welcome to the real world," Alex said. "And, we're done by ten, out of here by eleven. Flying looks better all the time, doesn't it?"

"How do they do it," Jeanna said. "When is this strike going to be *Over?*"

We had grown closer: Maurice, Alex, me—Jeanna too. I'd insisted Jeanna be included; she needed the distraction as she was jammed about the strike and about our future with Gateway. Maurice didn't need the money—Sergio made plenty, but Mo loved being with me and with Alex, so he came out to join us, every morning, rain or shine.

As word got out, some of our friends came by to point and laugh.

"You guys are *takin' care of business,*" one said.

Most were troupers and even bought a hot bun. 'Good luck,' they'd say. Later, when we'd go back to Maurice's and count our cash, we'd be the ones laughing because they had absolutely *No* idea how much we were making; and it was all tax free!

"Look at me," Maurice sang, lifting his pile of bills, *"I'm self-employed. I love to work at nothing all day."*

"Good show," Sergio said on a Thursday afternoon after we'd raced through our early morning routine. I'd fallen asleep with Maurice on their L-shaped couch. Jeanna was passed out in their guest room while Alex snoozed in the master bedroom. Sergio eyed the stacks of bills. "What's everyone doing tonight?"

"I'm going back to our apartment," I said. "Sorry Sergio; I know your home hasn't been the same since we started this."

Two weeks later, we sat in the same spots after watching the TV show, "Dallas," now in its second season. Mitzi, Danielle, Bonnie, Tom, Georgia and Yosef had joined us. My three classmates had recently started showing up at S & M's. No matter what was going on in the world, conversation always made its way back to the same topic: when was the strike going to *end?*

Alex and I made it home in spite of how tired we were. I was looking forward to curling up with some of my favorite books: *The Ghost of Flight 401* and *Coffee, Tea or Me,* because I missed flying so badly and longed for my 'flying' life back. It sounded funny to call it that—I'd been a flight attendant for less than a year, but already I couldn't imagine doing anything else.

Friday after 'work' we headed downtown to visit Danielle's husband. I'd never been to Wall Street. As Jim spoke, I stared at a picture on his desk. It was of a woman with huge breasts in a low-cut, almost non-existent, see-through tight blouse.

I couldn't stand it anymore; I picked it up and asked, "Who is this?"

"That's Candy Samples," he stated proudly. "She's a porn star. Danielle had her on a flight a few years ago. She knows I love her so she asked for her autograph."

"No way," Jeanna said, taking the photo from me. We stared at it together.

'To Jim,' the buxom star had written. 'Breast wishes, Candy Samples.'

"Booby-bragging-rights!" I said with a laugh. Jim obviously liked big ones; his wife Danielle was well-endowed. "If Danny ever saw this, he'd be copying it in no time."

Into week five, business was better than ever. We knew several customers by name. People who usually bought one roll were buying more and taking some to their offices for friends. *Life was good.* Maurice did an inventory of our product. "What time is it?" he asked.

"Nine," I answered.

"We need more," he said. "Run and get another four dozen," he told me. "Tell them tomorrow, we'll need twelve dozen on our first pick up," he said.

I took off. I liked the running. It made me feel better, as I was eating so many pastries. I came back with three boxes. "They only had these left. Said tomorrow they'll only charge us twenty cents each instead of a quarter."

Later, from Jeanna who was on the lookout, we heard, "He's coming!"

Maurice shoved empty pastry boxes into a large trash can. I folded up the checkered cloths. Jeanna collapsed one of the tables and Alex took care of the other. As the cop turned the corner, Jeanna and Alex slid the tables behind them; they were clearly in view. Then the two of them began flirting with the cop—it was nauseating, but effective. Eventually he walked on by. He smiled, but he was clearly suspicious; he kept looking back at us as if he knew we were up to something. We were there every weekday!

"Ten o'clock on the dot," Maurice said.

And thus, the weeks passed. The union and the company were both standing firm—unflinchingly devoted to not caving in. Even in New York, the unofficial laissez-faire-est domicile of all, we were getting antsy. No one believed that the strike would last into a seventh week, but it had. Mom and Dad urged me to come home, but I couldn't; I had to do my part.

'*We're self-employed* now,' I'd explained. '*Working overtime.*'

Our five days a week stretched to six. We woke by four. By five thirty we claimed our corner and began selling.

One unseasonably bright but cold spring morning, a long limousine approached; it seemed that whoever was inside was curious about us.

"Probably an undercover cop," Jeanna speculated.

"In a limo?" I said, squinting at the car. I wasn't in a good mood; I'd forgotten my sunglasses and the sun's glare was bothering me.

The driver got out and bought a half dozen pastries. We watched him walk back to the car.

"Whoever it is, isn't leaving," Maurice pointed out.

"Maybe he's going to proposition us," Jeanna said. "Tell us how we can make a lot more money."

Then the car slipped away.

"That was weird," Alex said.

Within ten minutes, the car returned. The back door of the spotless car opened and the passenger stepped out. It was Roman. He walked toward us with his right hand outstretched. "Think you need these," he said, holding out a pair of sunglasses for me, the price tag dangling from a string. I tried not to show how excited I was, but found myself throwing my arms around his neck anyway. Then, everyone else was hugging him too.

That night, Roman treated us to a fancy dinner. We treated him to The Pyramid Club. It was screamingly funny to see the look on his face when he realized we were surrounded by drag queens. After squirming around uncomfortably for a while, he did settle down.

Roman picked up his glass to raise a toast. "If you can't beat 'em, join 'em." Then he whistled and cheered along with the rest of us. "Can't say I've ever been in a place like this before," he admitted.

"What a tedious dull life you've led," Maurice said.

"What if someone I know sees me?" Roman said, looking around self-consciously.

"What if? You're seated with three knock-out 'real' women," he pointed out. "Look at how scrumptious they are." Then he added, "At least I think they're real women. Do I have first-hand knowledge? Can't say that I do. Each one of them can certainly be a *drag* at times."

We whooped and hollered as we witnessed hilarious impersonations of Barbra Streisand, Joan Rivers, Bette Midler, Dianna Ross, Cher, Tina Turner, Debbie Reynolds, Ann Margaret and Lena Horne. They were beautiful; we truly were being entertained by the right bunch of fellows.

*   *   *

Roman was staying in a small suite at the Plaza; it had become my favorite New York Hotel. I stared out the window as I usually did. The city lights and the park were magical.

"What is it you want?" he asked me as I stared out.

"I want my old life back; my 'new' old life," I said. "There's still so much I want to do and explore. To have it yanked away makes me realize how much it means. That's not what you want to hear; is it?" I turned to look at him.

He raised his open palms, a questioning gesture, but said, "I won't ask you to give it up. Not yet anyway."

"What does that mean?"

"We can talk about it later," he said.

"We don't really talk though, do we? We fight."

"We'll work it out." He came over and slipped his arms around me from the back. I leaned my head into his shoulder; it felt wonderful; the familiarness of him soothed me. "Would you consider coming out to LA until the strike is over?"

"God Roman. I never even thought about that. How could I possibly drop a bomb like that on my parents?"

"Seriously?"

"Yes seriously; I couldn't disappoint them. Announce I was openly living with a man I wasn't married to? My parents would be hurt; they might disown me; I wasn't raised that way."

"You really are young. Sometimes I forget how much so. Let's take a trip. We were going to ring in the New Year together—I want to make that up to you."

"I can't commit to a trip now," I said. "This strike won't last forever. Flying will be a fiasco when it's settled. Gateway will be scrambling to get all their planes in the air again—I won't have time off—none of us will."

He pulled me close, watching to see if I wanted him to kiss me; I did. Then we heard the 'just in' special announcement blare from the TV.

"The nearly eight-week long Machinist Strike at Gateway Airlines has finally been settled," the excited news anchor announced.

"Bet the mechanics won," I said hopefully.

"When the machinist union returns to work at Gateway Airlines," the TV anchorman explained, "they will be paid for their half-hour lunch break," he said. "This is an unprecedented…"

I smiled, thinking about Quentin and all of his co-worker friends. *Bravo to all of you. You stayed strong; you stayed United. Good show.*

Chapter 22:

My Cherie Amore

ROMAN AND I SKIPPED INTO A waiting taxi on a gorgeous, breezy evening. We'd just seen *Deathtrap* on Broadway; it was as funny as Maurice and Alex had promised. "I loved it," Roman confessed. He looked refreshed; not as tired as usual.

"It's good to have you here for more than just a night," I said as he snuggled in close.

"It is." He pressed a quick kiss on my cheek and closed his door. "That play was hilarious. You hungry?"

"No; I don't want a heavy meal now."

"We can have room service later if you change your mind. Plaza please," he said to the driver.

I did love my lifestyle when I was with Roman; who wouldn't? But sometimes I felt like a phony. I got uncomfortable with the overboard doses of limos, hotels with doormen and bellhops bustling and fussing. We stayed in our share of exclusive hotels with Gateway, but I was a crew member; I wheeled my own suitcase; I let myself into the room and got my own ice.

With Roman, employees fell all over themselves, asking if we wanted them to turn on the TV, pull down the bedding, open the curtains, retrieve ice or water—anything. It didn't suit me twenty-four/seven. Seemed as if it should have been reserved for vacations and special events; but that was Roman's style. We'd argued about that—as well as other things, often, as Alex had pointed out to me. How had I missed that?

Jeanna rolled her eyes when I tried explaining—just like when her date Brad had waltzed us into Studio 54—she didn't get it. Neither did Maurice; he always wanted to be on holiday. I didn't mention it anymore; I'd learned a lesson from Alex. The fighting was over; I was biting my tongue more. I tried to appreciate instead how he was always nice to the staff and how he was a great tipper. Did I want to live in the same city as he? I needed more than a girlfriend label to move all the way to the West Coast, away from my friends. I was working hard to ensure that it didn't become an argument. LA was even more senior than New York; I really wouldn't ever get off of reserve out there. Instead of flying two-day cushy coast-to-coast trips with one leg a day and nice layovers, I'd be flying early crack-of-dawn turn arounds with no meal money; that's what the reserves in Los Angeles usually flew.

In Roman's room, I slipped into something more comfortable and joined him. "You happy tonight?" I asked.

"Yes."

"You look… good. Rested, calm, something's going right. And we got to spend so much time together. This is the third night in a row I've seen you; a record!"

"Work is fabulous right now." He picked up my hands happily, as if to lead me in a dance and said, "I have a surprise. I need to go to Milan. Have you been to Italy?"

"You know I haven't."

"There's a perfect spot I love off the coast of Naples—an Island called Capri. I think it was a getaway for Julius Caesar. I've arranged to spend a few nights there; of course, I want you to come with me. No work, just R & R. It'll be our first trip to Europe and I want it to be memorable."

"When?"

"When will you have your June schedule? I'll keep my dates flexible until you tell me what works."

I clapped with glee and broke into child-like laughter. "Italy! How romantic! I can't wait… that's just… *Perfect* Roman! I can usually hold a reserve line with five days off in a row. Our bids come out Wednesday; they're due Sunday. I'll know three days after that!"

"Say the word, and that's when we'll go. *Cherie amour, pretty little one that I adore.* I know that's the wrong language but I don't know any Italian."

"Yet!" I corrected. "Ciao, arrivederci, prego, e cappuccino! We'll practice."

"You always make me so delighted Sherri; you're easy to please," he said, grabbing me as I spun around the room. "You really are the *only girl my heart beats for.* Come here."

• *Dear FlightLog. I'm finally going SOMEWHERE ABROAD! Italy!!! And it's not a layover! Got a guidebook from the library because even though I've heard of Rome, Venice, Florence, I've never heard of Capri. It looks like it might be the most beautiful place ever. There was a picture of Jackie O walking down a curved cobblestone street – if it's good enough for American 'royalty' then it's good enough for me. There aren't any cars on the main part of the island; you take a ferry over. Since it's so cliffy, the luggage goes up to the hotels* via a tram car while you ride or walk... oh wait, you don't 'walk' on the isle, you 'stroll.' It all looks like an Agatha Christie Novel setting. I'm SO EXCITED about this trip! Did you know there's a real 'Blue Grotto?' I thought that was just an expression like 'golden sand' but no, it's technically called: Grotta Azzurra, and it's a cave overhanging you can only enter for a few hours on calm days by small boat during low tide. Once inside, all you see is electric blue water from the way the sun filters up to the water line – it seems outrageously cool and I'm going to jump right in – what a perfect place to be a mermaid. Roman can be so wonderful; suppose this has anything to do with his name? He can be so romantic! This trip is going to be extremely special; I just know it. He sang to me last night. Made me laugh because a few months ago, Danny was singing that corny, 'Sherry, can you come out tonight' song which I loathe, but Roman sang 'My Cherie Amour.' I like that one. I love how the French say my name: 'Cherie' with the accent on the second syllable. Taking me to Italy and singing to me in French; I wonder if he's going to ask me something while we're sailing around the Mediterranean? I don't feel old enough or ready for that; oh, this is happening fast. What would I say? What a nice problem to have, huh?

Roman and I talked every night on the phone, making our plans; it was costing him a fortune in long-distance bills. I couldn't think about anything besides our trip. The more excited I was, the more he started sounding like it was going to be the best trip ever for him too. *This* was how I'd pictured my life all those years dreaming about working for the airlines! Further, I'd just called the reserve tape to get my assignment. I was going to have my twenty-first birthday in: LOS ANGELES! Now *that?* That only happened in the movies. *'Kismet' as Danielle would say; life is a fairytale come true; I'm a Disney Princess!*

"We'll celebrate your most-special birthday—the first day you can legally drink in California—as well as your one-year anniversary with the airlines," he said.

"What are we going to save to celebrate in Italy?" I asked.

"We'll think of something," he said in his soothing voice. "Where would you like to eat? Tomorrow night after you land?"

"A nice place but not over-the-top. No sommeliers or anyone scraping bread crumbs from the tablecloth with strange tools; no sorbet to cleanse the palate—how 'bout a good seafood place with a great view?"

"I'll take you to the Chart House in Redondo Beach. You'll love it."

"If I'm with you, I will," I said.

Since I'd been laying over in cities like Seattle, San Francisco and Baltimore, I'd discovered how surprisingly delicious well-prepared seafood was. Roman was an expert anyway—he was always introducing me to things I loved more than I could have once imagined. Growing up in my house, 'fish' meant heated, frozen fish sticks. My new tastes weren't helping me keep the weight off—with all the wining and dining—but it was all still so new and rare that I couldn't muster up the discipline to just order salads.

The next day I floated up and down the aisles; nothing was too much trouble; nothing was too hard. I was in the best mood ever, even though it was a long duty-day. I didn't get a nonstop flight to the coast as I'd hoped. I had to fly from LaGuardia to Chicago, to Denver, to LA on small crowded planes.

Roman was there when I arrived, waiting to whisk me off. Sometimes he'd send a car for me, or pick me up later at the hotel. But I appreciated it most when he came himself. And now that I was sensible enough to wear flat shoes inflight, the recovery would come quicker; I'd be a fun date.

* * *

"Owww, my birthday! And I'm in beautiful sunny Southern Cal with a gorgeous guy…"

"Who loves you…"

"Who loves me," I repeated. "And I'm going to have the *Best* time." We were seated just in time to enjoy the sunset on the water and everything at the Chart House was delicious. The cute waiters all wore Hawaiian shirts. They looked like 'The Beach Boys'—young, darling, tan surfer guys who must have all been lifeguards in their teens and I was happy.

"Roman?" Another nice-looking fellow in a Hawaiian shirt, though older than the waiters I kept eyeing, stopped by the table and shook hands with Roman. "Lovely to meet you Sherri," Glen said as he readied to leave. "I won't keep you two from enjoying your meal. Roman, can I call you about that group? Seventeen of them; I'm having a hard time getting them all on the same flights."

"Sure," Roman said.

"Should I call you at the office, the house or the condo?"

"At the office," he said. He cleared his throat and moved his chair several times.

When Glen stepped away, I asked, "What house?"

"I bought a house; I've been working out of it sometimes. It's mostly empty; I'm thinking about getting rid of the condo."

"Since when? I never heard you talk about getting a house. Why haven't you given me that telephone number?"

"Sherri…"

"Where is it?"

"It's… it's here actually, in Redondo Beach."

"Happy birthday to you, happy birthday to you!" Approaching our table were several waiters and cocktail waitresses. One held an enormous piece of mud pie: coffee ice cream in an Oreo cookie-crust, smothered in whipped cream, hot fudge and sliced almonds. Several long thin candles lit up the face of the waiter carrying it toward us. I kept a smile glued to my face, thanked them all, took one bite, then got up.

"Where are you going?" Roman asked.

"To the washroom. Gonna buy some cigarettes too." I found a payphone and a cigarette machine. I asked one of the cocktail gals to make change, bought a pack, and with my hand shaking, slipped a quarter into the phone and dialed: 213-555-1212. I knew most of the area codes around the cities Gateway flew into by heart. Everything in Los Angeles was a 213 area code.

"Information, what city please?" The operated asked.

"Redondo Beach."

"Go ahead."

"I'm looking for a listing for Roman Palermo—'P' as in Paul, 'A' as in apple, 'L,' 'E' as in echo, 'R,' 'M' as in Michael, 'O' please."

Roman came around the corner. "What are you doing?" he asked me. He was frowning; he still hadn't been able to clear his throat.

"Something I should have done a long time ago."

He took the phone out of my hand and hung it up. There were already tears in my eyes when he said, "Alright Sherri, alright. I'll tell you everything."

* * *

I wouldn't leave with him after he'd told me *'The Truth.'* We almost got into a physical fight outside the restaurant. There was *No Way* I was going to let him take me anywhere; and at that moment, I didn't care that my suitcase was at his condo.

"Maybe this is all for the best," he said. "You're so young… it really hit me when I suggested you come stay with me and you said you couldn't 'do' that to your parents. Made me feel like a dirty old man. We live 3000 miles apart. You probably should be dating boys your own age. I didn't mean for this to happen; she's an old girlfriend from college and we ran into each other. Remember; *You* were the one who needed 'some time'; it's not all my fault! You wouldn't return my calls. She was someone to talk to who listened. I was going to tell you about it after our trip. You and I are supposed to be leaving for Italy in three weeks…"

"Why didn't you tell me before, why would you take *A TRIP* with me when you're dating someone else? That's just… *Wrong!*"

"I don't know the answer. I don't know which of you, or even if either of you, is right for me; I've been confused too. You asked me to understand when you were confused, now I'm asking you to understand that my head was spinning too. Do you think this is easy?" He moved toward me with outstretched arms.

"Is she living in that house with you? You said you were thinking about getting rid of the condo."

He didn't answer.

I pushed him hard. "Get away from me!" With fury and hatred, I picked up two handfuls of sand and flung them at him.

The aim was pitiful; I didn't even come close to hitting any part of him.

I did hear him say he would get my things to my hotel that night and he'd wait for my call, which he hoped wouldn't take too long. "I really do love you Sherri. I love you, and I'm sorry."

I stayed on the beach for an hour, crying, yelling at the water, kicking my shoes off in front of me, smoking, sitting in the sand and… thinking. This certainly was *another thing of the movies;* young girl gets swept off her feet by older, sophisticated man, then finds out he's a cheat. Oh… *Poor Roman!* Such a *Difficult* decision for him! My heart bleeds for the tortured lover! She was just someone to talk to… *does he think I was born yesterday?* Was this how the rest of my life was going to be, every birthday a disaster? Killing passengers during my mockup quick and dirty when I turned twenty in training, and now this betrayal on my twenty-first?

A cab started to leave the front of the restaurant; I ran over. "I don't have any money," I said, poking my head into the open passenger window. "Would you take me to my hotel and I'll write a check when I get there? I work for the airlines. The front desk will cash a check for me," I told him honestly (it was in our contract; thanks Gateway).

He leaned toward me and put his arm up along the back of the seat. "You got something I'll take in trade; don't have to cash a check."

When I reared back with a look of horror, he tried to apologize and said he was only kidding. I ran to the cab behind him and got in. More tears poured.

The driver said kindly, "Having a rough night Miss? I'm sorry."

"Me too."

I couldn't sleep. I called Alex, Maurice, and Jeanna which was stupid, because I renewed my sobs with each new conversation.

Then I went down to the pool and dove in even though the lights were out and the pool was closed. I swam underwater, crisscrossing the length of the dark pool over and over; the cold water felt wonderful on my hot swollen face.

The next day I worked two early legs home, walked into my apartment, and flung myself into Alex's arms. Maurice—sweet Mo, was there too. I could see in their faces how sad they both were; it took me by surprise. They both looked like they had been crying. Wow, they really loved me! Alex held me close; we talked and laughed between tears. Then, they delivered the day's news, positively stunned that I'd been able to race home from LaGuardia without hearing about it already: a full American Airlines DC-10 airplane had crashed minutes after takeoff from Chicago's O'Hare International airport when an engine had fallen off; everyone was dead. The revolting tragedy put everything into perspective; what the hell did my foolish love woes matter?

Sean flew on the 727s, so it wasn't with too much trepidation that I thought of my dad. Putting self-pity aside, I remained calm and pretended I wasn't concerned. No news is good news, right? Then from the television we heard that several American Airlines non-working crew members had been deadheading on the flight. I jumped up and called home. The line was busy; I tried again and again; I couldn't get through. I kept trying in vain. Finally, after two hours, thirteen minutes and fifty-two seconds, I heard a dial tone and a click as someone picked up the receiver.

"Van Ness residence," my handsome father said slowly. He sounded exhausted.

"Oh Daddy," I blurted out; tears of relief poured down my face; I was sobbing again.

Chapter 23:

I Will Survive

THE MONTH OF MY ONE-YEAR anniversary turned out to be an occasion no one could have predicted. The FAA grounded all DC-10s after the engine had fallen off the American Airlines airplane. They were doing thorough inspections of all 10 aircraft for all airlines, as well as checking each company's DC-10 maintenance procedures. Since no one knew when they would be cleared for travel, Gateway had not taken the trips off the lines of flying. DC-10 crews were deadheading all over the system so that flight crews could be in place to go if the planes suddenly got clearance.

So far in June, I had flown one regular trip and two jumbo trips, where I had deadheaded every leg; I hadn't worn my uniform once. Because reserves only received half credit and half pay for deadheading, junior attendants deadheaded while senior attendants worked the flights. *I remembered Darryl and Louise's argument the night after I'd graduated, while working my 'pass-riding' flight into LaGuardia. 'This is going to be an issue!' Louise had said.* The whining from our senior ranks was unparalleled. 'Thank you Gateway Airlines!' Jeanna had said. Like me, she was deadheading, a lot.

At Kennedy, I checked in for my fourth trip of the month. I was deadheading to Seattle to work a—scheduled DC-10 flight home, which would probably cancel. I raced into the mailroom, grabbed my latest revisions and found a company addressed manila envelope from Cleveland. Inside was a pretty envelope with some kind of lacy fabric and a note.

'Dear Rejects; Surprise! Thought of you the other day when I saw this; couldn't resist. Wear it in good health. Guess what? It's been a year; we 'officially' started flying June first last year. Time to fly back to Cleveland for Recurrent training. Let me know what day you're going to bid for so we can go together. Give me a call some-time… and… Happy Birthday Miss all-grown-up-now. Want to buy you a birthday drink too—legally this time. Hugs and kisses, Danny.' The gift was a beautiful, delicate, blue and white garter.

I couldn't believe my twentieth birthday, which had taken place during Emergency training, had already been more than a year ago. We were required to keep up our FAA certification by attending a day of recurrent Emergency training once a year. Gateway only had one facility for that training—the Cleveland hangars. We would evacuate planes and review safety measures, for eight hours. I filed the idea of calling Danny in the back of my mind somewhere near my medulla.

The other reserves flying to Seattle were junior to me; Bonnie and Kurt were among them and friendly as ever. Deadheading out together, we talked about all sorts of things and agreed to meet in the hotel lobby later.

No one needed more food; we'd eaten our way across Amer-ica, sampling Gateway's 'Sea to Shining Sea' spread, but no one was worried about drinking too much before flying, as we 'knew' the 10s wouldn't be cleared overnight.

In a bar downtown, the whole story about Roman's and my breakup and our cancelled trip to Italy came out. I wasn't sure how it happened—though I took full responsibility for it later, but at some point, we ended up in a beauty salon. With my female co-workers urging me on—Kurt remained quiet—I let a hairdresser I would never see again, cut off all my long hair and give me a trendy perm. I even pretended to like it and was surprised by how much it didn't bother me, even though I found it dreadful.

When we strolled into the tiny ops center in Seattle the next afternoon, a crew scheduler called out my name. "Van Ness!"

"Yes?"

"Need you in San Fran," he said, handing me the meter with my trip information.

"Oh," I really *Was* surprised. "Why am I the one getting reassigned?" I asked. "I think I'm the most senior reserve here."

"Not my call," he said. "We didn't do this reassignment; it came from your domicile. You'll have to take it up with them. Want me to dial?"

"No," I said. "My roommate's a union rep; I'm conditioned to question first. Frankly, it'll be nice to get back on my feet," I said, only halfway meaning it.

"Did you even bring your uniform with you," he teased. "Don't change yet; you're deadheading down there. Working the all-nighter back to Kennedy. Sorry you didn't have more warning; it's going to be a long duty day."

I had plenty of time to change into my uniform in San Francisco. In the crew bathroom, I kept staring at my reflection in the mirror. My hair was so weird! Not becoming at all. *I look like a drowned rat.* Jeanna and Maurice were going to skin me alive. I went into the terminal and bought a few loaves of San Francisco sourdough bread. It was the best, and would comfort me later.

When I stepped into the briefing room in San Francisco for our 747 flight home, I found a good ol' New York crew waiting.

Danielle was at the helm, again, holding all the A stew paper-work. "Well hello Sherri; this is becoming a norm for us," she said. "Is that a wig?" She pointed to my curls and frizz—which had taken over my head from Seattle's humidity.

"Wish I could say yes." That made her smile. "It's kind of a rebirth," I said.

"There's a first-class aisle position open…" she started, look-ing at me with a knowing look.

"I'll take it."

Breaking in my after-take-off cigarette-holding garter was going to have to wait. We didn't smoke on the jumbo jump-seats—we smoked downstairs in the pit, so I raced downstairs after lift-off and enjoyed a smoke there. All twenty-six first-class seats were occupied and though it was an all-nighter, they were a lively group that wanted cards and pre-departure champagne. Ellen, the most senior attendant in New York, was pass riding; she, another S & M's regular, was in 1C. And seated right next to her in 1D was the adorable, Mr. Anderson Jeffries.

"*What* did you do to your hair?" He cocked his head and furrowed his brow.

I bent down in the aisle so that Anderson was looking down at me. "It's not my hair—it's a dunce cap," I said, again, surprising myself that I wasn't in tears over the self-imposed scalp-and-hair-frying disaster.

"Oh?"

"Roman?" I started, "You were right about him. Turns out—he's… in another relationship."

"Married?" he asked.

I shook my head. "No. Well, guess I'm not sure… know what? It doesn't matter." A call button in the front section of coach went off. I peered down the aisle but didn't see a coach attendant anywhere, so I excused myself. A poor woman had her pet cat in a carrier under the seat in front of her. The animal was in terrible distress.

"If I could just take him out and hold him, he'd calm down," she whimpered. "He's shedding so much hair because he's so scared." Passengers around the woman were throwing her dirty looks. The cat was making sickening guttural sounds.

"I understand," I said. "But we can't let him out; the lawsuits… oh, I hate the world sometimes."

"What do you mean?"

"If he got loose and accidentally scratched someone; if he got near food; the list is endless. Even if he didn't do anything except curl up into a ball—if he frightened a child…" She started to cry. Her cat gave me the most pleading looks. It was all I could do not to open the cage door and let him out. "Will he eat or drink anything?" I asked.

She shook her head. "I've tried."

"I know this is stressful," I said. "I'm so sorry. Let me think about it while I finish up a few things. See if I can't come up with something."

I asked the front pit attendant if she would let our passenger take the cat downstairs after the service. We only had snacks in first class anyway, there would be no cooking and there was no hot food in first, but she said, 'over my dead body.'

"Those are pretty big closets on either side of the front galley," Anderson said later when I told him about my shot-down idea. "You could take the garment bags out and let her sit in one of them with the cat."

"That is a *Damn* good idea," I said.

"Sherri I was kidding…"

Danielle didn't care; she turned a blind eye as I pulled everything out of the tall closet at 2Right. It was right beside my jumpseat anyway—and I let the passenger sit in the dark with her cat carrier. I made her swear she would not open that closet door if the cat was loose. After fifteen minutes, the meowing mercifully stopped. The passengers seated near the woman were relieved. It was an all-nighter; they wanted to sleep.

Anderson and Ellen hung out in the galley with Danielle and me.

"I'm still so *Angry* at him," I told them. "Even about—the stupidest things!"

"Like what?" Anderson said.

"Like… him ruining a song I loved—*My Cherie Amour*, how dare he 'take my name in vain' I said. That song is sacred to me and he was…"

"Take your name in vain?" Danielle said. "Darling, she giggled and held her hand to her mouth. "You don't speak French, do you?"

"No."

"It's… MA Cherie amour; 'My cherished one,' not 'my Sherri.' This is not necessarily a girl's name he sings of," she touched her belly as she laughed with amusement.

Anderson saw the look of embarrassment on my face. "Sherri's name *Means* cherished one in French," he said. "That's the way I'd look at it," he said.

"Thanks And; nice try," I said. "According to my mom, it means 'white meadow.' Now I know that was never my song after all. And he was never my guy. And I have to grow up! I've been flying a year this month. I haven't gone to Helsinki or Reykjavik like you," I nodded at Danielle, "or to the Galapagos or Tibet like you," I nodded at Anderson. "I haven't even gone to Mexico or Canada—countries on my own continent, and I'm realizing that I have a hell of a lot more to learn and I want to change my life. I want something more in the order of *Your* lives," I said pointing at both of them.

"Ah! So you gave yourself an Afro?" Danielle touched my out-of-control perm.

"I'm taking a year off," Anderson said. "Going to Hawaii to train for the next Ironman. You been there?"

"How are you managing that?" I asked. "Didn't you just do that in January?"

"No; I wasn't ready, but I will be. As far as the time off, I put in for an educational leave. Going to Grad School in the fall. In the meantime, I'm training for the race till classes start," Anderson said. "When it's over I can focus on school."

"Wow; a year off. Sounds wonderful. Get your masters, train what… eight hours a day? I gotta admit it And, I'm impressed." Ellen was quiet. I remembered Mo being annoyed with me for challenging her. She probably didn't like me very much. "What about you Ellen," I asked, "what great places have you traveled to in your extensive career?"

That got her talking. She was actually very funny and loved sharing her stories. Soon we were back to chatting about the company.

"Is it true you guys had girdle checks?" I asked her. "That supervisors pinched you to see if you were wearing one?" I had heard that in training.

"AB-SO-LUTE-LY," she exclaimed. "We had the craziest rules! If we wore a pony-tail, we had to have a ribbon around the rubber band—one infraction if it wasn't covered. Our eye shadow had to white on the lid, brown in the center and white under the brow—only acceptable color combo. There was a list in the appearance room letting us know EXACTLY which brands and shades of lipstick and nail polish we could wear; if we deviated from that—another infraction; it was abuse! Think we got paid for sitting around on reserve? Honey—not ever! We could sit there for days and days, and if we didn't fly, we didn't get a dime!

You reserves have it so good with your 'minimums and your guar-antees' and you don't even know it."

"I see movement up front," Danielle warned me. "You might want to see if anyone needs anything."

First class was fine. Anderson stayed in the galley. I started into coach to check the bar cart at door three when And pulled me back. "Sherri?"

"Yes?"

"You're still *lovely as a summer's day.*" It sounded sweet but then he laughed too hard. I walked away but glanced back—he was watching me.

I found a mommy in the back with a restless baby in her arms and two young, overtired children seated on either side of her. Both were trying to get her attention. "Would you like me to hold your baby for a few minutes so you could tend to the others?" I asked.

Her mouth dropped. "That… would be…"

I reached down and picked up the little girl. She wasn't dis-tressed to be with a stranger. Her older siblings smiled happily when their mother put her freed arms around each of them. I walked a few rows away to test the separation; the baby was still fine. I kept going, right back to the galley where Danielle, Ander-son and Ellen helped me entertain her.

"The crew's meeting for brunch in the city after we land," Danielle announced. "You all should join us."

"Sounds fun," said Ellen, "I'm in."

"No I can't…" Anderson started.

"Come one Anderson," I said firmly. "You're leaving for a year; we never see you! Come have a goodbye meal with us before you start your navy seal training. Please?"

"She's right," Danielle agreed.

"Sherri?" The first-class passenger in 6D stepped into the galley. His name had not been on the manifest. I had not worked that side of the aisle, where the DEF seats were, so I had not asked him for his name.

"Yes?"

"I'm Owen Hurst, Supervisor out of San Francisco. I did a check-ride on you tonight. Would you please return the baby and come have a seat with me so we can review your evaluation?"

So that was why I had been reassigned out of seniority order! This was my one-year annual evaluation and it was a 'ghost' ride—as in—unannounced and secretive. When he returned to his seat, I knocked on the closet door and urged the passenger to cage her cat and return to the cabin. We only had an hour left and I was feeling uneasy about having a supervisor onboard with a 'cat out of the bag.' There was a quick orange juice and sweet roll service in first class before landing, just as we flew into the sunrise, but Owen instructed Danielle to do the service without me. I popped a fresh piece of gum into my mouth, put on some lip gloss, pinched my cheeks and took a deep breath.

"Your instincts with passengers are wonderful," Owen said. "I will be reporting that I found you to be a very sincere, attentive attendant who watches, responds to the need of her passengers and crew and hustles. I watched you work the other side of the aisle and heard you using everyone's names; marvelous! I'm sure everyone wants to work with you Sherri. You obviously like the job. Now, let's move on to the areas that need improvement. *What* were you thinking when you let that woman take over the closet with her cat?"

It didn't matter what I said, Owen was grading me down for my poor judgment and worse, a 'safety violation' which was far more serious. Further, he felt that it might be dangerous to hold someone's baby inflight in case there was turbulence and I dropped it.

"You would be putting Gateway at great risk if you dropped the child," he said. I did not roll my eyes but looked at him as if he were *so wise*. Gateway would be at great risk if the mother dropped the child in severe turbulence too, but I didn't say that. "As for your appearance," his voice dropped as he looked down. "Your uniform is neat and tidy, as is your apron. Your hair is terrific." Again, I contained one of my 'not-so-great' instincts and didn't laugh. "Does anyone ever tell you that you look like Marie Osmond?" He grinned, but didn't wait for a reply. "However…"

I held my breath.

"This is not easy for me to ask you," he said slowly, "but would you mind getting on the scale when we get to Kennedy operations?"

"I just weighed in on my last trip," I said. Which was the truth.

"Were you at least ten pounds under your max?"

"No."

"As a supervisor then, I have the right to check your weight. I find it hard to believe that you're below your maximum right now," he said, while raising his eyebrows. "We'll just take care of that quickly. Is there anything I've overlooked?"

"Yes. You didn't give me an outstanding for 'frequently reapplying lipstick and blusher,' and I think I deserve that." I pointed to the area on the performance sheet that listed that responsibility. *At least I can rock my vanity.*

"Point taken." He found the box on his sheet, crossed out the 'meets expectations' notation, and put a check mark in the box for: 'outstanding' effort.

* * *

The brunch spot we picked in the city was jammed after a dozen of us had taken our seats and tossed our belongings onto the floor. It looked like a jumbo jet briefing room; crew luggage was everywhere. The tables were round, so putting two of them together to seat all of us was awkward; our chairs stuck out in the aisle. The poor waiter watched with resignation as we settled in. Most of us were still in uniform with only the thinnest of disguises: we took our jackets and vests off, and donned T shirts or sweaters over our uniform shirts and blouses. We were never, ever, supposed to drink alcohol in uniform. But… this was a New York crew, and, we did things a little differently.

I *really* didn't care, seeing as I was just informed that I would have a mandatory three weeks off without pay. I would also be getting a letter of warning in my file and I was at high risk for losing my job, not only for my weight, but for a 'safety infraction.' "Champagne for everyone," I told the waiter. "I'm getting the first round."

An attendant named Carrie asked me, "How does time off for being overweight work? What do they call it again?"

"Being beached," I said. "Like a whale. For every pound that you're over your max, they give you a week off. Five pounds over, five weeks off without pay. It's meant to be a punishment as well as a time off to get thin—thus, unpaid. Here's the thing though; when the time period is up, if you haven't lost the weight you're *Fired*—Done. And if you're on time-off for weight more than twice in your entire career—you're also fired. I weighed in three pounds over, so I'm off for three weeks. If I don't weigh at least three pounds less in twenty-one days, I'm gone."

"Believe me honey," Ellen said. "They *Will* fire you! I have seen many good flight attendants lose their jobs over this during my career. Another example of abuse this company gets away with. Why aren't pilots or gate agents weighed? It's total discrimination."

Everyone was quiet. *I should know how to bum out an entire table.*

"It's alright everyone; I've had this problem for months," I said, glancing at Anderson who winked at me. He wasn't going to give me away. "It's time for me to beat this. I need to lose the baby fat and the childish attitude. If this supervisor had caught me during probation, I wouldn't even have the option to lose it; I would have been fired on the spot. I took that chance too many times. He was even 'kind' enough to reschedule me for recurrent in three weeks, because he said he 'knew' I would make weight. I was supposed to fly into Cleveland tomorrow."

Everyone stared, some frowned, some smiled.

The waiter had heard me and said, "You *will survive* girl-friend! I'm a model; I know all about the pressures of staying thin honey."

We ordered Eggs Florentine, French toast, sausages, fruit and sweet rolls. We traded the champagne for Bloody Marys and Screwdrivers. The waiter/model stopped the music and put on another song. He cranked up the volume.

"At first I was afraid, I was petrified!" Gloria Gaynor began her new chart-shattering hit.

"Oh Lord," one of the stewards wailed. "Why does every woman in the universe *Love* this song?"

"Because," Danielle exploded, "we can all relate to her words!" She stood up and moved around the table, singing along and breaking into a line dance. Every female attendant got up to join her. We circled the tables screaming to the poor defenseless, innocent stewards and on-lookers, that we wanted them to, *"Go! Walk out the door!"*

"Weren't you the one who tried to hurt me with goodbye; you think I'd crumble," we sang as best we could. *"You think I'd lay down and die? Oh no not I! I will survive..."*

* * *

"Thank you for the sourdough," Anderson said, as he and I walked up Second Avenue toward his car. "Good luck Sherri. I do think you'll be fine. You're not that little girl from Kansas anymore. You're a lot…"

"Smarter? Not yet."

"You'll be back," he said. "If what happened with that supervisor today had happened when I first met you, you would have dissolved. Now you're handling it; and being—yeah, smarter; taking responsibility."

"Good luck to you too Anderson. Sorry to see you go." I hesitated, then asked. "And, can I ask you something?"

"Sure."

"Did you really call me?"

I knew the answer before he said it. "No; wanted to, but you're so young. Didn't want to be that way. Wasn't thinking clearly in Vegas. You were…"

"I'm twenty-one now," I said defensively, surprising myself.

He laughed. "How'd you figure it out? That I hadn't called."

"You didn't know Alex was my roommate. If you'd gotten our number, someone would have told you it was hers. Everyone in New York knows her number; she's our union rep."

"See, told you—you are smarter."

"And older!"

"Ok Sherri," he laughed some more. "If you find yourself in Oahu in the next year," he said, "look me up." He gave me a half-assed salute, turned, and walked into the parking garage.

I shouted at him, trying to sound funny. "Watch out for jellyfish Anderson!" But it was me who was stung. Once, I had walked away from him. I thought about adding, *'If I get to Hawaii and call you, will it be a date?'* But the moment and my courage were gone. I looked up at the bright sun, reached for my sunglasses and yawned widely. I realized, suddenly and overwhelmingly, I was exhausted.

- *Dear FlightLog; It's been over a year now that I've been writing to you — the 1st year of my flying career (which might be over if I don't watch it) has 'flown' by. Sorry for the lame pun — again. And, well, I don't have a lot to show for it, considering all I've been exposed to and considering I'm now a 21-year-old adult, except to say that I finally caved in and chopped off all my hair and have a 'stew do' like they nagged me to get in training. It's really ugly. A year ago, I'd have cut off both arms before doing it. Doesn't seem possible that it's been a year! Know what I did? I read my first entry. 'Danny is a dork.' How funny, because it's me who's the dork. I give myself credit for being a great crew member, for going all out, being nice and caring, but I haven't taken seriously one of the things Gateway asks: that I stay real thin. Whether or not it's right for them to be so strict, I knew that requirement and I've been lucky, reckless and foolish. It's 'career-resolutions' time! I'm going to drop to 115 pounds in full uniform, and be ten pounds under, and I'm going to STAY there, even if I have to fly to Hawaii and have Anderson Jeffries put me on a workout regime. Ok, so there's another area I feel totally foolish about: LOVE!*

FlightLog, let's talk about it. I gave myself to a married man – then, I broke up with an older man who was probably going to dump me anyway – 'You're so young' he said. Eight months I dated him. I would be heading for Italy soon if I hadn't found out about the 'other' woman. I'm humiliated, I feel dirty, cheap, cheated on and lied to – I think I HATE HIM! But what I really want to do is forget him. After all – there was New Year's Eve; I wasn't exactly a saint. I want to stop thinking about him, about us, about all my girlish fantasy dreams and the life I thought we were going to have. Since we're on the subject – how about all the nice guys I ignore? Why can't I swoon over Danny? Yeah, he lied too – but he's a prankster, not a cheat. Why can't I swoon over Eric? Know what? Everyone tells me that they're a great judge of character and that's why they like me. So... if they're such great judges of character, why can't they see that I'm not? When was the last time I – Sherri Ann Van Ness – was a 'good judge of character?' WHAT the HELL do I know? Who am I and where is my life going? I'm tired of feeling and being so STUPID! Those same people who say I'm smart, that I learn quickly because I memorize names, books, movies, don't realize that I'm just... dumb. I actually was a good judge of character once this last year – when I met Anderson. I knew he was special – not just because he helped me, it was more than that. So what did I do? I over-reacted and blew it; we flirt, but then he backs off. He said I was too young too. Now I see him, and instead of being able to laugh that he's reciting lines from a Stevie Wonder song – I'm wishing he'd sing me another line. 'How I wish that you were mine!' Why didn't he sing that? I would have jumped into his arms. I could be on plane RIGHT NOW headed for Hawaii. I just got three weeks off for crying-out-loud! How do I mature? I don't want Anderson to think of me as too young.

Oh boy! Wow, I do know, YEP. Sometimes, when I'm writing, it comes to me; guess that's why they say this is therapeutic; I connect the dots – it's crystal clear. I know EXACTLY what I should do. I need to go home; I need my mommy. Good grief; I've been terrible about visiting – think I've popped in – maybe two or three times for a couple of days in the last year? I want to go home. More than one person has called me 'Dorothy from Kansas' – maybe it's true. Maybe like her, it's time for me to click my heels together, put my tail between my legs, get some family time in, tell my parents – who are smart – about Roman; and about being burned. And, about agonizing about my weight EVERY SINGLE DAY, WEEK, MONTH – being unable to nip that – yep. Thank you, Gateway Airlines! Looking back, I was too young for this job; I was too young to race off to New York City and *now, you're giving me a chance to work it out. I want to ride bikes around the block with my kid brother; I want to go shopping with my sis. I want my mother to cook me breakfast and I want to watch Wimbeldon (Wimbledon?) with my dad. I want to hug and squeeze all of them real hard while telling them face to face how much I love them, how much I've missed them, because I haven't done that for a very, very, very long time. Thanks Gateway and Roman; and even you Anderson, for going away – for making it easy by wiping my slate clean. My schedule is wide-open. Like Scarlett O'Hara, realizing she needs Tara, I realize I need the home I grew up in too – and that's where I'm going: I'M GOING HOME!!!*

*   *   *

"Wake up! Wake up! Sherri." Maurice was pulling my arm as I lay sleeping.

"Maurice? What… did I miss my check-in?" I sat up quickly; my heart was racing. Was Dorothy waking from her dream? Then I remembered everything. I was officially off the line; I couldn't have missed a check-in. I had collapsed in a heap in my bed. Staying up all day in Seattle before working the San Fran all-nighter had caught up with me. The champagne brunch had helped cork me too.

"No," he said.

"What time is it?" I asked, slumping back onto the bed. Maurice was setting something up in my bedroom; he was making a lot of noise. I couldn't see what it was.

"Eleven-thirty," he said as he connected two planks or boards together.

"In the morning?"

"No again," he said. "It's nighttime."

"What's that?" I asked. "Please don't tell me you bought a scale!"

"It's a sunglass stand. Sergio got it; he's got connections in retail. You say you don't have a collection of any kind, but you do! You collect sunglasses; you need a proper place for them."

"Oh my God Maurice! Only you would think of that."

"Thought of something else too," he said. "We're going to Central Park. I've already picked out your ensemble." He tossed the flowing, thin, silky shirt and skirt I'd worn for New Year's Eve onto my bed. "Come on," he commanded, pulling me to a stand.

The abduction was on. Maurice directed the cab driver through Central Park, telling him exactly where to stop. He propped up a battery-powered ghetto-blaster tape player and put on Credence Clearwater's "Green River."

"Barefoot girls, dancing in the moonlight," blared from its speakers; it sounded wonderful.

"Kick off your shoes," Mo said. "Look," he pointed up to the cloudless sky. "A full moon. Given everything that's happened to you in the last few weeks, I think this is the perfect night for this overdue indulgence. Let's set this daring-damsel on fire. Dance Sherri." He put out his hand, which I took, and twirled me into him. Then he whispered in a sexy, husky voice, **"Like nobody's watching."**

Acknowledgment of the Bragging Rights

Airline employees love to boast about meeting celebrities. Even famous people love sharing stories about meeting celebrities! If you finished *FlightLog*, you know that Danny took *'The Bragging Rights'* to a remarkable level. I promise I won't do that.

Listed below (in alphabetical order) are many of the famous people who boarded flights I worked on, and took a seat. Those who have an asterisk beside their names are celebrities I met at layover hotels, restaurants, bars, casinos or at airports—because I was working. I have not included the names of people I've met away from work, such as at concerts. I have not included the names of those I met at private exclusive parties/events who are: Formula One Race Car Drivers, Oscar Winning Directors, Artists whose works appear at the MOMA or Pulitzer Prized novelists. Ok, I haven't attended one of those parties/events... but don't tell!

Athletes

Mohammed Ali
Andre the Giant
Tracey Austin
Rod Carew
Chicago Bears Team including: Richard Dent, Coach Mike Ditka, Dan Hampton, Wilbur Marshall, Walter Payton, William 'the refrigerator' Perry, Mike Singletary, Matt Suhey
Chicago Bulls Team including: Coach Doug Collins, Horace Grant, Michael Jordan, John Paxson, Scotty Pippen, Will Purdue
Cincinnati Reds Team including: Pete Rose
Detroit Pistons Team including: Joe Dumars, Adrian Dantley, Bill Lambeer, Dennis Rodman, John Sally, Isiah Thomas
Hulk Hogan*
Bobby Hull—or perhaps it was Bobby Orr…
Phil Esposito
New England Patriots Team

Broadway/Comedy/Movie/TV Stars

James Amos*
Johnny Carson*
Richard Chamberlain*
Richard Dreyfus
Linda Evans*
Greg Evigan
James Franciosa*
Greta Garbo
Mark Hamill

Richard Jaeckel*
Mary Tyler Moore
Paul Newman
Pudgy
William Smith*
Robin Strasser
Danny Thomas
Dick Van Dyke*
Jimmy Walker
Joanne Woodward
Chuck Woolery*

Politicians/Public Servants

Congressman Daniel Crane
Secretary of State Warren Christopher
Political Activist Jesse Jackson*
President Richard Nixon
President Ronald Reagan

Singers

Pearl Bailey*
Tony Bennett*
Bonno
Chakka Khan
Willie Nelson
Oak Ridge Boys
Pointer Sisters
Bobby Vinton*

Andy Williams*

Writers/columnists

Dr. Joyce Brothers
NYT Food Editor Craig Claiborne
Chicago ST Columnist Irv Kupcinet*
Ann Landers (the original 'Dear Abbey')

Others

Playmate of the Month Candice Collins
TV Producer Mark Goodson
Artist/Painter Leroy Neiman
Fitness Guru Richard Simmons*

www.ingramcontent.com/pod-product-compliance
Lightning Source LLC
Chambersburg PA
CBHW021216310726
48971CB00006B/1583